Dominion of Midgard

Year of Olympus 539

MW01103659

A Note on Pronunciation

y pronounced like *i* in *grin* (Dryn, Rychard, Rysarius)
Double consonants separate syllables (Ker-res or Tan-nes)

A Note on Dates

Years are recorded from the founding of the Dominion's oldest city, Olympus. The Year of Olympus 0 was its establishment and the end of the Age of Myths. Shadow Glyph was set in the Year of Olympus 588.

A Note on Maps

For better resolutions, please check www.ithyka.com

Gothikar Family Tree

*Royal Names in **bold** and dates in Years of Olympus

- ❖ Veldar ten Gothikar (m. / 404-501) married Nara ten Heth (f. / 446-493)
    - ❖ Parcep Gothikar (m. / 431-463)
    - ❖ Tamese Gothikar (f. / 478-514)
    - ❖ **Akheron** Gothikar (m. / 484-527) married Reya Edemar (f. / 497-543)
        - ❖ **Periander** Gothikar (m. / 519-) married Catlin ten Joran (f. / 520-558)
            - ❖ **Artemys** Gothikar (m. / 545-)
            - ❖ **Pyrsius** Gothikar (m. / 558-588)
                - ❖ Lanteera "Iris" Gothikar (f. / 572-)

Second, mercy.

1

Year of Olympus 539

The mountain men were howling again. Trembling in frosted metal helmets and thick pelts, the terrified troop ascended a rocky slope like an injured cockroach. At its head, Periander Gothikar tried to lead the best way up into the Maker's Forge, every stiff step of his mule bringing him closer to those rocky heights. Echoes reverberated down the pass for another hour before that mad shouting ceased.

"What do they say?" a voice asked.

Periander glanced at Mordus. The fellow easterner's gaunt face peered from within the thick bear pelt he wore, the question written in his concerned eyes. "Nothing. They are men without minds, cast out of their tribes and preying like animals in the valleys."

Mordus turned his eyes back to the jagged horizon ahead, the sun shining off of the glacial peaks. A moment later, he sneezed deeply and caught his helm before it crashed to the ground.

They had seen smoke ahead a few hours ago, but it had stopped seeming like they were moving toward it.

Periander concealed his reaction to these mountains. He recalled a month spent in the Southern Spine, touring his fiefdom before ascending the Avernan throne. Those mountains had humbled him with their size, dwarfed him with their awesome strength. It was thousands of miles away now.

The Maker's Forge was a leviathan to the minnow of the Southern Spine. The gargantuan peaks on either side of their winding road gave way to greater heights and in turn rose again like a stairway unto the heavens. The teachings of the late Kinship of the Maker seemed justified in the face of such an inexplicable... creation.

No wonder the tribes lost men to madness.

"Oban Ford is only a day's march," Mordus said, staring at the smoke.

Periander glanced at him. Mordus remained silent, his words left in midair like the wisps of cloud weaving the mountaintops. "And?"

"And we've been riding for a whole damn day!"

Periander smiled. "Ask the guide."

Mordus cursed, but reluctantly picked up his pace. Periander was the only one mounted; he watched Mordus pick his way uphill to a lumbering giant of a man. It was summer, and the frost on these slopes had irrigated the soil. Sprouts of grass were beginning to emerge from the dirt, but Periander knew that the next winter would strike before anything else grew.

Trelkl stood a head taller than anyone Periander had ever met, his arm nearly as thick as Periander's torso; even by the mountain men's standards, this man was massive. He had met them at the far side of Dagger's Edge, standing there amongst the statue guardians, disguised like them with the hilt of an axe protruding from his shoulders.

Periander could hear Mordus's barked questions, and Trelkl's rumbling replies. The barbarian's tribe was *nalk-dfar*, a state that was akin to "destruction" or closer to the word "lost".

Mordus stopped walking alongside the giant and waited until Periander and the troop caught up beside them. "Says over the next hill."

Periander nodded, and glanced along the fringe of the small woodland between the ridges. The trees were far too small at this altitude. Periander wondered how the mountain men could grow in lands where the trees could not. The slope they were climbing met the nearest mountain a mile to the west, but peaked and declined ahead.

The troop crested the hill, and as promised, the valley opened for a large camp. The foliage had been cleared away for more than a hundred tents. Periander estimated that the camp spanned at least a mile in each direction from the hill.

It was scurrying with Trionus soldiers. Periander was surprised to see others too: several dozen mountain men navigated the camp as well. Both races sat around fires, and a variety of stoves had been built in a section of camp cordoned off for the tradesmen; smoke hung in a cloud above the camp.

Trelkl sank down and folded his knees on a rock at the top of the hill.

"You're not coming into the village?" Periander asked.

The massive man tilted his protruding brow just enough to meet Periander's eyes. "I hold no interest in water-walker meets. And those of my kind will not have dfar walk in their midst."

Periander shrugged and stepped past the giant. They were called water-walkers as all their towns were built beside water. Mountain men claimed to only need rock.

He led his men down into the camp, greeting the soldiers with a wave of his hands. None of them would meet his eyes though; he dismissed it as his youth. He had met many veterans twice his age who wondered how an 'untested youth' decided where they should march.

In answer to that—Periander was not untested. He had killed three men when he was ten. When Akheron Gothikar was assassinated, Lord Ivos tended the throne of Avernus as steward. Periander was sent to the village of Bertren to spend his coming-of-age years at a family estate. Two years later, he set off on a tour of the Avernan fiefdom with the Captain of his Guard. Captain Joran was slain when they were set upon by assassins, and Periander only survived by killing their assailants.

Now he was twenty, and he was marching into a camp in the middle of nowhere.

The camp, however, was well organized. There were wider aisles between some of the tents, roads that cut lengthwise across camp so anyone could cross camp easily. From the main road, Periander saw winding paths between the tents that did not border the roadways. That made sense; allow the troops to set up their tents how they want, near whom they want. It boosted morale, while the wider roads maintained efficiency.

The command pavilion was on the south side of the camp village, so they did not need to march far. It looked large enough for two dozen men and was decorated with the black and yellow patterns of House Trionus. There was a wide swath of empty grass around the tent for audience to wait. Periander raised his hand and turned to his troop. All eyes fell on him. "Wait here," he directed them. "Rest at ease...Mordus, with me."

"Sir." Mordus followed him up the last slope to the Imperial pavilion.

Periander threw aside the tent flap. There were three inside, a man and two giants. The tent was full of colours; there was an artistic map across a nearby table, a four poster bed with yellow sheets half hidden by a yellow curtain, a rustic red chest on the opposite side of Periander, and a rack of armaments near it. Near the table was the man, seated in a wood and gold-gilt throne. He had a curly, short beard around his face and a hooked nose. *Ernes Trion, Lord of House Trion and Trionus City.* On either side of the Lord were mountain men with burgundy mantles— tribe leaders. Their balding heads brushed the ceiling. Their skin was greyer than Periander's, but their eyes held the same certainty that Trion's did.

"What's this then?" Periander asked. "You've dressed yourself up as the Prince and made these your Nobles?"

Ernes scratched his beard, then stood. "Not the Prince, young Gothikar. The King."

"And you've requested the youngest politician in the hopes of tricking him?" Periander returned. "I'm afraid I must disappoint—"

"Periander, come now. You need not be so defensive, Prince," Ernes Trion said, walking down from the throne and toward Periander. He glanced at Mordus, then put an arm around Prince Gothikar. The mountain men raised eyebrows and stirred in surprise; enemies were not for touching. "Listen, Periander. At the end of this, there will be the two of us. I invited you here to respect you as an equal, not to keep you in the dark like a child."

Periander separated himself from Ernes's grasp. "Speak then. Why have you fled from your city into these mountains? Why do you use these treasonous words?"

Ernes sat upon his throne again and let out his breath. He was a grizzled man, who led his House from Galinor into the north and founded the city of Trionus in his own name. Now, thirty years later, he had demanded the audience of a Prince, namely Periander, and the Triumvirate had agreed. Periander's wife, Catlin, had not.

"Your father changed the Dominion, Periander," Ernes told him. "Akheron Gothikar burned down House Aristorn and, only getting started, set to work on the Kinship of the Maker."

Commotion at the tent flap interrupted Lord Trion. Periander turned to find Lord Ivos meeting his surprised glare. "Ivos," he barked. "What finds you in these mountains?"

Lord Ivos was equal to Trion's seniority, but far less accomplished. While the latter had built his own thriving city from a wasteland, Ivos sat in the spoils of his House as a bachelor, an outcast, and a coward. Ivos had once been a Royal House—one of his predecessors had ruled as Prince, but this man's forefathers had lost the Princehood to House Theseus a hundred years ago. Ivos now lived as a disgraced, minor House.

"Periander," Ivos returned, "I had heard of your arrival. I've thrown my lot in with Trion. He recognizes my strength."

"You have no strength," Periander retorted. The mountain men reached for weapons, and Mordus followed in turn. Ivos and he had history. He wondered how many of Trion's words were his own, and how many were Ivos's thirst for power speaking through him. If the two were allied...

Ernes raised his arms and stood again. "Lords, please. Let us act as men, not boys." That meant nothing in context to the mountain men, but after a moment they calmed.

"You promise these men riches, but you have not explained why," Periander said. "Instead you tell tales of my father, tales we all know."

Ernes nodded. "I only bring up Akheron because he was a man not unlike myself. He knew the world was for the taking, and he took what he pleased."

"If my father believed that till the end, he died a fool."

"Did he? Have you not, in your short reign, helped Gothikar thrive even more by that same belief?"

Ivos chuckled, at which even Ernes glared. Ivos had refused to relinquish the Avernan Princehood to Periander when he had come of age. In front of the entire court, Periander had banished him from the fiefdom and taken his rightful seat as Prince. Everyone in the tent knew the bad blood between them.

"The world is not mine to take. The only truth my father knew was that you can choose to make the best of what you are given, or you can let it all waste," Periander explained.

"The only difference is in semantics," Ernes dismissed with a wave of a hand. "My point, Periander, is that this 'wilderness,' as we have called it, is a kingdom of mountain tribes. We have dismissed them as barbarians, but there is power in them. Strength."

"Strength, but not society. They are not members of the Triumvirate of their own request," Periander said, looking now at the tribe leaders in their midst.

"We are not part of your government, but we require land nonetheless," one of the mountain men grumbled with his low voice. "My forefathers would have made a much different arrangement with Tiberon Odyn if..."

Trion raised his hand and the giant looked at him. He met Periander's glare again. "I speak not of the Triumvirate nor the Dominion, but of a new order, a new... Kingdom."

"What, with you at its helm?" Periander questioned. "You promise these tribes a place at your side, and you promise Ivos the riches he cannot live without? Heed my words, friends—these are lies."

Mordus coughed as weapons were stirred once more.

Periander continued, intentionally ignoring their threats. "You have invited me here to make an ultimatum. I have travelled from the far East to the West. Make your demands and I will be on my way." *Back to my dear Cat.*

Ernes stood. "Grant us the Cerden Mountains, and Galinor, then acknowledge us as a fellow country, or face the hammers, axes, and fury of a *million* mountain men."

Periander turned away and looked at Mordus to collect his words and warn his friend. When he turned back to Lord Trion, he spoke with certainty and purpose. "You and your deluded dreams will die before crossing the Strait of Galinor. Return to your city and dismiss these mountain men. Do this now, and I will not have your head for treason."

"You were promised safe passage, Gothikar," Ivos said. Ernes turned his back on them, brooding beside his throne. "Leave now, before that is changed."

"I do not hear your words, traitor. I will not leave until Ernes Trion comes with me, back to the gates of his city."

Trion spun on him, snapped, "Kill them," and reached for a

sword. Periander kicked him solidly in the gut, knocking him back onto his throne and toppling with it to the dirt. Mordus crossed blades with Ivos as Periander faced two mountain leaders.

Then the screaming started.

Periander breathed a spell for smoke, and the pavilion was instantly choking with it. He had scratched the glyphs for the spell into the pavilion's canvas when they first entered, just in case. He slit the tent hide from roof to earth and stepped through. "Mordus!" he shouted.

Mordus smashed Ivos back with an overhand swing of his sword and then stumbled after his Prince, out into the open camp...

The sight before Periander would stay with him until his grave. His men lay strewn across the ground in a pond of blood, limbs scattered. The mountain men were still pounding them with clubs or axes. The few men still clutching life found themselves beaten until they released their holds and fled the world.

Periander froze. *I did this. These men came because of me. I ordered them. Maker! I am responsible...* He felt Mordus grab him, hauling him through the weaving paths between tents. Almost immediately they were set upon by attackers, and Periander was forced out of his horrified daze to strike them down with magic.

Somehow, they reached the struggling woodland. The thin foliage was easy to run through and the small trees easy to dodge between. Periander glanced up at the hill they had descended. There was no sign of Trelkl there.

They made good time toward the Strait, not stopping when dark fell. The sun was starting to rise, and it cast beautiful shadows between the mountains. It was tragic after the slaughter they had seen.

They reached the age-old bridge at Dagger's Edge in those early morning hours when the world was still blue. Periander stopped walking.

"Milord?" Mordus questioned.

"Ride for Galinor, good man," Periander told him. He still saw the bloodied carnage of his troop displayed before him by the barbarians. "Gather as many men as you can."

"You intend to hold this old bridge? Just as you told Trion?"

"We must."

"I cannot leave you here, on your own. You are a Prince whose father was assassinated. You cannot be unguarded."

"I have guards." Periander smiled.

"Who?"

"The giants that stand around us," Periander said, though he did not mean the stone statues of long-gone soldiers.

Trelkl had appeared from the mountain woodland. A dozen others approached with him, as more trickled out toward the bridge. "The other tribes have cast us out, but they are fools to trust promises of land and glory. We will stand with you, Gothikar. We nalk-dfar will stand with you," Trelkl said as he reached them. His voice was like thunder, his words blurred together but strong nonetheless.

Mordus galloped into the Cerden Mountains, riding straight for Galinor as Periander and a hundred "lost" giants stood against the hordes of the north. He knew now that it would be longer before he returned to Cat. He prayed not too long.

2

Year of Olympus 570

A wind was blowing through the peaks, desert sand and heat from the south in its gale. It whistled through the ruins of an old tower, built there in another age, and then continued through the brown and green valleys of the World's Foundation. By the time the wind reached the valley where Artemys had appeared, it pressed his cloak against his back, cold fingers grazing his neck like Kerres's words. He could not stop the wind with a shout of "He killed my mother!" like he had once silenced her. He *could* stop the wind with different words of a much older language. He chose not to.

Ahead of Artemys was the short wall of the village, stones piled and set into place with dirt and water, wooden palisades jutting out from the earth in front. He could see houses looming higher than the wall, though only a handful of them had second storeys. Above the houses was the huge stone building at the town's center. His visions could scour the town but could not pry open that massive block. Why?

He had to know.

Rising above the stone town square was the horizon, a mountain ridge held between two peaks, and a clear blue sky above that. The instantaneous change from his somewhat stifling Avernan quarters to this windswept valley made Artemys shiver.

Before walking towards the town, he glanced back over his right shoulder. There were four stone pillars, only one of which seemed its original height. In the center of the square, the columns formed a much older stone arch. Amongst the cracks hid many mosses—this side of the mountains was much more moist than the other. Artemys could not imagine how that arch was still standing. A dark cloth hung within. He stepped toward it when he realized otherwise. Within the arch was a shimmering arrangement of glyphs, held there in a magical void of light—the dark swath he had assumed to be fabric. The letters themselves seemed to emit an eerie glow. He recognized the complex spell of glyphs that floated there as a location, though he did not know which. He turned back toward the village.

The dirt footpath he had appeared upon was replaced by ancient cobblestones at the village gate. There were no guards at the opening in the waist-high stone wall. Artemys's arrival went unhindered, though not unnoticed. The handful of villagers to be seen were all robed in grey and turned to stare at him. There was only surprise in their expressions, no fear or hostility. Eyes widened, whispers exchanged.

Artemys was not such a surprising sight. He had unkempt brown hair hanging over his ears, the chiseled jaw of his father, but the green eyes of his mother. His features were distinct enough to be easily recognized, but none here knew him as the son of Prince Periander Gothikar.

Soon, Artemys reached the two-storey structure in the middle of the village, the fortress even his spells could not gaze within. Like the village gate, there were no guards near the building's arched, wooden doorway. Artemys suspected there was no need for security in such a secluded village—he could find no trace of this place on any of the maps in the Avernan Palace. He opened the wooden doors, the metal hinges not even whining as he stepped inside.

"Who are you?" someone blurted. The two men seated at the table within rose to their feet at the sight of this stranger, a young man garbed in an Imperial beige cloak.

This room was just as Artemys had seen it when he had first scried this village. He looked to his right, at the stairwell descending to the deep layers beneath the ground. The secret room was there, hidden from the entire world. He turned back to the two men. One's hand hovered by the table, likely to write a spell should Artemys turn hostile. He held his hands out in peace. "My name is Artemys Gothikar. I'm here to see Weveld."

Both stared at him in shock.

"How did you find this place?"

"Who are you," Artemys asked them, "that I would explain myself to you? Will you take me to the Crown Magician, or will I find him on my own?"

The two glanced at one another. There was a moment when Artemys thought the man whose hand was ready to write spells would, but then the hand disappeared into the folds of the man's grey robe. His friend, the one who had asked him how he had come here, tipped his head and said, "This way."

Artemys followed him toward that staircase, his heart pounding. A curtain hung halfway down, covered in stitched glyphs, the spell that hid the lower storey from the prying eyes of the world. The other man held the curtain open for Artemys. He took a deep breath and stepped through.

The basement was much more elaborately decorated than the village itself. The town had resembled any village: wooden shacks hastily thatched, muddy clothes. This hidden area was in fact more than a room, but rather an entire complex. The first chamber was an anteroom, bookshelves containing books Artemys had never seen. The furniture was as high in quality as the wealthy estates he had visited in Olympus.

Another robed man was seated at a table amidst a pile of parchments, scrolls, and volumes; he glared up at Artemys's entrance, though directed his expression at his guide. "Who's this?"

Artemys's escort did not blink. "Periander, Gothikar's son."

The glare vanished, replaced by the picture of interest that had been on the man's face when he was reading from his piled table.

The guide grabbed Artemys's elbow before he could speak. "This way."

Artemys followed into the next room. This was a hall of some kind. At a quick guess, Artemys figured that it could seat about a hundred men, though only a handful could be seen. They all watched Artemys as their peers had, some talking openly about the appearance of a stranger.

He was ushered forward towards a doorway on the opposite side of the hall. There were three doorways on either side of the chamber, separated by curtains. Artemys was surprised by the apparent size of this secret group: a hall to feed a hundred, an entire sanctuary hidden from history by magic that rivalled Artemys's.

"In here."

Artemys was shoved through another curtain, into the room opposite the anteroom and stairwell. His guide did not enter.

There was a long moment of silence when he met the questioning glance of the man across the room. Weveld was seated at a desk that was just as cluttered as the one in the antechamber, his snowy beard pressed between his robed torso and the tabletop. The top of his head was nearly bald; Artemys had only ever seen it covered by a hood or a hat. Weveld came to his feet with a tremble that Artemys could notice even from the dozen feet between them.

Artemys stepped towards him, sandals sinking into a thick, fur rug. He glanced to his left and right—they were the only ones within the room.

"Artemys," Weveld mumbled, his voice as rough as his skin.

"Weveld." Artemys nodded. "Crown Mage?" *Master of the Order of Magic... which I* resigned.

"Not here." The old man's face was set like stone, his expression nearly blank, yet threatening.

Artemys nodded again. "What is this place?"

"How did you find it?"

"You have always underestimated me. You and all the others of the Order. I could be a master mage. And I proved it, but that, apparently, was not what anyone wanted," Artemys said. He could recall the looks on their faces after he had burnt Master Kaen to the ground. As they used healing to bring him back from the brink. No one admired Artemys's power. They feared it. How could he do anything good or *useful* with it, if it only instilled fear?

"I've never underestimated you. The day you left, I asked you to join my evening meal...you turned me down," Weveld said. He had a scar on the left side of his balding scalp. How could he have scarred? Healing magic left no scars. It looked like an axe wound. His voice cracked as he continued. "I was going to tell you the truth."

"What truth?" Artemys took another step closer, his hands

resting on a chair across the desk from Weveld.

Weveld closed his eyes for a moment, preparing his words. "The Magician's Order is a nest of schemers and factions. It has nothing to do with power or merit."

"Then clean it out. Empty house."

Weveld shook his head, his beard swaying back and forth. Could it be any less ridiculous? "No, we need it that way."

"We?"

"Sit down, Artemys."

Artemys meandered forward, sinking into the chair as Weveld did the same. Their eyes met. There was a spark in Weveld's gaze, something Artemys had not noticed before. A strong life, where before he had only seen an old man waiting to die.

"We are the Disciples of Andrakaz. I am the Prime Zealot—the leader," Weveld said. "For centuries, the Crown Magician has also served as Prime. This knowledge is one of the closest guarded secrets in history. No one outside of this village knows what I have just told you."

"You are saying that the Order of Magic has been commanded by a sect this whole time?" Artemys asked. In all of his visions, all of this scrying, he had never seen this.

Weveld's face was a block of stone. He gave one stiff nod.

"Why?"

"Look around you," Weveld said. "These books...and the brothers you saw outside...this is the truth of magic."

"What truth?" Artemys asked. He had already said this once. The shelves were just as cluttered as the ones in the antechamber, the brothers did not seem distinguished, and Weveld did not seem wise.

"Magic *is* a gift from the Maker. Though not without strings attached," Weveld said.

Artemys shook his head. He had seen the invention of the Maker, when the Kinship had resolved to teach of him. There was no more truth to the Maker than there was to Weveld's role of Crown Magician. If Artemys believed in any gods, they were the ones worshipped before the Kinship. "I do not believe in the Maker."

"Then it's a gift from the gods, or from the spirits, or whatever you believe!" Weveld's face was finally moving, an expression mixed of frustration and hope. What hope? What did Weveld want? The old man said, "My point is...there would be no Magic Order without the Disciples. There would be no peace without us."

"Your zealots? Andrakaz?" Artemys had read the name once in a historical tome. He had seen the man supposed to be the great wizard Andrakaz in his visions. Ending the age of myth and beginning their age with the founding of Olympus in Year 0. Nothing Artemys had seen gave him reason to believe Andrakaz had any real *greatness*. "What does he have to do with the Order of Magic?"

Weveld bowed his head, apparently at a loss for words. After a drawn out moment, he looked up. "You have to believe me, Artemys, though you won't. The gift of magic was the gift of creation. Our world was made from nothing, from the void. Writing an earth spell creates earth in as real a way as the world was built."

Artemys nodded. This much was believable.

"The human race would have destroyed itself centuries ago. Do you honestly believe that power-hungry, devious, violent people would be able to preserve the world with the gift of creation?"

Artemys frowned. "You're telling me that you *keep* the Order of Magic from being too powerful on purpose? So we won't destroy ourselves?"

"No. Even then, the cults and sorcerers that operate outside of the Order would be enough. Andrakaz foresaw this. He created a spell that would limit the creation of magic, allowing only a certain amount of energy to be created at any given moment of time," Weveld explained. "The Disciples use an analogy of a Hunter for this. It hunts its prey, but leaves enough that the prey is not extinct. In a similar way, Andrakaz's Spell allows magic to exist, but keeps the amount of creation at a safe level."

"Ha!" Artemys rose out of his chair and stepped away. He began pacing. How could this be? Was Weveld just trying to trick him? What would Weveld gain by creating these lies? "You're telling me," he said, feet shuffling through the fur rug, "that even if I wanted to, I could only do so much with magic?"

"Yes."

"I already know you're lying."

A smile cracked Weveld's stone visage. "Your storm? At Delfie all those years ago? You believe that means you can do anything?"

"You know about that?" He could remember that day. His mother dead. He had conjured a storm of anger, a hurricane crashing upon the island of Delfie. Even the great Order of Magic, whose headquarters were held at the School there, had done nothing in the face of that onslaught.

"Why do you think I did not stop it?" Weveld asked.

Artemys froze. If Weveld had known the storm of Delfie to be Artemys's doing, why would he not have cast a ward to defend the School? A month of repairs and a small fortune were the cost of the damage. Why would Weveld not have intervened?

Weveld leaned back in his chair. "I'm not trying to win you over with fantastic stories. Your storm used a huge amount of energy, and a ward would have used an equal amount." He did not mean physical energy—magic drained none from its user. Such was the gift of creation, Artemys supposed. Weveld continued, "We measure the amount of creation in years. For that year, your storm and my ward would have used roughly a tenth of the magic energy that could be expended. Not nearly all of it. But there are thousands of magicians in this world."

"And they would have noticed," Artemys finished. He now understood what Weveld meant by "you have to believe me, but you won't." This would change his entire understanding of magic, if he accepted it. He would go back to the learning stages.

"Artemys."

He continued pacing, feeling his heart pound like a hammer in his chest. It was almost painful. If he did not accept this truth... how could he compete with the realm, and the Order, and Weveld? How could he even plan to fix things if he did not accept the way things were?

"Artemys!"

He froze. He had been pacing so fast that his breath was a hoarse pant. The room seemed larger now, like Artemys had shrunk. He shook his head to clear it. "I cannot fathom what any of this means." That was no more than a whisper. "And if I enact the changes I plan to..." Had he really just said that aloud?

"Changes?" Weveld asked. "We know of some of your plans... you desire power? Both political and magical, do you not?"

Artemys shook his head. "No. Not for me. I have seen the past, a repeating cycle of imprisonment. The people deserve mercy, and the Triumvirate system *cannot* give it to them. They *deserve* more than they have, and I *will* give it to them."

"You think that changing the government will help them?"

"They are yearning for the old ways. They need a king. They deserve it."

"You think that becoming king will fix these problems?"

"If I doubted it... I would not suffer the burden I do."

"You truly believe all of this?" Weveld asked. He looked confused, slightly disappointed, yet deeply ponderous.

"With all that I am," Artemys breathed. Now, more than ever, he clung to these beliefs, and they were as strong as a mountain. No, stronger, if magic could create mountains with the breath of a few words.

Weveld slumped back into his chair. "Very well," he said, contentedly. "I won't press you about it now, though at some time we will discuss this again. What I can offer you is help. You asked how to understand what I have told you, how to "fathom" it. We can help you. We can teach you. That's the reason we were watching you; not to spy on you, but to recruit you if you showed the interest." Weveld chuckled. "Instead, *you* found *us!*"

Artemys sank into the chair again, his breath still laboured. He would learn again. He had to. He had to accept what Weveld taught him, and learn how to use it. He knew that the key to his plans was hovering within this Discipleship. It would be the first step of his plans. Part one.

3

Year of Olympus 540

The city of Trionus was built on three plateaus: the Lower Wall, which loomed above Periander's army; then the Mountain's Grief, a sagging cliff on the city's namesake mountain; and finally the Strait's Sentinel, a massive keep overlooking the Strait of Galinor.

Periander would have to burn through the Lower Wall first.

"Cowards and scoundrels all of them," Odyn spat, storming into Periander's tent. He was a broad man, with a barrel for a chest and a boulder for a head.

Aghast, the herald proclaimed, "Odyn the Tenth, Prince of Olympus, Victor of the Tourney at Quintus, Wisd-"

"And so on and so forth. Be gone with you. or I'll have your tongue," Odyn rasped. He turned to Periander, who glanced up at him, feigning amusement. "Theseus sent word, green as the pine tree he is."

Periander nodded, and let his mask of humour drop. "He has reached Dagger's Edge?"

Odyn nodded. It had been a month since the unfortunate meeting at Oban Ford, and now they besieged the city of their enemy, where it lay on the wrong side of the Strait. Trion and his armies needed to cross before they could come to its aid. "As I was saying, those cowards on the wall won't even let us speak to a proper commander."

"There probably isn't one here."

"They're still cowards."

Periander grinned, and continued taunting his cohort. "It

takes a fair bit of courage to stand against an army of this size."

"Blasted seafarer," Odyn laughed. It was a nickname he often called Periander. "In a city like that? It doesn't take bravery. It takes a spear, a helmet, and a piss bucket to stand against this army."

Periander stifled a laugh. "Oh, I forgot this was an Olympian army..."

"Damn blasted seafarer," Odyn boomed, slamming a meaty fist against the table. "You know your Avernan drunkards would have no other effect on these cowards!"

Periander laughed, took a drink of lukewarm mead, and leaned back. Odyn grabbed another mug off a nearby platter and took a mouthful, then spat it out in a spray. "What kind of dung is this? Bring me an ale!"

A trembling servant stormed in with a different mug, and Odyn grabbed it from the short man's arms. "We've got a fair number of cowards ourselves," he told Periander, even before the poor servant had left.

Periander raised an eyebrow. "It's not often one must serve the tent of two Imperial Princes."

"Soon to be worse. They say the snake Weveld is on his way."

Periander sat up. "He's coming here? We need him holding the bridge at Dagger's Edge, not sitting on his arse in the worst siege of the century!"

"Maybe he can break the siege," Odyn said.

"Perhaps."

Odyn put aside his ale and stood to his feet. Periander's map lay across the table, mugs and coin purses holding its corners down. He glared at it for several moments, muttering to himself and examining each hostile sighting closely. There were tags for ongoing conflict and smaller pins for alleged sightings of giants. It was a mess.

After a minute, Odyn lifted a hand to his cheek, setting it against his neck to give a ponderous look. "When old man Theseus appointed his son, I didn't think too much of it. But when your father passed..."

Periander looked up. His father didn't pass. He had been murdered. Assassinated. Akheron Gothikar had stolen the throne of Avernus from House Aristorn after leading a people's revolution against the Kinship.

Odyn continued. "I didn't know what I would do. An old man—part of a dynasty that has ruled since the Triumvirate was founded—and I'm now ruling with two boys."

Periander stood up. He was a year past his twentieth name day. Prince Theseus was a year past his twenty-fifth.

"I mean no offence, Periander. You're a good man, well worthy of your status." Odyn finally turned from the map toward him. "Which is why I bring it up. I've been through war before. But I am becoming so tired now. I will ride at your side as long as I can, but I have an heir."

"What are you suggesting?" Periander asked. "Would you step down?" He found himself terrified of the idea—three young Princes defending against perhaps the greatest threat the Triumvirate had ever faced.

"No, no. But whatever happens—you must watch my son closely. I won't have him ruin our name. If he is to become Odyn the Eleventh during this conflict, then so be it. But if he becomes Prince after, I fear he will only know a life of pampering on the Olympian throne."

Periander pursed his lips. "You could make him your general."

"Even this 'Olympian army' wouldn't follow the Prince's son."

"They follow me."

"Yes, but your father changed the world!" Odyn boomed, amiably. Then his face folded sternly. "They watch you, Periander. To see if you will best your father, or vanish in his shadow."

Periander found himself short of breath. As a child maturing without a father, he had often wondered if men would ever speak of the son as they did the great Gothikar Conqueror.

It brought up feelings from Agwar Marsh. Brought up that murderous shame and the hatred. *It was survival,* he told himself. But it was more. The assassins had killed Joran. They had killed him, so he had killed them.

Odyn threw him off of it. "I heard you were married before all of this *madness* started."

Periander grinned. In his mind's eye, the Marsh was replaced by Catlin, Cat with her glowing blond hair, those eyes that soothed his soul. "Aye." He nodded to Odyn. "How old were you when you wed?"

Odyn took a swig. "Twenty!" he laughed. "First two children were stillborn. Third turned out a bit better though," he said.

Before Periander could reply, a sound like thunder made both of them jump. Periander grabbed a token from beside the map and broke it, watching a prepared scrying spell shimmer into his vision.

He could now see the frontlines of his camp and most of Trionus's Lower Wall district. As he watched, he saw the thunder strike again—a massive burst of red and orange burning through the streets. The spell faded.

"Glyphs, that fool Weveld is attacking already!" he told Odyn. The large man stormed from the tent without a word. Periander threw open a chest beside his cot and shouted, "Squire!"

A man came at once—not Periander's normal squire, but neither of them said a word. The man helped Periander into his breastplate. As the Prince slid vambraces up his arm and yanked on the leather straps, the squire tightened the ties on his back and helped him into greaves.

Finally, Periander took hold of the Avernan handblade—a sleek, one-handed weapon.

"Milord," the squire said. "Your spells."

Periander accepted the belt-full of tokens. "Other way," he told him. He kept elemental attacks on his right side and defensive spells on the left. The squire corrected his mistake, and bid Periander luck and the Maker's blessing.

Periander didn't wait for the blessing to finish. His father had destroyed nearly every Stead of the Maker, so why the squire would invoke him was a mystery.

His soldiers were in disarray. Half had followed the Crown Magician on this hasty assault of the city, while the other half had remained. Such a division could break morale—Weveld would have some answering to do.

"Captain Illus, how many men do you still have in your command?"

The Captain was still being armoured by his squire, but was walking toward Periander nonetheless. "Nearly all of them, milord. The Crown Magician's gate opened on the other side of camp, not where our tents are."

"You will defend our camp. I'm taking the rest of our men into the city. If you see any other captains, tell them to rally their men and follow me."

The Captain nodded, and, swatting his squire away, strode briskly towards his troops.

Periander bellowed summons to the rest of the soldiers, found himself surrounded by a group of Captains, and began his march into the Lower Wall.

Weveld had left a smouldering hole where the gate had been, burnt and desiccated corpses littering the ground around it. Periander's men entered it ahead of him. By the time he reached it, Avernan soldiers had panned through the streets inside, the slums of Trionus. Thundering booms still echoed off the mountain cliffs; Periander looked up and watched the crackling energies of a magic duel near the entrance to the Mountain's Grief.

It took him close to an hour to climb the steps and reach the next district. The fighting was still in play, both magic and blades leaving a trail of gore as the Imperial troops slowly forced their way towards higher ground.

Periander saw very little combat himself, only once did the fighting get close enough to his guards, and even then they could deal with it. Battle was nothing to enjoy, but it was even worse to simply watch.

There was a major crossroads in the midst of the Mountain's Grief, a square that divided to a north road around the mountain's shoulder to the Strait's Sentinel, and a road that ran the rest of the way through the Grief towards the old ruins of a Stead of the Maker.

Most of the soldiers continued pressing the soldiers of House Trion in the latter direction, though Periander led his guards onto the north road. Here there were more scorches and burns of magic. The gates into the Keep were gone—dissolved perhaps, for no trace of them remained.

The sounds of battle seemed to fade as he led his troop up the stairs and around the mountain's shoulder. The Strait's Sentinel was a massive block of bricks and mortar built on a cliff top. From the battlements on the east side, it was a direct drop into the Strait of Galinor, direct enough to drop a rock cleanly into the water.

Periander strode into the Keep's great hall, and his soldiers fanned out into the adjoining hallways. At the far end of the great hall was a pair of massive doors. Periander stepped through them and onto a wide balcony. There was artwork on the walls of the Keep, and a bench against the edge of the balcony.

He put his hands on two battlements and leaned between them, staring down at the distant water. He could hear arguing voices from the rampart above him and fighting somewhere nearby.

He could feel that guilt again, tugging beneath the surface, confusing him. A family had lived here. Children had grown here. And Ernes Trion had thrown it all away.

What could be so wrong with this? To toss it aside and wage a war?

"Sir?" a voice asked.

Periander turned from the parapet and smiled. Captain Mordus stood with hand on sword, dripping with the blood of their enemies. "Mordus," he greeted, clasping hands with his subordinate and friend. "The city is ours?"

Mordus nodded.

They both started at a loud thump. Turning, Periander saw the arms and head of a torso slumped across the rampart where he had just stood. Its weight pulled it off a moment later, and it disappeared into the void. A streak of blood stained the crenel between battlements.

"That was one of ours," Mordus snapped. They ran across the adjacent great hall to a stairwell. Mordus always seemed fast to Periander, ever since he had ridden the length of the Cerden Mountains to fetch the reinforcements for Dagger's Edge.

They stormed into the chamber directly above the battlement, finding living quarters. A woman was standing in the doorway to the balcony, a blade in her right hand. Her sleeve was drenched in the blood of the man she had slain and tossed into the Strait. Her back was to them.

"Hello?" Periander asked, giving Mordus a warning glance. They approached her slowly. Periander could tell from the decor of the room and the woman's garb that she was nobility.

She turned at the sound of their voices, a blank gaze that

seemed to look through them. There was blood on her forehead, though it was only a smear from rubbing her hand there.

"Perhaps you should accompany us," Mordus suggested, stepping closer.

She didn't speak, and didn't move, but continued staring at them darkly.

Periander grabbed Mordus's arm. "Close enough," he said, but it was too late.

The woman lunged toward them, the blade disappearing into Mordus's gut. He gasped in shock. Periander smashed the woman away with a backhand. He pushed Mordus's stunned form back onto the nearby bed, and yanked the knife out of his spilling gut. He traced glyphs into the floorboards, and breathed, *"Telvyn al'ross. Azur neeros dei."*

Mordus gasped as the spell sewed the wound shut.

Periander stood to his feet. The crazed woman was lying against the wall, the wall tainted with red from the concussive blow of her head against it.

Periander closed his eyes. The rage was there, same as when he had killed the men in Agwar Marsh.

And the guilt.

A robed man stormed into the room. "Prince Periander. Are you all right?"

Periander spun on him. "Weveld! The Maker's curses upon you!" He stepped toward the man angrily. "What were you thinking? Even if you can burn this city yourself, you made two Imperial Princes look like fools!"

Mordus had finally sat up, and stumbled out into the great hall to give the royals their privacy.

Weveld frowned. "That was not my intent."

Periander could recall Odyn's words. "That snake, Weveld." Periander spat to one side and turned away from the Crown Magician. He glanced at the gruesome spectacle against the far wall, then back to the snake's eyes.

"Burn this Keep into the Strait."

"Milord?"

Periander nodded and strode for the door. "You heard me, Weveld. The Dominion must know that treason bears the highest price."

He heard Weveld following him out of the great hall. "I

will have soldiers escort the prisoners—"

"No prisoners. We must wound Ernes Trion. Wounded animals may be dangerous, but they are also reckless," Periander said. He knew hunting. He knew logic. His father had been a great man, perhaps the greatest, as Odyn had said. Listening to that voice of guilt would not lead him out of his father's shadow. This conflict against House Trion might.

"Very well," the Crown Mage said, his head bowed. Though he shared some authorities with the Princes, he also served them.

The soldiers feasted after the battle, as was the custom. Their campfires all dwindled in comparison to the Keep. Pigeons from Edessa would later confirm that the flames were visible from the outlying villages in the Sinai Foothills. When the sun rose in the morning, the city of Trionus was built on two plateaus: the Lower Wall and the Mountain's Grief.

Ч

Year of Olympus 552

Artemys was on the stairwell leading down to the kitchens, ready to break his fast, when something else broke. He was seven, his mother was lonely and his father was in the West, in the War. The stairs he descended were in the Gothikar estate in Bertren, several days south of Avernus. The smell of bread was winding up the spiral stone steps, drawing out those who got to eat it. Artemys's mother told him that not everyone could eat when and what they want. Artemys did not think that was right.

A large hand grabbed Artemys's small one and shoved him back against the pillar around which he was walking. A man was holding him and crouching next to him. Some men bowed to Artemys; that was not what this man was doing. "You're what, ten?" the man asked, his words slurred. He spit to one side.

"Seven." Artemys's knees trembled.

"Seven. You're seven, but you're as bad as any of them. Odyn, the family that has ruled since the dawn of time... Theseus, the righteous pigs... and the worst of them all: your daddy. Periander, Prince of the whole Maker-damned world..."

Artemys could not speak.

"Glyphs, you've got even less guts than your old man. Guess that's what you get for being raised on milk, not mead." The man released Artemys and stood again. He was wearing the green and black tunic of a Gothikar guard, chainmail, and a hood.

"Sorry, sir," Artemys tried, whispering a prayer.

The man laughed, and spit again—onto Artemys. Artemys

flinched and moved his head away from the drips on his small waist jacket. It stunk.

"Let's see what you Princes are made of." The man struck Artemys with the back of his hand. Everything went white. Artemys felt the steps beneath him. They felt sharper than they had when he was just walking down them. When he stopped rolling, he had a fire in his side. He tried to push himself up, because he could not see anything but a blur, but a boot pressed down on his back.

"Ah-ah-ah," the guard whispered. The boot disappeared and then reappeared with a lot of sideways momentum. Artemys felt a crack in his side and did not even feel himself roll this time. He blinked and was staring at a blue sky. When had he made it outside? Why did his leg hurt?

The man's hand grabbed the front of his tunic and hauled Artemys's limp torso until their eyes met again. "What gives you the right to being Lord Prince Gothikar any more than me, huh?" he asked. Artemys could tell he really wanted to know. "I'm an Aristorn, somewhere back there. I'm as much royalty as you, earth-scum. So. Tell me. What's so special about you?"

There was shouting somewhere in the background, help. Artemys stared at the guard and tried to understand what he was saying. Everything pulsed with mind-numbing pain.

"Huh!" his attacker breathed, rattling Artemys with a shake of his left hand. The right hand raised. "The answer," he whispered, "is *nothing.*" Then he slammed his chain-mailed hand into Artemys's jaw. Everything went black.

Year of Olympus 555

Artemys sat in yet another class on the basics of magic. Outside the stained glass window was a pacing shadow, one of the few guards at the School of Delfie. Usually there were none, but these were the years of war.

His father had killed the man that had attacked Artemys. No one would let Artemys know that, no one would tell him when he had asked about it. But he knew it, because his father had known it when he looked Artemys in the eye after it was done.

Artemys already knew everything his teacher was saying.

He had read it in a book during the year after that incident. The year he had not left the library. After two years of study, his father had deemed Artemys worthy of the magician's gift. So now Artemys could speak the glyphs and his spells would control magic instead of staring at him from the page, silent.

"Artemys," Master Kaen said, "is there something outside?"

"No, Master. I was just looking at the stained glass window of Rearus Vel, the great commander."

"Are you trying to impress me with your knowledge of history?" Kaen asked him.

"No, I—"

"Perhaps if you wish to impress me, you should explain magic to me."

Artemys smirked. "As you will, Master." He glanced at his peers. He knew he would only stutter his own words, so he quoted something he had read once. "'There is a glyph for everything, categorized as internal or external. Glyphs for the world are external: fire, water, earth, air. Glyphs for behavior, perception and such are internal. Each glyph must be written and spoken to be activated. The only limits to magic are the imaginations of the spell-casters and their knowledge of all the glyphs.' The School knows only one thousand and *twenty-seven*. But it is very possible to know more. That would be... *impressive.*"

Even Master Kaen was silent for a few moments after that. "Please see me after class," he said at last.

They negotiated to have Artemys moved ahead in his years at their school. He could remember glyphs after looking at them once and his Masters told him he was also turning out to be quite creative.

Year of Olympus 558

"She is close now." A man was speaking to Artemys's father, but Artemys hung on every word.

"May I see her?" his father asked.

The man's face folded. "You know it to be ill fortune."

Artemys's father nodded. The man left, letting a small breeze through the door. They stood in the Delfie School, where it seemed they had stood for years. Artemys took his father's hand.

"Hello there, young man. Sorry I just arrived now."

Artemys shrugged. "That's not a problem. How many giants did you slay?"

"None, this time. The war is done, Artemys," his father said, sinking down onto the bench beside him. He sounded tired. Artemys's mother had sounded tired too.

"Father," Artemys said. "Were you there when I was born?"

Periander smiled. "Of course I was. But I only saw your mother before and then after. You know the custom."

"That's a bad custom."

His father laughed.

They waited in silence for several minutes.

"Father," Artemys said at last. "Are you done fighting?"

There was another stretch of silence, long enough that Artemys thought of repeating himself. Finally, his father stirred, moving off the bench and to his knees in front of Artemys.

"Listen to me, Artemys. I never loved fighting. I never loved the war. I love you, and your mother, and...your new brother. That's *why* I was fighting. For you."

Artemys nodded. "Yes, but are you done?"

His father chuckled again. "Yes." His eyes were distant now.

They sat side by side again, and many minutes passed. It had been so long since the last time they had. Artemys could hardly remember.

Finally, his father asked, "How's your schooling? The wizards of Delfie are some of the best in the Dominion. One of the reasons it was easiest to have your mother brought here for the baby. Both she and I could get here quickly."

Artemys nodded. His mother had arrived two weeks prior to prepare. His father had come only yesterday.

"Well?"

Artemys stood to his feet, and with barely contained pride told him, "Master Kaen has asked me to be his Apprentice!"

"What?" His father's jaw dropped. "Master Kaen! You've been here three years and you're already becoming Apprentice?"

"The ceremony will be in two weeks."

"That's astounding! You must be the youngest...?"

Artemys, swelling with joy, breathed, "Second!"

His father grabbed him beneath his shoulders and lifted him into an embrace. "Artemys, I am *so* proud of you!"

Artemys rested his head on those rock-solid shoulders and lost himself in his father's strength. He did not know how much time had passed, until finally he spoke again. "Father, those men do not look happy." He pointed past the embrace, through the window at the cluster of dark-clothed men.

His father set him down again. "Stay here, Artemys."

As soon as the door closed behind his father, Artemys leapt onto the bench, put his knees on the window sill and watched. His father approached the men cautiously; they turned and presented him with a bundle of linens. They were smiling now, patting his father's back. Artemys smiled. That was his brother in those linens.

Now their smiles faded, and they exchanged words with his father. Those shoulders slumped, and the bundle passed out of his hands and into a servant's. They again patted his back, but differently now. Artemys frowned. What could it mean? Was his brother sick? The servant holding him seemed concerned. Where is Mother?

Artemys slid off the sill, dropping his rump onto the bench again.

Many minutes passed until his father returned. He brought the baby with him, crouched beside Artemys and told him, "This is Pyrsius. He's the youngest Gothikar now. Say hello to your brother."

"Where is Mother?" Artemys asked.

Year of Olympus 563

Artemys was tired of entertaining his brother. He was tired of pretending that leaving the School of Delfie had made him happier. He was tired of deluding himself that Kerres actually loved him. He was just tired. He had that same slump to his shoulders that he had seen in his father.

He sat in his grandfather's study of the Avernan Keep, a room full of bookshelves, expensive rarities, and comfortable furnishings. When the Aristorns ruled the Avernan lands, this entire storey had not existed. Artemys's grandfather had added it and the storey above. Artemys had never met his grandfather, but many people talked about him.

Outside, a riot was ruining the streets of Avernus. Artemys could hear the shouts and screams and the crash of wood dropped from windows. Food and resource prices were on the rise; the government had no way to fix it, because the source of the problem was in their very society. Things had been like this since the war, since one or two rebellious lords had plunged the entire realm into eighteen years of bloodshed.

"There's no such thing as trust," Salantar said. Artemys's father nodded to his wartime friend. Salantar had scared Artemys when they first met, but he was much safer than his scarred exterior looked.

Artemys had been listening to their conversation instead of reading the thousand page tome on the table in front of him. That had started him thinking this way. The sounds of riot did not help.

Artemys's father sighed. "My father once told me that—"

"Your father once told you a proverb for every day of your life! I thought you only knew the man for a year or two!" Salantar laughed, a welcome chuckle to bring relief.

Periander only shrugged it away. "He said that the times when men and women need to trust each other the most are the times that we do not."

Salantar again piped up his wit. "If it makes you feel any better, I trust you fine."

"I am certain that will solve all of our society's problems," Periander rebutted dryly.

"What will?" Artemys asked.

Salantar muttered, beneath his breath, "Oh, *all* the Gothikars are a serious lot..."

"Something new. Something to distract them. I don't mean another hardship. Just a new leader, a new passion, a new dream. It is not hard to agree that most men and women deserve better than second guessing their brothers and keeping a wary eye for the dagger in their back."

They do, Artemys agreed. *We all deserve better than this world.*

Periander and his friend took a drink from their flagons.

Salantar was older than Periander by several years, but they were both marred and battered men, long after their prime.

"Maker," Salantar cursed, "I thought the war was over."

Periander shook his head. "We thought the high cost of it was something else. The real cost to the war is that it may never end. All I see is damage. And none of it caused by a giant with an axe."

The two warriors stared down into their ale. They had already been out to try breaking up the riot. But only so much could be done.

Artemys rested his head in his hands and wondered, in all of his knowledge of glyphs and magic... *Where is the answer? Where does the war end?*

5

Year of Olympus 541

The valley of Dagger's Edge was a sight to belittle any man. An Imperial military camp spanned from the narrow crossing of the Strait of Galinor up the slopes of the Cerden Mountains, each tent a link in the chainmail of a god. There were three camps within, like the two halves of the god's breastplate and the torso plate below. Each camp consisted of several thousand tents. This camp covered several miles, though it still lay in the distance.

A procession of soldiers, guards, merchants, and wagons were the sleeves of such a set of armour. Here, Periander and his men rode, descending the slopes toward the camp, a long line of men and carts.

From this vantage, where Periander regarded the fortifications as the armour of the gods, the namesake bridge seemed to indeed be a dagger, an infernal blade thrust into the body of the titan. No records remained of the crossings's construction; historians believed some of the eroded inscriptions to be an early form of the Old Tongue, though its translation escaped them.

"*Korbios decadus abyron*," Periander murmured beneath his breath. The Old Tongue was strange to him, though his father insisted it be part of his education all those years ago.

"'Conquest stands alone?'" Mordus quoted. "From here it seems conquest is a camp of knights."

Periander smiled. Mordus had been inseparable from his side since Periander had healed him during the Battle of Trionus

City last year. As Prince, Periander was certain he could order the Eldisan native to leave, but Periander didn't mind the camaraderie of the common soldier.

They began their descent into Prince Theseus's camp. Dagger's Edge had been built in the years before the Dominion had been united beneath the Three Princes and the Triumvirate, perhaps even in the Age of Myths a hundred years before that. Periander had read a chronicle of the great explorer Oban Hokar, who claimed he had found the ruins of a great city in the World's Foundation, a city five times that of Olympus. Periander doubted such a city could sustain itself so far inland. It was after this very explorer that the ford where this war had begun was named.

Periander had to pause on the thought. Contemporary historians were only beginning to refer to is as a war, as there had only been one true battle—the taking of Trionus.

"Sir?" Mordus asked. "The messengers from Theseus bade you hurry, if I recall."

Periander nodded. "I'm aware," he said, and they continued down the slope. Behind them, several hundred of Periander's troops were marching out of the Cerden Mountains, making the dirt trail into a muddy road as the columns reached the camp.

"Is this war?" he asked Mordus.

The man let out a hearty roar. "Look around, my Prince. This is not a camp of peacetime. Can you hear the blacksmith's pounding metal? They are making swords, not plows."

Periander nodded. "I had hoped it would not come to this. I told Lord Trion he would not cross the Dagger's Edge."

"He hasn't. And you had better hope he doesn't," Mordus replied.

They soon reached the entrance to the camp. There was an array of twenty guards at the opening in the palisade wall. They had a campfire burning nearby where several of them huddled. A few men came forward to speak with Mordus. They eyed Periander in surprise when they were told who he was. After a quick conversation, Mordus returned to his Prince's side and led the way once more.

They were now in the camp proper; Periander's horse wove its way through the muddy intersections where soldiers jumped out of the way of its steel-shoed hooves. From his mount,

Periander could see over some of the tents. He could see the camp stretching uphill on three sides of him. On the fourth was only the sky and the distant glaciers of the Maker's Forge. That was the north, that was Oban Ford, that was the war.

. . .

The next day, Periander awoke early. He had been on the road for days, and his legs ached. He ate a quick breakfast alone, served by his attendants, before setting out into the camp. The sun had just begun to peak over the Cerden Mountains. It seemed odd to Periander to be seeing the sunrise in the east over these mountains... to him, there was nothing farther west than them. Around him, the camp was beginning to awaken. Few wagons were rolling between tents but there was already smoke rising from the cook fires and the forges.

By the time he got out of the Gothikar camp, the entire military town was abuzz. Some men were sparring, some were running messages, some were working on their equipment. Blacksmith anvils echoed around the valley.

Theseus's tent seemed tranquil in the midst of the camp's chaos, set apart like a pendant hanging beneath the chainmail of the god. Unannounced, Periander stepped within.

"Periander! At last!" Erykus Theseus cried, rising off a stool and stepping past his table to clasp arms with Periander. He was only a few years older than Periander, so in the years since their Princehood they had become fast friends. Now, after more than a year guarding the bridge, Theseus sported a large, matted beard, giving him the appearance of age.

"These mountains are like a maze," Periander replied. He gestured at the book Theseus had been reading. "They say when my father was a boy, a tome was worth nearly five hundred gold. You and I are blessed to read as easily as we do." Midsentence, Theseus's distinct features clouded, so Periander asked, "How is *your* father?"

"I'm afraid he passed last cycle," Erykus murmured, stepping back. "I recently returned from the ceremony in Athyns, where he has been laid to rest in the crypt of our household."

"By the Maker...did this have to happen in these troubling

times?"

Erykus nodded. "I had only enough time to hang a wreath by the plaque, "Verin Theseus," before returning to this accursed camp."

Periander sat as Theseus did, placing his hands on the strategic map on the table. "I vividly recall the day we buried *my* father," he recounted. "It was the first snowfall of the winter. He had passed a week earlier."

"They say the killers were not caught for a year afterwards."

"More than a year. And even now, we have not caught those truly responsible. The men were hung when Lord Ivos was still steward and I was still a boy, but they were hired men."

"Our Houses have many enemies." Prince Theseus took a drink from a mug on his desk. "It is an unfortunate consequence of ruling."

They mulled through their own thoughts in silence until finally Periander asked, "What was the urgency? Your courier urged us to haste."

Erykus nodded. "There hasn't been an attack in three months."

"Good!" Periander regarded his friend's concerned features. Theseus took another drink from his mug. He was reminded of Odyn swigging ale before Weveld destroyed Trionus. "The longer it takes them to rally assaults, the better."

"No. Before that there were attacks every week. They didn't run out of giants, they decided to stop attacking."

"Send out scouts. They are likely trying a flank."

Erykus shrugged. "I've sent out close to a dozen scouts. Not a single one has returned."

Periander stood up, almost knocking his chair back. The tent was low, the canvas brushing his matted dark hair. He had been riding long hours, and had not slept since before the sun rose that morning. "So we have no idea what is out there?"

Theseus nodded, leaning back in his chair. "Is Weveld with you? Perhaps he can determine what lies north of the Strait."

"He left with Odyn. They intend to examine the defences in Galinor and then Edessa."

Erykus scowled. "You were given magic, were you not?"

"My father insisted my education include a study of

glyphs."

"He destroyed the Kinship of the Maker, yet agreed glyphs are important?" Erykus asked, tracing a finger along the map's coast on the table between them. Periander finally sat down, and Erykus leaned toward him.

"He never doubted the Maker, or the glyphs. He simply allowed the people what they wanted," Periander explained. "After my years of study, the Order of Magic recognized my position and my knowledge with the gift of magic. But my abilities are basic."

"Sir, permission to enter?" a voice called.

Theseus barked an affirmative, and a small man appeared. "Captain?" Erykus asked the newcomer.

His captain bowed his head; his gaunt features were no less concerned when he rose. "My Princes. A rider has been spotted."

They leapt up from the table and followed him outside. Theseus's pavilion was closer to the bridge than the area Periander's men had been told to camp at, so it was brief walk to the Dagger's Edge Bridge. There was already commotion, men pointing and exclamations drifting from beneath matted beards and rusted helms.

Theseus followed his captain to the opening in the palisades, still sliding his fingers into leather gloves. The air was much colder here than even in Athyns. They stood at the foot of Dagger's Edge. There were three steps up to the bridge where a line of stone statues faced east along the river. They were sculptures of soldiers, standing watch over the Dominion, it seemed. A few dozen feet below were the silent waters of the Galinor Strait.

Periander followed Prince Theseus's gaze across the bridge to where a horse galloped. As it came closer, the soldiers sucked in their breath and even Periander muttered, "By the Maker..." as the rider came into focus.

A headless corpse was tied upright in the saddle, bobbing sickly as it was bounced toward them. A spearman grabbed the bridle once the mare came close enough. "One of the scouts, sirs." He spat off the bridge into the waters below. The gruesome sight was unbound and let gently off the horse. The crazed animal was foaming from the mouth and stepped around erratically, hindering the process.

Periander examined the body before the soldiers bore it away. The hide tunic the man had worn was split with crisscrossing red lines, lashes that had torn flesh from bone. Several fingers were also missing, and the letter T had been carved into the poor man's palms.

Erykus paled and turned away. "What cruelty is this?"

"A message," Periander told him. "He wants us to cross." He strode towards the palisades and glared up into the hills beyond the bridge. "Theseus, ready your troops."

"It's provocation!" Erykus retorted. "He wants us to come onto his battlefield."

"No, he wants to catch us on the bridge," Periander explained. No sooner had the words left his mouth than battle horns echoed the skies. Theseus spun as the sounds continued, wailing cries that rose hairs on any man's arms.

Then the pounding started. It could have been drums, but the earth seemed to tremble with it. A sea rose over the hilltops and, as though released from a reservoir, flooded downwards to drown the god Periander had imagined. To drown their camp in blood and steel.

The mountain men were howling again as they stormed in the thousands down the slopes toward the Imperial camp. Each stood two feet taller than any of the Periander's soldiers, each carried a sharpened axe or mace, each ran among a crowd of his kin.

Periander was already storming across camp, bellowing, "To arms!" Men scrambled from tents, plunging feet into studded leather greaves or heaving chainmail onto their shoulders. Cooks and servants fled toward the back of camp. Somehow, amidst the chaos, Mordus appeared at Periander's side as quickly as he always did. He helped Periander into his plate armour, buckled the straps behind each knee. Periander slid his gauntlets on, fumbled with the clasps on them, and then reached through the loop of his shield.

"Trelkl is running to his camp," the fellow easterner boomed over the din. "We'll need some giants, I suspect."

Periander peered back across the Strait, where Trion's tribes were still pouring out of the mountains, crammed shoulder to shoulder. "Maker guard us," Periander breathed. Trion had said "millions," but that could not be possible, could it? He slid his right gauntlet through a leather string and gripped the pommel of his sword. The string would help him from losing his blade in the melee. "Let's go."

The next half hour was a blur. The bridge was already packed with soldiers when the mountain horde stormed onto it. A host of Imperial infantry waited on the southern shore of the Strait. Theseus appeared at Periander's side; together they watched the bodies fall amongst the stone statues, sliding on slick red trails, and plummeting into the waters below.

Giants fell near as often as their soldiers, but Periander did not stop praying beneath his breath. There were still men cresting the foothills on the other side of the Strait and Periander could still feel their pounding march in his bones, a dull ache forming in the back of his throat.

"Where are the magicians?" Periander asked as the mountain men advanced step by step across the bridge.

Erykus spat. "I have only two at this camp. Weveld deemed this camp was safe enough."

"Find them," Periander said. Theseus bristled slightly at the order, but shook himself when their circumstances sunk in again.

Periander and Mordus were able to advance as far as the palisades. Both slain and living soldiers were knocked off the bridge to make room for more.

Theseus finally returned with his magicians. "This is Daren of Cuross and Kronos Accalia."

Periander nodded to them. "We'll use air."

"What spell?" Daren asked.

"Any. We should focus the attacks in the middle of the bridge," he said, pointing with one hand, "so the force will knock them off the sides. Mordus, have our archers line these cliffs. Anything moves in the water, shoot it."

They nodded. Periander had a moment of hesitance. What did he know of strategy? He was no veteran. He had only seen one battle. Theseus regarded him with certainty, eyes meeting his with a nod. Periander shook himself. This man knew nothing more than he. None of them did.

"We need some soldiers to stay off this ground." He gestured to the dirt around them. Men instantly vacated the spot he had indicated. He watched Kronos and Daren write their spells, then copied them. He did not know this spell, but he knew the words to control these glyphs.

Finally, he looked up at the bloody wall, where giants and men met in a flurry of blades and the screams of death. He took a deep breath, then roared, "Fall back!"

The soldiers were hesitant at first, but soon ran past the ring of men around Periander. The mountain men roared in triumph and stormed forward. He waited as long as he could so their men would survive, one hand stretched toward the bridge. At last, he breathed, "*bor'sab irkono ob ogar*," and a blast of air pierced the approaching charge. Several soldiers still fleeing the bridge were caught in the gale, but a dozen mountain men were knocked out of the path of the spell, falling against their companions and then into the void. They hit the water below with roars of anger and pain.

"Daren!" Periander shouted, bending to write another spell. Daren repeated the words, and another storm smashed across the bridge, knocking more mountain men off the bloodied stone.

A moment after Daren's spell, Kronos's sent more to their grave. The archers were peppering the water with arrows, picking off any men who survived the fall. Periander and the two magicians advanced onto the edge of the bridge, tracing more glyphs and continuing their assault. The other shore was packed from the ridge of the foothills to the steps of the bridge, and every giant blown from the bridge was replaced by another.

Periander knelt to write another spell, but a bang louder than thunder stunned him. He felt stone hit his back, *hard*. Someone was shouting in pain. It was his voice. He was rolling around in pain without willing it. He forced himself to a stop. His fingers clawed the stone of the bridge as he raised his head from the ground. Kronos was lying two dozen feet away, half-wrapped around a stone statue, and Daren was nowhere to be seen.

Everything went black for a moment.

Mordus grabbed his hand and pulled, though Periander didn't even try to stand. He could see Mordus's lips moving. He could see the archers releasing volley after volley in the background. But the only sound he could hear was a whine. Mordus's grip tightened and Periander was hauled to his feet.

Then, with Theseus's roar of "Charge!" the din of battle crashed back into Periander's head. Imperial soldiers rushed past

Mordus and him, regaining the ground they had lost on the bridge. The giants had been pushed halfway across again by Periander's assault.

Periander shook his head to clear it once more. "What happened?" he shouted.

Mordus led him back toward their shore, though they were moving against the grain of the charge and did not make much progress. "A magic strike!"

"Trion doesn't have magicians!"

Mordus shrugged. "Are you hurt?"

Periander lifted his sword and winced. He had probably broken a rib. "Not bad. Where are the others?"

"Kronos is there." Periander glanced back. There was a line of fighting to distract him, but sure enough Kronos was limping a few paces to Periander's right. Mordus said, "Daren was thrown into the Strait."

Periander peered over the edge. The water was tainted with red, blood spreading around the fleet of corpses and flailing injured. Mordus was still holding his arm and abruptly yanked him back.

"Relax, I won't fall—"

Mordus was not looking at him. A giant with a beard as long as Periander's arm hammered downward with a blurred weapon. Periander raised his shield. He was knocked to the stones, his arm jarred by the strike of a mace. There were two holes in his shield, on either side of his handhold. He rolled to one side as the weapon smashed the stones where he had lain. He slashed his sword horizontally and the mountain man teetered away from his feet before disappearing from Periander's view.

A spearman charged over Periander, thrusting at the next attacker. After what felt like minutes, Periander reclaimed his footing. Mordus was dodging thrusts from a giant. Periander grabbed a pike from one of the many fallen men nearby and hurled it into the giant's shoulder. As Mordus stepped back to catch his breath, Periander yanked off two plates of his armour from beneath each arm and discarded a layer of chainmail with them. Against that giant's mace, this armour would be crushed as easily as flesh. The only way to fight them was dextrously.

The spearman that had charged past them was soon

gruesome decoration for the gargoyles that served as railings on this cursed bridge. Mordus and he drove forward with thrusts that splattered their legs with blood, then stepped back to dodge the angered onslaught.

Out of nowhere, a war hammer smashed Periander's shield from the right side, catching it against a statue and splintering his arm with slivers of wood. He dropped to a crouch to dodge the next swing of the hammer—which decapitated the weathered statue—and stumbled backward as quickly as he could. The giant kept swinging the weapon like a sling around his head, and the next blow struck Periander's raised sword. The blade went flying, nearly dislocating his arm when the hilt caught on the leather strap he had put around his gauntlet. He found himself fumbling on the bridge for his weapon as the mountain man raised a final strike.

The butt end of a spear was all he could see when he looked up again. The weapon had been thrown with such force that it had all but disappeared through the giant's chest. The beast of muscle fell back against the halved statue with a loud thud. Periander stood shakily to his feet and glanced in the direction of his savior.

Towering over the carnage, Trelkl advanced toward the battle with a massive axe clenched in both hands. As he neared Periander, he ignored the Prince's astonished thanks and grunted, "Leave."

He looked around. Mordus was already stumbling toward camp. There was only a short span of bridge left. Only a few dozen paces until Trion's giants set foot on the south shore of the Strait. New giants were still striding down the distant hills. "Maker..." Periander trailed, and the world blurred.

He eventually found Theseus clasping his shoulders, though he could hardly feel it. "... Just that we don't have enough men," his fellow Prince was saying. They were climbing. Periander glanced back over his shoulder. Trelkl and his lost tribesmen were the only ones still on the bridge in the onslaught of the horde. The remaining Imperial soldiers dotted the hills, crawling like bugs as bedraggled as he. And the Strait of Galinor had turned the colour of blood.

Year of Olympus 570

The sun rose much later than the villagers of Attarax. The self-named haven of the Disciples was scurrying with activity by the time the mountainous horizon bled light upon the crude buildings and dedicated magicians. Ovens were beginning to heat up, animals were being fed, and the looms were a blur. When it did break over those high ridges, the sun could not penetrate the void on the edge of town, the stone arch at which Artemys stared. Within that ancient structure, the glyphs continued to glow, unaffected by rays from the sky. They beckoned him.

Not to step within the arch. It was a Glyph Gate. Artemys understood how it worked. It was the same as travelling, crossing from one location to another. If he stepped into the Gate, he would appear near Elysia Port on the northern coast of the Mydarius Sea. No, entering the arch was no temptation to Artemys.

It was the mystery of these Gates that lured him. He stood with a bucket in each hand, paused between the well at the southern corner of town and the roadway that led to the bakery. From here, he had a clear line of sight to the Glyph Gate. Though the water was a heavy burden, he could not step away.

Weveld and the other Zealots claimed that the Gates had been built by Andrakaz. Artemys could scry Andrakaz, he had in the past, but it revealed nothing. Andrakaz was only as talented with magic as Weveld or Artemys himself. The Zealots claimed that the great wizard and father of their order had warded his life with the same spell that protected their stronghold.

The Great Glyph was the Maker's scroll, and each letter upon it a part of their world. Artemys could not fathom how something could exist without being seen within the Great Glyph.

But that was why he was here. To understand. He was a different man from the one who had challenged his own master to a duel. He was a different mage from the apprentice he had been at the Order of Magic.

Or he tried to be.

He set the buckets down. There were no ants here. He stared at the dirt. It was dry and dark. No movement. He could recall watching ants for hours at their family estate in Bertren. His mother had raised him there, before he even had magic. Before he had been *lost* to them. Ants weren't important to him. Not anymore.

The Gates were. They taunted him because they were proof. Proof that he did not know everything. *Proof that I cannot.* He inhaled at the thought. Someone had made the Gates, and no matter how many hours he searched the Great Glyph he could not find who had. *Why must I—*

"Artemys!" Hevarus ten Lak wandered towards him. There were only three roads in Attarax, with several smaller ones connecting them. Hevarus came from the bakery, and Artemys knew why. "You won't get the water to Ossus by letting the sun dry it up."

"Hev," Artemys nodded. "Weveld did not tell me those laws of nature had changed too. I know energy is monitored and certain elements draw more, but the sun is hardly a threat to these buckets."

Hevarus shrugged. "Ossus will have your hide anyway."

"Fine." Artemys knelt and heaved one from the dry earth. "Grab the other."

Hev sighed deeply, but complied. At first, none would listen to him, but they were used to having him around now. He did not have a "ten" before his name, but most of the other Disciples did. There were a couple nobles among the Zealots, their leaders.

They set off into the village, following the road towards the smoking ovens that marked the bakery.

Weveld was no commoner either, of course. The Crown Magician of the Order of Magic could not be a commoner. Artemys wondered if the Disciples had similar rules, though he had heard of none.

During his days in Avernus, or at the School of Delfie, Artemys had only known nobles. Well, aside from Kerres. Kerres ten Rysarius. Daughter of Varlin ten Rysarius, one of the most successful merchants of Avernus. But still commoners.

Kerres. He said the name in his mind for the first time since joining the Disciples. When they had all neglected him, she still welcomed him. Until he had realized the truth. Until he had told her the truth. *By the Maker...why does it have to be the truth?*

They soon reached the bakery. The only buildings outside of the stronghold were to help it run. Almost everyone lived inside the large structure, so only a few of the buildings surrounding it were houses. They passed the blacksmith, then a couple storehouses—with harsh mountain winters, these were valuable—and finally reached the bakery.

Ossus was within, and, with the tendril of smoke above, he was preparing a new batch of bread for the ovens behind his shop. Artemys could not shake the thoughts that boiled in his mind, so he handed the other bucket to Hevarus and told him, "I'll be in to help in a moment."

Soon he was alone outside, leaning against the building watching the sun try to leave the horizon.

Kerres, he repeated.

"I spend each day wishing I was away. But then these evenings, I wouldn't leave for the world," he had once told her. She had kissed him when he said it. Though he longed to leave Avernus, he had no other place to go. She had used it to persuade him to stay.

One day he had realized, after countless such debates between them, that she did not want *him* to stay. She wanted his power to stay. His status, his wealth, his magic. She had seduced the son of Avernus, the future Prince! What did it matter, if she loved him or not?

"Maker," he cursed. *Why must I remember it all?* He ran his sore hands down his grey robe, to smooth the creases he had made with clenched hands and painful memories. Their parting had been followed by tears.

Ossus and Hevarus had nearly finished the dough when Artemys entered. "Dreaming, milord?" Ossus asked. The baker was a very tall man, with a remarkable beard of nearly every hair colour Artemys had seen. The man called him 'milord' as a mockery. It was truth, though. Ossus had a lord serving him.

"I apologize," Artemys said. He rolled the sleeves of his shapeless grey shift up to his elbows and prepared to join them until Ossus held out a hand and shook his head.

"We've got this covered. Nalaf needs a hand."

Artemys glanced at Hevarus, who shrugged with a small smile. Artemys shrugged. "All right, tomorrow I shall be more prompt."

"I hope so!" Ossus called out the door after him.

Artemys walked down the street towards Nalaf's carpentry shed. The buildings on either side of him were built out of clay, wood, and thatch, unlike the sturdy, grey bricks and rock of Avernus. He was not surprised that the buildings had clearly been built by hand. Though the Order of Magic built with spells, creating rock and carving it with air into the great keeps they named Schools, the Disciples of Andrakaz used as little magic as they possibly could in their day-to-day lives.

"Artemys." He glanced up to see Weveld striding past, a cane supporting him, and two other Disciples in tail. "Walk with me, Artemys."

Artemys matched their pace. "You have just returned?"

Weveld nodded, his white mane quivering. "Promoted a new Master today," he said.

A Master of the Order of Magic, like Kaen, Artemys's master. He had defeated Kaen in a duel, to the shock of all who watched.

They reached the doors into the stronghold and Weveld took a breath. "You must return to Avernus."

"What?" Artemys blurted.

"Not to stay," the Prime Zealot clarified. "It has been three weeks. You father has sent pigeons across the Dominion. The realm fears your whereabouts."

"I am finally learning," Artemys said. "I had grown bored in Avernus. Bored and angry."

"I know," Weveld said. "Which is why you will continue

your studies here in Attarax. You know that the Zealots are granted the privilege of teleporting, though our concerns for energy have prohibited most of the Disciples from it. We are making an exception for you."

They descended the stairs into the subterranean level of their fortress. Weveld continued, "Your father and his nobles will believe that you have returned to the Order of Magic. You must visit him occasionally, but you will spend most of your time here, as you have in the past weeks."

Artemys nodded. "Very well. What of the Order of Magic? Should anyone contact them, they will know I am not at Delfie."

Weveld nodded. "I will tell them that I have given you a personal assignment, to keep track of you. Such an accomplished magician is dangerous without the Order's guidance," he said sarcastically.

They reached Weveld's chambers. Artemys did not miss Avernus, though he understood the reasoning for his return. Most of the Zealots lived double lives; why should a Prince not? There was no way to explain his utter disappearance. *Avernus, Periander, Pyrsius, Kerres...*

"How will we explain my three weeks of absence?"

"I have arranged a plan, using one of my operatives in the city. I have a letter here, we shall place it in your quarters. It is a request for a magician's assistance. You can tell your father you accepted a commission from my agent, and have been in the countryside with him for some time."

Artemys frowned. That would work. But it did not provide any advantage or gain. One of the few lessons his father had been there to teach him was, "Set your mind to something and you can achieve it." *Setting one's mind on power means all decisions must lead to it. And power is the only way to get rid of the Triumvirate.*

"Perhaps," he began, "that is not the best plan. There is no change then. We have an opportunity, here, to change something from the way things are now."

"You value change more than anything. This is one of the things I have observed in the past few weeks," Weveld said. "What plan would you suggest then?"

Artemys sank into one of the chairs in Weveld's sitting area, at the table where he had first encountered Weveld as the

Prime Zealot. What would Weveld value? *Information*. Artemys would be best for that. He could provide insights into the Prince's dealings, the Nobles of Avernus, truly anything within that third of the Dominion. *I want to learn from Weveld, not spy for him. He needs someone to replace me in Avernus.*

"You said you have agents in Avernus," Artemys said. "Are any of them lords?"

Weveld smiled. "No."

"My return shall establish a new lord in Avernus, one who we can rely upon," he explained.

"Who? What is your plan?"

Artemys shrugged. "Kerres."

"Kerres?" Weveld asked. "Your...friend from your years after the Order? You split ways, I thought. You realized she did not seek you, but your status."

"Exactly," Artemys said. "I will give her what she seeks. Her family will join the nobility of Avernus in return for saving my life. And when she is Lady Rysarius, *then* she will love me."

"You would..." Weveld trailed off. "*Use* her like that?"

"No," Artemys said, with a small smile. "I am just letting her use me the way she wanted to." *It's true,* he knew. *She showed me no respect before, barely even veiling her intentions...*

Weveld nodded. "That's a formidable strategy. Have you thought about this before? There are many details to make such a plot work."

...so I will give her what she wishes. "No, but I have an idea of what to do. I will take my leave now. Avernus awaits," he said.

"You are going to orchestrate this entire plot yourself?"

Artemys smiled, then nodded his head in a bow and turned away. *Kerres awaits.*

• • •

There was a ship moored in the port of Avernus, the *Valharyn Venture*. During the summer it set sail for Tarroth, but the winter storms that broke in The Gate of the Seas kept it at port this season. It was not yet winter, though the weather had turned grim. The *Venture's* crew spent their days frequenting the inns or working seasonal jobs in local lumber yardsand granaries, or even as guards. Most of the Avernan port rumoured that the *Venture* was a pirate ship. Tarroth boasted safety in its docks for any boat, and many crews that travelled there were bandit crews. But there was no proof against the *Venture.*

Artemys was marched towards it with his hands bound and a large armed sailor on either side. Mud was smeared upon his face, his hair was dishevelled and torn in spots, his clothes in tatters.

He had not looked so terrible since the day one of the guards of his family's estate had beaten him to the brink of death. He had been seven years old, but it felt like yesterday even after eighteen years. The pain and trauma barely entered Artemys's head, but those eyes remained there always. They were frightened eyes, pupils so dark they drowned Artemys. As these pirates marched him toward the *Venture*, his mind found itself back there, under the fist of that guard, clawing in the dirt and praying for his mother.

No one in the crowds that surrounded them could recognize this as the son of Periander Gothikar. The man on his right side, whose large, brown beard was only dishevelled because of the three scars on his left cheek, had told him if he made a sound he would lose his tongue. The man meant it.

The port of Avernus was built on the low shore, a mile below the city itself. Half of the buildings were cut into the cliffs themselves. The Avernan Point was like a massive rock jutting out into the sea. They passed a warehouse, one of many that the city's merchants used to store goods that would be shipped from the port. The large building was guarded daily, and the sailors that had captured Artemys steered him clear of the building.

Through the crowd, another party of the same numbers appeared: a woman leading two guards nearly brushed Artemys's captors. Those guards wore black and white cloaks; they were mercenaries, not green-garbed Avernan defenders. Their employer was a tall woman, strikingly beautiful, with shocking black hair and a fair complexion. This was the merchant and her guards of that very warehouse, attending errands for their next shipment of exported ore and imported grains from across the Gate.

This merchant, or her father, could be found in the port

yard during any morning of the week.

Her eyes met his, green meeting green. Hers widened.

The two pirates kicked him forward and he nearly tripped. His thigh could barely support his weight, swollen as it was. Someone called, "Stop!"

Scars, the man on his right, grabbed his arm and began to run. The other sailor soon joined them, forcing the crowds apart with shoves or shouts. Behind, someone bellowed, "In the name of the Prince, stop!" That only urged Scars to run faster. Artemys found himself jarred by the shoulders of each pirate. His lungs could barely inhale without the air being knocked from him.

Out of nowhere, a foot appeared and Scars slid onto the cobbles. Artemys found himself hauled sideways by the other pirate's yank. He tumbled to the ground, drawing blood from one knee on the rough stones. Scars reclaimed his feet, but found himself facing the charge of a black-and-white caped mercenary. The ringing of swords was loud enough to echo across the open port yard. The crowds fell back like water from the drop of a stone, fanning away from the conflict.

Artemys caught a glimpse of the fight as his other captor yanked him to his feet. Scars thrust forward with a short sword, and the mercenary stumbled backwards. The crowds continued to seethe around them, wary of the waving swords.

The pirate that still held Artemys hauled him back into the crowd, and, like a man with wide eyes beneath the sea's surface, the skirmish was blotted out. He saw the shocked stares of men and women watching the battle. The cobblestones beneath his feet seemed to shake with each step the onlookers took. An elbow caught him in the jaw; he felt a loud crack but could not raise his bound hands to the injury. He felt blood on his chin.

The pirate was running now, smashing a tangent across the crowded yard. The rooftops that marked the boundaries of the market street soon gave way to the open air and occasional masts of the docks. Artemys slid in the wet mud more than once— there were no more cobbles here. The next time he was tripped, his knee dragged against wood, rough cut planks that left an inch-deep line of slivers.

Out of nowhere, an oar caught both the pirate and Artemys against the chest. When next his eyes opened, he sat up from the grimy wooden dock and sucked in air to fill his winded lungs.

The second of two black-and-white mercenaries was finishing off the pirate with an overhead hack. The defeated crook was halfway to his feet and, as though time had slowed, blood fanned out from his chest with a splatter and his corpse toppled to the muddy ground.

Artemys gasped again, his chest tingling where he had been caught by the mercenary's ambush.

The mercenary turned to him and slowly took off the steel cap helm he wore. The second mercenary soon arrived with their original leader. The tall woman stared at Artemys like she had between the carts and crates of busy passersby, and asked, "It's you?"

Artemys accepted the hand of the mercenary who had tripped him. The man had a sharp look to him, though his brow was furrowed in apology. The man cut the cords binding Artemys's arms and Artemys spread his fingers. As he turned to Kerres, he ran a hand down his chin and cracked wind-dried blood off. He tried to open his mouth in reply, but it only made another cracking sound. He held up a finger as his opposite hand searched his shoulder satchel. They had only checked it for weapons.

"It is you," she said.

He cracked a healing token and, with both hands, quickly snapped his jaw to one side as the spell took effect. The healing energy muted the pain and quickly sewed the swollen tissue around the newly located joint. "Yes," he said at last. "Thank you."

She laughed. "I haven't seen you in months. Hardly expected this."

"Neither did I," he said. He patted his robe down but it was in vain; the outfit was ruined. Kerres, on the other hand, was the epitome of her class. Only the upper class, the nobility, the lords of the Gothikar court dressed better than the silk skirt or the white fur scarf she wore. "You saved my life."

She eyed him, her mercenaries slowly returning to their places at each of her elbows. "You have been missing for weeks... Your father has search parties in the countryside and has sent pigeons to most major cities. Who were these men?"

"Crewmen of the *Venture*," Artemys said. "I must let my

father know of this rescue at once!"

"Of course." Kerres turned to one guard and said, "Run ahead and fetch horses from the port guardhouse. Tell them Artemys Gothikar has been saved. I will accompany him to the Palace."

"Thank you, Kerres. They threatened to kill me if my father did not pay enough ransom... They said there were men who wanted me dead and would pay them better," Artemys explained. He rubbed his jaw. It did not hurt anymore, though it still reminded him how close that had been. Under an assumed identity, he had hired the pirates to capture and kill Artemys Gothikar. The stakes had been real—if any detail did not seem true, his spider-web would collapse. They had been clever enough to keep his hands bound the entire time so he could not cast spells and escape.

Kerres gestured ahead of them, though Artemys glanced back. The *Venture* had already set sail. The galleon had two decks and two masts; as he watched, he could see the men on-board, crawling like ants. They had their pay, they had found the crumbs they so searched for.

"How long have they held you in the Port?" Kerres asked as he finally joined her walk back along the docks. The crowds had dispersed. After the thrill of open conflict had subsided, the workers and tradesmen escaped the intervention of guards by disappearing from the streets.

"Two weeks. The first week, they kept me in an inn. Up in the city." He glanced up. The road from the port wound back and forth as it climbed the cliffs to the city high above.

"Hopefully not the Bard of the Valharyn."

He glanced at her hesitantly, then let himself smile. That was the inn where they had once met when they did not care for the watching eyes of nobility or parentage. "No, not the Bard."

She returned his smile, though it faded as the mercenary appeared with at least a hand's count of horses, two Avernan guards, and a servant in tow. The latter insisted on helping both Kerres and Artemys onto their steeds before vanishing.

Their escort formed around them as they rode toward the Port Gate, though they had to collapse to double-file after setting off on the cliff road. They spent the rest of the ride in silence, accompanied by the echoes of words exchanged in the past. The moment he had realized the truth about Kerres he had called her on it. *I thought you cared about me. The only one who did.*

. . .

They had been at the Bard, lying side by side as the sun rose one morning. He traced a pattern across the bed sheets. Not glyphs, just a design. It was an ill habit he had developed. "My father and I fought again."

"Bad?" she had asked. He nodded. "What about?"

His finger stopped its tracing. "He is going to make Pyrsius Prince. I'm the heir but he said that he had planned for my success at the Order of Magic. I ruined that plan."

"I'm certain he doesn't think you *ruined* it," she returned.

"You weren't there. You did not see the look in his eyes. He said, 'It was not supposed to be this way,' and I knew it was with disappointment he spoke," Artemys said.

"But he can't control you, and he's told you before that you decide your fate."

"He changed my fate the day he gave me magic," Artemys said.

"He made you powerful."

Artemys's index finger became a fist, pressing into the mattress. "He made me distant. He took away my friends. He took away my humanity. He took away *my brother.*"

"What?" Kerres asked, sitting up to face him with the bed sheets clutched around her. "You've accomplished so much with magic. He didn't give you it as a curse."

"Then why is he *so* frustrated that I ruined his plan?" Artemys retorted. "What do you care anyway?" She had never shown an interest like this in his ranting.

Her jaw dropped. "You loath yourself so much for your *gifts* that you don't see how they have opened the world to you!"

"Opened the world, Kerres?" He backed off the bed, sliding trousers up about his waist and buckling them with a narrow belt. "I've lived my life *alone*. You've been the only one who can stand me! There is no *world* for me, Kerres. My father made certain of that. Pyrsius gets the world. Pyrsius is his heir."

"So, what?" she asked, rising to her knees to keep at his eye level. "You're giving up? All of this has been for nothing?"

"All of what?" His voice choked on the last word as he

realized what she had meant. "Oh, that's strong. That's royal. You're here for the world you thought I could open. You're here for the heir. You're here for the magic...not because you know who I am beyond 'the magician', but because I *am* the magician..."

She was crying now. "Wait, that's not true..." It was a lie.

"By the Maker, Kerres, you're just like the rest of them!"

. . .

The cliffs lay behind them, and the guards at the north gate of Avernus watched in awe as their escort rode through. The city was the smallest of the three fief capitals, but it was also the strongest. The walls were high enough to seem like mountains. The bailey between the outer wall and inner wall was wide enough to be a town of its own. Within the walls was the sprawling metropolis of an Imperial City.

They emerged from the gates into the trade district. The city was divided into quarters, with the Palace a towering intersection of the district walls. By the time they crossed the Merchant's Quarter, full of towering warehouses, bustling markets, and crowds of men and women in search of something, the sun had begun to dip on the horizon.

At last they neared the Palace gates. The Palace had a few outlying buildings, but the central Keep, several storeys tall, was considered the Palace proper. The first two floors had been built ages ago, while the magnificent layers above had been added by Artemys's grandfather, Akheron. Those displayed the true wealth and influence of the Gothikar household, looming over the nearby gates.

The guards let them in with looks of surprise. Despite the grime on his skin, the missing hair, and the blood on his chin, these men recognized Artemys.

"By the Maker! Artemys!" a servant exclaimed. Dobler Rewan strode up and helped Artemys down from his horse. "You look as rough as a winter storm! Do you need medical help or healing?"

Artemys smiled politely. Dobler had been their servant for many years and was one of the few men that did not treat Artemys any different after the gifting of magic. He had dark hair held in a knot at the back of his head, though its square frame around his face was beginning to grey. "Thank you, Dobler. It's already been taken care of."

"I'll fetch your father at once!" He disappeared, slightly dragging one leg with a limp he had developed.

The healing had only been a minor drain on Artemys's energy—he had felt much worse in the past. He helped Kerres from her horse. Unlike the bed sheets Kerres had worn in his recollection, her flowing silk skirts and the sky blue blouse that pressed against him when she landed on the cobble stones were the image of a Lady. Best officialise it.

"Artemys! Thank the Maker!" his father blurted, appearing from the arching doors of the Palace Great Hall. "Are you unharmed? Your mouth..."

He ran a hand around his chin, but the blood stain would require more. "I am fine, Father."

Periander Gothikar nodded and grasped Artemys close to him for a hug. He smelled of ink, strong enough to choke the senses, and his skin was as rough as the wooden docks. "What happened? Where were you?"

"I was captured. It seems you still have enemies, Father. If not for the quick thinking and courage of Mistress ten Rysarius, they would not have escaped the Port with me their hostage," Artemys explained. "They have held me for weeks! In our own city!"

"How did this happen?" his father asked, with only a brief glance at Kerres. "You disappeared three weeks ago, though for the first couple days we assumed you were off on one of your missions." Artemys used to plan outings to other cities or towns in search of books he could not find or imagination he needed to inspire.

"I was. I went south to Coastspine village. I was on the road back. I saw some riders in the distance. I knew it was not you, or your men, and based on their speed, I chose to flee." The locals in Coastspine would swear they had seen him. He had done more for them than any of his Father's men.

"But they caught you?"

"They had men in the foothills, waiting for me." Artemys had set up a few small camps there, after opening a gateway from Attarax Village. Camps that were concealed enough to be connected to bandit activity.

His father frowned. "I told the Nobles we needed more patrols throughout the fief, but they refuse to fund it. They claim there is no danger."

"There is, Father. Twice, they held a knife to my throat. Twice, they were willing to finish it, if not for my bribes and pleas."

Dobler walked up, having stabled their horses. "Sir, a guard from the Port just brought news that the *Valharyn Venture* has, in fact, set sail. First ship to leave the port. Without cargo."

"The Buccaneer Navy, perhaps," Periander said. The rogue fleet had been antagonizing Imperial coastal regions for the last several years. "They have not bothered our fief so directly yet, and I had reason to believe they wouldn't... but what rogue crew would be willing to risk such a kidnapping?"

Artemys frowned. The point of choosing pirates had been to frame the Buccaneer Navy—an illicit organization that would not soon be questioned about a kidnapping. But his father had accepted the rest of his story.

"It is my honour to meet you, Prince Periander," Kerres said, finally approaching their reunion.

Periander nodded. "ten Rysarius, I presume. You must be the daughter of Varlin, yes?"

She nodded. "Kerres, milord."

"I would like to offer you and your house a deep thank you from myself personally, and from the Fief of Avernus. And, of course, I'll have Dobler deliver the reward for my son's rescue."

"Father," Artemys said. This was the important part. "She saved my life. Certainly a larger reward would be acceptable."

Periander raised an eyebrow. "It is a sizeable amount of gold, Artemys."

Artemys nodded. "But the Rysarius family are some of the best traders in the city. They do not need our gold."

"Well then, what do you suggest?"

"Welcome them to the nobility of our fair city. They have already made a large contribution to the city, both its economy and the influence of our social power. Now, they have saved my life as well."

His father could barely conceal his surprise. "Artemys... that is a—" He paused. "A moment, please," he told Kerres, and took Artemys aside. "That is a much larger gift than the gold we offered. It is not your place to suggest this."

"But I have," Artemys said. "I knew the Rysariuses a long time ago, and I have presented reasons for such a boon. It is your decision, but it was my life that's been saved."

Periander stared at him, expression still broken by surprise. "Very well," he declared, loud enough for Kerres and Dobler to hear. "Dobler, I believe the Nobles are just inside the Great Hall. They have been present to advise me on the search. Have them join us."

"Milord," Dobler said, and strode toward the Great Hall. The arched doors creaked as he entered, and then there was silence. Kerres was staring at Artemys, though it was Periander who had made the declaration. There was a gleam in her eyes.

The Three Nobles of Avernus appeared, though they each looked bothered by this turn of events.

Periander glanced at Artemys once, as though probing for something more. Then, they began. "Kerres, kneel before me."

Artemys held his breath as Kerres sunk to the ground without a word. It felt like this moment would never end, as the three Nobles slowly walked to corner Kerres. Once they had taken the shape of a triangle, they each drew a sword.

The three blades settled on her shoulders, as Periander stepped closer to Kerres. Artemys could barely hear what was said. "Kerres ten Rysarius, I, Periander Gothikar, recognize that you have served the Dominion and House Gothikar, and have decided to grant you the privilege of service in my court."

Artemys's father drew his blade, an old, battle-marked sword that Artemys had never seen him wield. He set it upon her right shoulder. "This blade represents the power of the Dominion, and I gift you with its power. We remove our blades, but remember that you wield the power of the Dominion through their steel embrace." The swords were sheathed again. "Now rise from your knees as Lady Kerres Rysarius, and may your House never again bear the symbol of the commons. Rise, Lady Rysarius, and take your place at my side," Periander commanded.

She stood up and glanced at Artemys again.

"You had best hurry home to inform your father. I'm certain there will be a feast for the occasion," Periander said. "A chance for him to meet his fellow lords."

Kerres nodded and, still holding Artemys's eye, rode off.

Periander stepped toward Artemys and said, "We shall see in the days ahead if that was a mistake."

Artemys nodded.

"I am glad you are safe, Artemys," Periander said, walking with him toward the Keep. "Your brother has had a rough month. We attended a feast in Eldius. A riot nearly overthrew our escort on the way through the city! The ringleaders were executed by the magician's cloister there, but Pyrsius did not take that well. He is not fond of magic."

. . .

The Bard of the Valharyn was a large inn built against the district wall between the Merchant and the Residential Quarters. The building had three storeys—a tavern and two floors of guest rooms. The steps leading to the front doors were wide enough for four abreast, the common room could feed a hundred, and the faces of crowds that frequented it could not be recalled.

For this reason, Kerres and he had once chosen the inn as their meeting place.

Artemys stepped inside from the dark. At this hour of midnight, the inn was surprisingly empty. There were only about ten people in the common room, not counting the barkeeper and two barmaids. At the bar, a woman sat with her back to him, black hair knotted behind her head. He touched her back as he approached and whispered, "Kerres Rysarius," in her ear.

She smiled at him, but held her tongue. For a moment, they sat in silence until the barkeep asked Artemys for his preference of a drink. After the man had left them, Kerres finally spoke. "I know what you did."

"What?" *Did I overlook something? I planned it all. I'm safe. The scheme will work.*

She smiled, this time the look of someone taunting a precious secret. "I was in Coastspine three weeks ago."

Curse me. Artemys sat for a moment, thinking. She knew. *By the Maker, she knows I planned the whole thing... What now?* He needed her to keep it between the two of them. He needed her. *Like the herder needs the sheepdog.* "It was a gift," he said, praying she bought it.

"A gift?"

"Of many to come."

Kerres laughed and took a drink from a mug. "You made me a Lady, as a gift?"

"Yes. So long as you do not ruin the gift."

"I certainly don't intend to do that," she said. Another sly smile. "What do you *intend* to do?"

Artemys blinked. "About what? You?"

"Ha, I already know what you'll do with me. I mean, what are you planning? What's the goal? If you gave in to me, you did so for a reason. What do you intend to do?" Her face was flushed red, though not due to her blatant taunting.

He sat back. He could tell her many things. He intended to fix the Order of Magic. He intended to fix his father's city. He planned many things. For once, though, he told her the truth. "I intend to be King."

7

Year of Olympus 545

Frost. It breathed from his lungs, froze in his beard, collected on his clothes, shivered on any exposed skin. Periander hated it. He held his hands so close to the fire he imagined they should catch aflame, if not for the cold. Winter was *only* frost in Avernus, two thousand miles away. Some years it just rained. He had never hated the frost as he did now.

Periander sat on a keg from their wagon, though he was sure the contents were frozen solid. Around him was a bank of snow, high enough that he could barely see over the surface. The fire in front of him was a poor excuse for heat, a sputtering, crackling mess that licked the nip from his fingers. His beard was long and dirty enough to keep his chin warm. The condensation that formed around his mouth and nose felt like icicles as long as the ones that hung from the wagon.

The flames were a poor excuse for light. Night fell quickly in these mountains, too quickly. Periander peeled a tendon from the roasted rabbit leg he held. The meat was tough and tasted worse than he imagined boots did. He tossed the bone onto the snow nearby and watched it melt a halo for itself.

Across his small fire sat Mordus, his hair longer than Periander's, his furs scanter, his beard longer. Mordus's features had been set in a perpetual scowl for the past few years. "How old are you?" he asked.

Periander would have grinned, but his face was numb. "Twenty-six."

"I did not realize you were so young, my Prince." Mordus

had not called him Prince in a year.

Periander shrugged. "And you?"

"Thirty. Today."

"Today?" Periander asked. "You know what day it is?"

Mordus smiled, then visibly shivered. "One of Captain Illus's fellows carves sticks with a notch for each day."

"And what day is it?"

"The nineteeth day of the tenth Cycle," Mordus replied. A small flurry of snow brushed past them, and Mordus leaned closer to the fire.

"I'm surprised the man can keep track of the moon." Periander looked up at the sky. He could only see a few stars through the canopy of clouds. For what seemed like a year, there had only been clouds, snow, and wind. He closed his eyes, but then he was left with images of bodies, men raising axes and clubs, red water in the Strait. He shivered again and leaned over the fire, trying not to cough from the smoke.

Mordus had finished his rabbit before Periander. He patted his belly and said, "I should retire. My tent seems awfully warm now."

Periander nodded, gripping his beard in a glove to shake the snow from it. "We ride at sunrise." He watched his friend stand up. As soon as leaving the small ring of firelight, Mordus faded into the night. Periander took a deep breath of warmth, then stood up. He kicked snow onto the flame, clenching fingers and toes as the cold set in. He could see Mount Cerde, a dark contour against the clouds. During the summer, on a clear day, Mount Cerde was easy to spot from the Imperial Tower of Galinor. Tonight, it was the only thing he could see in terms of horizon.

His pavilion was pitched on the opposite side of the wagon. He did not know who had left the wooden cart there, and did not care. As he brushed past the rough, wooden wheels, he felt splinters cling to his cloak. During the winter, these wagons only lasted one trip. They had learned to tie bands of cloth to the wheels to keep them from falling the whole way through the snow. Otherwise, it would be impossible to make any progress with it.

He parted the folds of his tent, closing them as quickly as he could after himself. The tent was pitch black. He stumbled to his left and knelt. He could feel the warmth from the fire brazier. He yanked the moss canvas back, letting air onto the still warm coals. A bit of kindling from the box on the ground was enough to get the flames going. *By the Maker, this snow sucks the moisture out of everything.* Periander felt like his skin was as brittle as the twigs he threw on the fire.

He glanced around his tent. It had been hastily set up: to the right, a bed cot dragged from the wagon, blankets in a pile on top, the chest with his three outfits and another with his armour. He could dimly recall a wardrobe in Avernus, a hundred sets of clothes, all in better condition than those he wore. Cat was in Avernus, too. *Maker, I miss you.*

His cloak and tunic he threw into the first box, then sunk beneath the blankets with only a pair of breeches around his shivering thighs. He fought with the pile of blankets until they covered him. It took almost an hour for the tent to warm up. He tried reading, peeling open the tome he had been trying to read for the past five years. It was a history of House Theseus, the founding of Athyns, and the gain of their Princehood. It was one of the few changes in Princehood that had been a decision of the Nobles to elect a new House to royalty. That was the day House Ivos fell.

But there wasn't enough light to read. He set the book aside. Once the tent was warm enough, he dropped the moss over the brazier again and hurriedly jumped back beneath the blankets.

Thoughts of Cat kept him warm. He visited her once a year; he could not be away from the troops more frequently. Such a visit required him to travel to the nearest magician, which was often miles away, in Galinor. He had been nineteen when they wed, but he had known her since telling her of her father, and Agwar Marsh. Those thoughts chilled him and he longed to light the tent's brazier once more. He forced his mind back to Cat. Only a year passed after their marriage and he was summoned to meet Lord Ernes Trion in the Maker's Forge.

He had always believed in the Maker, but rarely prayed to him. Religious practice was a thing of the last generation. Nonetheless, Periander breathed a prayer as he fell asleep. He prayed to survive the war, to live with her, not a Dominion away.

"Dawn has come, my Prince," someone said. Periander rolled over, pulling the blankets tighter. The cold felt like tendrils of cobweb or smoke, creeping at him from every crack. Pulling the animal furs closer around him didn't help at all. Frustrated, he rolled back and opened his eyes. One of his pages was holding a tunic already. Periander cursed beneath his breath and slid away from the cot.

The frost had him for a moment until the tunic was on and a thick hide cloak above that. The material felt softer than skin after the rough furs draped across his cot. As the page scoured the chest for Periander's next article, more servants entered, folding up the blankets and hauling the cot away. The page draped a large, fur scarf around Periander's neck. Another man entered and dumped the coals from the brazier into a box. By the time Periander was ready to leave his tent, there was nearly no tent left.

The skies, in contrast to the previous night's flurries and winds, were whiter than snow, almost blinding after the shadows of his pavilion. He prayed it did not snow today.

As the page disappeared, Captain Illus arrived. Periander had six captains in the West, while his seventh remained in Avernus to serve as the city guard. Five of his captains were under Theseus's command, fighting the giant's horde with stand-and-retreat tactics. Illus was the only one still riding with Periander. "Milord, there was a rider in the night," his captain said. Illus was a tanned man, a seafarer, with his eyes set far back beneath his brow. A spider-web scar emerged from his right ear, lost in his grey hairline. It looked like the work of a mace.

Periander was shivering, but locked his knees in an attempt to hide it. "From Theseus?"

"Aye, sir. The horde has stopped its advance. The few scouts that survive tell they are dividing."

He almost said "Why?" but did not bother. Thoughts of that monstrous wave coming over the mountain ridge at Dagger's Edge... Periander was filled with dread. "Are the men ready to move?" He spotted Mordus approaching with two horses.

Illus's face never changed, but held the grim expression it

always did. "Certainly. I'll give the order, milord."

At his nod, Illus strode away and began bellowing orders. They would reach the coast today, where the mountains fell down into the Mydarius at the mouth of the Strait of Galinor. And tomorrow they would sail across to Edessa.

Mordus handed him the reins of his horse. Even trained steeds like these did not last long in the mountains. Periander had brought a royal warhorse from his stables in Avernus, but it had lasted no more than a few months after the ride north to hear King Trion's ultimatum in the Maker's Forge. Periander climbed into the saddle of this latest steed. "Sleep well, Mordus?"

His friend forced a dry laugh. "Did any of us?"

Captain Illus took the lead, the soldiers forming a loose tail behind him. They counted forty-seven. Another man had died yesterday to a coughing, shivering fever. They had departed Theseus's camp a week earlier with fifty.

Periander and Mordus rode behind Illus. He was the only other with a mount. The troop marched on foot, and the wagon took up the rear, pulled along by a pair of donkeys. It was incredibly slow travel, forcing each step through knee-high snow. The sun provided little warmth, only glimpsing through the clouds at rare intervals and feeling far distant even then.

Again, Periander was haunted by death. It seemed whenever he shut his eyes, there were bodies there. Men he had killed. He had never asked for a war.

"We've spoken on many things," Mordus said.

"Yes."

"But never politics."

Periander smiled. "You've been on common terms with a Prince for five years, Mordus. What's on your mind?"

"All Three Princes are in the West. Odyn, who normally rules Olympus, is waiting for us in Edessa, Theseus of Athyns is on the front, and you are the farthest from home." Mordus's back was slumped forward as he rode, though he leaned a bit toward Periander as he spoke. "Who rules your cities now? Or each of the fiefs?"

Politics were the focus of Periander's education. He could remember his tutor's swaying, grey beard, almost twenty years ago, explaining these very things to him. The Avernan fief covered the dozens of tiny villages from the Southern Valharyn

Coast to the village of Lydion. It was the rockiest regions of the Dominion, save the unsettled west where they now fought. "Currently, the Nobles. Each city has three. By law, they are responsible to elect the Prince of that city, and therefore have rights to rule it when needed."

"I've never heard that," Mordus said.

"That's because the last time the Nobles decided to elect a different House was when they demoted House Ivos and granted the Princehood to House Theseus. Two hundred years ago," Periander said. The Odyn family had ruled as the Princes of Olympus since the Triumvirate's establishment more than three hundred years ago.

Mordus mulled this over with his bottom lip stuck out. They were now riding through a narrower pass, two large cliffs of rock on either side. Sheets of ice hung down the ridges where trickling streams and waterfalls had frozen. The slope was much steeper here. They had been riding for most of an hour, and Illus suggested, "We should dismount here."

Periander slid off his horse into the deep snow and used his horse's reins to lead it after Illus's mount. He felt the cold begin to seep through the high riding boots he wore, like water soaking through one's hair. Behind him, Mordus cursed as he forced his steed to follow him.

They were low enough in the mountains now that small trees were sprouting through the snow all around them, pine branches bowing beneath the weight of snow. Periander could not see where his feet met the earth beneath the snow and nearly fell when he stepped on a round rock. He remembered the naked slopes of the Southern Spine, the crowd of stones that rolled down the mountains, there one month and gone the next. The remains of rockslides.

"But the Nobles can't rule the cities forever. They don't have the authority of the Princes," Mordus said, his voice loud enough to reach Periander ahead.

Periander just nodded. It had been proven over the years. The longer the Prince was gone, the more unrest perpetuated within his fief. But they could not return now. King Trion and his tribes would not be content with the borders anymore. Those had been the terms of his ultimatum: give up the borderlands all the way to Galinor, and they would have peace. But in Galinor was the Throne of Midgard, the ceremonial meeting place of the Princes, the capital of the Known World. There would be no surrendering it to the barbaric hordes.

It took the troop an hour to descend the steep pass. The pine forest that now surrounded them was the foot of the mountain. The smell of seawater was now palpable. It was, for Periander, an aroma that reminded him of home.

The snow was shallower here as well. They mounted their steeds again and the troop picked up a brisker pace. They now travelled north towards the point of land jutting into the mouth of the Mydarius Sea. There was a small town on the peninsula, built there simply for the sail to Edessa. As they crossed the snow-laden woodlands, the column of smoke from the village of Helius was the only thing visible through the snowy canopy. The heavens remained as luminous as when Periander had awaken, the sun setting the white clouds on fire from above though only blinding to those below.

The tin buckles of his cloak were dull with frost. By all accounts, even the giants could not fight in the snows of winter. His fellow princes and he had spent six years fighting during the summer, plotting during the winter. Or just simply travelling. Periander slumped his shoulders as they rode. There was no comfortable way to travel in the winter.

"Milord." Illus's face was turned to one shoulder, his voice drifting back to Periander.

Periander clucked to his horse, nudging its sides with his boots. As he reached Illus's side, he asked, "What is it?"

"Look."

A man in orange robes stood out against the trees, wading through the snow on foot. He had his hood up, wolf fur draped around his neck, and a sheath on his back. That was the traditional colour of a Master of the Magician's Order. The troop was less than a mile from town, and the wizard had likely been watching for their arrival. Periander and his fellow riders dismounted when they were close enough. Illus called out, "What business do you have, mage?"

The man drew off his hood. He looked somewhat like Mordus without a beard. He was thick, wrinkled, but not from age, and perpetually scowling. Periander noted the few whiskers on the man's chin. He had likely just departed his home, travelling with magic to the western mountain ranges. The wizard smiled to them. "I've news for the Prince. Good news." He directed the last comment at the wary Illus, whose hand sat on the pommel of his sword.

"I'm Gothikar," Periander told him. "What news? If it requires privacy, you must wait until we arrive in town."

"My name is Kaen, milord. I bring word on behalf of Lady Gothikar, milord's wife," the magician said. He spoke with a stammer that bothered Periander half as much as the frost. "Your wife is having birthing pains and shall give birth today."

Periander froze, though not from the snow. He stared at the stranger. *Cat is having a child?* He had to correct his own thoughts. We *are having a child.* He closed his eyes as tears sprung to them, but didn't like the horrors he saw behind his lids. Instead, he glanced away from the others, and took a deep breath. The snow on the trees looked like the clouds, as light as the sky. *By the Maker, Cat's with child?* He had not heard from her since his last visit in the east. Nine months ago.

"Mordus," he blurted.

The others all seemed to be holding their breath, waiting for his reaction. He heard them exhale as Mordus's hand clasped his shoulder from behind. "Yes?"

He spun to his friend and said, "I'm going to be a father!"

Mordus embraced him briefly. Kaen and Illus were grinning now.

"I'm going to be a father..." Periander trailed off. Reality submerged him again in a rush of blood to the face. He looked around. There was a troop of soldiers waiting patiently in knee deep snow. The sun was at its peak, held between the icy peaks, noon was upon the mountains. "Illus," he said, "start the march again. Let's get these men a camp outside of town and some food."

Kaen stepped closer to Periander as the Captain began bellowing orders. Illus's voice was rough, but carried far. Speaking loud enough to be heard over the noise, the magician said, "Milord's wife was brought to Delfie. I will be—"

"Delfie? The School?"

Kaen nodded. "Royal lineage is of greatest importance, and my Order's care is the best in the Triumvirate. Heirs have been delivered this way for centuries, my Prince."

"Of course." Periander was not thinking clearly. He was staring at the men as they walked past, the frost-coated armour, and grim beards. Occasional smiles passed him as they heard the news. He could not believe it himself! *Cat, my dear Cat...*

"I will be returning to Delfie momentarily, milord, and you are welcome to join me," Kaen told him.

"Yes!" Periander nodded fervently. "I want to see Catlin at once!" He paused to catch his breath. He yanked a knife out of his scabbard and proceeded to cut his beard in half. The hair was matted from days of travelling, cleaning or cutting it was a good way to lose heat. He had heard a soldier's joke recently, that by the end of the war no one in the Dominion would recognize the difference between the mountain men and the Imperial soldiers.

"Mordus," he said, as he continued his sloppy shaving job. "I will return as soon as my family allows. Tell Illus to cross the Strait as soon as the weather allows."

Mordus nodded. "You will meet us in Edessa then?"

"I will be close to a week. For the return journey, I will use gateways to reach Galinor, but will have to sail the rest of the way after that." He sheathed his knife. He still had a beard, but now did not look like a barbarian. Or so he hoped. "How do I look?"

"Like a warlord." Mordus shrugged, then they laughed. "Give my regards to Cat."

Periander nodded, joined hands with his friend. "When I return, I'll tell you of the newest Gothikar." He turned to Kaen and bade him to open his gateway. He remembered Mordus's date the day before. The nineteenth day of the tenth Cycle. *My son*, he thought, *will be born on the twentieth of the tenth cycle.*

Kaen wrote a lengthy spell into the snow, constantly pausing to warm up his finger. Finally, he returned to Periander's side and read his spell aloud. Some of the words made sense to Periander, but not all of them. He was no wizard. At last, a shimmering hole opened in the air, growing in the shape of a box around them until they were no longer standing shin deep in the snow.

Periander glanced around. They were in a courtyard, the sky dark grey overhead. The Isles of the Mydarius Sea were always rainy it seemed. But at least there was no frost. The School of Delfie looked like a small, stone village. There were

five buildings, two of them significantly larger than the others—
the Archives, to his right, and the Hall, on his left. The thatched
roofs were in disrepair. He imagined they had to slave on the
buildings after each storm season. No trace of the sun breached
the clouds. Instead, the air itself seemed to glow. He had to
wonder if it was the wizards' doing, but he knew it was just the
telltale signs of fog in the air.

He glanced back at the courtyard they had appeared in, the
stone slab that had been placed there for arriving travellers. *Cat
is here. Somewhere. And my son. Or daughter?* Only the Maker
knew. He glanced at Kaen and said, "Lead on."

They crossed the courtyard between the two large
buildings, and entered the smaller building on the north side. His
heart was racing by the time he stepped inside. "I want to see her
at once."

Kaen shook his head. "You know the traditions, milord.
Ever since the death of Tiberon Odyn's wife and heir, it has been
an ill omen to—"

"No. Unless the baby is being pulled from her at this
moment, I will kiss my wife." He closed the thick door of the
building with more force than he had intended. This drew
glances from the half-dozen old men inside. The antechamber
was a broad area, likely a meeting place of some kind.

"Very well," Kaen said. "This way." He looked inside the
door on the left side of the room first, to be safe, then beckoned
Periander to enter with him.

Cat sighed when she saw him, trying to lift herself off of
the bed she lay on. He crossed the room in one step and held her
tight against him, careful of her swollen stomach. When they
separated, he stared at it with a whirlpool of thoughts. He had
never seen her like this, large enough to shock him. He looked
back into her teary eyes. This was Cat. His Catlin. She sobbed in
joy, trying to speak, still clutching her belly with each pang, but
he embraced her again and their mouths met for a brief moment.
She caught her breath when he withdrew. "Thank the Maker,
Periander. You came..."

"No number of barbarians could keep me from this." He
was breathing heavily as well, both from their kiss and from the
drain of everything going on. "Oh Cat," he whispered. "You
could have sent a letter! Something!"

"How could you fight then?"

"Sometimes you are foolish." He was grinning, not serious. They touched foreheads. She flinched away though, one hand on her stomach.

"Not foolish," she whispered. "Scared."

He grabbed her hands. "Listen to me, Cat. You are the strongest woman I've ever known. *You* have *no* reason to be scared. If my father was still alive, the great Akheron Gothikar himself would name you his ideal, his role model."

She laughed, then grabbed her belly again. Kaen touched his shoulder. The other magicians in the room stared at him. It was time.

He turned her head towards him once more. "Your father... he would be so proud. And I am the proudest of them all. Because I married the right woman, and we are going to have a child! Don't be afraid. Next time I see you, we will be parents."

She smiled, tears mingling with all the sweat. He stood up and his legs forced him to pace backwards toward the door. "I love you, Cat."

Abruptly, he found himself standing in the anteroom again. There were old men staring at him. Maker, his knees *hurt*. He had only been kneeling for several moments and didn't even recall dropping to the floor. He slid into a chair at the table in middle of the room. The table was so smooth compared to anything he had sat at in years. *What am I doing here? How did I get here? I'm just the son of the great Prince. I'm not... a father!* Now he was afraid. Maker, he was terrified. He took a deep breath. Kaen had disappeared. He wasn't even helping with the delivery. He had just been sent to fetch the soldier-father.

"Milord," someone said. "You may return. You have a son."

Already? Periander didn't recall running, or even walking, back to Cat's side, but he remembered the moment he saw his son. A tiny nose, a rounded, white head. He reached out. Silently, he drew a breath and felt the baby—*no, my baby*—touch his callused hand with a tiny wave.

He stared into Cat's eyes, and then kissed her until they couldn't hold their breath anymore. She looked exhausted. Periander couldn't imagine how he looked. But he did not care, and he knew she didn't either. They whispered quiet words between them, cried that their parents could not see them now, smiled at the tiny life, love incarnate. *My son...*Periander breathed.

He closed his eyes to clear his head. In his mind, he could only see that tiny hand held against his own.

8

Year of Olympus 571

This time, Artemys and Hev were tasked with cutting firewood. They followed the path behind the Attarax stronghold until it bent away from the village and descended a small hill. At the bottom was a brook, which they stumbled across on stepping stones placed there by the ancestors of the Disciples. Hev had a wagon in tow, a small hand cart for hauling the wood back to the village; he had to yank it through the stream with Artemys's help. The sun was blocked by the clouds for most of the spring; occasionally finding holes in the grey cover, the sun gleamed down and set Artemys's blond hair aglow.

Most of the Disciples demonstrated at least a basic physical dexterity, though Artemys spent the most time reading books and the least time sparring with swords or, coincidentally, cutting wood. He barely had enough patience to eat, let alone sustain a strong vitality. *Why sit and dine, when you could be creating?*

"At the School," Artemys told Hev, "you cut wood with a spell. And then you quickly grow a new tree and cut it down as well."

Hev glanced over his shoulder. They had just reached the clearing where a chopping block and a few fallen logs lay. The sky seemed so open compared to the Southern Spine of Avernus, where such grand pines grew. "Waste magic like that here, and you're bound to be penalized by Dalon or even by Weveld."

Artemys nodded. He spoke often about the Order of Magic and now wondered if it bothered Hev. Artemys had been spending a week at the Order and then a week in Attarax for months now. In two or three days he would return to the School of Delfie.

"You going to help?" Hev asked as he hefted up an ax. Artemys nodded and scooped up the other.

It was hard work. Artemys had hardly done a day's work in the first ten years of his life. He was occasionally trained in sparring and running, but when his father granted him magic he immediately enrolled in the Order of Magic. Only a few years of training in the local guilds passed, and he was accepted by the School of Delfie.

In the past year though, he had been working as hard as the rest of the Disciples. Being a noble, a Prince even, did not mean any refuge from hardship in this version of civilization.

He arced the ax down and halved a log. He set the next log onto his chopping block and split it in two as well. After five logs, he began cutting the halves into smaller pieces and then stacked them in the wagon. Then he went back to chopping log sections. Hev was in charge of finding new logs, whether that was by dragging previously fallen logs into the clearing or cutting down new trees and hacking the branches off one at a time. Hev was much better suited for this work than Artemys.

Once he got into the motions of it, Artemys fell into the repetitions, his mind wandering. With work like this, enough of Artemys's mind was free to call upon his gift. Years ago, he had discovered the Great Glyph.

He could recall every moment of that night. It was after he said farewell to Kerres. Their fight has escalated until she tried to leave. He had grabbed her by the throat and pressed her back against the wall. "One more kiss," he said, his mind a cancerous knot, "for the memory." He had pressed his mouth against hers, felt her knee in his groin, felt the floor as he fell back. He had lain there forever after she had left, and wandered the streets of Avernus for hours after. As he lay in one alleyway, his mind had snapped—not like the senses of magic, or anything he had ever felt. In that instant he had beheld the world. All of the complexities, the patterns, the chaotic peace, and the peaceful chaos. It felt like he had sunk so deep into the water he could not breathe, and beneath it all he found a web, leeching into the corners of his mind to sustain itself. It was not pain, it was a *stretch*. Like his mind had expanded.

That night, he had beheld reality, driven to insanity and back again.

He stacked another group of split wood into the cart. After that night, he had realized how small he had become. No matter how shallow Kerres might be, there was a much better way to deal with the situation. What had he gained from treating her in such a way? Nothing. There was no reason for such attitude, such anger.

Even his duel with Master Kaen, years before that night of the Great Glyph, seemed insignificant in the sea of history. If he wanted to make a splash, he needed to do more than prove his magical prowess by defeating a weak, old man.

He had spent a year after that night in the alleyways of Avernus studying the Great Glyph. He scoured for religious texts—the Glyph had been the focus of the late Kinship. Artemys's grandfather Akheron had led the People's Uprising that ended it, and most of those records had been burned in the Revolution. The Order of Magic had a few mentions of the Great Glyph in their tomes, but this was long after he had left the School amidst the controversial battle in which he had bested his own master and he was denied access to some of their libraries.

"Where are you, Artemys?" Hev asked.

At first he thought Hev was in the woods, calling for aid in finding the clearing again, but realized it was a rhetorical question his friend posed. "Just thinking."

"We've got a full load." Hev pointed to the cart, piled high with wood. They set off for town, Artemys still stirred by memories.

After years of studying the Great Glyph, he had travelled to a village in the southern fief of Olympus. An old man in Nim's Run had spent his life telling fortunes. He told Artemys that these things concerned the True Name. Artemys had questioned him intently about the man's training—had he attended a magic school to learn of the True Name? He explained what Artemys already knew; the True Name was a name specific to each individual, a series of glyphs that described both their physical and internal make up, their abilities, their fate. The granting of magic was a simple act of adding another ability to one's True Name.

"What is the Great Glyph?" Artemys had asked then. This man had been abounding on the internal, personal, small glyphs.

He recalled the man's words to this day. "The Great Glyph is in us all. Some of us are unaware of it. Some of us use it. Some of us see the past through it. Some of us see the future. We are the Great Glyph."

Artemys had avoided a debate with him. He did not know enough of the Great Glyph to decide such a thing. Instead, he discussed the middle claims thoroughly—how do we see the past? The future?

The man explained that some people are born with a reference to the Great Glyph in their True Name. This meant they were born with the ability to access the Great Glyph—the organization of the world in the form of glyphs. The Maker had spoken the Great Glyph into existence, each word an element, a person, a land. Those with the reference to that universe in their Name could access it at will. No spell would be required.

Artemys had nodded. That night, in the alleyways after his last kiss with Kerres, he had not conjured any magic, though he had seen the world.

Hev and he reached Attarax again. The small village was bustling by this time of day—every man and woman with a task. Some attended training, but that was scheduled to not interfere with the daily functioning of the stronghold.

Once the cart of cut wood had been emptied into a storage shed, they began the venture back to their clearing. "How long are you staying this time?" Hev asked.

"A couple more days yet." Artemys helped him haul the cart across the stream. A bird had nested nearby and kept calling at them each time they passed. He had once been out here during the rain—though it rarely fell this far into the mountains—and no birds bothered him then.

"Then back to Avernus or Delfie again?"

"Delfie," he said. "Lady Rysarius still spies for us in Avernus."

Hev nodded. The Disciples were the most dedicated people Artemys had met. The schemers at the School seemed like squawking gulls in comparison. There were very few secrets kept by the Zealots, for all the Disciples led lives of purpose; there was no reason for living in a hostile mountain range like this, without purpose. "I heard a rumour that you used to love her. And were willing to abuse that connection to turn her into one of ours."

Artemys smirked. "Partially right. I did not abuse any love. I let her have what she wanted—power. She's willing to do the rest."

"But you *do* love her?"

They reached the clearing, and Hev stared at him, waiting for an answer. "I do," he said, surprising himself. *Why?* "Because she's me. She acts to change. She has a goal and will do anything to accomplish it. We cannot be together if our goals do not match, but I *do* love her."

Hev nodded. "That makes a lot more sense than it should."

Artemys laughed and handed Hev the other ax. *I did not know that about Kerres,* he realized, *or myself!* How could such revelations come with a burst of words? *Did the Maker know what he was going to say when he spoke the world into reality?*

Soon he had fallen back into the methodical hammering of ax into wood, and his mind summoned the Great Glyph again. Though he could feel the rise and fall of the ax in the physical world, his mind observed much more and much farther. An ocean of glyphs filled his eyes—the rock of the mountains, the air in the sky and the life in the trees. He could think *wider* and see from coast to coast. The present world around him formed a layer like a scroll. Beneath it was a tower of scrolls dating back into the past, each parchment a moment of time. He thought *back* and flipped through the pages of time to that conversation with old man Nim.

"Some True Names are limited to seeing the past. Those with a strong gifting in this can even travel there," the prophet claimed. "That is rare though. Some True Names are limited to seeing the future. Those can also travel through time, to the places they see."

"Is it possible to do both? See both, or travel through any year of time?" Artemys asked. All of this was theory to him. How could he travel to the past? He had never seen the future.

Nim had explained, "It is possible, but only in a thousand-thousand years."

"Is it possible to learn these abilities?"

"Your True Name includes your potential."

He had questioned the prophet further but learned nothing more. That moment of the past faded from Artemys's mind. The vision of the Great Glyph faded and he knelt to pick up the pieces of wood he had finished. He could sometimes see through the Great Glyph, watch both it and the world his physical eyes perceived. This allowed him to multitask, making progress with a job in the real world while learning from the past. He only had that ability. He turned back to the stack of uncut logs.

After he had discovered gateways—the spells to travel from any point in the world to another—he had tried to travel into the past, using coordinates in the Great Glyph as his destination. None of those spells had worked. He had not been born with such a gift.

"Artemys!" Hev called. His friend was staring across the clearing past Artemys's chopping block.

Artemys glanced behind him. Weveld was standing at the edge of the clearing, immaculate grey robe hanging into the moss and sweat beads dripping into his white beard. "You think I don't know what you're doing?" the Prime Zealot questioned.

In an instant, Artemys found himself pinned to a nearby tree, Weveld's forearm braced across his chest, and the old man's face a storm of fury. "Do you think you're above us? You consume more magic than I! Constantly watching the world. You think that we hadn't thought of that? You think we *want* to use spies when we could just scry all we need to know?"

"What are you—"

"We live and toil beneath the sun for a reason, Artemys! We slave to survive because we *don't* use magic. Because someone has to keep it, someone has to sustain it. Protect it. All you care about is yourself!" Weveld's eyes were filled with the same darkness that Artemys saw in the face of that guard in Bertren, fist falling on Artemys's childish form until he was drenched in his own blood.

It was not hard to shove Weveld away from him. He leaned away from the tree, fists clenched. "All I care about is the state of the world! Unlike you and your petty order! Plotting in the shadows, fooling with the world like it dangles from your puppet strings!" Artemys returned. "It disgusts me."

Weveld was flushed red in rage. "Ha! You're the same as all of us. It was not I who suggested a scheme to convert your once-lover into a spy! The only difference between you and the Disciples is that *we* actually have discipline! Dedication!"

"And I do not?"

Weveld patted his robe off where Artemys's shove had wrinkled it and rose back to his level. "I was sitting with the Zealots at the weekly Session—we monitor the current usage of magic. How was I to explain what we saw? Watching you consume days worth of magic as you explore! Such scrying consumes more magic than some of the Order's Apprentices have ever used!"

"I am a prophet!" Artemys declared. Both Weveld and Hev stared at him in shock. Hev looked just as winded by the fight as those who were actually arguing it. "You would silence my voice?"

"Why do you think anyone with the gift of time-sight ends up as a small village soothsayer, using his abilities only for the occasional foretelling and predicting the weather?" Weveld breathed.

Artemys froze. "The Disciples... *limit* them like that?"

"We must, no matter what we want to do."

"And me? Now that you know I am one of *them*." Artemys slumped back against the tree Weveld had thrown him against.

The Prime Zealot sank down onto the chopping block, winded. He took a deep breath, trying to calm himself. "That's entirely up to you, Artemys."

Can I do it? he asked himself. *Only use the Great Glyph when I must?* Even with Kerres as a spy, Artemys spent hours watching the lords and ladies of Avernus, Athyns, or Olympus. They were the rot at the heart of the Triumvirate, living leisurely lives and withholding the wealth that the commoners generated. With a single ruler, there would be fewer individuals at the top, less wealth being wasted by the upper class. In order to maintain his awareness of the Triumvirate on a government-wide scale *without* the Great Glyph, he would need to work around the clock and develop a new set of methods. Which did not depend on magic.

"I will play by your rules," he told Weveld. "I see the need for it. I will only use my gifts when it is required. To tell you the truth, if it means anything now, I had not considered the possibility of my innate scrying using energy..."

"Most do not." The Prime Zealot stood. "I apologize for my outburst. I remember feeling this same rage at your father during the war. He was *perpetuating* our hardships, I thought. But I remember the night after the assassins almost claimed him, as he lay on the edge of death—so frail! I sat at his bedside and realized that I had been all wrong..." He trailed off, gazing into secrets only he knew. He glanced back up at Artemys. "I simply had no other reason for your use of energy than the things I accused you of just now. How long have you known of your time-seeing talents?"

Artemys sighed. "Long before I found the Disciples. That is how I found Attarax initially."

"Some of the Zealots discussed that possibility, but we had no proof. We had to assume that you had used standard scrying spells and had luck on your side."

Hevarus was still staring at them. "You can see the past? Tell me about my parents or the farm I grew up on."

Artemys glanced at him, then back to Weveld. The Prime Zealot's eyes were narrowed. This was a test. Artemys turned back to Hev and took a deep breath. *How I have dreaded these words...*"I do not know," he replied.

. . .

Four days later, Artemys returned to the School of Delfie. Travelling was the one use of magic that the Disciples sanctioned, if only for a select few. As he prepared the spell, Artemys reflected on the first question that new Disciples asked: what's the point of magic if no one is permitted to use it? But the question relied on flawed logic. The Disciples did not demand their magic laws of everyone, only their own Order. They kept a system of management in place to access many different social structures in the realm, but they did not stop the use of magic. The Disciples, as Weveld had first told him, were tasked with balancing it.

With his gateway spell ready, Artemys stood up from the dirt outside of Attarax and whispered, *"Osh hayen loraz zar heega."*

The glyphs he had drawn into the soil were activated one by one as he spoke their names. Once he finished, an area shaped like a crate or a small room began to flicker around him. The vertices of each corner began to change from the grey sky of Attarax to the blue of Delfie's air. The ground beneath his feet—the bottom dimension of the area his spell had affected—began to change from the dirt he stood upon into the ancient stone slab that welcomed all travellers to Delfie. The spell changed the air around him slowly until, with a quiet bursting sound, the colours and conditions of the area around him snapped to mimic those of Delfie, and no indications of Attarax remained.

"Welcome, Artemys!" Caius stood up from the wooden stool he sat on against a pear tree.

Artemys glanced down long enough to descend the old stone steps. The stone platform had been there for as long as the teleport spell for this location had been known. Surrounding it was the School's orchard, though he could see the rooftops of the Hall building, the Archives and, of course, the Tower looming above the tree tops. The latter was used primarily for quarters, though Artemys would not find his way there for a couple hours.

He clasped hands with Caius. The mage was serving as the Sentinel of Delfie, an honourable position defending the Travelling Pedestal. He had a small mustache and long sideburns, his hair the same dull orange of his robe.

Weveld had used his role as Crown Magician to convince the Order's council of Artemys's return. Better than that, even, they welcomed him as a magician, not an apprentice. Artemys had jokingly told Weveld that it was because of how well his first apprenticeship had gone. Weveld did not laugh.

Artemys had also been the youngest Apprentice in the history of the order. He had been only thirteen when he was assigned to Master Kaen. Artemys's dedication to magic was unparalleled, which was perhaps another reason he could skip the Apprentice stage now, when he was twenty-six.

He brushed past Caius after a brief welcome and made his way toward through the orchard. The Archives sat quietly to the left of the looming Hall. To the right, some workers were repairing the thatched roof of the School Storehouse clouding the air with the din of hammers and saws. He strode along a narrow footpath that led him through the fruit trees to a gate in the wall between the Archives and Hall. Leaving the smell of fruit and the buzzing of bees behind, he set off through the second courtyard. This one was formed between the Tower of the Order, the back of the Hall, and the classroom buildings at the back of the campus. He was on his way to meet an older wizard with whom he would be working for the next several days.

Ringing in his ears was the debate about Weveld's accusations, still as fresh in Artemys's mind as that day earlier in the week. Weveld held control of the two most important forces in the Triumvirate. While the Princes made the political decisions and defended the Dominion, Weveld controlled the powers that shaped the world itself. While he spoke the truth of magic—that energy creation was limited and thus must be governed—his status was much greater. Artemys now knew that the Prime Zealot and Crown Magician controlled what magic was accepted, what spells were prohibited, what men were great, what men were petty.

Artemys would have to do something about that.

Year of Olympus 547

Tiberon Odyn, the tenth of his name, the Prince of Olympus, the Champion of the Southern Tournaments, and the Wisdom of Vero, was dead.

Periander planted a foot in the center of the door, the wood, which he had already splintered with a sword, separating beneath his kick. The door caved in, his leg jarred from the impact. He limped for the first step, then, ignoring the pain, flew through the frame into the next room. A man in chainmail stood alert above a bloody corpse, its tunic bearing the insignia of the Three Towers of Avernus just as Periander's own. Periander raised the buckler in his left hand to send the man's hasty sword swipe reeling to one side. Another powerful hack of Periander's blade forced the man to release his sword and clutch his arm in agony. Chainmail was a challenge to cut, but a strong enough blow could either shatter bone or grind the links of metal into flesh. Periander smashed his sword's pommel into the man's face, splattering blood onto the floor as the enemy collapsed.

Thankfully, that had not been too loud. Below him, enemy soldiers scoured the streets and forced doors open to find the Prince that had escaped, to find Periander.

Beyond the corpse of the Avernan soldier was a small window. The shutter was hinged only in one corner as the window was shaped like a diamond. He swung it open, letting the din of dying men and fighting metal echo into the room. Smoke was rising like a cloud above the city of Edessa. Even as he watched, a building collapsed into rubble, spilling outward, and crushing the men and women who ran through the street. Occasional shots from a catapult would blast into the rooftops. He could not tell which way this window faced. He could not recognize any landmarks, though the ones he might have remembered could have burned down.

"How did this happen?" Periander breathed. It had been nearly three years since open battle with the advancing mountain horde. And now this: King Trion and his personal guards had seized Edessa.

He had to get higher to get a vantage point of the battle. Next to the window was a door. There was a small balcony, and nearby a ladder to the roof. This was not the tallest tower in this vicinity. Many of the buildings in Edessa reached as many as five storeys into the air. Such marvelous architecture had been destroyed by the chaos of Trion's unexpected attack.

Periander took another breath and scaled the ladder, each step of his boots bending the old wood. If it weren't for the din of battle, he imagined he would hear each creak. The roof of the tower sported a waist-high battlement made of stone, though the central area, the open space above the tower proper, was made of comparatively aged wood. It looked as if it was rotting, though Periander's sight was blurred from fatigue and smoke.

He turned in a full circle, shocked by the devastation that greeted him in every direction from the battlements. Pillars of smoke rose from a hundred fires, bodies littered the streets, and the Keep was becoming a smouldering pile of rock as catapult after catapult fired upon it.

How did this happen?! Earlier he and Odyn had met for a noon meal. They recalled the mead they had shared at the Siege of Trionus. But on this foul day, their servants had drawn blades, and soldiers had stormed the door. Guards had been watching for giants, not for normal men in chain or plate. Periander had nearly been slain himself. As Odyn's corpse had sunk to the floor with two knives in his chest, the assassins then advanced on Periander. He had leapt from the balcony of the royal quarters of the Keep onto the thatched stable below.

The streets now swarmed with the black and yellow of Trionus soldiers, the red of Imperial uniforms fleeing the city, and the red of blood.

He should not be here. He was trying to distance himself

from this war. It was not healthy, and it was not right. He had a wife and a son. He should not be parrying swords with a buckler. He should not have been standing within the rain of flame and rock, choking on smoke, gasping for breath.

Without warning, he was knocked to his knees. The stone battlements wavered from the impact that had dropped Periander. He glanced over the edge; bricks were falling to the street below, where a large rock was rolling to a stop. The building quaked from the catapult shot, its structure beginning to buckle. Periander did not bother to stand up. He dragged his finger across the rough stone of the rampart, grimacing as flecks of rock and dust dug into his skin. It took him longer than it should have to remember the glyph for lightness—"feather" as the Order called it. He breathed, *"Hayen al'vanor bor ogar,"* as the building collapsed beneath him.

With the crashing noise of splintering wood and crumbling stone, the tower spread a pyramid of debris across the streets on either side. Smoke and dust wafted into the air with the gagging cries of men trapped within it. Drifting like a leaf in the breeze, Periander was blown lazily to one side of the collapsing block. He stumbled as his feet dragged atop the remnants of the battlements. Only a handful of bricks retained the square frame on which he had stood moments earlier. He lifted his hands to his ears. The roar of collapsing bricks had deafened his hearing. He shook his head and looked up with bleary eyes through the settling dust. He could not see the sky anymore, only a smoky, red haze. Earlier he had seen a different sky, alight with its own brightness. Though the colours differed, it had reminded him of Artemys's shining, green eyes.

He had been spending more and more time with Artemys. Instead of annual trips to the east, he had travelled back to Avernus four times this past year. His recent visits had lasted more than a week. He had held his son in his arms for hours, watched the small, sleeping face. So calm. How could something, some*one* be so calm?

Rising from the din of echoing ears, a scream drew him back to reality. Someone was pulling himself out of the collapsed building, legs a mess, a trail of blood behind him. He stared at Periander through the eyes of shock, speaking incoherent words. Periander knelt beside him and showed the dying man his knife. The man nodded with one shaky bop of his head. Periander made it quick.

He stood up again. Time to end *this* insanity as well. There was only one way he was going to escape the city. Only one way any of the straggled Imperial survivors would. He started walking, a slow and limping start, but soon a sustainable jog. He was wearing lamellar armour over his red tabard. He had found the vest of leather links in the stable on which he had landed when escaping the assassins. It was not strong armour, but its light weight was an advantage now.

Edessa was built like two overlapping, round shields. In the umbo of one was the Keep. At the center of the other was the Arena. Every street on that half of the city led directly to the stadium, like spokes on a crest on a shield or spokes on a wagon wheel.

It took him only ten minutes to find one of these main streets, but more than an hour passed as he tried to follow it. Enemies in groups would force him to hide in a shop or beneath an overturned carriage, waiting patiently for them to pass. Solitary soldiers, wearing black and yellow uniforms or mail byrnies, did not require such caution. He stopped to duel on several occasions.

When he had made half his course, he was met by a group of Imperial soldiers. Two of them claimed to be members of his regiment, some were infantry of the late Prince Odyn, while the remainder wore the emblem of the Edessan garrison, embroidered waves beneath a mountain.

Together they fought their way closer to the Arena. The Arena of Edessa was the largest in the Dominion. Although the Arena of Avernus had a dirt pit with thatching and palisade spikes surrounding it, and Olympus had an established tourney field, this stadium was a stone structure half the size of the City Keep. The exterior was square, though the central combat field was circular. The resulting corners made room for cells.

Periander pounded on the door without even pausing for breath, when his small troop reached it. There was a moment of silence, then a muffled: "Go away!"

"I'm Periander Gothikar, let me in."

"Right, and I'm Valik Aristorn," the voice retorted. One of the founders of the Triumvirate. "I'm not opening this door for anyone!"

Periander sighed. He was too tired for sarcasm. "Do you want to survive today, Valik Aristorn? If you do, you'll open this door. My men and I are leaving this city, and I'd prefer not to leave you, being such an important man and such." That was odd. His knuckles still ached from knocking on the door. He pressed them into the palm of his other hand.

There was a long pause. Finally, the door creaked open and a spear emerged. The spear pushed sideways until the doorway was open. The man behind the shaft was short, his face greasy, and eyes sunken from hours patrolling the dark cells of the stadium's combatants. "By the Maker," he breathed. "You *are* the Prince." The spear disappeared, behind the wide doorframe. "Come in, come in."

With Periander and his party inside, the guard lowered the bar across the door again. "I'm sorry, lord, I've turned away many men to save my own skin. Please sir, do not..."

"It's not important..."

"Pharas," the man said.

"Pharas. Tell me, how many men do you have here?" The room was small, an antechamber of some kind, though it merged into the next room like a hallway. Periander wandered forward. The roof was much higher in the next area, and a group of men and women crammed around a table watching the newcomers with snake-like eyes.

"Myself and five others. Then three of their wives, my lord," Pharas said.

Periander recoiled his head in surprise. "Five?" He blinked. Of course. "How many fighters?" he rephrased.

"Oh. Pardon, my lord. There are fifty-seven combatants, locked in the cells."

Periander nodded. "And armaments? You have an armoury, yes?"

Pharas bowed. "Through here." He gestured to a doorway. "Accessed through the Arena itself."

"And you have the keys?"

"My lord?"

"Do you have the keys?" Periander demanded.

"You can't intend to free them," Pharas said. "They would kill us, quicker than Trion's men."

"Give me the keys!"

Pharas's face broke like an overripe melon. He held them out, his hands trembling so the keys clanked against one another. "Please let me and my men leave first. We will flee..."

Periander shook his head. "You will not. These men, fifty of the most dangerous killers and magicians in a thousand miles... that's a troop worth gold. If you wish to live, you will stay with us." Pharas quaked as roughly as the collapsing tower had, and, in a similar way, he sank to a seat near his comrades. "Now, who is the reigning champion?" Periander asked.

"Arkius Salantar," came a quiet reply. Pharas glanced up. "His cell is directly across the Arena, on the second floor."

Periander gestured for two of his men to follow him. The arena seemed even larger within the stone walls than it had from outside. Flakes of ash were falling like rain from the buildings, but Periander marched right through it. There were stairs set into the stone wall, curving up to the second storey and higher to the third. The cells faced inwards, so the contestants could watch the fights as well as the audience could. The latter's seating occupied the front section of each storey, like balconies looking onto a courtyard, but this courtyard was the place where men fought to the death.

"Arkius Salantar?" Periander called as he reached the second storey. The man in the closest cell rose to his feet with the clank of manacles. Periander regarded him for a moment before speaking. Salantar wore sackcloth, though his features were as sharp as any nobleman Periander had met. Salantar had green eyes, as clear as Artemys's. He seemed to recall an Athynian noble with the name Salantar—perhaps a relative of this man. The man's beard was thin, missing in spots, as were his teeth. Periander imagined himself looking about as pleasant as this fellow. He had not shaved for two months. It was nothing compared to the cloak he grew during the winter.

"I'm him."

"I am Prince Gothikar of Avernus," Periander said. "I'm here to offer your freedom. In return you will accompany my men in a fight to the harbor. From there you are free to travel your own way as a free man."

"Hah," Salantar said. He spat beside Periander, a loud snap. "You open that door, I'll kill you and...these two, and take my freedom anyway."

"Then you'll stay there, and I will offer a similar deal to your comrades." This was a bargain, a trade. He had to convince Salantar to accept his deal.

"None of them will take your offer," Salantar returned. "They'll do the same thing I would. You want my *service*, you'll earn it."

Periander eyed Salantar stoically. These men would likely die if he did not free them. But on the other hand, that was their life already. "Fine. I'll humour you. How?"

"You see that cage?" The prisoner's muscular arm pointed towards the corner. Another man was standing at his bars, watching Periander. "His name is Berik. His brother, Orion, earned his freedom last year. Berik had already won more matches, but is still bound."

"Berik is angry?" Periander replied. "We could search for his brother after—"

"You will fight Berik," Salantar said, his grin a mix of rotting teeth and black gaps between them. "You will fight him down in the pit, like one of us. That will earn my service."

Periander met Salantar's gaze. The man's smile faded to the same analytical expression Periander's face must have borne. Without a word, Periander turned away from Salantar's cage and strode toward Berik. Berik was equal in build to Periander—he wondered if Salantar had chosen the fighter for that reason. The key had to be forced into the lock, then a quick turn and the cell eased open. More men were coming to their bars, interest piqued by this turn of events. Outside the rumble of catapults and the screams of slaughter could still be heard.

Berik stepped out of the cell. Periander followed the prisoner past Salantar's cell to the staircase and down to the pit. A look passed between the two—Salantar nodded to Berik's unvoiced question.

They reached the dirt floor of the central Arena and Berik tore his sackcloth shirt over his head. "Never fought a Prince before." His voice was slurred. "You bleed like the rest of us?"

"I've been practicing it today actually," Periander replied. He drew his sword. Pharas and his friends gathered near the hallway, along with the troop of soldiers Periander had commandeered. "Do not intervene. On pain of death, do not intervene," he ordered them. "Give this man a sword."

One of the two soldiers that had followed Periander handed Berik a weapon. Periander tossed his buckler aside, the small metal disk rolling into the sand. He paced backwards, his booted feet kicking the sand, then turned back to Berik with his guard up.

The fighter had kicked aside his own poor sandals, his bare feet curling into the dirt. He was bare save knee-length sackcloth trousers. Above them, the sky showered ash and smoke. Berik saluted with his sword, a custom which Periander had never really used. He returned the gesture and then, like the snapping tail of a scorpion, Berik's first thrust glanced off his sword. He had not even seen the man move.

He ducked the next slash and found a swinging foot at level with his head. Stars blurred across his vision as he fell solidly on his behind. By the time his senses returned to him, a chant of "Berik" was echoing from the jail cells above.

He clambered to his feet, much more wary of Berik's nearby pacing. This time the fighter waited for Periander to advance on him. Periander knew he could not move as fast as the seasoned warrior, but he had been trained by an accomplished Blade-master. His skills lay in form, not in speed. He swung right, left, then left again. Berik knocked the blows aside with experienced force though not with any trained manoeuvres. This man had learned to fight in the Arena most likely. Periander flowed into a more complex style. Every curving slash touched an imaginary line slightly to the right of his opponent. Close enough to warrant parries. Berik stepped back as he needed, blocking each of Periander's wide arching attacks. The roar of chanting warriors was lost as Periander layered his focus to cross the line and lash his piercing attack on the *left* side of his opponent.

Berik had become so used to blocking the right-oriented slashes that even his left block was too far to the other side. Periander's slash ran straight along his sword arm, shaving off a long strip of flesh. The man danced away on light feet, a trail of dripping blood following him, silent. His sword arm did not waver, despite the pain that must be wringing the man's body. After that blow, the arena was silent. Or Periander was still drowning out their chants. He did not know, but here Berik came with another lashing thrust like a scorpion, curving downward as though to impale Periander from collar to groin. Periander raised his sword like a horizon above his head, and instead of blocking the blow, stepped back. He smashed his horizontal sword down on Berik's thrust, his enemy's blade knocked even farther downwards, digging into the dirt.

Periander lashed out with his pommel, to knock Berik out with a blow to the unprotected head. Instead, Berik lunged forward with one shoulder, catching Periander in the gut and smashing him sideways. Gasping for air, Periander could barely raise his blade in time to parry Berik's sideways slash. Berik continued his zigzag assault, and Periander had to fall back, step by step. The chanting dug into his ears once more, "Berik, Berik, Berik..." Then out of nowhere, the fighter dropped to one knee, Periander's attack sailing high over his head.

He did not feel the stab until he tried stepping to one side. He glanced down, finding Berik's blade between two ribs on his right side. Still no pain. Then Berik rose from his knee, sliding the blade the rest of the way through Periander's torso, blood bubbling through his tabard. When it reached the exposed skin below his tabard, he felt how hot it was, his life-blood mingling with sweat, smoke, and sand. Finally the pain hit him, like a red-hot brand that had been placed inside his lung. He tried to inhale and could not get any air. He exhaled, and felt blood in his throat. He blinked his eyes. Why had the chanting stopped? Flailing, cheering arms were still snaking from the bars of the cages. Why was the world sideways? He could feel sand on his face, very distantly, and he had a momentary thought: *this is death.*

Then, ice crept through his side. Ice did not move like this though. It was water spreading through his chest. The hole the sword had left felt like an icicle now. He tried to grab it, but found another hand placed across the wound. He forced his eyes to see, and found Berik kneeling over him, no hostility in his eyes, no sword in view. *If he isn't finishing the job... then what?*

A jolt of energy surged through Periander and he sucked in a deep breath, air flowing into his lungs, and staying there. After a long moment, he exhaled. He grabbed his side again, Berik's hand gone. Smooth skin. No hole. Warm blood everywhere, but no wound. He gasped another thick breath, still not moving. A third, and he found the strength to sit up. "You healed me?" he breathed.

Berik nodded, one foot kicking the glyphs he had written in the sand away.

Periander took several more trembling breaths, and then climbed to his feet. He could barely stand, and, scooping up his sword from nearby, leaned on it like a crutch. He had not planned to die in order to escape Edessa.

His guards were scattered between where they had stood at the start and where he had fallen at the end. He smiled weakly to them.

"Well done, Prince Gothikar of Avernus," a voice echoed. Two storeys above, Salantar was laughing. "A commander who does not quake in the face of death. You have earned *our* service."

Periander handed the key to Pharas, who approached in a daze. "Free them," Periander ordered. *"Maker help us.* Free them." He stood no chance of escaping the city without them. He had news that had to reach the Dominion. Tiberon Odyn the Tenth was dead. And Periander Gothikar had narrowly escaped the same fate. Twice today.

He limped toward the table where the Arena's guards had been sitting at his arrival. He needed a drink. His throat still tasted of blood. He sank into a wooden chair. "I have a son," he said. He wasn't sure if anyone was listening, or even if anyone was nearby. He grabbed a mug from nearby, and regardless of its contents, took a long drink. "And a wife. Maker, what would Cat have done..." he trailed off, his eyes squeezed shut. He brushed ashes off of his arms.

Salantar sat down across the table from him. "That was an impressive fight. No one's given Berik a slash like that in years." In the background, the other fighter was writing another healing spell, his arm still dripping blood. He would be exhausted after the spells; healing—unlike other magic—drained both the caster. If healing was used on another, it would draw energy from both.

"You see the smoke? All that ash?" Periander asked. "And those screams? That won't happen to my home. I need you and your men to get me to the port. I'm going to sail to Galinor and ask that sorcerer Weveld where he was when Edessa burned! I'm going to call for the election of Prince Odyn's heir. And we are *not* going to lose this war. Tell your men they should help if they desire to save their home. Where are you from, Salantar?"

"Edessa," the man spat, looking toward the Arena pit. "Edessa's *my* home."

Periander stared at him. Even after the ordeal of collapsing to his death, Periander could taste Salantar's pain deeply. He hated to picture Avernus wrapped in the smoke of this place. And Salantar had watched it from a prison cell.

"Let's get to the harbor," Salantar said.

10

Year of Olympus 571

Every time that Artemys slept, he awoke with dreams of the past and worried that he had created energy by using the Great Glyph. It was on his thoughts all the time, beckoning for him to scry, taunting him with his knowledge, tempting him worse than anything he had ever tried to resist.

"How do I learn without it?" he asked Weveld, standing in the quarters of the Crown Mage.

Another time, in the study chamber of the Prime Zealot: "What do I do when no book contains it? How do I say 'no' to the truth of perception?"

Both times, Weveld beheld him with a skeptical eye and said something to the effect of, "You learned magic as a boy, before you ever saw the Great Glyph. You can learn without it once more."

Artemys did not need sage wisdom. He needed answers, a solution and a fix.

One day in the winter, he was sitting in the Delfie Archives, turning each page of a tome as he huddled against a table near a hanging black lantern. The warmth from the small magical flame was kept within the aisle by the bookshelves on either side. From the other side of the cluttered shelf, to Artemys's right, came the sound of books being stacked; one of the Archivists was at work there, a man by the name of Parsis.

The volume Artemys read had been a recent find by a travelling mage in Tarroth on the Valharyn Spine. Entitled *The Four Devils of Erkenkarl*, the chronicle told of four men during

Shadow Age, before the Triumvirate, who were granted the authority to enact any punishment on *any* man from the Valharyn Sea to the World's Foundation. In those days it had been the Endless Sea and the Mountains of Gevaraz, but Artemys had read enough to understand what the book spoke of.

The third chapter told of how they had achieved such a position. After sending gifts to most of the many kings across the realm, these men compiled enough information to blackmail, bribe, or threaten each of them into submission. Rather than claiming positions of royalty, the men simply asked for permission to do anything. To be exempt from any law. So long as this condition was met, the Four Devils kept a trust for the kings and did not use any of the information they had collected.

What interested Artemys was the manner in which that dangerous knowledge was obtained. By offering harmless or well received gifts, the Four Devils found their way into each ruler's inner circle. Artemys closed the tome and set it aside.

With the Great Glyph, Artemys did not need to be personal with the rulers. But gifts...they would be accepted by the high and the mighty of the Triumvirate. Strange, that nothing had changed in so many centuries.

"Master," Artemys said. He glanced up from the book.

Master Parsis stuck his head around the end of the shelf. He was one of the senior Archivists at the School of Delfie, though he was younger than most of the others. His brown hair was short, and he was just beginning to bald. He was clean shaven, though the scar on the bottom of his chin seemed worthy of a beard to hide it. "You have a question, Artemys?"

"Where could I find a truly remarkable sword?"

Artemys's question raised Parsis's eyebrows. "A sword? Why would you need a sword?"

"Call it a gift," Artemys said.

"You say a remarkable sword? Supposedly, that would be the work of a great smith, such as Breylin of Edessa or Ino of Tarroth. They say there is a newcomer to the industry in Port Elysia, a man by the name of Orestys whose gift in plying steel is unparalleled."

"In Elysia Port?" Artemys asked. *What are the chances? There is a Glyph Gate nearby I can use to return to Attarax.*

Parsis nodded. "I assume this 'gift' of yours was inspired

by that book you've been reading?"

Artemys frowned. Still open beneath his elbows was the *Four Devils*. "I assure you, I do not plan on blackmailing any kings this week."

"I should hope not," Parsis said curtly. He returned to his work.

Artemys worked a knot out of his neck with his left hand as he put the book away with his other. *Meddling magicians...*It was impossible to get any work done at the School without it becoming everyone's business. *Someone will have to clean house sooner or later. I should ask Weveld about it.*

Once the book was back in its proper place on the shelf, Artemys walked toward the door out of the Archives. He would need some privacy for his spell. According the Order of Magic, only five teleports were known—the ability to travel to Athyns, Olympus, Avernus, Galinor and Delfie. It was said that, when the Order had been established in the 99th Year of Olympus, close to twenty locations had been known.

Artemys had discovered the ability to learn any location's glyphs when his Great Glyph visions had first manifested. To travel to a location with magic, a magician had to write a spell referencing those glyphs. Now Artemys could open a gateway anywhere.

As a Disciple, Artemys was encouraged to use Glyph Gates more, but their destinations were limited. To travel *to* the Glyph Gate of Elysia, one would have to step through the Gate in Attarax. There was a Glyph Gate near Delfie, but it led to the swamps of Agwar.

Weveld had permitted him to use spells, if necessary. Only Artemys and a handful of the Zealots were so privileged.

Artemys turned right after leaving the Archive's arched doorway. The cold threatened him to bring a lantern, but he refused the urge.

If he had stayed on the footpath, he might've been able to see the rest of the campus, but he now walked away from it. There was a tall fence around the orchard to stop it from being overgrown by the thick foliage from outside. Artemys had once run through that foliage, the day his mother had died. The day the Storm of Delfie struck.

Today, however, he opened the gate of the fence and closed

it behind him. There was a thick layer of snow on the ground here. The School's grounds themselves were never snowy, but kept both illuminated and protected from rain or snow. Artemys only took three steps through the winter and knelt, one hand balancing himself against the trunk of a birch tree. He summoned the Great Glyph into his vision for only a moment. It had been weeks since he had, and the temptation to study it longer was almost painful. As soon as he saw the glyphs for a deserted alleyway within the Port, he let his sight return to normal.

He wrote several glyphs into the snow—the location of that small forest clearing at the center. His finger stung as though the crisp surface of the snow was cutting it. When he was done, he uttered his spell aloud and watched his surroundings change.

Now he was crouched between two brick walls. Where his hand had been set against smooth bark, there was now the rough texture of masonry. The snow he had knelt in was a frosty mud puddle, his feet not cracking its frozen surface. He glanced up at the clear, blue sky. It was such a deep shade it made Artemys think of the summer, though it was colder here than at Delfie.

The blacksmith Parsis had spoken of would have shop nearby—Artemys had travelled to the Craftsman's Village, a successful trades district built across the city from the Harbour.

The street at the end of Artemys's alley was nearly deserted. The snapping air kept even the children indoors. It never got this cold in Bertren, the town where the Gothikar estate was held, on the interior of the Southern Spine.

Artemys had been raised there. He could recall days spent running through the dirt with friends as equally sun-burnt and muddied as himself. They played at war, they talked of war. In those days, there had been war. None of them knew if it would end, or if they would champion within it.

And then, his father had taken it all away. He had granted Artemys the *gift* of magic. None of those boys would run in the field with him anymore. None of them would join him anymore. They feared him. They distanced him. There had been no nostalgia when he left Bertren for the School of Delfie and the Order of Magic—that pain had begun the day Artemys was given magic.

The hammering of steel interrupted his thoughts. That

would by Orestys's smithy; a cloud of dark smoke dissipating long after it formed hung in the air above a building up the street.

Artemys hurried his pace; it would be warm within the blacksmith's. The ground was not very snowy, though small banks could be seen at the corner of some buildings. The street itself was well-trodden enough to leave only a thin layer of frost and a dusting of white flakes. Artemys nearly slipped more than once, but made it to the metal worker's without incident.

There were two signs on the face of the building, each above a wooden door. One door was propped open with a shovel of some kind; the sign above it read "Smithy." The second door read "Private."

Artemys peeked inside the open door and called within. The banging of steel stopped and a voice replied, "In here!"

The shop was like any smithy Artemys had ever seen, cluttered and coated from ceiling to floor with a layer of black grease. The smith was the same—he was a man with a shaved head and a beard that was missing more than one spot of hair. Each line of his angular muscles was traced with soot and sweat.

As Artemys approached, the blacksmith wrung each finger in a cloth that seemed too dirty to do any good and then one hand shot out to take Artemys's in a hearty clasp. "I am Orestys ten Eledan, finest smith in Elysia. What can I do for a member of the Order?"

Artemys glanced at his orange and beige robe for the first time all day. He was too accustomed to the indistinguishable grey cloaks of the Disciples. "I am not currently on task for the Order, but for my House. And your reputation reaches further than Elysia."

Orestys sighed with a smile. His eyes were a clear, grey colour, but only when they caught the light in the right way. "Glyphs, I make no claims beyond Elysia, sir." He broke Artemys's gaze and glanced down, running a hand over his clear scalp and leaving smears there. He leaned back against a crowded work table. "I assume a noble House?"

"The noblest," Artemys declared. "I am the heir of House Gothikar."

Orestys's jaw dropped, those grey eyes flicked back to Artemys's green. "You're a Prince, milord!" he exclaimed, and hesitantly bent at the waist.

"None of that."

The smith turned to the table and lifted his arms in dismay. "This place is a mess! Please, sire, come into my residence...perhaps there is a measure of comfort there."

"I did not come for comfort," Artemys said. "I came for your work."

"You did not exaggerate when you spoke of my reputation beyond Elysia!" Orestys still appeared winded. "I have crafted weapons for lords before, but never a Prince. Sire, I am no royal armourer!"

"According to the records of my Order, your work has great promise." Artemys strode into the center of the shop. The bellows and furnace in one corner, a large shelf in the other. He rested a hand on the anvil and glanced back at the smith. "We are going to forge a sword fit for a Prince."

"I would be honoured," Orestys responded. "You said 'we'. Do you know the art?"

"Art?"

"Craft," the smith corrected himself.

"I am no smith. But I am a magician."

"This will be a magical sword? Is there such a thing?"

Artemys smiled. "They say that in the Age of Myths, men fought with swords made of fire and air. But that Age did not last—for a reason. It will be a weapon that cuts with steel but endures like magic."

Orestys nodded. He strode across the room and pulled a sheaf of parchment out of a pile. "This..." He hesitated. "What is the purpose of this sword, sire?"

"A gift," Artemys told him. "To my father, who saved this realm years ago. We are distant, and this sword may help." *That's no lie.*

The blacksmith held up the parchment again. "This is my masterpiece. We will use it for basis."

Artemys examined the page. It was the plan for a sword, with various numbers indicating dimensions and a sketch that meant little to his magician's eyes. "You have not made this weapon already?"

"No. I have neither the resources nor the wealth for such a project, sire."

"Please. I will be working with you until this weapon is finished. Drop the 'sires'. If you must call me, my name is Artemys."

Orestys grimaced. "As you wish."

"Do not worry about wealth or resources. I can procure ample amounts of both. Now, how do we begin?"

"We need to make the metal. A balance of steel, chromium, and nickel. It takes me weeks to reach the right combination for a masterwork blade—a sword for a Prince could take even longer."

"There are spells to conjure metals," Artemys told him. "And I can forge them into metal similarly. Explain to me the proportions of each metal, and we can move past this step by nightfall."

. . .

True to his word, Artemys provided Orestys with a balance of metals which the smith called "beyond perfection," and immediately set to work upon. Artemys sat outside on a small barrel to cool himself. He had used many spells, none of which created too much energy, but some of which created heat. The smithy was already hot and, by the time Orestys began his task of hammering the metal, Artemys's beige robe was drenched in sweat.

"You have any way you'd like to fuse this?"

Artemys turned to the open shop door. Orestys was holding the two pieces of the weapon in his hands - the hilt and the blade. Artemys stood to look.

"Normally we insert two or three pins within the hilt to hold the taper of the blade, but, being a magician's sword..."

Artemys nodded. He took the hilt in his hands. It was fairly simple at this point, just a metal cross with a slot on the surface at the top. Next Artemys took the blade and slid it into the slot until the tapered bottom widened into the sword's actual blade.

Orestys gestured to the open door and led Artemys inside. He had cleared one of his work benches, so Artemys set the blade down there. He made certain the blade was positioned correctly within the sword. The first spell he wrote was a simple set of glyphs on the table top, imbuing his finger with the ability to etch into the steel. Spells that were merged with their target were permanent spells, so the strongest enchantments of this sword should be carved upon it. Artemys had learned this many years earlier at the School of Delfie.

He read the spell aloud, touched his index finger to the steel of the blade, and felt it make way for his skin. To that finger, the steel had the texture of cake batter or wet mud. Careful not to go too deep, he traced two glyphs—one at the base of the sword blade and the other at the top of the hilt.

He wrote a second spell onto the table, which would cause fiery metal to join the two locations he had marked with glyphs on the sword. As he read this one, he eagerly watched the weapon. A thick layer of metal filled the slot, fusing the tapered length of the blade piece within the hilt.

"Like one piece," he told Orestys.

"By the Maker, that was incredible," the blacksmith told him. "How hot was the metal you created within?"

Artemys smiled. "Not hot enough to ruin the tapered end. I knew that is why pins were used. If the blade is built as one piece with the hilt, the weapon is more likely to break."

"You're a proper smith!" Orestys laughed. "Never imagined my day would involve this!"

"I'm no good with a hammer. But knowledge is the ultimate weakness and the ultimate strength."

"The hilt will take me a couple days." The blacksmith lifted the sword by the hilt to examine it. "You going to stay in town until then?"

"No, I have errands to run."

Orestys smiled. "It's clear to me that a man on your path runs *errands* out of town."

Artemys nodded. *A man on my path...* "I will return when you are done the hilt."

. . .

"So this sword," Kerres whispered. "You'll give it to your father?"

Artemys nodded. "And hear everything he says." He sagged back into the cushions more and wrapped his arm around Kerres's smooth shoulders.

She smiled. "But you could already do that."

"Not Weveld's way."

She leaned into his embrace and bent to face him. "You're letting Weveld control you? Your magic?"

"For now." He pushed himself up, pressed his lips against hers.

When they separated, she smiled and asked him, "Does the Order trust you enough yet?"

"Almost."

She slid away from him, wrapping the bed sheets around her as she sat up. "And the other princes?"

"Theseus is untouchable. His court magician—a man named Accalia—has an impervious reputation and an astute eye. Also, the two spend enough time side-by-side, it's a wonder they do not merge."

Kerres laughed. Artemys glanced out the window. The sun had just left the horizon, and, though it hurt his eyes to look, he could see the narrow blue band just between the grey sky and the gleaming rays of light. That light caught Kerres's green eyes and lit them on fire in a way that Artemys doubted his ever shone. "And Odyn?" she asked.

"The Prince of Olympus, like his predecessors, is controlled *by Olympus*. And it, in turn, is controlled by the wealthy. To get to Odyn, we must get to them."

"How?"

"Have your father begin a new mercantile enterprise in Olympus. One which demands his direct oversight. Within the year, he will be invited into the inner circle of the city's elite. Not many merchants are lords, after all."

"You're sending me to Olympus?"

"Oh, it does not matter to me where you choose to go. I can find you whenever you want me to." He sat up, the blanket falling down to his waist. He was both thinner and less muscular than most men his age and he often wondered what she thought of his appearance.

She smiled. "I know," she said, "but I can only guide my father if I am with my father. We are not all as swift *travellers* as yourself."

"I know. Do as you see fit."

"When has it mattered what I see as fit?"

"What?"

Kerres's cheeks flushed a bit. "Since the day I 'rescued' you, I have been doing as you say."

Artemys hesitated. "I thought you shared my goals."

"I do," she said, softer than her last comment. She glanced around the room, the clothes strewn across the floor, her wardrobe on the opposite wall from their bed, the locked door in the northern corner. Finally, she met his eyes again. "It just seems like sometimes, all you want is to use me. For these goals. I know that I once treated you the same way, but it feels like more now."

He slid across the bed and put his hands on her hips. "Listen," he told her. "You know that I value my plans above anything, but, the truth is, I love you the same." No matter how Artemys felt, he could look past their feelings. *The only reason she feels an emotional connection is because I have already helped her accomplish her dreams...*He had realized long ago that she would care for herself above anything else. *But I do love her. That's why this hurts...*

She smiled at the word love. He kissed her once more and then pushed himself away, to the bedside. "Now," he said and stood up. "I promised Pyrsius I would join his hunt today."

"Your brother?" she asked, confused. He heard her sliding within the sheets and then the thump of her back against the pillows.

"I do not spend enough time in Avernus. As much as our past differences kept us apart, he has potential." Artemys pulled his breeches up around his waist and buckled them. He had a soft cotton tunic he wore beneath his robes and shrugged into it next.

"Potential?" she asked. "As a friend or a tool?"

Artemys laughed. "Both."

He threw his lightweight, beige robe over his head and tightened a rope belt around it. "Until tonight, Kerres."

"Send in my maid!" she called as he stepped through the door.

He found the servant in the corridor outside, seated in a niche in the wall with a torn cloth on her knee and sewing needles in her hands. "She's ready for you," he said. She bowed as he passed.

Isn't Pyrsius too young for a full hunt? he wondered. He had to remind himself. *You communicate with him far too rarely... he's your brother!*

Pyrsius was a man now. It had been thirteen years since his birth. Between Weveld's Disciples and, before that, the Order of Magic, Artemys had only been in the same region as his brother for a few years.

Artemys had been thirteen on the day of Pyrsius's birth. He could recall that day so clearly—the dark expression on his father's face with news of Lady Gothikar's passing, the darker storm that Artemys had summoned. Their father had granted Artemys magic that year. As a *gift*. A gift that had stripped Artemys of his friends, distanced him from his home and ultimately left him with only one relationship—Kerres. Pyrsius had arrived in the world that winter and Artemys's mother had departed.

Striding out of the staircase, Artemys crossed the bottom storey of the Avernan Keep and entered the courtyard beyond. The Palace grounds held three structures: the Library, the Barracks, and the Keep. Here was the Great Hall, the popular hub of Palace activity, much unlike the calm tranquility of the Keep's housing accommodations. Artemys noted an empty chair nearby and a dog wandering idly toward the Barracks, nose to the ground. *Likely, my brother has drawn any idlers to his hunting preparations!*

"Brother," Pyrsius called as Artemys stepped out of the Keep. He was standing outside the nearby stables, wearing a rich, red cape and knee-length, leather hunting boots. He was stringing his bow as he called out to Artemys.

The courtyard was shaped like an arrowhead with the gates at its southern tip, the Keep where the metal would be joined to the shaft of such an arrow, and the Library and Barracks at the head's bottom prongs,. Artemys approached the stables against the Keep's looping wall. The Palace of Avernus was often referred to as the Three Towers of Avernus, after the Keep, Barracks, and Library which appeared on the city's emblem. Today, the towers cast shadows like scars across the city, lines of darkness that reached almost to the outskirts.

"Did you sleep well, Pyrsius?" Artemys's brother was standing next to his sandy- coloured courser, one hand stroking the horse's shoulder while stablehands and servants prepared the wealthy saddle.

Dobler Rewan was also present; the aging master servant and steward of the Gothikar household knelt with a rache, a running hound from the family kennel. He had dark grey hair and muscles as thick and sharp as rock. The dog was well behaved, long ears and stocky legs still. Dobler glanced up and nodded to Artemys.

Pyrsius smiled. "Perhaps more than you," he taunted.

"I do not follow," Artemys said. A stable boy was leading two more coursers out of the nearby stable. In the sunlight, Artemys could not see a thing beneath the weathered thatch. He took one set of reins from the servant, and Dobler took the others.

"I've heard you court the daughter of a merchant?" Pyrsius asked.

Artemys shook his head. "I spent the evening in the Library and retired to the Keep late."

"Sorry." Pyrsius frowned. He was facing Artemys now, though Artemys pretended to be examining his mount. Pyrsius's boyish expression seemed genuine.

Why lie to Pyrsius? Artemys wondered. Perhaps he wanted to preserve his young brother's view of him. They had communicated so little during Pyrsius's life that Artemys imagined a certain image that Pyrsius might perceive of him.

"My Prince, would you prefer a hound or hawk?" a servant asked.

Artemys frowned. He spent so little time on the sport, and had little love for it. "A hawk," he said. He preferred them to dogs. Dogs were always prowling in the shadows of the foliage while the birds soared on the winds, waiting for the proper time to strike.

"Tower-hawk or a bird of the fist, sir?"

"The latter."

Every few years, Dobler Rewan would review the estates and ensure that the hounds and birds were still familiar with their masters. If not, the Gothikar treasury could afford new ones. Hounds from Agwar were often of great value, closely related to the deadly and near-impossible to train moor hounds. The best birds in the southern realms were the falcons trained in Gev or the sparrow-hawk of Vero.

The servant brought Artemys a hooded sparrow-hawk, a falconry glove and a pouch of fresh rodent lures.

"I have been hunting regularly this season," Pyrsius told him, "but have not had a bird along once."

Artemys smiled. "Well, that is because Dobler, here, cannot see far enough for one. He would lose it in practice."

Dobler's expression did not blink. "Yes, milord."

Pyrsius joined Artemys's chuckle. "Tell me, Dobler," Pyrsius said, "how far will we range today?"

"Perhaps two hours across the Valharyn Chase, milord. My huntsmen have spotted a hart near the groves to the north. Against the Gate."

The Valharyn Chase was a broad swath of land that ran east from Avernus, almost to the Valharyn coast. It had been hunted by each Prince of Avernus since the Triumvirate's establishment three hundred years before, though Artemys had been trained to hunt on the Gothikar family estate in Bertren.

"We'll be careful of the cliffs, and pursue the stag away from them before going for the slay," Pyrsius said.

He has been well trained. If you want to be the one to defeat your enemy, first keep him safe. Artemys flexed his hand within the falconry mitt, then leapt into his courser's saddle. Finally, he accepted the small hawk from the servant.

The Chase was rocky, but not as rocky as the Valharyn Spine to the south. As they rode out of the city, they entered a land that Artemys often imagined once covered in rolling hills. By their era, entire surfaces of these rises had faded away to dust and exposed the rocky skeletons within. Growing up from any small vein of soil along the rocky ridges was a variety of shrubs and herbs. The only trees were small and broadleaved and grew in the grassy areas between hills or on the soft surface above. It was only a day's ride south that pine started seeping into the woodland. The Southern Spine of the Valharyn, looming in the distance, grew only needles.

The further across the peninsula they rode, the flatter the land became. One of Artemys's tutors had told him, at a young age, that the cliffs of the Gate sometimes fell, dropping entire hills into the sea and stretching all the nearby land to the edge. The wind was picking up, which only made their hounds more eager.

They travelled with Pyrsius in the lead—it was his hunt. Artemys followed, with Dobler Rewan, a few servants, and a packhorse taking up the rear. Artemys sometimes let his hawk fly, but it only caught a rodent once. It came flying back to him with a ferret pierced upon its claws.

They spoke little. Artemys spent the time in a quiet reverie. In the past few years, he had branched out from his own scrying. Kerres was establishing his ties in Olympus. Orestys was forging a sword fit for a king, as a gift for Periander, one which would give Artemys a way into his father's world regardless of their relationship. He had learned the truth of the Disciples, that they maintained the use of magic and had infiltrated all branches of the government, even commanding the Order of Magic. Weveld was the spider at the heart of a web that linked the empire. Once he had ties in each fief, he could find the weak thread in the web, pull it, and drop the Dominion into his grasp.

"I know you lied," Pyrsius said, reigns held in his lap. He led the way around a moss-eaten rocky bluff.

Artemys stared at Pyrsius for a moment, and then glanced behind them. Dobler Rewan and the servants had fallen back. He turned back to his brother. "About what?"

"You weren't in the library last night. I was," Pyrsius said, his expression blank. Artemys hawk circled overhead. "Father asked me to look over some documents. He has been training me in some administrative tasks, things Dobler usually handles but a Prince should know."

"With my ties to the Order of Magic," Artemys said, "I am unable to pursue our Princedom. You have my blessing, Pyrsius. I think you would make a fine leader. You already command hunts and the hearts of the commoners, and you have only just become a man."

Pyrsius smiled. "Your flattery is not enough, brother. Where were you last night? Are the rumours true?"

"I was with a woman named Kerres Rysarius. She is the daughter of a merchant. We have been planning a new enterprise for her and Lord Rysarius to begin in the Olympian fief," Artemys explained. "No one can know, or the Olympian merchants will attempt to close the business opening."

"Truly? You were working with her?"

"Why does it concern you?" Artemys replied. "Would you like to meet her sometime? That is actually an excellent idea. If you are to rule here, you should familiarize yourself with her family; they are some of Avernus's finest merchants."

Pyrsius pursed his lips for a moment. "I have seen them before. I remember your rescue from those pirates last year. Perhaps it would be beneficial to meet them."

"Enough of this," Artemys said. "To sport!"

"One other thing. Father told me you were angry after mother's death, that you were never quite the same after that."

Artemys looked down. His horse's slow trot lolled his head from one side to the other, showing him the rough soil and patches of grass. He looked back at his brother. "There is nothing either of us could have done. I can hardly blame you for being born."

Pyrsius nodded. "I know, but I wanted you to know that I don't take it for granted. I live my life with everyone that was there at the start still around. Father is here for me, you visit when you can, I have known Dobler Rewan and Archivist Ekar since I was a child. You spent the first half of your life with one parent, had her taken from you, and had to—"

"Enough," Artemys said. He had got through that part of his life because of Kerres. "Thank you for your empathy...but enough."

They rode on, in silence. Shortly after, Dobler reclaimed a place at their side and told them that they were nearing the scouted area. They let their hounds go out into the foliage around them. The stag was grazing atop a ridge and heard them below, getting a chance to run before they spotted it.

Pyrsius's dog led them after it though. The pursuit took them several miles from their first encounter; thankfully the hart did not charge up any of the ridges and fall to its own death. That would have ruined the sport.

Pyrsius knew what an opportune shot was. He only wasted two arrows during the duration of their pursuit. His third caught the majestic animal with fearsome precision. He waited longer than Artemys expected to put the stag out of its misery. The arrow had struck its front left shoulder.

Artemys and Pyrsius did not dismount at first, rather watched it flail the three legs that had not been caught, and pant until it started choking on blood. Artemys had expected Pyrsius to be quick and decisive, but for that first moment, Artemys watched an expression similar to his own cross Pyrsius's features. Peace.

The hart lost its footing. Pyrsius approached it from the side and deftly avoided a lunge of the animal's antlers. He got a grip on them, lifted them to one side, and dragged a knife across the deer's throat. The hunt was over. "Dobler. String this up. We will feast tonight."

"Of course, sir."

Pyrsius mounted again. "Shall we return?"

Artemys held up a finger. He could hear something. Someone shouting.

"What is it?"

"That way," Artemys said, and urged his horse in the direction of his pointing hand. The closer they got, the more it sounded like shouting. The hunt had taken them south; there was a small village south of the Avernan Chase. Perhaps it was villagers he was hearing.

"...think you can just run away, do you!?" someone bellowed.

Around the next rocky slope was a small dip in the land. A man was standing with his back toward the royal hunters, fist held above his head. It fell, then rose again. A cry of pain echoed the nearby stone. "I'll teach you about leaving, little coward!"

"Enough!" Artemys barked, before Pyrsius could even open his mouth.

The man turned to look at them, revealing a smaller man held down against the earth. His face had been beaten into a bloody mess, nose broken to one side. At least one limb had been broken.

Artemys had dismounted quicker than he thought possible. He strode toward the man. "Why are you beating this man?"

"That's my business."

"We're the lords of this land," Artemys retorted. He shoved the man away from his victim. "What did this man do to deserve such a vicious assault?"

"He left my land. He lives and works in my barn, and I never told him to leave," the attacker sneered. "I keep mine in line."

Artemys shoved him down into the dirt, muscles from chores in Attarax surprising himself. The man struggled against his strength, but Artemys scrawled a small glyph in the dirt and whispered a spell and the man could move no more. The victim had already started to drag himself away, as much as he was able to. Pyrsius dropped to the man's side.

The attacker whimpered as he realized he could not remove any part of himself that touched the earth. His eyes, though, were still as dark as when he was beating that poor soul, full of malice like the guard on the Gothikar family estate all those years ago.

Artemys lit a fire in his hand with a series of glyphs and some of the Maker's words. He extended his arm until the fire drew beads of sweat from the man's cheek. "Do you do this often?" he asked. *It makes me sick. Men like this...*

"I apologize, sir! I would not have killed him! Mercy!"

"Answer the question!" Artemys growled, and moved his hand closer. The flames began to lick the man's face and he started gasping in pain.

"Artemys..." Pyrsius said.

"Answer!"

"I cannot run a farm without keeping my workers focused!"

Artemys yanked his hand back. "Men like you are why there is evil in this world!" he hissed, then planted the palm of his hand over the man's face. He could feel the skin sizzle.

"Artemys!" Pyrsius shouted, voice hardly audible over the man's screaming. Artemys chose to drown it out. Pyrsius grabbed his shoulder, curled over the slaver, but it was a boy's grasp. Artemys moved his gaze, but not his burning hand, and shoved Pyrsius away with his eyes alone. "Don't do this," his brother pleaded.

Strong hands took hold of Artemys, and yanked him off the man, onto his feet. Artemys spun, stone tokens etched with glyphs held in his hands. Should they be broken, each of the brittle pieces could unleash enough fire to burn a hole in the earth where they stood.

Dobler Rewan stepped back from him. "Would you even treat an animal like this?"

Artemys let out a long sigh. He moved toward Dobler,

shoving him to the earth with both hands. "Him, and any like him, are worse than animals," he sneered. "As are those that would defend—"

Dobler had the nerve to interrupt, shoving himself to his feet. "I have served your father—the ruler of these lands—since before he was born. You will not push me down, boy, and you will not harm this man further without a lawful trial."

Artemys lifted one of his hands in front of him, carving-covered token held ready, then slowly lowered it and walked away, past his brother's terrified expression.

"Tie the poor man up," Pyrsius said. "We'll see what Father says."

"Where did that come from...?"

Artemys ignored the rest. He glanced at his hand, where the leather mitt was smouldering, leather cracking away and binding melting. It was nothing that could not be repaired, but Artemys tore the glove off his hand and hurled it at the hart as he strode past. *Dobler can try to harness the hawk again, Maker forsake him...*

11

Year of Olympus 547

Three times. Three times today, he had almost died. Periander slashed across his attacker's chest and stumbled backward, trying to catch his breath. Close to the nearby guardhouse, its door spilling orange flickering light into the dim street, Salantar sidestepped a man's spear so the man killed his comrades. Periander had never seen someone fight like that gladiator. He was still exhausted from his lost duel with Berik and his flight from the Keep before that. After seeing Salantar in combat for only a few minutes, Periander was certain the man could break Berik in half like a twig. As the day wore onward, he realized that not only could Salantar do it, but he could do it a thousand times over.

Salantar noticed Periander watching him and gave him a crooked smile. Then he was back in the battle, stepping forward to lob off a man's head from behind. For him, this was not a battle; it could not be defined in the way that word defined things. There was no honour, reward or enjoyment here. For him, there was also no strategic value. Even survival did not matter. This was not a battle, but a chance at vengeance.

"Prince, Prince," someone shouted ahead. The skirmish at this gate was drawing to a close, but the whole city echoed with a din of screams and metal.

Periander strode through the gateway, past the guardhouse. This was the gate between the Keep's Outer Wall and the Port District. If the city of Edessa was two overlapping shields, the Port District was the area belonging to both.

Ahead, was a mile long road to the harbour.

"Milord," a scout said, stumbling up to him. It was one of Pharas's men. The Arena master and his men were not warriors, so Periander had given them other tasks as they fought toward the port. The Arena's fighters and the Imperial soldiers they had rallied on the way: today, this was Periander's army.

"Report," Periander said, examining the edge of his sword. It was his second blade today.

"We are lost, milord. They hold the port. There is still fighting on the docks, but most of the ships are on fire," the scout panted. "And there is an entire regiment of Trionus soldiers between."

"Glyphs!" Periander asked, "How many soldiers?"

"Two hundred?" the scout guessed.

"Maker, now what?" Pharas gasped, wiping blood on his shirt, though it looked like his hand came away even redder.

Periander sighed. The city was already under siege. There would be no escaping on land. Again, he asked the question, *where was Weveld when Edessa burned?*

Periander had no way of knowing if Trion had brought his mountain horde along with his private army. "We go forward," he said. "We will punch through their soldiers and find a ship."

"We will perish, milord," the scout said.

"It is the only way. Salantar, do you intend to die today?"

"I got some debts to settle, yet," the man said, turning away from an execution. Blood pooled from a corpse behind him. "If I die with this city, so be it. I promised you a way out."

"You promised?"

Salantar stepped closer, wiping sweat away from his brow and leaving a red streak on his forehead. "I never met a lord who would die for his men, 'specially when he don't know the name of one of them. This lot and you've only met today, right?"

Periander smiled dryly.

"Right, and you fought a fight you had no chance of winning. So, you're a truer fool than I, or a rare saint."

"And..."

"And I've already said a word too many for today. Glyphs!" Salantar roared and turned back to his killing. There was a man dragging himself toward the guardhouse door. He was wearing yellow and black. Soon, he was wearing red.

Periander turned back to Pharas. "We have released fifty of those men on this world, Pharas. The Maker will cast us into the snows at the end of time for what we have done today. But it's our job to make sure Trion and his men go there too."

Pharas nodded, but Periander had started to look through him. *Maker,* he thought in a daze, *what have I done?*

"Sir?" Pharas asked. A moment had passed.

Periander drowned the philosopher within and replaced him with adrenaline. "Listen up!" he bellowed. It took a moment before the gladiators and soldiers gave him their attention. The last Trionus soldiers were being finished off now. It appeared a nearly clear stretch from here to the harbour. Smoke covered the battle there like a blanket. "They're waiting for us at the Port," he said. "Trion knew we would have only one way to go, so he cut us off."

A few shoulders slumped. Mumbles rose.

"He would have us surrender, or throw our lives away on his siege lines. He would have us all dead, and he would have our families," he said.

"Hey," someone called, then mumbled under his breath and turned a bright shade of red. Almost all of them were running on adrenaline and not much else. It felt almost like being drunk. Almost. The biggest difference was the pain.

"What Trion does not know," he said, "is that we have more than a group of soldiers here. We have a group of homeless!"

This time the rebuttals were real. The gladiators were not above killing their liberator.

"We are *all* homeless, if we let them win today," he said. "He will have taken our city, our land, our pride and, probably, our lives. Are we going to let him?"

They shouted, "No!" Fists were raised, swords clanged.

"As soon as we hit them, protect me. I will write a spell to let anyone still alive in the harbour know that survivors are coming. If all goes according to plan, we will be feasting on sailors rations tonight!"

They groaned, then laughed. One man said, "Still better than the slop they were feeding us back in there."

"Stow it," Salantar said. Periander was impressed. The Arena ring-leader ran a no-nonsense group. Earlier, some of the fighters had started bullying one of Pharas's men and his wife. Salantar had broken one gladiator's fingers and said, "Think about them when they save you, whelp." The man now walked, with a bowed head, amidst the refugees they had in tow. He could not fight with broken fingers.

The men were looking at Periander again, waiting for further instruction. He looked around. "Let's go kill them!"

They crossed the mile-length of road in what felt like minutes. The smoke grew closer until he could no longer define its starting point. When he glanced behind him, he could not see the wall they had departed.

Emerging through the smoke was a wall of yellow-and-black shields and readied spears. "On me!" Periander ordered. His fifty men stopped in mid-step, and, like a group of veterans, stepped inward. Salantar placed himself directly in front of Periander until Periander said, "Down," and lashed out with a hand.

"Bor'sab irkono shosa ob," he incanted. A blast of wind slammed forward—narrowly grazing Salantar's head—tearing away a cloud of smoke with it. By the time it reached the ranks of Trion soldiers, the spell was as wide as the street.

"Charge!" Periander shouted.

Some of the front ranks started to step backward from the spell, but found their comrades blocking the way behind them. The air slammed into them like a fist. The sound of the impact was deafening, a pop of the force against their shields. Some men were pressed down to the ground, while those in motion tumbled over the heads of those standing behind them. Spears and shields tumbled; more than a few soldiers took wounds from their enemies.

Seconds later, fifty furious swordsmen reached their fallen ranks. More men were dead before reaching their feet than Periander could count. As he strode into the melee, he found one man rising from one knee toward standing. He dragged his sword along the man's hamstring and then finished the reeling soldier off with a thrust. Two men stepped forward, both wearing the colours of House Trion. One took Periander's sword through the thigh, while the other's helmet was thoroughly dented by his a swing of his sword. The latter did not move as he fell to the ground.

"Protect me," he shouted, and stepped back three paces. Salantar and three others were there.

As he stepped back, he took a glance around. The first few ranks of men were dead and the remainder of this particular troop was scattering. Periander could see the opening ahead where the street reached the wharfs. There were more men there, some striding forward, some grouping up with their comrades.

He wrote a longer spell this time. He had to make sure it worked just right; without enough experience on these particular glyphs, he had to use more to make sure the spell would work the way he wanted it to. It was like in a conversation. He was describing parameters to his topic, to avoid misunderstanding.

He raised his fist in the air, and a column of fire, his signal for the ship, appeared. It wrapped itself around his hand, though he felt no heat, and continued to grow taller and taller.

Without warning, it became water and fell downward. Periander was stunned by its weight, and soaked to the bone.

"What?" he mumbled, shaking himself. Salantar stepped back from the conflict, staring at him with a look between concern and mirth. Then he realized the only explanation; his spell had been interrupted by another magician. "Brace yourselves!" he shouted and dropped to one knee, raising his dented buckling shield above his head.

A clack of thunder struck his ears almost as hard as the force that crushed him into the bloodied cobblestones. The magical blast caught Trion, Imperial, and gladiator the same. It knocked those closer to the walls of the street into them.

Periander recovered quicker than he had at Dagger's Edge. He leapt to his feet and ran forward. He glanced to his right. Pharas was on the ground, transfixed by his own sword. A curtain of blood was draping across his torso. Periander's teeth ground. *How does Trion have magic?* he wanted to know. The man's court magician had returned to the Order a few weeks before the war, citing stress as the cause. *Trion has no magicians!*

Trion's soldiers were pushing their advantage. Some of Periander's soldiers were already dead. He strode forward as quickly as he could. His knees cracked painfully. He could feel a bruise forming on the back of his head where his buckler had slammed off of his head. His arm ached.

He clashed swords with a veteran. He knew the man from the scars on his bare arms and the scowl on his gaunt face. They danced, stepping between bodies when they could and exchanging slash for parry. Their swords met, and Periander forced his blade toward the man. The man pushed their crossed weapons toward Periander. Then, Salantar's sword sprayed blood from the man's abdomen across Periander's lamellar tunic.

"Was your signal enough?" was all he asked.

"We'll find out," Periander said. "Glyphs, we need to find those spell-casters! Protect me, and I will maintain a barrier for our defence ."

Salantar nodded, and fell in step with Periander. He wrote a spell that should be able to shield the street from further attacks, if they were anything like the first one. Unfortunately, the spell required him to hold his arms up, to direct the barrier upwards. He sheathed his sword, raised his hands, and spoke the glyphs. The air above tinted green.

His troop and he continued forward, fighting their way toward the water one inch at a time. He saw multiple masts peek through the smoke as he got closer. They were on fire. *Please let there be a ship...*

Salantar cut him a bloody trail onto the main wharf, while the gladiator troop surrounding them guarded their flanks. More than a dozen of the fighters were down, and most of Pharas's men had fallen. Periander saw some of their refugees flee down an adjacent street.

"Gothikar!" someone shouted, voice amplified by a spell. "I know you are here!"

It was Trion, standing on the prow of a burning ship. A magician in black stood behind him, keeping the fires at bay while the self-proclaimed King bellowed down into the crowd. The man's hair, longer now than at Oban Ford years ago, was whipping into his face; the sorcerer must have been cast a wall of air between them and the inferno.

Periander's first thought was dread. *We are dead.* If Ernes Trion himself stood here, knowing he had Periander and his men surrounded, there could be no escape. He glared across the battle at the deck of that ship, bending his head to look past his sore, upraised arms. The man would have his entire guard, not to mention any more magicians he had mysteriously recruited.

Periander's second thought was much clearer. It was a thought descended from war, from death, from loss. *I can kill him,* he thought.

Salantar must have thought the same thing, for he doubled his pace, slashing forward. His sword took down enemies who had not even seen him. The few soldiers who gave him pause faced a blur of steel. Salantar parried very little; instead, he was always where his enemy did not think he was. Periander, arms occupied by his spell, could only watch—and analyze. A soldier's spear would thrust directly for Salantar, but the champion would always be a few steps away by the time the point could cause any harm. Then, before the soldier could see the gladiator's sword coming, Salantar would come slashing in.

A spear grazed Periander's side. He stumbled to one side, his arms wavering and the green barrier above them tilting. A Trionus soldier, having cut his way into their ring of safety, lashed forward again, and again Periander dodged, crying out, "Salantar!"

The gladiator turned and hurled his sword in one fluid motion. It struck the soldier in the shoulder with the hilt, but Salantar was already behind their opponent's spear, grabbing the man's head and snapping it to the right.

Without anyone ahead of Periander, the yellow-painted soldiers eagerly charged forward. While Salantar reclaimed his sword, Berik dashed forward from behind them, where the remaining gladiators were fighting. Together, the prisoners drove the line back along the wharf.

The dock was looking less and less like a battlefield and more like a smoky waste. There were more bodies lying like patches of quicksand, seeping through the cracks in the wood, than there were warriors. There was space to move now, while in the yard before they had been cramped shoulder to shoulder.

"Trion!" Periander shouted at the top of his lungs. "I'm here! Face me!"

With a shriek of rage, the man leapt from the prow of the ship and onto the wharf, a good ten feet drop, and landed with ease. For a man of his sixties, Ernes Trion moved like a young man in his prime. He crossed the space between them in four long strides, past where Salantar struggled against two attackers, and raised his sword.

Periander was ready for him. Striding toward his adversary, he slammed his arms downward in front of him, and the barrier of green energy arced with them. Trion found himself charging into a solid barrier of energy as Periander brought it to bear against him. The energy hit the ground with silence, fading to nothing as it did, but his charge caught Trion's headlong assault and sent him tumbling back.

Periander drew his sword and walked forward. "What have you done?" he asked. "You have ruined this city."

Trion was rolling away from him, recovering from the daze of his impact. He came up onto one knee and raised his sword just in time to block Periander's downward hack. Periander could see the madness in the man's face. There was an edge there, one that hadn't been when last they spoke.

Trion reclaimed his feet, forcing Periander's blade away from him. Then he stepped back, releasing their hold on one another and slashed low at Periander's hips. Periander parried and drove forward with an arcing swing for his opponent's opposing shoulder. Trion blocked with his blade, but attacked with his fist. Periander reeled back from a punch, but knocked away Trion's next hack and the one after that.

"You killed my family!" the man shrieked. "I was coming for them, my giants and I, I was coming to save them from your capture..." He paused while he dodged a stab Periander managed. *Maker, I'm tired...* He would have landed that blow if he had been fighting fresh. He had lost count of how many times his life had fallen into jeopardy today. Trion came at him again. "And you *killed them*, you earth-spawn!"

"To stop this war," Periander returned, and parried Trion's attack with his own slash. Toward the end of the wharf he saw the black-robed sorcerer kneeling in front of a wood and sail backdrop. *I can't keep this up,* Periander realized. *That magician... who is he?*

He stabbed once and Trion stepped backward, toward his wizard. He stepped forward, slashed, and then stabbed again.

Trion knocked this stab upward and drove his blade downward. There was a flash of blinding pain. He grunted reluctantly. It felt like Trion had stabbed him with a white-hot brand, not a sword. The blade had gone through Periander's booted foot and into the wood beneath. Instinctively, he yanked his foot backward. It was pinned.

Then Trion yanked it free and Periander cried out in pain, falling forward. He caught the wharf with his off-hand, holding himself up as his buckler clanged away across the surface.

Trion came at him to finish the job, but Periander had only a horizontal stab waiting. His sword cut into Trion's side. The man stumbled to one side. Periander slashed again, still not able to reclaim his feet. His whole leg was a slab of rock—smouldering rock.

The weathered man avoided the slash. He dragged himself back a few steps, feet kicking along the wood. He grabbed hold of a dangling rope at the side of the dock. Periander's eyesight was failing, his peripherals infested with dark tendrils while everything gleamed brighter in front of him. He turned his head. Trion was pulling himself up onto the side of the burning ship he had leapt from, but he was stopping and smiling. He was not escaping, just watching.

"Now!" Trion shouted.

A flash of light invaded Periander's peripherals. There was a bright fire down the dock near that cursed magician. It looked like the wood was turning to light. It surged forward like a tidal wave, and caught the Prince in its onslaught. There was a terrible heat, and then a terrible cold.

Periander was drifting. He was not breathing, so he decided he should. His mouth filled with water. In retaliation, a last wave of adrenaline rushed through him. He awoke him within a watery grave. The water was like ice, and, even six feet under, it felt like the weight of a mountain on top of him. He flailed out with his arms and brought himself around so that he could see the surface instead of the depths. He could taste blood in the water. It was his own, for his wounded foot had hung in this space before his head.

But he was still sinking. He tried kicking, but agony crawled up his leg with hands made of nails. Biting back everything, he tried with the other foot and rose a few inches. He kicked again.

It was the hardest climb of his life, across a space only as far his own height. He rose inch by inch. An errant thought made it through the panic and chaos: *If I'm to go, I'll go kicking and flailing!* But the pain in his limbs got worse as he got colder and the tendrils of shadow around the edges of his vision became tentacles, clawing at his sight. He kicked again.

And then he could swim no more.

There were sparkles in the water. He noticed them as he sunk. Golden rays that swam back and forth. They were playful. He wondered if they would be white without the red in the water. How could they be so playful, underneath the surface?

The world will just keep on going, won't it? he realized. *With or without us on it... the water will still dance and the leaves will still sing. They don't care who wins the war. They don't care...*

He opened his eyes to sunlight and air. He waited until he was not blinded by the sun. There were ropes and nets in the sky. There was a mast rising above him like an unnaturally straight tree.

"I didn't put you through that ordeal in the Arena so you could die on me later," a man said. It was Salantar, sitting nearby with his feet hanging over the edge of the ship's deck. Periander wearily remembered his lost duel in the Arena. It was hard to believe that it was still the same day. His scraggly, black hair was a soaking mop and his sharp muscles sleek. "The man who bought me told me that, a few weeks after my first time through the Arena."

Periander closed his eyes. Whether or not Salantar would demand the bargain be equalled, he had bought the life of a Prince today.

He realized that his foot did not hurt anymore. He opened his eyes and glanced down. There was a hole in his boot, but not one in his foot. He looked to his right, where another man knelt, pocketing a handful of spell tokens. He had a grey robe, bound at the waist by a rope belt.

"Thank you," Periander said. He sat up. They were already making good distance away from Edessa. He had almost died today. He stood up, and offered his healer a hand.

Weveld smiled and accepted it.

12

Year of Olympus 572

Artemys stepped through the Glyph Gate from warm sand to cold snow and followed a small trail without looking back. To his right was the gleam of sun on water—the Mydarius Sea. Across that void was Avernus, the Chase, his brother, his father. And to the east of that, Olympus.

The forest on his left was full of fog, the chirping of birds, and the silence of the north. Artemys had always found there to be something mysterious about the northern lands. Thousands of miles of unbroken pine forest; there was nothing like it in the south. And the snow that fell in this fief was more than the dusting Avernus got some years.

Olympus. Kerres, the brilliant creature she was, had only visited the city for a week before her father's trading and import business was set up. It had been two weeks since his hunt with Pyrsius and his encounter with that accursed slaver.

Now it was the new year, and he was now returning to Port Elysia. *Why does Kerres insist on staying in Avernus?* he wondered. She claimed it was because he visited the city more, not knowing he had sent her to Olympus so he would have a reason to visit it more. Her love for Artemys was the strongest it had been yet, for he gave her what she desired. *Gold and power.*

Pyrsius had met Kerres, as they had discussed. That night, the Gothikar brothers had hosted a feast of the stag they had captured. Kerres had demanded attendance, though Artemys was content to spend the time in their quarters. He sent her ahead of him, so it did not appear they had been together. When Artemys arrived at the feast, his brother had already seated her at the head table with his friends. Artemys sat a few seats away and watched in surprise as Pyrsius gave a good effort to charming her. *Why should I be so surprised? She's near perfect by any standards of beauty I have heard.*

Artemys knew it was his own fault; he had told Pyrsius there was nothing special in their relationship.

"Ho there! Is it friend of foe?" a voice called.

Artemys had nearly left the forest. He could see the beach ahead. There was a dark structure to the west: a wooden cabin with a deck.

"Friend!" Artemys replied. The ferry woman lived here. As Artemys drew nearer, he could see a giant stowing a proportionally-sized crossbow inside his homestead. He had never seen a woman so large.

"Not many of you this time of year," she called when Artemys drew closer. She was pulling an extra cloak around herself. Artemys glanced at his own clothing. He was going to be seen today, so he had changed from his grey Disciple's robe into Magician's Order orange. "Only the Zealots come now."

Artemys raised an eyebrow. This woman knew of them? She lived a short walk from the Attarax Glyph Gate—Maker, she could be one of them for all Artemys knew. He could easily check with the Great Glyph, but did not. All that Artemys knew of her was her name, Varana.

"Hopefully my last time through here in a while," Artemys said lightly.

Varana led the way onto the beach. She was a full torso taller than Artemys. Subconsciously, Artemys straightened his shoulders.

"Just heading to Elysia Port?"

Artemys nodded and climbed into the boat when beckoned to do so.

It was a full day's voyage from Varana's wharf to Elysia Port, across a cove full of islands. Behind them, the Glyph Gate was built amongst the ruins of a Keep that looked as old as the Age of Myths. The clumps of dirt, trees, and snow seemed to cling to the black stone architecture, curling up out of the glowing fog like wisps of night in the bright day.

"Have you ever wondered what happened to this place?"

Artemys asked.

Varana smiled. "Andrakaz."

Artemys froze. Again, the only sorcerer that confounded Artemys. He quickly summoned the Great Glyph. He could see this keep in its perfection, then in its destruction, but not the hour of its downfall. He could see the Glyph Gates after they were made, but not their crafting. He could see the footprints of Andrakaz, but not the man himself.

Varana smiled. "That's why it's called the Age of Myths."

Artemys was surprised that this big brute of a woman knew the words he spoke. Perhaps she did have ties with the Disciples.

By noon, the mist had dissipated. Varana made it a quick trip, arms as thick as Artemys's head heaving the oars with little effort. They reached the other side before dark. "I will eat at the Night Rat, an inn on the docks," Varana said, "and my passengers are welcome to join me before I return to my island."

Artemys shook his head. "My business here is brief, then I will be on the road."

Varana smiled. "Good journeys to you."

If Varana was a Zealot, or even a Disciple, she would report to Weveld. Weveld would want to know what Artemys was doing, and how he was travelling if not by Glyph Gates. The more that Artemys saw of Weveld's web, the more he hated the old man. Something had to be done, something had to change. The man was ancient, likely sustaining himself with the very magic he denied others.

Elysia Port was a silent city during the winter. There were three galleons tied at port, massive ships designed for crossing the Mydarius, and a few smaller boats. There were no new arrivals and no movement on the docks until Varana tied their boat in and they climbed out.

As the shadows lengthened, Artemys hurried to Orestys's smithy. The blacksmith answered his door quickly, wiping his mouth with a rag. He had just been dining.

"I was wondering when you would return! The worst feeling is to not be able to share the completed art."

"You can now! I am certain both my father and I will be pleased."

Orestys led the way through his home to his shop. The house was kept so much neater than the man's workshop was, but both felt tight and uncomfortable to Artemys's notion of living space.

Orestys had reorganized the smithy since Artemys's visit. The weapon was wrapped in a rag and set on a much cleaner worktable. "It is spectacular," he breathed as he unwrapped it.

Soon, Artemys held in his hand a jewel among swords. The blade shone like any new blade, but had an untainted, bright grey colour due to the perfect blending of metals. It was the length of a bastard sword, not quite as long as a long sword, but with better manoeuvrability. The hilt began with an inch-wide square around the blade, with a horizontal bar to guard the wielder's hands emerging from each corner of the square. There were etches of fire around that square plate and the faces of serpents on each hand-guard. The handle was long enough for a hand-and-a-half, a warrior's way of saying it could be wielded with one hand or both. The pommel was a three-pronged spike and a blood-ruby was set in the space between.

Artemys stood in a daze. He had never seen something like this. He considered himself a weapon, each hammer of this world sharpening him for his inevitable final battle, like the guard beating him or the slaver escaping his fiery hand. If he were a weapon, he strove to be this one, this beautiful and deadly thing he held in his hands. "It is...peace *and* war. Life *and* death..."

Orestys remained silent, perhaps uncertain what Artemys meant or perhaps in agreement.

"Can I use magic to cut into the blade? I mean to write spells into this weapon, but do not wish to ruin it," Artemys explained.

"With the strength of this steel...you could pierce through the heart of the blade without it breaking. Simply do not change the edges," Orestys told him. "I hope your father is as proud of the weapon as I am."

Artemys nodded. "I am proud already. I will send you a letter of the gift's success." He removed a pack from his shoulder. "Two hundred sovereigns as payment."

Orestys paled. "This is far too much! A fortune! Two hundred gold pieces!" With a reluctant expression, he accepted the bag, but breathed again, "Too much..."

"No. Far too little. This weapon has a destiny with my

father or with whomever it finally settles," Artemys assured him.

"Many thanks." Orestys bowed. "You do me honour, sire."
He handed Artemys a sheath, a strip of fine leather with similar
artwork scrawled across it.

While strapping the cloth-bound blade to his back, Artemys
walked outside. There were no longer any traces of sun on the
horizon, and the crescent moon had started its rise. Artemys
folded his arms and tucked his hands within his armpits. He
imagined a world where those who had earned it could use
magic for comforts like this, a spell to warm cold bones and
brighten the nights for the eyes of the great. A world not ruled
by Weveld, or Three Princes oblivious to the true workings of
the world around them.

He stepped inside the nearest tavern and called, "Anyone in
need of a spell to Avernus?" It was common for a magician to
offer his services for free or for charge. There were only five
known teleports. Artemys knew, and could discover, many
more, but they were secrets, for now.

The inn was crowded. A cloud of smoke hung from the
ceiling beams to the table tops where weathered men and women
drank ale and ate a variety of breads and fish. Elysia Port was a
fishing city, but the lands north of it were ripe with farmland.
These were working men and women; did they not deserve a
spell to warm their bones? They deserved someone to give them
that gift, someone who could see which were noble of heart and
deserving, and which were not.

A man seated near the furnace in the center of the room
raised his hand. A few others seemed to inch back from him, but
the man, rising to his feet, called over the din, "Let me grab my
things."

Artemys leaned against a wall and waited for him to return.
He appeared a moment later with a small chest under one arm
and a pack thrown over the opposite shoulder. He had brown and
blond hair, and a weathered appearance which made it hard to
guess his age. A narrow scar ran from his left eye to his
cheekbone.

Artemys was surprised by the power in those eyes. They
were probing him, watching his every move.

"Do not worry," Artemys assured him. "Magic is not
harmful unless I wish it to be."

The man did not react, simply followed him into the street. Artemys knelt and scrawled the horizontal phrase-line for his spell, then wrote the glyphs for travelling and the glyphs of his destination, the rooftop in Avernus.

The air flickered with the warmer colours of their destination as he spoke the words for each glyph. He glanced at his companion. "After you," he said.

The man eyed him once more, deep eyes piercing him. Then, with a shrug, he stepped through the opening. Artemys followed, and they emerged in the noticeably warmer air of Avernus. The moon was further overhead and there was no snow beneath their feet. It was not warm, but it would be indoors.

The guards recognized him and welcomed them both. They led the way down the staircase and into the street. It was a fair walk to the Palace grounds, but one that Artemys was used to. Teleporting to a specific destination required one to know the exact glyphs that represented that spot; Artemys had long ago memorized the Known Locations, but searching the Great Glyph for a place like the Palace itself was something he did not have the patience for.

"Thank you for your help," his companion said before heading the opposite way down the street.

Artemys waited a moment, in thought, and then approached the adjacent building. A stable boy handed him the reins of a horse for the journey to the Palace grounds. He mounted and shifted the wrapped sword so it wouldn't bother the horse.

It was an uphill ride, interrupted by a large crowd gathered by torchlight around a shop that had been shut down for the bandit operation it was running. The problem with peace—especially after a war as long as the most recent one—was crime. He had plenty of time to watch the guards escorting four men and a woman out of the house, mouths gagged and arms bound. Another two soldiers emerged with a cartful of woven sacks. No doubt full of some intoxicant or even poison. Eventually he crossed the busy section of street and continued on his way toward the Palace.

He needed some privacy. He had a few spells to write for this sword. This sword. He needed a name. He could not think of one until he reached the Palace; riding through those ancient gates, he glanced at the carved crest of Avernus above the portcullis and the honoured words of House Gothikar. *"Decadus abri-korbios,"* he read. It was the oldest dialect of the ancient language. Even Periander's flags read, "*Korbios decadus abyron*," a mode of tongue more familiar to the contemporary Common tongue.

Conquest stands alone. Conquest. This blade would be Korbios.

He slid off the horse and walked toward the Keep. The guards let him enter without a word. He shrugged out of his icy cloak as soon as he stepped into his chamber, taking the still-wrapped Korbios by the hilt. There were crackling embers warming the room from the fireplace in his study, so he paused on the threshold between his antechamber and the next room.

"Hello?" he called. He could see the open door to his bedchamber, but it was dark there.

"Artemys?" Kerres mumbled. She stumbled from his room, wrapped in only a robe bound in front, rubbing her eyes. Her bare feet seemed so small compared to the billowing robe. Above the robe, her chest, neck, and forehead shone blue in the moonlight. "I didn't think you would be back so soon..."

"You sleep in my quarters?" Artemys asked surprised. *She has her own quarters, her family estate...*

"Sometimes, when you're gone..." she whispered. "I miss you."

Artemys nodded. "I miss you too," he said.

He summoned the Great Glyph before his eyes for a moment, seeing more glyphs than any man could count, and sought Kerres among them.

There, while he was still across the sea, she was talking to Pyrsius, laughing like Artemys had never seen her laugh. They were sharing a meal, no more. His brother was smiling like the charming Prince he would become.

"Pyrsius..." Artemys trailed; he was back in his chambers—feeling foreign to them—and she was staring at him with his own keen, green eyes and bed-dress.

She stepped forward, wrapping the thin robe closer around herself. "What?"

For a moment, he decided that time could no longer pass. He needed a breath to think. His mind raced ahead of the room, ahead of the Great Glyph and all the rest. *I* know *she does not love me. I have known that along.* Had he lost his grip on things? Had the web he was weaving somehow slipped out of his grasp? Artemys had introduced them, and now she remained in Avernus to seek his brother? *She was supposed to stay in Olympus!* Even Pyrsius was sliding away, horrified by the torture he had seen his older brother commit and the magic which Pyrsius had come to know as a curse. Artemys had lost his clutch on his own plans, and unaware Kerres was just the first snapped branch in the canopy.

No.

Artemys looked to the sword in his hand, the greatest steel of their age. How many times had Orestys hammered the steel? Muscles and metal forced the blade into its shape, a grindstone had chiselled away the edge until only a sharp razor was left. Now Korbios was ready for magic, a spell to set it above any other weapons; its metals had been conjured by magic and would be sealed with it as well.

"Artemys?" Kerres asked. Her brow was slanted with concern.

He held up a hand. He was the steel. He was the magic. He was the spider at the center of the web, and anything that disturbed his creation would become caught within it. The hammered sparks and ground-away slivers of metal were deserved collateral for Artemys's victories, for the good he could do as a weapon. His father had fought battles to save the realm—and Artemys could too.

"Pyrsius will be a blade as well. I will make him one."

Kerres laughed uncomfortably, and stepped toward the desk in the center of the study. "What?"

"Periander, Odyn, Weveld, Theseus..." Artemys trailed. "All of them are key figures in the future of this Dominion."

"Yes..." She tucked her black hair behind her ears and crossed her arms again, leaning her thigh against the edge of the tabletop.

Artemys leaned Korbios against the desk. There was a bookshelf on either side, mostly spell books full of glyphs, and a simple armchair on the other side. The arm chair had been one of his early attempts to use the Great Glyph, so he kept it despite the discomfort of its seat.

He turned back to Kerres. "I forgot one," he told her.

"Pyrsius."

She smiled. "I know."

"What?"

She sank into the armchair across the desktop from him. There was a map in one corner and an inkwell near it. "I know Pyrsius is one of your *keys*."

Artemys parted his lips in a dry grin. "And you are going to tell me you have been staying in Avernus to keep an eye on him? Just for my plans?"

She snorted. "No. I've been staying in Avernus because it's my home. And Pyrsius... he is a friend. And he's fun. He's like you in a lot of ways, but less ambitious."

Artemys took a deep breath. This would hurt like Orestys's hammer, but it would have to be done. "You are better off with him," he said.

"What?" Kerres's jaw dropped. "What did you say?"

"If you want me to be king, we need to completely control Pyrsius," he told her as she slid out of the chair. "We both promised we would do anything in ord—"

"By the Maker, Artemys!" she breathed. She opened her mouth again, but now it was a shout. "Glyphs! Who do you think I am? Your slave? Your dog that you can just send off to any stud?"

Artemys shut his eyes. "He can stay in Avernus with you, like you want, your very own Prince."

She lashed out across the table, her hand catching him across his face. Off guard, he stumbled to one side, planting his right hand firmly against the wall so he did not fall; the wooden chair she had been sitting in toppled the whole way to the floor. "Great Glyph! I never said I loved him! I said I *missed you!*"

"I cannot do this anymore, Kerres." He could not meet her eyes. "I cannot pretend that we have a future. Do you not see what is happening to me? I am drawing you into something dangerous. Something unhealthy." This, after an entire conversation of lies, was the truth. He loved her enough to spare her any more of his plots. Together, she had to survive his plots. He would manipulate his own father. He would sharpen Pyrsius into a weapon that would one day become Prince. What if Artemys had to kill someone? What if he had to kill Pyrsius? *He's like you in a lot of ways, but less ambitions. He is a friend.*

She was crying now. She shoved him against the wall. "Unhealthy? Artemys, I have been here for you, for years, and now you're, what, throwing me away? Glyphs, what is unhealthy here?"

He did not reply, but remained slumped against the wall. He felt tears around his eyes. When was the last time he had cried? He held it. Steel did not weep. Korbios did not weep.

"Look at me," she sobbed.

Maker, what am I doing? he wondered. There was a pain in his chest, was it the intensity of this, the feel of himself on the grindstone? Or was it his heart?

She grabbed his shoulders and barked, "Look at me!"

His head snapped up, and he locked green eyes with her. They were red; there were tears everywhere, her mouth trying to breath with winded lungs. He looked into those eyes and saw that same pain there, the burning inside of him.

His own tears fell, for the first time since his mother's death. At first it was just a few drops, escaping the corners and following long-forgotten lines down his cheeks. Then his shoulders shook under the warmth of her hands and more tears welled up.

"Tell me the truth," she whispered. "Please, Artemys."

He took a sobbing breath. The truth. Which truth?

The truth of this conversation and Pyrsius's fate within his hands? She would say she would go to Pyrsius to spite him, but then actually would. She would hate him for years, but then remember that he had said, "If you want me to be king."

Or the truth of their relationship, that he knew she only wanted power? He now doubted that truth.

He told her the truth of his emotions. "I have become *too* attached to you," he said, blinking tears away. His eyes felt dry now. "There are too many plans for emotion. For distraction. For... love."

She flinched. She slapped him again, but he barely noticed it. "Maker, you *are* mad. I hope you are happy without me, but that's just a distraction, right?"

She was not there anymore. He was standing alone in his study, sobbing. Then she appeared again, a cloak thrown over her robe and a bag slung around her torso, wiping more tears away. "Maybe I will go to Pyrsius," she said to spite him. "He at least sees me as more than an animal."

Artemys heard the door to the Palace corridor slam shut. He sank to the floor. He could see everything differently from here: only the desk's legs, the tip of Korbios, the toppled wooden chair that he had first scried with the Great Glyph.

"Maker," he whispered. "Why?" *I did all of this... I did all of it...* A part of him said that it was no different from sending Lord Rysarius to Olympus, to keep an eye on Prince Odyn. There was a voice inside that compared the gift of Korbios to sending Kerres away and told him these things were for the best.

Years from now, all it would take was three words to turn Pyrsius's world upside down: "Kerres was mine."

But here and now, lying with feet spread apart on the floor of his study, he prayed, "Why is there no mercy in this world?" If there was, if the slavers understood the slaves and the princes understood ... their sons, Artemys would not need to hurt so much. Hurt himself and those around him. "How do I carry on?" he asked.

A single image rose in his mind. It was a guard wearing a green and black uniform, chainmail beneath the shouldered hood and cape. The man's fist cracked Artemys's ribs; the gauntleted hand fell again and again. "You have no right to be Prince, no more than me, little earthspawn!" the man had said.

It was what he always returned to. The memory became fiercer and fiercer until Artemys was clinging to the sword he had brought from the northlands.

Kerres was gone. As with every time something in life was taken from him—his absent father, his dead mother, the friends that had abandoned him when Artemys became a "wizard," and his beloved Kerres—he returned to this memory. The guard, the Imperial, the Triumvirate, was pounding him and claiming what its rights were.

Gothikars had been kings before there was a Triumvirate. Artemys knew right had nothing to do with the Triumvirate's governance. *People do what they must, and sometimes sacrifices are needed. Sometimes, swords are necessary.*

He braced the sword against the floor and levered himself upwards. He needed to do this now, when he had the strength to do so. He felt exhausted, but he also felt tense. Alive. He knew exactly which glyphs he would write onto this sword for his father to see, and he knew which glyphs he would conceal.

He needed to complete this gift for his father, so he could replace the hole Kerres had left.

He picked the wooden chair up, though he did not sit in it, and he set the sword onto the wooden desktop. First he unwrapped it and tossed Orestys's leather binding aside. Even after everything he had been through that day, he still caught his breath at the sight of his shimmering perfection. In the moonlight, the light grey steel looked white.

He whispered a spell to turn a narrow section of the blade malleable, like hot wax, and used a quill to write spells in it.

The first was a small collection of glyphs that made the sword lighter. Artemys was careful to keep the weapon's balance, but it should be as quick as an arrow.

Secondly, he added a spell that would use the air around the blade to help its puncturing. This was a more complex spell; essentially it would use new spells whenever the sword encountered an object to cut deeper into it. A sword hitting armour was still a sword hitting armour; this spell could not change that, but it would mean any contacts with cloth, leather, flesh would be much deadlier.

The third spell was not quite as complicated, but it was the most important. It made the blade permanently sharp. Any damage sustained to that straight edge would fill with new metal instantly. The blade could never be unmade now. It could not be chipped or scratched away. Artemys, comparing himself to the blade, felt that he could be. He needed a spell such as this.

These spells were part of the gift, but the final one was Artemys's reason for this entire process. He wrote a spell onto a spell token. The small pieces of stone were a staple of spellcraft. The spell allowed the holder of the token to hear anything said near the secondary object. The secondary object was marked with a tiny, circular glyph at the top of the line of glyphs on the sword's blade. Now, whenever Artemys held the spell token, he would hear those who held the sword.

Tomorrow, he thought. Pyrsius and Kerres would be nowhere to be seen, but he could find his father easily enough. Periander, Prince of Avernus. Artemys would need his best half-truths to succeed. His father would catch any lies, but Artemys was tired of lies and plans. *Tomorrow, I will convince my father that my time in Avernus and the School at Delfie have made me his equal. Tomorrow, I will convince him to believe in the threat I face.*

Artemys held the sword in front of him, hands sweaty from that pain in his chest. The steel was brighter than many swords and the weight lighter. There were three sets of glyphs; each set a line of delicately inscribed and spoken glyphs. Above that was a small circle, the key to this third of the realm. A key to his father's world.

Korbios was conquest, Artemys's conquest. It was the blade that cut deepest as a gift.

13

Year of Olympus 548

"I'm scared," Cat said.

Periander sat on the bed with one knee tucked under his chin, looking down at his foot. Sometimes it chilled him, looking at where a scar should be. Did scars not serve some purpose, some warning, some lesson? What did it mean then, that some scars were hidden? Healing spells cleaned them; the severe wounds that should have killed...the ones only survived by healing magic, these ones never left scars. *It must mean something...*

"You're so thin," she said, snuggling closer against his side. She had one hand wrapped around his shoulders, her other folded in her own lap, while she pressed her torso against him. Her sandy hair pressed against his shoulder. "What if they had taken you from me?"

Periander squeezed his eyes shut. It was not the first time he would face this price. His service of the Triumvirate would demand his life again, he knew it.

She ran her palm along his right arm, the one closest to her. Where once his arms had borne muscle, hard and thick like a soft-barked tree, her hand had no contours to trace. Could she feel the bone?

He had fallen ill after Edessa. He had spent months under the care of magicians. The Princes did not fall ill often. Complex healing spells were too expensive a service for most in the Dominion, but would always be a privilege of the leaders. When Periander had asked why he trembled, wheezed, and wasted,

Weveld had explained that this was not just an illness of fever or infection.

Periander should have died in Edessa, and he was brought back by spells. Spells demanded energy be drawn from the target and the caster. First, Berik had healed him from the brink of death. The long day of fighting was enough to exhaust him for days even without that additional drain. And, at the end of the day, the flames of Trion's sorcerer had singed him, and the waters of the newly christened "Blood Strait" had frozen him. The drain on his body had sucked away his fat and his strength like a leech seeks out blood.

"You should have returned sooner," she whispered.

"Cat." The bed sheets were a mess, the blanket thrown all the way back on the foot of the four-poster bed.

She raised her chin from his right shoulder. He shivered. "The others can fight the war, can't they?"

After the fall of Edessa, the Imperial armies had months of work to do. There were new battle lines to draw, new regions to scout. Suddenly, the entire Sinai Mountain Range seemed like it could be the next battleground of this war. Without Edessa, no fortifications stood between the Maker's Forge and Athyns.

Thankfully, the giants did not want Athyns. They wanted the western mountain ranges and Galinor, as Trion had demanded.

He had waited far too long to return to his family. "I'm sorry," he said.

She started to shift away further, opening her mouth to speak. She would say that he should be *more* apologetic, enough to stay with her. He had a son! He had a city!

He had a wife.

"Not now," he whispered, and, with his left hand, pulled her back against his right. "Please, not now."

She wept. "Sometime," she said. "If not now, then sometime else."

He nodded. He wished he had something to tell her now. He would shift onto his knees, turn to face her, take her hands, and kiss them. He would console her. He would promise her the safety she wanted, the safety of a husband, not just the safety of peace.

But he wouldn't tonight, for he did not have any other

words other than, "Not now."

After his first two hour sparring session the next day, Periander went straight to the kitchens. Often, the cooks were astonished to see their Prince in person. He needed food as much as he needed exercise. He was used to the dull ache in his legs and arms; that was the cost of recovering what he had lost. He was used to being sore from wooden blows landed on him by his blade master.

But he could never be used to the pain in his stomach when his muscles consumed more energy than his last meal could provide. He wolfed down whatever they brought him: a variety of fruits from Olympian orchards, breads from his own lands, wine from the Elysian Point—though Trident wine was finer, none could be acquired when the Trident Rivers fed the their armies.

"Would you like more, milord?"

"Meat!" Periander told the chef. "Who serves a Prince a meal without meat!" He laughed so they would not fear his demands.

Minutes later, they brought out a pig. He had no idea how they managed it, but suddenly there was a cooked suckling pig on the table. The chef cut into it when Periander did not, and offered him a sizeable slice.

He felt much better after eating. He still had a few hours before his afternoon spar, so he looked for his son.

From the Great Hall he climbed the steps to the second floor. This was still old brickwork and wooden beams from centuries ago, not the newer architecture above. Though in style, the Keep looked magnificently designed as a single achievement; a close examination could spot the differences between the old storeys and Akheron's additions to it, especially in the interior.

While his own quarters were on the third floor, a variety of communal rooms occupied the second. He found Cat transcribing some numbers in a ledge book in her study. "Where's Artemys?" he asked her.

She smiled. "Asleep, probably," she said. "It's midmorning."

"That's fine," he said, "I could use a nap too."

"Check the nursery. Gosa should be keeping an eye on him."

"See you for dinner," he said.

She smiled again, a bit weaker.

Artemys's nursery was a cozy room, full of fabrics and cushions. It was guarded by two stoic soldiers, two of Avernus's best. As the royal child, he had the best instructors on all things. Though he was not learning combat or history yet, his teachers encouraged him to do things like running and balancing, and he had a language tutor. After all these strenuous things, the young boy needed sleep.

"You can find food if you want," Periander told Gosa. She glanced up from the sewing she was doing. "Have a break."

"Thank you, highness." She rose out of the armchair.

Periander approached Artemys's bed. He had only just graduated from a crib. The tiny person was only three years old now, and Periander was still in awe that this was his son. *One day,* he realized, *you will be a man. A good man.*

He lay down beside his son, and put a hand around him. He ran a hand through the messy brown hair and Artemys stirred, rolling toward him and tucking his head into the nook of Periander's arm.

He had no clue how long he lay there. The breaths blurred into minutes. He woke up a few times, having not realized that he had fallen asleep. Artemys mumbled, "Father," and wrapped an arm around Periander's stomach.

This is worth it, he decided. *This hour of bliss is worth whatever Trion wants to throw at me.* Something in the thought disturbed him. He did not fall asleep again. Trion had a son, more than ten years older than Artemys, a wife, and a younger brother, and Periander had ordered them burned to stop the man. What disturbed him even more deeply than what he had done was what had driven Trion to start this war. Had Trion never cradled his son, felt this embrace? If he had, what could have been so wrong with the world to require him to abandon it and forge an army?

"When did you come?" Artemys asked, more conscious now that Periander was awake too.

"Last night," Periander said. "Late. I came and saw you. You looked sleepy."

Artemys murmured, "Yes, I was very sleepy."

Periander continued petting his hair.

"Do you have to go again?"

Periander paused, then ran his fingers through again. "Yes. Artemys, you will understand someday why I must. But one day I will stay."

"Good," Artemys said, and snuggled closer.

Periander remembered the last time he saw his father. Akheron had sat him on his knee in his study after tiring of a book and told him, "Anything you want to be, you can be. Just make your own place in the world. Choose what you want and how you want to get it." Then he had left on the tour from which he had never returned.

"You can do anything you want," he told Artemys. "All you need to do is try."

Artemys looked up at him. "Do you want to go?"

"No, son," he said. "Of course not."

"Then why do you?"

Periander remained silent. After a minute, he swung his feet over the edge of the bed and sat up. His shoulders slumped. "Because I want peace," he said. It was something he was hearing for the first time, at the same time as his son. "And I want right."

Artemys swung his feet over, though they only made it halfway to the ground. He embraced his father's arm. "I think you're a good person," he said.

I hope so, he thought.

That evening, they hosted a feast in the Palace Great Hall. The Three Nobles were most significant guests; it was important for Periander to keep them vested in his wellbeing and his contribution to their lands. Cat sat at his side. She hid the last night's doubts so well that Periander felt like these were days before the war: she laughed at his jokes, teased him with her own remarks, and made good points in their discussion with the Nobles. She seemed to thoroughly enjoy herself, and Periander felt more alive because of it. She had to excuse herself early though, to join Artemys for his own meal and help Gosa take him to bed.

Periander continued talking to the Nobles. Ino talked about

the stories he had heard of Edessa and how surprised he was that Periander had survived. Ahryn was concerned with the state of the city's treasury; he kept asking Periander about the funding of the war. Odyn's estate was funding most of their expenses, "for the wellbeing of the Dominion," and Ahryn was concerned they would eventually turn that into a debt. The new Odyn XI was selfish with his money. Even Periander agreed that that Prince was still a boy. Edemar, like usual, said almost nothing. He mostly just agreed or disagreed with his comrades via noncommittal murmurs.

Sore from his slowly recuperating strength, he climbed the three storeys of stairs, spiralling around and around and around. His quarters sprawled for half of the level, while his study occupied a lot of the remaining space. Where was Cat? She must have already gone to bed.

He sat down in the antechamber and unlaced his boots.

"Tonight was good," Cat said. He smiled and pulled off his second boot. "At least we make the best of things when you are on this side of the land."

He glanced up at her. She was wearing one his tunics, but her legs were bare. They spent most of the nights of these visits together. They missed each other so much when they were gone.

"You're amazing," he told her. He stood up and asked, "Did you want to talk? I'm feeling stronger tonight, if you wanted to discuss what you said—"

She shook her head. "You'll need that strength for more than talking." She grabbed his hands and pulled him toward her.

14

Year of Olympus 572

The day after Kerres left him was warm. It was like the summer, even though the winter was in full swing. The snow began to melt, and the city of Avernus seemed to come out of hibernation. Wagons began to roll down the streets, all the shops opened their doors and windows, and some merchants even set up shop in the streets. It was the calls of bartering and the hammers of smiths that woke Artemys.

Groggily, he arched his feet to seek that warm spot under the blankets. What dream was just beyond his memory? It had felt right, like finding that comfortable position in a warm bed. Everything had been well in the world. Even now, he could hear some shouts from the streets beyond the Palace walls. Fighting. There had been none in his dream, he was certain of it.

The distant commotion was not loud enough to be another riot; more likely it was just a murder, some drunk done in by his once-comrade. During the war, any Triumvirate malcontents had kept silent for their lives' sake. But now, anyone disappointed by the outcome of the war had become brave enough to argue or fight for it. And no Triumvirate patriot could trust such a brother.

Another day. Artemys rolled over. *I wonder what my father's agenda is for today.* He would need to interrupt it, likely. He had a very special gift.

He finally sat up. The sun was casting a slanted square across the floor. The rest of the room glowed with the slight grey of smoke from the embers in the fireplace. His bedroom had a smaller fireplace than his main quarter, and both required tending.

He hesitated before ringing the nearby bell. Should he kindle his fire himself? He believed in equality, not slavery. But some members of society should deserve the service of others, the respect they have earned.

He lifted the bell from the dresser by its long, looping handle and rung it loudly. There was already a pile of clothes on the stool by the dresser. Artemys stepped into a fresh pair of breeches and then into a pair of shallow boots. He sat down on the wooden trunk next to his bed and began tightening the shoelaces when his servant entered. The man was short and thin, but angled with muscles. He set about the fire immediately.

"I trust you slept well, milord?" he asked as he lifted back the moss covering on the fireplace's embers.

Slept well? I hardly slept at all! Last night was both a dark haze and a sharp splinter of glass. "I was plagued by nightmares, but it was no fault of yours," he said.

"I'm sorry to hear that," his servant said. He seemed earnest. "Perhaps your lord father's healer could brew something to ease your mind?"

Artemys planted his boots on the floor. Before he could brush away the suggestion, a burst of cold air nearly extinguished the servant's sputtering flame. Weveld stood in the doorway, the wooden hall door slamming shut and echoing from the antechamber.

"This is a warning, Artemys." The Prime Zealot wore a dark brown cloak, dishevelled to one side by running or activity. His trembling, white beard was shorter than the last time Artemys had seen him. His fists were clenched, and his eye nearly blocked by the steep angle of his bushy eyebrows. "You won't get another."

"Leave the fire," Artemys told his servant. The poor man somehow managed to fit between Weveld and the doorframe without bursting any personal sense of space. All of the sorcerer's attention was focused on Artemys.

Once they were alone, Artemys stood up. His hairy chest was still muscular from the months spent working the village of Attarax. He had seen a merchant staring at his calloused hands the last time he went to the market—lords did not lower themselves to the level of manual labour. The only muscles they should have are those for wielding swords or wooing ladies. Artemys was certain he had lost both, but he was certain his aggressive rise to his feet would deliver the intended rebut.

"Get out of my quarters," he said. The roughness of his own voice surprised him.

Weveld took another step into his room. It was Artemys's bedchamber, but the unmade bed made no difference to him. "You've been travelling coast to coast, with *magic*. You take the Glyph Gates when you can, but if there's none near enough...you just cast a spell! Maker burn you, Artemys...you are making a mockery of our doctrine! Magic is not some free gift! If the Maker wanted us to use it like a second pair of legs, we'd be born with it, instead of earning it with years of work."

Artemys lowered his voice. "Get out, now."

"And you continue to scry the whole world when it pleases you. When we invited you—"

His father's sword was sitting in the other room, but Artemys's magic was far more powerful. "You did not invite me. Last warning, *Crown* wizard. Get out of my quarters."

Weveld carried on, face red, lips wet. "You play your own game of cat-and-mouse with the pretty lords and ladies... we're trying to maintain *order!* I should have known that the great Prince was too good for it! Your father should never have given a pampered brat like you the ability to crush an ant with magic, let alone travel the realm! You're the same as the earth—"

Artemys put his finger on the nearest post of his four-poster bed. He wrote five glyphs: movement and air, and three glyphs to denote a destination. Weveld was staring at him in shock. Would this earth-spawn dare to cast a spell against the Prime Zealot himself?

Artemys's voice maintained its earlier growl. *"Bor'elep lorazar,"* he said, and a section of air around Weveld flickered. The man's furious words were still echoing when the air flickered closed and Weveld was gone. He was back in Delfie. Perhaps he should try being Crown Magician before he tried any more of his cult-rules cursing.

There was a green shirt folded on his dresser. He snatched it off and sank back onto his trunk. *I just teleported someone else.* He shrugged through the sleeves and neck of the shirt. It was softer than his other clothes, he noticed. He examined the knit and found it to be much thicker thread than the usual wool or cotton clothes he owned. *Good choice, poor servant.*

His thoughts returned to his spell. He had never heard of such a spell. He had just wanted Weveld gone. He did not even remember choosing a location. *The School of Delfie is a good choice though. Weveld often forgets he's the leader of both orders.*

"Time to visit my father," he decided, standing up again. He grabbed the sword from the next room and a cloak from his antechamber.

Prince Periander Gothikar was returning from the Great Hall when Artemys found him. His clean shaven jaw broke into a grin when he saw Artemys. He strode briskly across the cold stone corridor and embraced his eldest born.

"Artemys! I didn't even know you were in Avernus!"

"I arrived last night," he said. He had strapped the sword Korbios to his back, and his father did not notice it.

His father gripped shoulders near his neck and said, "I'm glad you're here, and I'm glad you're visiting me first thing."

"I sometimes miss this city," Artemys said. He remembered the years he spent here after leaving the Order of Magic. That was back before finding Attarax, the Disciples of Andrakaz, and before he rejoined the Order. "And of course, I miss the company of my family also."

"Ah," his father said, and added, with a much blunter attitude than Artemys remembered his father possessing, "We have only been close enough for company for a handful of years throughout your life. That is something I've been regretting more and more each day."

Artemys was taken aback. "I like to think that the times we shared were important though."

Periander smiled; though they were walking, he met his son's eyes. "Oh, they were. But I was at war for the first half of your life!"

"And I have been gone for the second," Artemys concluded. "I am as much to blame as you. I am very glad that Pyrsius has had the opportunity to grow up with your more direct attention."

Periander bowed his head in thought as they climbed a

narrow spiral staircase.

Artemys's grandfather had added two layers to the top of the Keep using building methods much more recent than the Avernan Palace's ancient origins. One of the rooms he added collected so many treasures during the years since that it was now a legend among commoners. It was just as valuable to scholars, full of one-of-a-kind books and other rarities. There was even a collector's wine rack in one corner.

The Prince swung the door to the Gothikar Study open and Artemys turned to close it. One of Artemys's thoughts bubbled up from within the shell he had built to contain them. *Here comes his regrets. Here comes his apologies. Why bother?*

Periander pulled off his gloves and tossed them onto the desk in the middle of the room. "I know you were frustrated with me for choosing him to be my heir. Your pursuit of magic leaves little time for rule, let alone learning statecraft."

"I understand completely. To be frank, I am far too busy to have any interest in being a Prince," he said, with complete honesty. *I do not want to be a Prince, playing a game of power with the others... I want to control them. Let Pyrsius replace you...he'll be much easier to control. No subtle gifts for him.*

Periander leaned against the desk. It creaked under his large stature. Some might say he was a giant among men, but the war that Periander had fought had made it a comment of ill-taste. His father was starting to show the signs of age, with wrinkles creasing his forehead and under each eye. He ran a hand through his brown hair and said, "Your brother is doing very well in his studies. I have actually brought him along to some discussions with our Nobles. Perhaps next year he will come with me to the Meet of Eldius."

The Meet of Eldius was an annual gathering of the rulers of the Avernan fief to discuss matters of state and economy. The southern half of their lands was still plagued by unrest leading to a resource shortage across the fief. This would be the topic of debate at next year's Meet. "Do the Nobles like him?" Artemys asked. He grabbed a chair from the corner and sat down.

The Nobles of each fief decided who would replace the Prince. It was not a matter of birthright. Another family who served the people well would be selected should the Gothikar name fall out of popularity.

"I think so. I hope so. Pyrsius is ambitious and would be disappointed if not. But throughout the history of the Triumvirate... there have only been a handful of Princehood changes," Periander said. "I think we'll be fine."

"Is Pyrsius a good man?" Artemys asked. He had not willed himself to ask it. He had not had one of these conversations with his father in years—they had discussed what made a person good many times. Back when he had understood the world as black and white. *There is no black and white,* Artemys thought. *Only grey.*

"I believe he is. He's young and rash, but he makes good decisions."

"Actions..." Artemys murmured. His father thought it was only a man's actions that made him. Artemys knew that his father's perspective overlooked the most important factor: how a man thought.

Periander smiled, standing. "Can I get you a drink?"

"I would like that," Artemys said. He had not consumed a thing all day.

As watery ale filled two cups, his father continued, "You scared him. That slaver that you assaulted—"

"The slaver that I stopped," Artemys corrected. "Is that action not a good one?"

Periander glanced at him, the gilded pitcher paused briefly. He raised an eyebrow. "Let's not get into *your* actions now."

Artemys snorted and looked down. He heard the trickle of ale continue and then a pottered vessel appeared in his vision. The carving on it was rough and the ale a dull red. He took a drink and looked back up at his father. His mouth tasted like watered down barley. Certainly, the Gothikar treasury could afford better.

"He's scared of magic," Periander told him. "He wouldn't admit it—he's trying too hard to be a man, but he's—"

"Enough about Pyrsius," Artemys said, meeting his father's eyes. "Let this action speak for itself." He pulled the sword from his back and, pulling away the wool and leather wrap from the hilt, held it toward Prince Gothikar.

"What's this?" Periander asked, lowering his drink.

"A gift," Artemys said. "Befitting my lord father, the High Prince and Hero of the Trionus War."

Periander scoffed, but his eyes were glowing. He gripped the hilt and gasped. "It's warm," he murmured and pulled the sword free. "By the Great Glyph!"

In this light, Korbios shone with a quiet blue. The rising sun gleamed off the blade, and, with its perfect blend of metals and the magic-enhanced finishing, it reflected like moonlight. The glyphs were a darker colour, but as Periander shifted the blade into his other hand they caught the sun too.

Noticing them, Periander moved the blade closer to his face to inspect them. "Maker, these are glyphs!" He tried to read them, but turned to Artemys with a quizzical look. "I haven't the knowledge for these."

"The sword will not dull," Artemys said, "and cannot be undone by magic, at least, none that I have heard of. As far as I know, this sword will outlive any man alive." He took another drink of his ale.

"This is incredible!" his father exclaimed, and gave it a swing in the direction of the window. The blade was a blur. "The balance...!"

"You can thank a blacksmith named Orestys for that."

"I'll remember to do so. Does this masterpiece have a name?" Periander finished his ale in one chug, his eyes not wavering from the blade.

Artemys nodded. "One I think you will appreciate. I have named it Korbios."

"Korbios!" his father laughed, delighted. He gave it a spin. Most of the Imperial houses had the word in their name. For Periander, this was a sword of the Triumvirate.

Prince Gothikar turned to his son, with tears in his eyes, and asked, "Why have you done this? Prepared so much work, for me? Glyphs, I'm not even at war anymore..."

"'The real cost of the war is that it may never end,' you said," Artemys quoted. "It never did, did it?"

Periander flinched at the quote and lowered his gaze as Artemys had done minutes earlier. "We lost," he said, words retched from somewhere deep. He set his cup on the table. "We lost the war. I don't know how! How could I have done better?"

Artemys stepped closer to his father. He felt awkward; this was something his father and he had never shared. "You did ten times what anyone had a right to ask you for," he told his father.

"But then it came time for everyone else to do their part. And no one did."

Periander looked up at Artemys. "Of everyone, *everyone*, I didn't expect you to be the one to understand. I didn't mean to raise you a soldier in this war."

"You did no such thing. You hardly raised me, Father. I was raised *by* this war." He held up his hand so Periander would not interrupt. "It is no fault of yours, and, frankly, I would not have it any other way."

"This sword, this gift... why did you make it for me?"

"So that we would be alone no longer," Artemys said. His reply had a double meaning, but he denied it a place in his mind. "We can both fight this war. Every time you don or even look at that sword, remember that you are not alone. In Weveld's inner circle, the Council of the Order of Magic," he paused. *What?!* He had very little desire to sit on the Council. That was a game of petty inconsequential politics. "I could influence the Crown Magicians and the other Princes. The riots have to stop. Our people, our citizens need to know that they are safe from one another, from us. Maker, it was one of their "lords" who caused the war. They have every reason to hate us! We need to give them reasons to *love* us!"

Periander smiled. He lowered the blade horizontally, resting it in his empty hand. "To battle?" he asked with a half-smile.

Artemys smiled. "To battle."

15

Year of Olympus 549

The Triumvirate met in Helius this time, instead of the Tower in Galinor. It was only a few days march, but no one wanted to lose the war because of a few days delay.

Periander rode through the woodland. The winter had been warmer this year, so his horse had an easier passage through the snow. The pine trees around him still huddled within white robes, and the clouds still obscured the sun above, but the steed could trot instead of stride. Mordus and Salantar rode side by side behind him. They were laughing to some joke the former had made; Periander had missed it under the noise of his troop. They were singing a refrain, a marching chorus about Hokar the Explorer.

They had thirty soldiers with them, a small battalion by any standard. Periander's armies were still camped further inland along the Blood Strait. The trip to Helius was the shortest for him. It did not even fill the week.

Theseus had travelled south through Sinai, and sailed across the mouth of the Strait. Earlier, before descending into the forest, Periander had seen the masts of his ship docked on the peninsula. He could see nothing man-made now, except some smoke trails ahead and occasional tracks in the snow.

Odyn could not have spared the time to travel from the south slopes of Cerden the whole way to Helius, so his court magician had teleported them to the Known Location in Galinor and marched the three days across the Crossing and toward Helius. Periander wondered if the Olympian Prince had arrived yet, or if their official meeting would have to wait.

"Will you spend the night alone, again?" Salantar asked, riding a bit closer to Periander. For some reason, the gladiator was the only one whose lack of royal address bothered Periander. He told most of his comrades not to: Dobler, Mordus, even his more familiar captains addressed him as Periander.

"Leave him alone," Mordus said, chuckling dryly.

"I have a wife, Salantar," Periander said.

"So do half your men, but these are the wilds! No one will know," Salantar said. He had become more talkative since his release. Sometimes, Periander wondered if he was trying to get himself imprisoned again. "You spend most of year in a camp with next to no women. At least enjoy them in the town, when we get to sleep in comfortable beds again!"

Periander shook his head. "I would know," he said. "And truth be told, I would think of my wife the whole time."

"You're a fool," Salantar said. Mordus breathed a curse beneath his breath.

Periander looked at him. "So are you," he returned. "But you're also the first person to call me a fool."

Salantar burst out laughing. "The things I learn from you," he said. "Princes, Nobles... I'm glad I don't have your life, Periander. It wouldn't agree with me."

"What about the wealth?" Mordus asked. They were riding past a small lumber camp. There was a yard full of stacked wood and a few large saws leaning against a shed nearby. Only two men were there, they waved as Periander and his men passed.

"You don't know me, if you think gold does it for me," Salantar said, stroking the beard he had grown this winter. His hair as darker now, reflecting his better health. It bothered Periander that the fighter was healthier in a winter wilderness than in his prison.

"Then you're both fools," Mordus replied, "and I'm the only sane one here."

They all chuckled. Ahead, Helius appeared through the snow-draped trees. The town was larger each time Periander saw it. The first time he had been here, there were only four or five buildings and a few docks. Now, there were short streets of houses, shops. There were a few inns and several brothels. The villagers had built a large barn in the center of town and called it the Town Hall. Their mayor, Nal ten Tarcep, was a decent administrator, despite his greed.

The Captain of the Guard gave them a stern look over. Unlike the lumberjacks earlier, the guards could not afford to accept someone's identity with the emblem they bore. He spoke to Mordus, but then addressed Periander directly. "Your peers have already arrived, Prince Gothikar. Shall I send word to them, highness?"

"Tell them I will meet with them in an hour if they are ready," he told the guardsman with a nod of thanks.

Periander turned in his saddle, patting the smooth back of the horse he rode. His troop stood shivering in the snow, sore from the long day's march. "Listen up, men!" he called. "You have at least a day's leave while we're here. Check in with your superiors in the morning. And enjoy your rest!"

Periander led the way down the main street. The first shop they passed alive with commotion. As Mordus passed it, a young man came out into the street with a platter of fresh bread, "Get warmed up from the long march!" he cried. "My master has just finished a large batch of his famous baking!"

Each place they came to advertised their wares. Innkeepers led some of the foot soldiers away, smiths brandished shields and helmets for the veterans of the troop, working women showed off various parts of themselves that Periander tried to ignore and even a few scribes appeared to write letters for any men who could afford it. The war-town opened up for the troop and closed its mouth behind them.

Periander glanced at Salantar, who still rode by his side. The man had said he was not interested in wealth. "What does 'do it for you'?"

"Killing," Salantar said. "That's all I have left. So I'll go find something else to distract from it. Probably a brunette." He rode away without another word.

Mordus watched him go, frowning. He looked at Periander with a raised eyebrow. "Quite the find, my friend, quite the find."

"We need killers," Periander said. *We're all killers.*

"Is that what he did?" Mordus asked. "To get imprisoned in the first place?"

"He stole his Lady-aunt's jewelry case. He was kept in a

commoner's jail, and then bought by the Arena," Periander said.

"Maker," Mordus said, running a finger along the scar on his forehead. He had gained that one in a smaller encounter in the Cerden Mountains while Periander was on leave.

"Indeed."

An hour later, Periander had moved his belongings into a guest room at the Town Hall and found himself something to eat. He found Tarcep speaking with Weveld outside of the designated meeting room. "Welcome, my Prince," Weveld said, while Tarcep bowed. "The others are here."

Periander stepped into the room as the spell-caster opened the door. Their summit was held in a larger room than the usual Council Chamber in Galinor. There was a long, rectangular table made of varnished pine wood. The light shone off its smooth surface; it was probably the most expensive piece of furniture in Helius.

Young Odyn lounged in his chair to the right of the head of the table. He glanced up at Periander but did not move. He was a larger man than his father, but not as fierce. The late Prince Odyn had been a dangerous warrior and a fiery man. Odyn the Eleventh had more than his father's stature, but none of his application.

"Periander!" Erykus Theseus stood at Periander's arrival and leaned forward to clasp hands with his friend. Periander accepted the gesture, and then offered Odyn a similar one. He took it, but with less enthusiasm, as Theseus sat himself down opposite Odyn, folding his arms on the tabletop.

"Theseus, Odyn," Periander said. "I trust your travels were smooth?"

"There's nothing smooth about these mountains," Odyn said.

"Nor the seas I sailed," Theseus said. "A storm delayed our departure from the North, and we only arrived yesterday because of it."

Weveld was already taking a chair a few seats down on Theseus's side of the table; it was tradition for the Crown Magician to keep some distance from the meeting of the Princes. He was here to advise and provide a less biased opinion should bias arise.

Everyone was looking at Periander. The head of the table

was empty, intentionally. The Council had looked to Periander since Dagger's Edge. He did not know why; they had lost that battle disastrously. Theseus had just as much experience as him, but they both had respect in their eyes when they looked at him.

He stepped past Odyn's chair and sat next to him, on the length of the table. They were equals, and they must remain that way. They were princes. None of them had been elected High Prince, none of them had claimed to be a king like Trion. He got a nod from Theseus.

"Where do we stand?" Odyn asked.

"Trion's men remain at Edessa. They have repaired the walls and set the refugees to work again," Erykus Theseus said.

"Really?" Periander asked. "Are they slaves?"

"My scouts could not say for certain. They have not seen any abuse of the citizens aside from theft of property. Trion's troops are well-behaved."

Periander pursed his lips. "If they have sealed the walls again...I doubt we could retake it without significant costs. Even Trion's troops diminished in that battle."

"Doesn't matter," Odyn said. "He could win this war without a single human. There are mountain tribes scattering across the Cerden Mountains. I engage them where I can, but in bulk they outnumber my armies more than ten to one!"

"Are they advancing?" Theseus asked.

"No, just enforcing the areas they have and manoeuvring armies."

Periander pursed his lips. "I wish your father lived," he said, thoughtlessly.

Odyn glanced at him with a look of irritation.

"He has—had fought enough battle to know which ones we could win and which ones we can't," Periander explained. "We cannot kill all of the giants, so we need to choose where to fight them and when."

"How?" Theseus asked.

"I have not been at this long enough."

"It has been ten years," Weveld said. "Ten years of war."

The Princes glanced at him.

"We need to learn how to fight this war before it continues another ten years," Weveld said.

"If this war continues for another ten years, we will have

lost Galinor by then. We don't have that kind of time," Theseus said, nodding.

"I must admit," Odyn said, "I admire Trion's success."

They all turned their eyes on him.

"He knows power," Odyn said. "He truly does, and it has taken three fiefs and thousands of lives to try to stop his power, to slow it down even. How do we fight this man? You killed his family and he still hasn't broken!"

"I'm not certain about that," Periander noted. "When I fought him in Edessa, he seemed half-crazed."

"My point is, Periander," Odyn said, "that we have fought him with steel, politics and emotion...and his onslaught has not wavered. It only a matter of time before he strikes again, and we cannot afford to keep this many soldiers marching back and forth across the wilderness indefinitely."

"How does he?" Erykus wondered.

"If it comes to a fight of survival, our men will not require pay," Periander said. "If it truly comes to survival."

"But we are the ones who would die," Weveld said. His brown hair was greying and his beard looked wirier than when he rescued Periander. "Look at Edessa! Our soldiers eventually will. Trion is providing for that city. Do not stop providing for our soldiers, for they will find someone who will."

Periander paused. There was sense there, but it infuriated him. "He's providing for the city, but he also *burned* that city!"

"Not everyone would make the sacrifices you would to stop a bad man," Odyn said.

"Sacrifices?" Periander asked. "I swore oaths to die before failing in my duty!"

"We all did," Odyn said, bristled. "But you would also sacrifice your duty to the Triumvirate."

"What!"

Theseus leaned back in his chair, sighing. He, apparently, knew where this conversation was going. How much did he and Odyn communicate without Periander? There were no laws between private communications, only private plots.

Odyn turned in his chair to face Periander. "Our treasuries are depleted. Our resources are quickly depleting, and our soldiers are falling. Your insistence on conscription—"

"Which was your father's also—"

"—is drawing out most of the capable men from across our lands. The economy of my fief is failing, and I know mine is not the only one," Odyn said. "I am no longer convinced that you are fighting for the Dominion. Rather, you are fighting *against* Trion. And you would sacrifice the Dominion to stop him."

Periander stood up, placing his finger on the table and leaning forward at Odyn. "And you would rather stop conscripting men and funding the war and what? Let him take our homes from us? Trion is an oath-breaker, a madman, and a murderer. The lives of our men are not on me, they are on *him*."

"I am not suggesting we let him take the Dominion. I am not suggesting surrender."

"Then what?" Periander asked.

Weveld cleared his throat. "You should be seated, Periander."

He reluctantly sank back into the chair, still fuming at Odyn.

Erykus finally leaned forward again. "We would all die for the Dominion, correct?"

Weveld said, "Yes."

Cat and Artemys forgive me... "Yes," Periander said, at once with Odyn. Periander doubted the honesty of the Olympian Prince's claim.

"Then we must consider the middle ground," Theseus said. "We concede to Trion's terms. Give him the Maker's Forge, Cerden, and Galinor. All of his actions support his honesty when he says he will stop there. He will likely execute everyone in this room. But we must consider this as a legitimate option. For the Dominion."

Periander stared at him. "Ivos will persuade Trion to break the peace again."

"Ivos again..." Odyn groaned.

"He is a coward and his leech. This entire war is his doing, I suspect, though he would rather Trion take the fall than risk it himself." Ivos had denied Periander his own Avernan seat when Periander was a mere boy. He had abused his responsibilities as steward to make a grab for the throne.

"Enough of Ivos," Odyn said.

"Fine," Periander said, grinding his teeth together. "Trion accepts our concession and sits in Galinor. And every other power-thirsty man in the Dominion tries what he tried! We must *win* this war, not just end it. This is the first time the Triumvirate has been tested so completely, and we must make sure everyone knows that they cannot usurp it!"

Odyn chewed on his words for a moment in silence. Periander saw the look in his eye; Odyn would be one of those power-thirsty aggressors, he suspected.

"Doing what is *right* should be enough," Periander said, "but if it's not, we must do what is reasonable. And letting that madman have our capital would not be reasonable."

Theseus was nodding. "I agree."

Odyn threw up his hands.

Periander caught Weveld watching him, his eyes alight with some sort of surprise. Periander's words must have impressed him, for he had clearly changed his mind about something. He bowed his head and continued pondering his own mind in silence.

Theseus replied to Odyn's frustration. "If we continue failing against Trion, we will pass the point of reason, and on that day we will speak of this again. I only pray it is not too late."

"Weveld," Periander said after a moment of silence. "Do you have any news on the magicians we have seen serving Trion?"

"Still none, I'm afraid," the Crown Magician replied. "On that front, I have recently recruited a cult, the 'Disciples of Andrakaz', to provide more magicians on the battlefront. My Order is already stretched so thin; this could effectively double the number of spell-casters at our disposal."

Periander raised an eyebrow. "A cult? Why would they agree to help? Are we paying them?"

"Can we trust them?" Odyn added.

"Since the fall of the Kinship, there has been no organized system of belief for those who see glyphs as proof of a divine force. Dozens of groups have appeared, but they are harmless. The cult of Andrakaz has deified an influential sorcerer from the Age of Myths. They believe he still exists, giving strength to the glyphs."

"And I suppose he 'told' them to help us?"

"To the contrary. Their deity is imprisoned and unable of

giving them direction. The funding I promised them will allow them to spread their beliefs wider."

"Is that wise?" Theseus asked.

"No," Odyn said. Their treasurer did not approve of any unnecessary expenditures.

"It is harmless," Weveld said. "Akheron taught the people that no one can tell them what to believe. Allowing this cult to spread their message will not result in the growth of their cult in the way they think."

Periander nodded. "Very well. Their magicians will fight for us?"

Weveld nodded. "It should equalize the disadvantage Trion has us at, though the mystery of his servants still remains."

"Can we agree to this?" Theseus asked.

Odyn and Periander both agreed.

"Anything else that requires a proper meeting?"

Periander shrugged. "I will continue travelling along the Strait. Perhaps we can force their hand by holding our lines but prodding forward in one spot. The rest can be communicated via letters."

Odyn nodded. "I have the longest journey ahead of me, so I will head out first thing in the morning."

"I will remain a few days for my men," Periander said. "My Captain Illus has things under control."

"I'll take my leave this evening," Weveld said. "I will teleport to the School and tell the zealot of Andrakaz our offer."

They stood. Odyn paced away quickly, with Weveld only a few steps behind him. Erykus walked beside Periander as they left. They were only a few years apart: Periander was thirty and the Prince of Athyns five years his senior. Odyn XI was just past twenty. Theseus had not married though, to the dismay of his Nobles. They had probably already decided on the next Prince of Athyns, for the current one had no heirs. He had a younger brother who now fought as one of his Captains. Perhaps he would be a suitable leader should they decide to maintain a Theseus in charge of their city.

"I fear for Odyn," Erykus said.

"He is too quick to give up," Periander agreed.

"And you are too slow to."

Periander looked at his friend. "Perhaps, though I did not

expect *you* to say it."

"I trust you, Periander," Erykus said. "And I will support you no matter what you decide in these next few years. But I will also provide insights when I think you might need them."

"Despite my reaction," Periander said, "I do appreciate your support and your advice. When will you be leaving town?"

"Not yet," Theseus winked. "I have enough time to grab an ale with one of my oldest friends, if he wants."

Periander smiled. "I would like that," he said.

16

Year of Olympus 573

Eldius's rooftops, in the distance, glistened with rainwater. Each of them was a small, black square gleaming whenever a nearby torch flickered or a lantern-bearing passerby let their light rise high enough. The billowing grey clouds seemed close enough for Artemys to touch as he rode at his father's flank toward the city. The hills around Eldius were evenly divided by farmland and copses of spruce, while their right side was an open blue nether. Artemys could see one or two ships following the coast, but no sailor wanted to be out on a day like today.

Ahead of him rode two horsemen: Prince Periander and the younger Prince-to-be. His father wore an elaborately embroidered, dark green jerkin covered by the evenly-spaced tower designs of golden thread. Each design was three decorated squares attached to a line: the Three Towers of Avernus that appeared on the Gothikar emblem. From his shoulder hung a bronze riding cape, and a black hood kept the rain from his face.

On his father's back clung Korbios, the sword inseparable from the Prince. He wore it whenever he went out, like a trophy of some kind. It was wrapped right now, against the rain. Every word his father spoke, though, vibrated inside of Artemys's head.

Pyrsius was of smaller build, but with just as sharp of build as his Gothikar kin—shoulders jutting and torso angular. He wore a brighter green tunic with a thick and high-collared black coat of the contemporary style. He had a thin sword at his side, a slashing sword that could be used from both horseback or on foot, with one hand or with two.

"At least the journey was smooth," Artemys called ahead of him, tugging at his own brown fur hood. He grimaced at the cloud of water droplets he shook loose. "If a little damp..."

"Seems like this Meet is always wet," his father called back. Artemys heard the words twice, once from the air and once from the sword. He had listened to half a dozen of Periander's meetings this way. Sometimes he could block it out when he did not want to hear double.

Pyrsius shrugged, "I haven't been to this event until now, but I know the spring always bring showers."

"We could have stayed dry..." Artemys leered. He had suggested a ward against water, and had offered a gateway straight to Eldius before that. His father had insisted against any tampering. He had reminded Artemys of his many tours around the fief, to survey and visit his lands. Even his father would use magic for comfort on occasion, but never on such a venture. "The experience of nature is best left to nature," he had said.

What of human nature? Artemys had nearly replied.

"We'll be within the city soon," Dobler Rewan called back. He rode ahead of Artemys's father with two guardsmen. Three more rode behind Artemys. They'd gone ahead of their slow-moving wagon, leaving several soldiers with it to carry on as it could. The roadway was scarcely more than a winding belt of mud.

Artemys's horse, Rook, walked on the grass where it could, but the sloping hills forced it onto the mud frequently. Artemys patted her sides and elicited a larger cloud of vapor from her nostrils.

Ahead were the smaller shacks and stingy markets of the slums. They could be found around nearly any city now, a first generation of muddy buildings gripping the city's walls and its descendants wandering outward from the city gates in clusters.

Artemys felt their escorts tense and saw hands hover near weapons. This was the most dangerous stretch of their journey: not the roaming bandits or the elusive Buccaneer's Navy on the adjacent sea.

"At ease," Periander urged. He glanced past his shoulder at Artemys, his expression blank. "They won't trust us if we don't trust them."

"Can we?" Pyrsius asked. There were groups of men and women watching them, some armed with weapons, others with farming implements, and more with empty hands clenched into fists. Their eyes were sad, though, not angry. Not yet.

They were almost at the gate when a woman stumbled into the dirty roadway ahead of Dobler. "Copper, all I ask fer is copper!" she cried, holding her cupped hands out.

Dobler snatched a pouch from his saddlebags and tossed it to her. Two men leaning against a nearby general store stirred, but Dobler raised his hand to point at them. "Give those two a coin each," he told the woman. He called toward the men, "I have no more pouches! She will share with you."

As soon as they were out of earshot, Pyrsius asked, "Was that wise? She's in danger because of your gift."

Dobler glanced back at them, holding his reins loosely in front of him. *"We* were in danger until I gave that gift, I'm afraid. I like it no more than you."

Periander said nothing.

They reached the city gates a moment later. There were ten guards out front, six pressed against the guardhouse nearby, while four stood in formation at the gate. Two were armed with spears while their two companions had loaded crossbows. Artemys had seen similar weapons before, but they were as clunky and useless in his eyes as the first ones to have been invented, when he was a boy.

"Welcome to Eldius. You'd best afford the visitor's tax or bear an invitation," the right spear-bearing guard declared. "Though your entourage looks equipped for both."

Dobler dismounted and brandished a folded and sealed parchment. "You have the privilege of addressing his lordship, Prince Gothikar of Avernus, High Prince of the Triumvirate, and Champion of the Trionus War. Here is our invitation to the Meet."

"Your highness," the group of guards gasped, lowering themselves in a bow. Artemys worried their helms might be claimed by the mud. The group of guards loitering nearby was suddenly alert. Some rejoined their comrades while a few wandered past their mounted group to keep an eye on the slums.

The guard captain rose from his bow to take the parchment. He gave it one quick look and returned it to Dobler. "I am

Sergeant Illius ten Taryn, and I will serve as Captain of the Guard for the Meet and for yourself and your sons, if it pleases your highness."

Periander nodded. "Very good, s ergeant. Lead on."

Eldius had been a village, then a town, and now a city. There were three roads leading away from the gate, one significantly wider than the rest. This main road was actually part of the Imperial Highway that ran from Olympus to Avernus. The town had started around an Inn, the Great Gambit; its original proprietor, Nallar ten Eldian, had spent every coin he had to build a highway-house halfway between Olympus and Avernus. Now his son, Lord Branok Eldian, ruled one of this fief's greatest cities from the comfort of the Great Gambit's north wing. From any point in Eldius, the newer buildings of the Great Gambit could be seen as towering, wood-shingled roofs, though the original one-story inn remained at the city's heart as well.

"I still remember the first time you brought me to Eldius," Pyrsius said. "I couldn't imaging leaving such a large legacy after only one small inn...it is still an inspiration."

Periander chuckled in reply.

They heard a woman's scream echoing through the gate from behind them. An anchor pulled Artemys's gut downwards, sickening him. Those men, watching, craving. The woman who had begged for coin. Why would Dobler give her coin? *If he withheld, there would've been a riot...It would have been just as bad...worse than this.* Artemys knew it.

Periander paused, his halted horse giving their whole escort pause. Artemys saw his head bow, and then they were moving again. The screaming cut quiet.

No. I will not let this go. If this is human nature, I will change *it.*

He turned his horse. He spurred it toward the gate they had just come from. The steed travelled at a startled trot, briskly returning to the guards. Artemys glanced behind him to see his father staring after him, concern spread across his clean-shaven face.

Artemys shook his head and turned back to the road ahead of him. One of the guards dared to speak up, "We sent some men to investigate the crime, my lord!"

Artemys ignored their calls to ignore the screams and turned left to follow the city's wall. A small, mud roadway led across the slums; this was the direction the woman had come from and returned to. His pounding blood was not the only reason he could not hear a thing, so he slid from his saddle. His boots hit the muck with the same anchor's weight he felt in his stomach. There was a loud squelch as he pulled his feet free and proceeded forward, his horse forgotten.

The rain had not let up, pounding off of everything and filling each dip with a puddle. Artemys splashed forward, ignorant of a destination until...

A final, blood-curdling howl streaked like lightning through the air. There was a meat shack three buildings down. The door was stained with blood already, despite the water that ran down the wood. Artemys squeezed his eyes for a moment. He almost lost his lunch and knew that he could not open that door in this condition.

Korbios. Kerres. Weveld. Pyrsius. Triumvirate. Order. Chaos.

Enough, Artemys decided, setting his jaw. *This is why I fight. This is why I must.* He pulled a spell-token of air from his belt's pouch. *This is all I must be: enough.*

He lashed out with his boot, shattering the wood near the door's latch into sopping shards of moss.

The two bearded men within stood over her twisted body. One held Dobler's coin pouch. The other held a knife. Both held hate.

So Artemys held it tighter. He clenched his teeth harder and broke the token. The shack creaked with the pressure of the air that exploded outward from Artemys's fist. It knocked Artemys backwards, through the door.

He picked himself up from the mud. The door of the shack fell into the mud. Broken glass, chunks of beef, and broken wood lay in the dirt all around him. Soaking, Artemys stepped forward on sturdy legs. He was purpose. He was hatred. He was the fight.

The man with the knife shoved himself off of the floor within and was right in front of Artemys in an instant, blade shooting for Artemys's rocky heart.

Artemys stepped aside and snapped his elbow against the

man's torso as he stumbled, off-balance in the mud. While the man picked himself up from the earth, Artemys wrote the glyphs for wood and changing on the ground and jutting his finger in the man's direction as he spoke the words, *"Heega oesa zar!"*

The man became wood. He looked like a carving, an expression of shock chiselled into a cracked and rotting wooden surface. Rain water pattered off the hard surface of hair turned into strands of bark, and dripped from the pine-wood knife clutched between solid, brown fingers.

"You done, now?" He shouted at the unmoving and unworldly corpse. He had *killed* a man. He felt sick again, but he had only one reply for his sickness. He raised his hands, fingers clasped together, and took a swing at the man's head.

There was a loud crack and pain shocked down both of his arms. The wooden frame toppled to the ground. Artemys went down with it, hands clasping the head still. There was a large crack in the wood, like when a heavy branch broke. The head hung away at an odd angle from its body. He tore it away, splintering wood around the neck.

Distant to his senses, a heavy weight rammed into him, knocking him and the wooden head into the muck. He lost his hold on the head, found a man on top of him. The first man's accomplice. *The first animal's pack-mate.*

Artemys gasped as he felt burly hands clutch around his neck. The man screamed, "Damned spawn! I'll pull your head from your shoulders—" The rest was lost in an incoherent bellow.

Blinding pain filled Artemys's body. He traced a symbol in the mud that he could not see, the glyph for fire, and roared with all his strength, *"Oken!"*

Everything went red. Not blood-red. Pain red. Artemys was burning. Everything was burning. He rolled across the mud until finding a pool. He rolled blindly.

When he finally pulled himself up, his clothes hung in singed strands from his shoulders, and the second animal was crumbling ashes nearby. Artemys rose from his knees. He dragged himself toward the shack again, what was left of it. In the distance was the sound of fighting and shouting. Artemys ignored it. He picked up the coin pouch from the threshold of the shack and stared at it in confusion. The woman lay in front of him, legs spread amidst the tattered remnants of a dress, throat pooling red all around her.

Maker burn these monsters. He threw up into the mud. *Maker burn them all.* He wiped his mouth and turned around.

A crowd of tattered men and women stood there. They were armed with knives, clubs, forks, shards of glass. They saw him, the Lord Gothikar, and two dead bodies, and a pouch of coins in his bloody hands. Somebody shouted, "He just wanted his gold back!"

Someone else shouted, "Get him!"

Artemys next inhaled when he was shoved to his knees in ankle deep mud to the terrified reactions of guards. Glass soared through the air, shattering against a line of shields in the city gate. There were corpses around Artemys and rough hands held him down. He was shivering, soaked, and dirtied. His skin was singed in spots from his own fire spell.

"I lost my son to this plague on the land! He *starved* to death!" the man that held Artemys shrieked.

There, Artemys could see his father and his brother, their eyes pits of terror. All around Artemys was the mob, shouting murder at the top of their lungs. The man that held Artemys shoved him downward further. Artemys found his face in the mud and he coughed water out of his mouth. All he could taste was blood and dirt.

"Enough!" Periander bellowed, but a block of wood nearly struck the guard directly in front of the Prince. Captain ten Taryn pulled him further behind their protectors. "Please!"

Pyrsius was in tears. A crazed man ran past Artemys and took a spear to the gut. More projectiles arced forward, some bursting with fire upon impact. The fires were quickly doused with rainwater.

Artemys could see three wizards standing near the Imperial Prince. He recognized Theos of Galinor and Queres of Orlin, two Masters of the Order. Another magician stood nearby, likely one of their apprentices. Queres was looking at a token in his hand, his face slanted with thought.

"Please," Artemys mouthed. They tried to look away from him, but the man holding Artemys pulled him back up to his knees. Cold steel pressed into Artemys's neck, and he felt the prick of blood being drawn. His arms were bound. There would be no spells for him.

"We want food!" someone shrieked from the back.

"The Lords cannot—"

"Glyphs, this Meet is nothing! You're all earth-spawn!"

Periander shoved his way forward a few steps, but the guards were persistent on his safety. Artemys could not meet his gaze. He had caused this. He had caused all of this. *No! Look at this! These men are the earth-spawn! They have caused this death... all I did was try to save a woman...*

"Kill them," Artemys mouthed toward Theos and his fellow magicians. They were trembling, staring at the infuriated crowd. They would do what he said. They had to.

"I'll give your son a quicker death than my son!" the man screamed, raising the knife for a stab. All the guards stepped forward, Periander cried out, Pyrsius turned away in horror.

Artemys threw himself into the mud and screamed, "Kill them all!"

He felt the fires. He felt them as a searing wave across his back. He shrieked as flame burned his skin. He rolled across the mud again, extinguishing the corner of his robe.

An inferno blazed above his face. He remained lying the mud so he would not touch the gouts of flame shooting from the magicians into the crowd. Artemys's scream was lost in theirs. A burning hand grabbed his right ankle; he kicked it away with his other boot, trying to close his eyes to the sight of its peeling and blackening.

When Artemys finally sat up, the crowd was nothing more than slumped remnants of bodies, embers rolling down into the mud as rainwater doused them. The man that had threatened Artemys's life had melted to nothing. Only his dagger remained, forgotten in a pile of ash.

Artemys's throat caught with a gag. He had no thoughts. He had no epiphanies or hopes. He had only the divide between his father and himself. He wrote the glyphs for Olympus into the dirt. No one would look for a Gothikar in the city of Odyn. He spoke the words and left Eldius in a shimmer of the air.

17

Year of Olympus 550

Periander and his army were marching south on the double. On their left was the Blood Strait, waves lapping the shore below them. There were higher cliffs here than the ones at Dagger's Edge. On the right side was the towering side of a mountain. From here, the base was just a forest sloping upward, but above him he could see a rock cap, like a cloak around the shoulders of the mountain. There was snow and ice up there. Thankfully, there was none down where the army marched.

It was spring. The pine trees were quiet and still, something that seemed incredibly more ominous to Periander than the shedding leaves of Avernus during autumn. His feet were killing him, but he did not complain aloud. His horse had become so ill that his quartermaster had advised they put it down, so now he marched like his men. Mordus, Salantar, Captain Illus, and Captain Kaid strode around him.

He prayed Odyn and Theseus had received his messages.

The giants were coming. He had first known it two weeks earlier. Only a few of that week's scouts had returned alive. Some had returned as mangled as the one that had forewarned the Battle of Dagger's Edge. Periander could not understand why Trion would send the scouts ahead like that. Sending scouts—alive or dead—to your enemy let him know you were coming.

It was not a strategic tactic, but an effective one; Periander glanced at the grim faces around him, his friends and his subordinates. Whenever a scout returned with his tongue cut out, a defeat followed. They had lost Oban Ford, they had lost Dagger's Edge, they had lost half of the Cerden Mountains, and they had lost Edessa. Whenever they lost a scout to Trion, he traded it for their lands and their lives.

Enough, Periander said. *We* must *win a battle.* If they lost the war and Periander could not kill Trion to teach the Triumvirate that traitors would not be tolerated, he must at least win a battle to teach them that betrayal would at least cost the treasonous. He knew it had cost Trion. *You took peace from me, and I took your family from you! Glyphs, I will take all of your life from you before I am done.*

This time he did not stop his thoughts from wandering toward Ivos. The true traitor had no life left to take, only a beating heart to stop. *You took Trion's world away from him before I even could, didn't you, my old enemy?* Syril Ivos, this man's forefather had been one of the founding Princes of the Triumvirate. *You have sunken far, earth-spawn. And I will exact your predecessor's vengeance on you.*

If you survive, another voice told him. *If you survive today.*

"A scout," Mordus said. "Alive." His friend's relief was an illustration on his face. He sighed heavily, and his step picked up.

Periander followed his arm. There was a man on a horse trotting down the slope ahead of him. The land sloped up into a mountain that sat directly in their path, rising from the Strait up to its peak without a friendly slope. On the right side of Periander's view was a wider slope, leading around the inland shoulder of the mountain. The forest here was more scattered, affording him a better view of the approaching scout.

"Prince Gothikar, Prince Gothikar!" the man called as he approached. "An army flying Odyn's banners is a few hours south, travelling toward the Strait!"

"Thank the Maker," Periander breathed along with his Captains. His message had reached Odyn. "Is Weveld with him?"

"I did not speak to anyone, save their scouts, sir," the man said.

"Burning fool," Illus said. Periander did not join his voice to the reprimand.

"Should we hold here?" Mordus asked.

"Let's climb this ridge," Periander said. "Then we can judge if this stretch is best or the next."

His captains nodded like it was their idea and they set off. Under Illus's direction, the scout rode off again to examine the woodland ahead.

They're terrified, Periander realized. *We are losing the war, and they are having the human reaction. Why am I not?* Periander felt little fear; he only felt anger. When their first thought was distress, his was vengeance. Their first thought was flight, his was murder. *Trion, Ivos, the tribal chiefs!* He unconsciously gripped the hilt of his sword. He was ready.

They climbed out of the valley and into the mountains. The afternoon was approaching, and the shadows of the peaks around them were drawing shorter. The day was heating up, and Periander started to break a light sweat as he climbed. Some of the men were eating; they knew there might be no pause for lunch today.

They reached a bit of a clearing that sloped upward. The dirt was rough; big clumps the size of Periander's head dotted the hill, though they were all grown over with moss and grass.

"Tell the men to stop here and eat. They will probably fight this afternoon, so do not eat enough to make yourself sick," Periander said. "Pass the order. Then we're going climbing."

It only took a few minutes for Illus's orders to spread far enough down the line. Even after half an hour, some of the army was still climbing the earlier ridge. The Gothikar army was several thousand men strong. As they spread across the field and the fringing woodland, Periander called his comrades to him and began his ascent.

A few hundred feet above him, the forest ended. From there, he would be able to see both sides of the mountain, the lowland to the southeast and the ground they had already covered to the northwest.

Mordus, Salantar and his two primary captains accompanied him. They hiked across the grass and moss until they reached the forest again, and then climbed using trees where it helped. Periander scraped himself more than once by peeling the flimsy pine bark away and fumbling with sharp branches to avoid losing his footing. Mordus found himself on his knees more than once.

At last they emerged from the short forest and climbed above the foliage. The ground was all moss and shrubs now and rock. It was uncomfortable footing, so Periander led them a few moments south to a flat, rock ridge.

From here, he could see clear to the valley floor a mile below them.

"It looks uneven," Kaid said. "There's a lot of rocky hills and burrows down there, I'd gamble."

Periander nodded. "The last valley was smoother. Would that work in our favour?"

"Against giants?" Salantar asked. He had yet to cross blades with the mountain men and knew them only from hearsay. "I hack at their head, not shins."

"Good point," Illus said.

Mordus grunted. "As frustrating as uneven ground is to fight on, it may work to our advantage."

Periander nodded. "Very well, we will hold our ground there. But where should Odyn enter the fight? It might serve us well to harass the giants from two sides."

"That pass is wide enough," Salantar said.

Kaid nodded. "He'll need to field a lot of men in wide ranks to hit the mountain men hard enough."

"Salantar," Periander said, "You're the only one here who does not have men to command when the battle starts. You're also the only one I think could sway Odyn's mind should he decided to deploy his own strategy."

"I'm to be errand boy to the Princes?" Salantar said. He tugged at his beard, still looking toward the pass that he had indicated.

"I could always have you thrown into an arena as a prisoner."

Salantar turned and looked at him for a minute. They held one another's eyes and grim expressions as their companions gripped their weapons in caution. At last, Salantar laughed and said, "Glyphs, you would have been chief of our ring had you been there. Much better than I."

Periander wasn't sure about that, but he was glad the moment had passed. Salantar started down the slope. "I can hear the drums now," he called a minute later, pausing. Periander could hear them too. "You lot better still be standing when I get back." He turned his back and continued down the hill. If Odyn's army was still a couple hours distant, the gladiator would need to make good time. Periander found himself praying again.

Over the next hour, the sound of drums grew gradually closer. Periander had a few soldiers stand on the ledge and return to him when the enemy was spotted. They would come striding across the ground that Periander's army had already covered.

He picked his way down the slope again. Ahead, through the woodland, he could see the dark green and black of his soldiers. They blended with the forest quite well, only the sunlight on their steel made them stand out.

Periander slipped in the mud, but grabbed a nearby spruce branch and slid to the left. He recovered his footing and massaged his hamstring. Mordus, hiking behind him, avoided the mud and eyed the Prince in concern. Periander found himself praying again. Salantar had to reach Odyn quickly, and Periander had to hold the next valley or else Odyn's men would be outmatched and unsuccessful.

And there was still no word from Theseus.

He reached the camp and barked out his orders. Most of the army would take up their positions below, in the rocky stretch of lowland beyond the valley. A handful would remain with him on the hill, waiting until the lookouts spotted the advancing horde.

The drums echoed louder, and Periander saw his men on the ridge, pointing. They waited a moment and then came clambering down toward Periander. It was an impatient quarter hour before they reached him.

"They're here, sir," the first panted as he reached Periander.

Periander patted his shoulder. "Good job."

"We only saw giants, no soldiers," the man said, removing his helmet and wiping sweat from his brow. "Lots of giants, sir."

Periander nodded. "We're going to hold the next valley, and smash the giants from the side when they think this hill is safe," he said. "Glyphs, time to make them hurt a bit."

The soldier smiled weakly, and joined his fellow a few feet away. Periander glanced at Mordus and said, "Let's go."

"Listen up, you lot," the Captain called. "Time to go. On the double down the hill!" The forty or fifty soldiers that remained followed Periander and Mordus down the slope. This side of the hill was even more barren than the other side. There were short cliffs of brown rock running the height of it. They were forced to divide the men up into lines and fit into each of the openings between ridges. No wander it took Periander's army so long to trickle off the hilltop.

"This will work to our advantage," he told Mordus. "The giants cannot bury us with their numbers."

They eventually reached the forest floor below. Kaid's men had drawn up some ranks of archers in spots that had a line against the side of the ridge. As the giants climbed down, some would fall before they could fight. Further back were lines of infantry that would charge the giants as they reached the forest. The rest of the army was scattered across the land. Some were hiding on top of rocky shelves so they could attack the unsuspecting heads of the mountain men while others were fortifying the trails between hills with spears and quickly assembled palisades.

Periander and Mordus positioned themselves with the infantry lines and waited mostly in silence. There were no words to say now, only minds to prepare. This was the calm before battle: not just the calm before a conflict of metal, but a struggle of mind. Even the animals of the forest had seemed to withdraw; all was quiet.

And then the mountain men appeared. The war drums were drowned out by their battle cries; foreign tongues that made even Periander tremble. He could not see the slope from this position, but he heard Kaid bellow, "Ready, aim, release!"

Bodies slid down the rocky hillside. Kaid shouted again and more appeared. Some stirred and were finished off by a select group of archers tasked with defending their lines.

Again, arrows flew through the trees.

"Look out!" Mordus shouted and shoved Periander aside. A boulder landed where they stood, along with a whole salvo that crushed infantry men in some places, archers in others. Their army was scattered enough that only a few men were taken out by the rocks.

"Maker," Periander breathed. "Let's hope they did not bring too many of those."

His archers released another volley of arrows and more giants came rolling down. Periander drew his sword with a rasp of steel. "Won't be long now," he said. It made him anxious not being able to see the enemy on the ridge.

One last chain of arrows flew, and then Kaid shouted, "Fall back to second positions!"

Periander shouted, "Infantry advance!" and strode forward. The archers nodded or bowed swiftly as they ran past. Periander was wearing chainmail this time; he had begun to favour its mobility against the giants while it still provided a safety net against any Trionus soldiers he faced. He wondered if Trion was here this time. Or Ivos.

The giants reached the bottom of the hill, stepping across the last trickling stream on legs as tall as Periander's chest. Their skin always seemed greyer than it should; there was now a wall of grey muscle slamming into Periander's frontlines.

Mordus and he reached them within seconds.

The first mountain man who Periander fought was a bit shorter than Trelkl had been, but still loomed several feet over his head. The creature wielded a simple metal pole, thick as Periander's forearms. He whirled it toward Periander, his deep-set eyes almost hidden under a furious brow. Periander threw himself to the ground. The rod blinked past overhead, and he shoved himself back to his feet with a heavy shove of his arms against the ground. As the giant brought his pole back toward his small opponent, Periander slashed upward with his sword. It shaved along the giant's right leg and nicked his torso just under his rib cage. The giant roared and lashed out recklessly with a downward hammering attack. Periander side-stepped and sprinted forward, his chainmail bouncing with every step, and stabbed his sword at the giant's lowered neck.

Dark blood, almost brown, gushed across the blade. Periander dodged backward as one of the tribesman's comrades charged forward with an axe. Giant by giant, lost step by lost step, Periander and his men fought to keep their enemy's advance slow. Some of Kaid's archers claimed ground on the small hills of this valley and pelted the giants with arrows when their line of sight did not put other humans at risk. Some of Periander's men fought with spears, taking on the giants in a small ring of antagonizing thrusts. Others fought like Periander and Mordus did, ducking and weaving as they could.

Regardless of how the men fought, it made it impossible to

hold a steady line. Periander's strategy books told of battles fought with men shoulder-to-shoulder in ranks, shoving forward while the men in front did the killing with little more than twitches of their pikes.

The giants could not be fought this way, for their strength could easily break shields and thus shatter ranks. Instead, the Imperial armies fought them in a dance, slowly falling back but killing hundreds nonetheless.

At some point, while Periander fought a one-armed brute hours after the battle had begun, a cry went up from the ridge they had given the tribesmen. The warriors on the ground began to advance more slowly; some turned back. Once Periander had finished off this war-scarred giant, he paused to listen.

There were war horns amidst the drums. He only heard the sound once or twice between the roar of dying giants and the clanging of metal. The air had started to smell like death: stale, nauseating, and bloody.

"Prince Odyn has come!" Periander shouted. "Fight hard, men, we'll win this!"

His men felt bolstered by the thought of victory. None of them had fought in proper battles outside of this war, and none of the battles in this war had ended well yet. They fought harder. Periander saw a man jump off a small rocky ridge and stab his sword into a giant's back, riding the unfortunate warrior until he fell.

The giants began to fall back.

Periander breathed deeply as he saw the feet and backs of giants instead of their weapons and angry faces. He smiled to Mordus, who was wiping black blood away from his eyes. "We've done it," he said. They charged after the giants, killing a few that turned to protect their tribesmens' flank.

Before they even reached the mountain ridge they had paused on earlier, arrows began falling from *above* and killing the fleeing giants as they climbed. Uncertain what to do, the creatures became divided. Some tried to climb, some ran toward the straight, and some stood to fight Periander's advancing army. All of them fell before Periander could even join the fighting.

"We've won it!" he shouted. "The giants may hold Dagger's Edge, but we've won the Strait!"

His men cheered, clasping hands with their comrades and

throwing their helmets down. Even Mordus raised his hands with a delighted shout and ran his hands through his sweaty, brown curtain of hair.

Salantar met Periander on the middle of the ridge. They embraced with a pat on the shoulder of the former. "Good job, man!" Periander said. "You have won this battle for us!"

"It was your call," the gladiator returned. He was drenched in sweat himself. He must have run to Odyn in order to divert the Olympian army in time. Periander looked up toward the top of the ridge: the sun was on that angle now and obscured the view, but he could see the banners of Olympus up there, the empty, red circle on grey with lines of red around it like the sun.

They reached the top of the ridge together and found a grinning Odyn there to greet them. His grey tabard was soaked with dark blood while his red cape made any on it invisible. He was sheathing his sword as he walked toward them. His beard was well-trimmed by comparison. "When your man here started giving me orders, I thought to have his hide," he told Periander, "but then he threatened to teach me the proper chain of command by drawing his sword *in my tent!*"

Periander stared at Salantar who was only smiling. "You did *what!*"

Odyn burst out laughing and held his arm out, folded at the elbow, for Periander. When he clasped it, the young man said, "Glyphs, I am glad he did. We have won a great victory today!"

Periander grinned and swatted Salantar's arm. "Not all nobility will treat you as we do," he warned his friend. He glanced back at Odyn who was still fidgeting with his sword. "I would not call it a *great* victory. These were not all the giants. But it was *a* victory."

Odyn grunted. "Bah," he said, turning toward his men. The ridge was decorated with giant corpses, some still crawling or moaning while the red-garbed soldiers of Odyn's army spread across the area. "Any victory is great victory for us, my friend."

"Sir!" someone shouted. Both Odyn and Periander turned, uncertain who was addressing whom.

A man appeared up the hill, climbing the last few steps as Odyn and Periander waited in confusion. The man was wearing teal: the colour of House Theseus. *Did Theseus arrive?* he wondered. The fighting was done.

"We must move at once, my Princes," the messenger mumbled as he reached them. "There are more giants, many more."

"Explain yourself!" Odyn spat.

"Where did you come from?" Periander asked.

The messenger managed a weak bow as he came to a stop. "The Blood Strait, sir. Theseus has arrived with enough ships to ferry your men to the other side. He has arrayed his men to build siege lines a day south of here to slow their advance again. He said that your victory here will give them further delay and gives you his congratulations."

"We have to fall back?" Salantar asked, looking incredibly winded once more.

The messenger nodded. "This battle was a trap, sirs. The bulk of their army will be here in an hour."

"Maker burn them," Odyn growled. "Captains!" He strode away to give his men the foul news.

"What now, Periander?" Salantar put his hand on Periander's shoulder to shake him from his daze.

The sun was starting to sink: fighting in the night would be difficult in this terrain. They had to fall back. Periander spat to one side and shook off Salantar's grip. "One day we'll win a real victory," he said. "One day."

18

Year of Olympus 573

Odyn was one power-hungry earth-spawn. As the eleventh of his name, the Prince of Olympus had nearly a dozen shadows to try to distinguish his legacy from. His father had tried as a warrior. He had won tournaments regularly, hunted the Buccaneer's Navy with a fury after their first appearance. When the legendary Akheron Gothikar had left the world, Odyn X had caught the culprits. And, as the West rose with Trion, he had not hesitated to ride forth to war, despite his age. Even the tenth Odyn fell short in comparison to the first. Tiberon Odyn had built the Triumvirate from scratch. He had conquered a dozen kingdoms and convinced all the others to join his new age of peace. If anyone were a great man, Artemys thought, Tiberon Odyn was.

Odyn XI was not. And, likely, he never would be. He spent his days hiding from the rotting city he ran. Even before their present age of unrest, Olympus had festered under his rule. But oh, he craved greatness.

Artemys's connections in the court were weak when he first arrived in Olympus. He had one guaranteed foot in that door: Master Rysarius would still answer his requests, even with Artemys's relationship to Kerres stretched thin. From that connection, he made more. First, a ring. Gifts were the key. Artemys spent a small fortune on purchasing a ring of great value. Upon it, he laid the glyphs he had written upon Korbios.

Now, Artemys could hear things that Odyn said, even from the low end bar where he sat. He had learned, in the weeks since the "Meet" of Eldius, that Odyn ran a vast network of spies across the realm. He had an ear in the court of every major city, even Tarroth, the self-proclaimed free city on the Valharyn Coast. It was like Odyn was just waiting for one of them to give him they key to a conquest, whether it be economic, simple information or political. Judging from the Prince's regular bouts of sparring, even a military conquest was not out of the question.

Artemys had long since learned that patience, like Odyn's spy game, brought about no change to status or power. Only frustration. He stared into the ale he drank. Only frustration.

But Odyn's thirst for power would be useful.

"Can I get you anything else?" the barmaid asked, smiling at him.

Thoughts interrupted, Artemys stuttered a moment and then said, "No." He immediately wondered if he could get something from her that she wouldn't be able to grab from under the bar. He was lonely. He had not seen Kerres for most of the year, since their fight, though she also had come to reside in Olympus.

He had also kept his distance from his family. His father and brother were unaware of his location. He had grown a beard to conceal his identity from anyone who might recognize the absent son of Avernus. He could not face them. Pyrsius had not trusted magic since Artemys had burned the slaver on the Avernan Chase. Then, he had watched a trio of magicians tear an angry mob apart with fire. Likely, he was glad of Artemys's absence.

Periander... Artemys could not face. Not after they had agreed to work together. Not after the riot.

Artemys finished his drink and walked out into the street. He was more careful now. No more causing fights. Simple justice was his game now. He walked the city and watched for the animals he knew lived behind some men's faces. When he found them, he tracked them and killed them once they were alone. Already, the guards were abuzz with word of criminals falling by the dime.

It made Artemys stand a bit taller. He was actually making a change for good now. He still bore weight on his shoulders: he had now killed seven men and two women.

Today he spotted a thief, a young woman in the crowd who darted between market stalls and came away with full pockets.

He followed her throughout the district, careful not to veer too close. Eventually she turned south, away from the docks.

As he followed her up the gradual slope toward the wealthier districts, he wondered if she planned to steal from one of the larger estates. The only things in this direction were mansions and the Palace of Olympus rising above the city.

As they neared the small wall that divided these lower end buildings from the estates, she doubled back, quicker than he had thought, and passed him. She was close enough to touch. She had short brown hair, bright eyes, and a small mouth. She winked at him as she passed.

When he dared to turn after her again, she was gone. He spent the next few moments searching the busy street for her. He thought he saw her sitting beside an older woman riding a horse-drawn cart, but only the woman was there when he got close enough to get a second look. How could she so brilliantly vanish? For a thief like her, he meant only to give her a scare, a warning to change. Then he would watch with magic and see if she did.

He had done this with two of those he had executed, and another one that had actually stopped selling illicit potions in the city after Artemys's threat and growing reputation convinced him.

But where had this thief gone?

At last he spotted her, ducking from a cluster of knitting women into an alleyway. *Perfect,* he thought, and hurried after her.

The alleyway led further from the street than he thought. It opened into a wider courtyard with a grated sewer entrance in the middle. She was walking toward it. The traditional flat rooftops of the surrounding buildings were all abandoned, thankfully. She had chosen the perfect spot for him to confront her.

"Wait," he said.

She spun, but the light seemed to glimmer in an odd way, and it was no longer the thief.

Instead, Hevarus stood in the space before Artemys. "Artemys. I knew you would not see through this ploy."

"Hev? What are you doing here?" Artemys blurted. He quickly scoured his glyph-sight for the actual thief and was relieved to find she was not an entire delusion, but had actually sidestepped him in the crowd. "Why would you impersonate that thief?"

Hevarus was still wearing the robes of the Disciples. "I've been sent to stop you Artemys. You have lost control of yourself."

"I have done nothing of the kind."

"The riot in Edessa was the last straw. We have been looking for you since."

"Looking for me?" Artemys questioned. "Glyphs, Hevarus. You and your Disciples are rotting by the day. Would you like me to send you back to Attarax? Or would you prefer to *conserve magic energy* and all that foolishness and hike back?"

"If I am returning to Attarax, it is with you."

"What if I resist?"

"Dead or alive," Hevarus said. "You are a danger to the peace, and to both the Orders you are a part of. Weveld is done offering you chances to reconsider. Surrender to me, now." His face was calm, collected. This was a much different Hevarus than Artemys had known. This was a true Disciple, or perhaps a Zealot.

"You will have to take my body, then," Artemys said, and turned his back on the fool.

To his surprise, Hevarus attacked him. A wind spell yanked him backward into Hevarus's hands. With Artemys back still facing the other magician, it was easy for Hevarus to grab his arms and force them behind his back.

Artemys shoved his legs against the ground and threw them both at the sewage well. Hevarus cried out as they slammed against the rock. Artemys rolled away from him and snatched a handful of glyphs from his pouch. The first he used at random, something to distract his opponent. A blast of lightning shot from his hand toward the Disciple, but it was snatched away by the metal grate.

Hevarus released another torrent of air toward Artemys. This time, he was ready. The spell yanked him toward his old friend, and Artemys lashed out with his knife.

Caught off guard, Hevarus tried and failed to avoid Artemys's blade. It grazed his shoulder and knocked the other magician backward.

Artemys quickly snapped another token. This time, a cloud of dust appeared between them, thick enough to obscure them both. Artemys stepped backward and began writing a series of glyphs on the ground, a spell more complex than his tokens.

A blast of fire shot through the cloud, several feet above Artemys's kneeling back. *Exactly as planned,* Artemys breathed, hurrying to complete his spell. Hevarus charged through the dust toward him, but Artemys was ready, raising his hand and breathing a line of ancient words beneath his breath. He stretched his hand toward Hevarus and watched as the air in front of it turned to stone. The effect spread out from him in a cone until it reached the building's wall behind his opponent, turning all the air to rock.

Hevarus would not be harmed by it, but would be trapped by it.

To his shock, the huge stone shape became water and splashed down. Hevarus's knee caught Artemys in his gut and knocked him backward. Keeping a clutch around Artemys's neck, the Disciple shoved him down to the soaked cobblestoned and then reached for his belt.

Artemys watched him try to unstring a dagger's sheath from the corner of one eye. He broke his second last token. A length of ice appeared in his hand, dwindling to a fearsome point at its tip. Braced against the ground, Artemys had to stab it blindly backward. He got lucky again. Hevarus grunted and stumbled away from him.

Reclaiming his footing, Artemys scooped his own knife from the pool of water beneath them and strode toward his opponent.

Hevarus yanked a length of icicle from high on his left shoulder, blood dripping from its point. Artemys charged at him with the knife, but Hevarus swung his arm with the same piece of ice held at an angle to impale.

Artemys had to abandon his knife stab and instead threw his shoulder into Hevarus's midsection. They both tumbled backward again, in a pile.

Hevarus must have broken another token, for something smashed Artemys in the side hard enough to send him into the air. He slammed against the sewer entrance, hard. Lights flashed across his vision. He had not trained against a magician in so long. He had forgotten that winding an enemy did not stop his spells.

"Don't make me hurt you worse," Hevarus said. His voice was rough. He was feeling his wound and bore an emotional pain too. They had been friends.

Artemys had lost his final token somewhere. He had dropped it. Still reeling from Hevarus's last spell, he reached out for his knife. He had lost it again.

Hevarus grabbed him by the collar, and shoved him back across the sewer grate. They locked eyes. Both of them were wincing from pain and daunted by the identity of their opposition.

"I—" Artemys said, smashing his only free hand into Hevarus's shoulder as his friend cried out with pain, "—am *very* tired of your Discipleship."

Hevarus fell back a step, and Artemys flung his arm around for the same target, this time knocking his friend down to his knees. Hevarus shouted in pain at that blow. He lowered himself further to begin writing glyphs, but Artemys lashed out with his boot. He pressed down until Hevarus screamed at the breaking of his fingers.

Artemys knelt too, and drew Hevarus's own dagger from its sheath where his opponent had fumbled with it earlier. "I am *very* tired of Weveld..."

"You won't kill me," Hevarus said. "You've sunken to murder, but you will not sink any lower. You still have good in you."

"Everything I do is for good," Artemys said. "I am stopping monsters!"

"You are the monster," Hevarus gasped, cradling his hand. Blood was spreading from his shoulder wound. "You are the..."

"...and," Artemys continued, "I am growing tired of this *fight*." Tired of fighting Hevarus and tired of fighting the Disciples.

He stabbed Hevarus in the chest with the dagger and stood up. His friend toppled forward, his face falling to the cobblestones and blood spreading into the pool of water around them.

Artemys sank wearily back against the edge of the well.

"Time to do something about the 'Prime meddler,'" he

decided. "I'm coming for you, Weveld."

He teleported with Hevarus's body back to his small inn chamber. The corpse threatened to set his stomach off like his first kills had, but he fought it. Either way, it set him on edge. The eyes he had closed still felt open, the wounds he had made stared at him just as sharply. He changed into clean clothes and quickly summoned the Great Glyph before his eyes.

Tired as he was, the sheer amount of information teetered and tried to bury him. He quickly fought for control, his head pounding as he sensed every glyph everywhere: every piece of wood in the walls around him, each torch flickering outside, each cobblestone in the city, every drop of water in the ocean...

Weveld, he thought. The vast amount of glyphs vanished out of his mind as his focus narrowed to the School of Delfie. There were glyphs for trees, glyphs for leaves, glyphs for buildings, and glyphs for people. There, the glyphs that represented Weveld walked toward the Council Chamber of the Order of Magic. Some of the other Master Magicians were already there, and others were moving across the campus toward the room.

Artemys let the Great Glyph fade from his mind. There was his inn room again, wide enough for him to stretch his arms and long enough for him to pace one or two steps. The bed was about the most uncomfortable thing he had ever touched. But this inn, the Croaking Palm, afforded him indiscriminateness. For him that was more valuable than comfort.

There was a small table, a single chair in the corner opposite the bed, and a body on the floor in between.

Weveld thinks he can hide from this, does he? That Council Chamber was the most secure place in the world once it was filled of the Order's greatest wizards. *But Weveld does not realize what security is. Unification.* Weveld would never have that security, not as the head of two organizations, not as a connoisseur of information.

Artemys dragged Hevarus's body back over his shoulder and wrote another spell, this one taking him to the Known Location for the School of Delfie. He appeared on the wide stone disc in the campus's courtyard and strode purposefully toward the Hall building. Caius stood guard again, hands clasped behind his dull orange robe. He was good at his job: dedicated, dangerous, but friendly for the many gusts that arrived and meant no harm.

He stared at Artemys. He had seen many strange things here, but this might be the strangest. Artemys did not pose any open threat though, so he asked, "Maker, a body? Where are you taking it?"

Artemys kept walking, and said over his shoulder, "The Council Chamber." The Sentinel of Delfie did not stop him.

The Chamber occupied most of the Hall's third floor. A spiral staircase led up to there from both corners of the building, and a corridor ran parallel to the chamber, connecting both stairwells. Artemys walked half the length of the hallway to the heavy wooden doors. This room was not guarded, for any that could possible defend it would be weak in comparison to those that occupied the chamber. Artemys had heard a saying from the Arena in Edessa: *no need to guard the gladiators.*

The doors were decorated with the engraving of a giant oak, trunk along the edge of each door, where they met in the middle. Artemys paused for a breath; the body was heavy, and he had walked a lot today.

Then he split the oak carving and entered the coliseum.

The Master Magicians of the Order sat in a circle of chairs, almost twenty of them. They were evenly spaced, save a wider aisle for entrance from the Chamber's door. There was a broad area in the middle where speakers could hold the audience, and Artemys certain held their eyes as he strode boldly into their midst. He met Weveld's horrified eyes, though the man wore a mask of confusion to mimic his lackeys. He had trimmed his long white beard to give himself a sharper look, though his age showed more than ever. The others stirred in surprise at his arrival; they stood, leaned forward or stiffened their posture in his peripherals.

He reached the middle of their circle and let Hev's body drop to the floor with a thud.

"What is the meaning of this intrusion?" the woman on Weveld's right snapped. "Prince Gothikar, you have no position at this meeting, and... what is this?"

"Mistress Aella," Artemys said, finally breaking Weveld's glare. "I am here to show you the traitor in your midst." Weveld's mask almost slid from his control.

"Traitor?" Weveld asked, mustering his facade. "Who would betray us? And who would they betray us to?" His tone summoned a chuckle from one or two of the other Masters. Artemys could see his white knuckles digging fingertips into the wooden armrests of his wooden chair.

"Master Magicians," Artemys said, turned around to meet each of their gazes. "I apologize for my interruption, but I hope to show you all how necessary it was. Let me begin my explanation. I was assaulted in the streets of Olympus by this man," he knelt to the body. "I survived. I defeated my attacker."

He rolled Hevarus onto his back as they reacted to the beginning of his story.

"How is this relevant to us?" Aella asked. She was one of the strongest magicians to arise since the Trionus War. Her husband and daughter had been murdered during the Sack of Edessa; she had sought magic as a means of defending herself and others who had lost what she had. Her success had been unprecedented for one that began so much later than childhood. More importantly, she could sway this Council as much as Weveld could.

"I invite any of you who wish it to scry this body. Follow his life before I took it. You will learn that this young man did not attack me on his own instruction, but under the guidance of another. In truth, I was assaulted in the streets of Olympus by... Crown Magician Weveld," he declared. Weveld shot to his feet amidst a chorus of shock and disbelief from all around the Chamber. Slowly, Weveld sank back down to his seat. Those eyes were red-hot coals, burning hotter and hotter. Ice cold, Artemys met that fury. "I survived. I *will* defeat my attacker."

"That is a heavy accusation, Artemys," Aella murmured. "Especially for one whose ties to this place and Weveld have always been strained."

Artemys laughed. "Mistress, and my fellow magicians," he nodded to his old Master Kaen, the wizard who had trained him until he realized Artemys knew magic better than he. "There is nothing that I can do or say that will convince you of the truth. However, you each hold the power to find the truth regardless."

Aella leaned forward. Her short, grey hair was knotted behind her head with a golden pin. "Weveld, you have been silent. What is your reply to this?"

Weveld smiled, and glanced around the room. "This is foolishness. Artemys has always been a sinking ship to us. He showed great potential in his youth, but has drifted further and further from us. This attempt at attention is unbefitting for a Prince's son, Artemys. Please, leave us."

"I seek no attention. I have not said or done anything yet that does. Please, Masters, use a scrying spell. See for yourself who this... tragedy at my feet was."

Aella glanced across the room. "Vardin and Parsis," the respective magicians rose: the Master of Information and the Master of the Archive. None could doubt their abilities of siphoning fact from fiction. Aella took to her feet and stepped toward Artemys. "Step back. Three of us will scry."

"Nonsense," Weveld snapped. "Enough of this mischief!"

Aella turned back toward him. "Crown Magician, it is you who insisted on scrying the members of your Council before accepting them. Your own creed instructs to learn everything, no matter the risk. You have nothing to fear if Artemys's claims are nothing more than 'mischief.'" With that, she turned her back on him and knelt to Hevarus's body.

Artemys had stepped back as instructed, allowing all three Masters who came forward to kneel. Parsis finished his spell first, with Vardin and Aella following shortly. The Order had long possessed the ability to conjure visions that followed a target glyph as it interacted with others. It was nothing compared to Artemys's Great Glyph ability, which allowed him to see *every* glyph and control the vision with a thought.

The room was silent. Stiflingly silent. Weveld's glare shouted murder at Artemys, while he met it with calculated satisfaction. He had let Weveld maintain control of this Order for too long. *You are a taint on magic, a* leech. *I do not care if a little salt hurts; it is time for you to go.*

Aella stood. "All that I have seen is a distant village in the mountains. This boy was just a villager there, then travelled by wagon to Olympus. There is nothing here..." She met Artemys's eyes with a look of scorn. "This interruption is completely unwarranted—"

"Good," Weveld muttered. "Get out of here, Art—"

"Go back further," Artemys interrupted. Parsis and Vardin were still scrying. "How would some villager from a mountain village learn magic to fight *me?*"

Aella frowned and rejoined the others in searching Hevarus's past to the stuttered objections of Weveld. As Artemys's point sunk in, the other Masters shifted in their seats uneasily. The entire issue was horribly uncomfortable for them.

This time, a longer moment passed. Parsis blurted, "This young man was here!" and returned to his spell. Two magicians nearby stood, tokens in hand.

Weveld took to his feet again, striding forward to interrupt Aella with a hand and some argument. He got about halfway when she, rising from the ground, grabbed him by the robe and drove him backward into his chair. "What is the meaning of this?" she snapped. "Artemys seems to be speaking true! This man was not just in a village and Olympus, but he visited you in your quarters here in Delfie! And you visited him in that village!"

Weveld was flushed red, not just from anger anymore. "He was a strong magician! I was considering taking a new apprentice or at least inviting him to the School!"

"And he just happens to attack Artemys, without ever meeting him?" Aella and the others would have to look a lot further back before they could see any interactions between Hevarus and Artemys.

"How should I know?" Weveld retorted. "This is madness!"

"That village," Vardin began. He had dark brown hair, almost black, and a thick moustache. He looked like a Westerner, and was big enough to have some giant's blood in him. "It is almost in the Southern Waste! How did you stumble upon it?"

They all waited for Weveld's reply, but he only gave a stutter.

Parsis walked toward Weveld and traced an invisible glyph on the arm of his robe. He whispered the words under his breath and scried *Weveld*. "How do you vanish from my sight in that village? Scrying shows you anywhere, but you vanish from the world there."

"Should we go there?" someone else suggested. "We should send riders!"

"It would take weeks," another argued.

Artemys cleared his throat. "That village does not matter," he said. He received a surprised glance from Weveld, one that read "you do not want to destroy the village? the Disciples?" "Trust me, Masters, it is just a hiding spot. It poses no threat. Weveld, however, does."

Aella turned her head back from Artemys to meet Weveld's gaze. "Answer our questions, Crown Magician. Answer, or face judgement."

Weveld visibly trembled. "I— It—" There was a drawn out silence. "You have heard of the Disciples of Andrakaz, correct?"

That brought a nod and a cringe from around the room. To them, the Disciples were a cult that had been hunted to extinction for their actions in the Trionus War.

Weveld nodded. "I am a member of their group, for they treat magic as their central goal. They provide a service to it, without them—"

The room burst with outrage as the Masters all rose to their feet, shouting at their leader. Aella yanked him up amidst the commotion and forced both his arms behind his back. "Why, Weveld, why?" she asked. Artemys saw her writing a spell that would bind his hands there with the air itself. "How long?"

"The whole time," Weveld said. "We are good, we do good..."

"He doesn't even count himself one of us," someone said.

"Maker!" Aella exclaimed. "You have led us astray, Weveld. You are Crown Magician no longer!"

"No!" Weveld shrieked, struggled against the ropes Aella had tied around him. "Listen to me, please!"

Artemys said, "There is nothing to hear."

"*He* is the one leading you astray!" Weveld said, thrusting his head toward Artemys. "I will not have my *legacy* forgotten! Will you really execute the Hero of Galinor's Crossing?"

Aella's shoulders were slumped. "I held you as a hero, as a brother, and as a man. You are none of these things." She paused, as the room hung on her words, "You would rather hide in the shadows than face the light. You would treat us all as strings, and only save us for your own use."

"But I still turned the tide of battle. I still helped the Triumvirate through the war," Weveld argued. "Who cares where my allegiances lie?"

Aella spat to one side. "For your victories in battle, I will postpone your demise. Instead, you are banished from the lands of Triumvirate. On the authority of this Council, you will never return to our Dominion, and will suffer the ultimate price should you ever be caught."

Weveld exhaled with relief, but still trembled and stuttered, "P-Plea—"

Aella raised her hand. "Go live out your final days on the hills of your mountain village, old man. May the Maker have mercy on you. You will need it when you face him."

Vardin and another younger Master led Weveld from the room with force. They would take him as far as the Known Location, so he could teleport closer to his destination. What a sight it would be for Caius!

As Aella returned to her seat beside the now empty Crown Magician's place, Artemys heard her mutter, "What a waste..."

The room very slowly returned to a semblance of order. Parsis and another Master moved Hevarus's body away as silence began to encompass the Chamber.

Artemys broke it. This thought had seized him in the moment, and he let his mind follow it. "Fellows and Masters, you need leadership now. You need a strong Crown Magician to repair Weveld's damage. Someone who will not hesitate to undo things he has done, to protect us and ours. More importantly, you will need someone who is... *powerful*. Who knows what trials our Order will face now. We have enemies again. The last time we had enemies, our own leader knew them and could keep a void between us. This time, we have *true* enemies. *I* will protect us. *I* am strong enough, and brave enough. *I* will lead us."

The room erupted into a second round of chaos. This time it was surprise, instead of anger and betrayal. Artemys was not even a Master of the Order! How could he even suggest such a preposterous idea?

Artemys forced himself taller. "I demand the Trials of the Crown Magician!"

19

Year of Olympus 551

A line of Everwood trees grew along the Royal Walk of Galinor. Periander had always been amazed by the massive trunks. Who planted them there was a mystery from the dawn of the Age; no one knew where Everwood was from, or how to plant it. The trees had large branches like an oak tree, but the leaves turned the colour of gold this time of year and fell around Periander's escort as they moved, like little floating stars in the night.

They were called Everwood because no one knew how to cut them. Periander had heard a story about Odyn's predecessor, the gruff man who had won the Battle of Trionus City with him. When that Odyn had been told it was impossible to cut the wood, he had found a moon-blade axe bigger than he was and gave one of the trees all his might. Even that massive man had only broken his axe swinging at the tree and left no mark. In the foundational days of the Triumvirate, an explorer, Oban Hokar, had found a dead Everwood tree on the Galin River, in the World's Foundation. With great effort, carpenters were able to make a few items from the dead wood—once dead, Everwood appeared to weaken. They crafted three statues: the Three Princes of their day. There was Valik Aristorn, Tiberon Odyn, and Syril Ivos. Then, they had made a table and a chair. All of these Everwood furnishings decorated the Imperial Council Chamber in the Tower ahead of Periander.

But these trees, looming above him, they could live forever as far as anyone knew.

A gleaming, golden leaf landed on Periander's shoulder. He brushed it aside and watched as it joined by others and settled on the ground. He was here in Galinor, but as he watched, he was back in Edessa and flakes of ash were settling on his shoulders and floating to the ground. Ash...

Anyone else would be astounded by the beauty of this, he thought. *But I only have horror left to me.* Something inside asked, *What about Cat?* but it was a quiet voice, and she was a distant thought.

"Sir," one of his guards said. "The road ahead is blocked by a wagon."

Periander followed the man's hand. There was a covered wagon ahead, set directly on the cobblestones of the road. "Well, perhaps we can lend a hand," he told his guardsmen.

One of the wagon's wheels was on the ground, not the axle. Someone was climbing out of the cart's bed with a wooden box under one arm. "Hello!" she called when Periander's escort came into view. "Evening to you, sirs. My wagon has lost a wheel."

"It is past curfew," a guard said.

"I know that, sir," the woman said, turning to them from the back of the wagon. She had frizzy, grey hair, but a youthful face. "I was on my way to an inn, sir."

"I understand," Periander said, frowning at his guards. "Perhaps my men can lend a hand."

The four of guards bowed and set to work, prodding into the woman's wooden box for tools while one man held the wheel up. The woman sighed, slouching her shoulders a bit. It took Periander a full minute to realize that she was not just relaxing her shoulders but reaching into the tattered brown cloak she wore.

Before he could react, she threw off the cloak to reveal tight black leather and metal plates in select spots. She plunged a knife into the back of the guard's necks and turned on Periander before he could blink. A line of blood had splattered the wagon's cover and dripped from the knife she calmly gripped.

He stepped back quickly, grabbing at his belt for his offensive tokens.

She was smiling as she pranced toward him. She knocked off her wig; the assassin had a shaved head and a face just as smooth so she could become anyone. She gripped the base of her bloodied blade with a thumb and index finger and dragged the knife between them, smudging the thick blood and dripping it to the ground.

She lunged for him, and he broke the first spell token he could. Smoke exploded around him, obscuring her from view and him from her sights. He immediately ran to the left, toward the Everwood trees they had been walking beside. He drew his sword.

Who is this? he wondered. Not the woman. She was an assassin to the core, he knew. But who had sent them?

She came out of his fog and charged him with a scowl on her face. He threw up one hand and whispered, *"bor'sab irkono shokin ob."* As soon as the burst of air struck her, he was running forward with his sword. Her flight blew a hole in the cloud of smoke that was still dissipating near the wagon so he could follow where she landed.

She tumbled across the cobblestones and skidded to a halt against the still loose wagon wheel. Periander plunged his sword into her torso and twisted until she went still. He yanked it out and cleaned the blood off on the cloth covering the wagon.

He had not killed a woman with his own sword before. Now that he had, he realized it was just the same as killing a man.

He sheathed the blade and left the wagon at a slow jog. He would need to get to the Tower quickly and bring guards to secure this area. The leaves kept falling like golden ashes and the rock in Periander's stomach continued to sink. *Who wants me dead? Could Ivos have hired assassins even out in the mountains where he hides? Perhaps he hired them from Edessa.* Periander knew it was not Trion. Trion wanted to kill him personally, not send others to do it. Only Ivos was enough of a coward.

Periander paused for a breath of cold night air. He should have brought more men. He had a troop of a few hundred camped outside of the city, but had chosen to enter with only a handful.

He was halfway to the Tower's grounds. He could see the market district ahead, a few torches flickering amidst empty stalls. He pressed ahead: perhaps there would be guards in the market. *There must be!* He ran ahead, his wool tunic rubbing against his neck as he did. *Must I wear armour even in our own cities now?*

The guards in the market were dead. He found them collected in a red pile in the middle of the square and froze in his tracks. There were shadows on the fringes of the torchlight, moving toward him.

He drew his sword again and turned to look into his blind spots. This market was a wide area, with neat rows of counters and shelves where merchants could attract the commoners. Now it attracted a different customer.

There were four of them, men wearing black robes from neck down, arms concealed. These men did not disguise their faces. They were calm, he noticed, as they walked slowly toward him. Periander felt a wave of dread. He was outnumbered and could not expect any reinforcements: he was not expected at the tower for another half hour.

"Come on, then," he said. "Let's do this." He threw fire at the first man who dropped under it. Suddenly, they were all there, blades hissing at him. Periander blocked and parried and spun and dodged. He got a nick on his left arm, then his right. A blade cut his back, but he stepped forward before it could do him any danger.

He kicked one of the shadows when he knew he could and the man tumbled back, creating an opening. Periander dashed away, slashing down at the man he had knocked down. He was rewarded with a shout.

He hid behind a market stall and grabbed a spell token from his pouch. He did not look for a specific one, as long as it could distract his enemies. He glanced at the first one that came out into his palm. It would create a lot of noise and light, perhaps enough to attract guards. He heard footsteps nearby and snapped it.

A blast of invisible energy shot outward from around him and obliterated the wooden structure beside him with a bang. Two of the men were in a pile of wood while a third was rolling to his feet a few feet away. Periander yanked his knife from his belt—the opposite side than his tokens—and whipped it across the distance. It struck the man's upraised arms and danced away across the cobblestones.

Periander was there a moment later, slashing downward with his sword. The man raised his own smaller blade to block the blow while he spun his legs toward Periander. His own blade dug into his chest under the force of Periander's attack, but then his feet swiped Periander's out from under him.

He hit the cobblestones hard enough to wind himself and found an arching blade aimed for his chest. He rolled away. The assassin's knife punctured his left arm with a red-hot flare of pain, and Periander heard metal strike stone. Crying out from the pain, Periander stabbed blindly in the direction of the man and was rewarded with a grunt. The man's hand released the knife in Periander's forearm.

The other two assassins—covered in splinters—were charging at him. Periander was forced to release his sword. It was pinned in the body of the man he had just killed.

Periander grabbed the hilt of the assassin's knife and yanked as hard as he could. With a shriek drawn from his throat unwillingly, he yanked it free and stabbed upward as the first of his remaining enemies leapt at him. Having not accounted for Periander's attack, the man's curved knife cut too high and missed the Prince altogether.

Periander's weapon got the man in the stomach. The dead weight of a falling corpse took Periander to the ground quickly again and dazed him. He fought his way out from under the man's body, sucking in breath. There would be one more yet, the last assassin.

A strong arm grabbed his arm before Periander could make a stab. He felt something cold in his lower right side and lashed out with another kick. His attacker stumbled back, but stabbed again. This one caught Periander in the upper thigh, and he shouted in shock. The third stab, as the man continued to stumble back caught his shin and, hooked in the flesh, cut from bone to cold night air, and sprayed Periander's blood across the bodies on the ground and cobbles beneath.

Everything went white for a minute. When black returned: the black of the cloudy night sky, Periander found a man looking at him like a vicious mountain cat. The man's claw, his knife, was laid across Periander's throat.

There was something in Periander's hand. What was it?

"Prince Gothikar, I presume," the man said, pressing one

knee into the hole in Periander's side. Everything went white again.

It was a spell token in his hand, he realized. When had he grabbed it?

"Aristorn has its revenge," the man said.

Periander broke the spell token and the man was blasted away by fire.

Gasping, Periander propped himself up on his right elbow. The last man was flailing around, screaming and burning. The assassins were done. Periander sucked in breath. He had to analyze his injuries like a healer. His left arm was pierced through and through. His right leg had two wounds, one a deep stab, the other a slash to the bone. Above was the most worrying: judging from the amount of blood pooling around the wound, one of his kidneys had been caught.

He put his finger to the cobblestones and, around the central spell line, wrote the glyphs for healing there. Then he paused. He had more wounds than any time he had healed himself. He coughed and almost lost consciousness as he pulled himself back from the fit.

Self-healing had to drain all the energy from the caster. Periander scratched out the spell he had been writing.

Healing himself would kill him.

He knew what he had to do next. He couldn't walk; he would have to drag himself with his good arm and his good leg. *Just a moment,* he thought. *I just need to catch my breath before...* He cut the thought off like the lives of his enemies. *No. I need to fight now as hard as I was moments ago. This is the end if I don't.*

He clenched his teeth together and pushed his right elbow ahead of himself and then, with his leg, pushed himself after it. His leg wound sent tingles of fire up his leg. Agony. He ground his teeth and blinked past the tears.

He shoved forward with his elbow again, and then raised himself on it to move another half foot. He left a smudged trail of blood.

Aristorn has its revenge? This wasn't even about the war! Periander's father had convinced the Three Nobles of Avernus to elect him to be Prince instead of another of House Aristorn, when Prince Olles Aristorn had been killed by bandits. Thus, the

Princehood had passed to House Gothikar. No recognized Aristorns were left.

Periander laughed, but it made him weaker, and he had to stop. His vision was pulsing between light and dark as he shoved himself along the ground. "Maker," he breathed. "All this for the sins of my father?"

He tore off a strip of cloth from his bloody tunic and wrapped it around his leg. It was bleeding too much. Then he kept going. Inch by inch across the ground. He was a slug pulling itself through the autumn leaves. In his wake he left gold ashes and red blood.

Above, the stars kept turning across the night sky.

Catlin and his son had seemed such distant thoughts an hour ago. Now they were very close. As tangible as the rough cobblestones beneath his trembling hands. He slid his elbow forward and pulled his body after it.

"We would all die for the Dominion," Erykus had said, and Periander had agreed. *I must not die tonight,* Periander decided. *For this would not be a death for my land.*

His elbow began to bleed from the grinding of the ground beneath him. He started using his hand to grab at the cobblestones ahead. He got less leverage that way and had to move in smaller increments, but it was all he could manage. Glyphs, it hurt.

Would he truly die for his land? Periander paused and felt a twinge of irony. Like they had turned gold into ash, his thoughts had again twisted his world. He had decided to fight tonight, not to live and return to his family, but to die another day when it served the land better. *I so thoroughly accept that I* will *die for this Dominion, that I have forgone thoughts of life altogether.*

But tonight, no giant had tried to kill him. Only men. Not Trion's, not Ivos's. Some nobleman, lord, cousin, or attendant of a late Prince had tried to kill him. Not the *enemy*.

Tonight the Dominion had tried to kill him.

Would you truly die for this?

He stopped crawling. His side hurt, the side that was dragging along the ground. His shoulders ached from the pain that danced up his ribcage and into his skull. It was getting harder to see. Were there fewer torches? Or was there less world? He rolled off of his side and onto his back. Up above him, the trees swayed gently in the breeze and a golden leaf let go of its branch.

"I was going to die for what is right," he said aloud, though his voice was rough. He didn't care that it hurt to speak: he wanted these words to enter the world before he left it. "But that's not possible. There is no right, is there? You set the world in the heavens so you could send all that isn't right somewhere other than your heaven. You wanted it to kill us, so it wouldn't kill you."

There was something cold about what he said. He shivered. It was a sharper cold than the steel that had pierced him time and again. "Well, I may never see paradise, but I'm done with this hell," he told the night.

"Your son isn't," a voice said.

He wasn't sure if it was just a thought in his head or the shape of a man he thought he saw sitting nearby him. "Glyphs, no. Don't say—"

"He's just entering the world."

Periander curled his hands into fists until the fingernails hurt. "Don't give me a reason to stay," he pleaded.

There were no more words spoken. A minute later, Periander reached out and dug his claws into the cracks around a road stone. He pulled himself ahead again. And again. And again, until he got close enough to the Tower yard's gatehouse.

He shouted, "Help! Please!"

There was motion, guards with wide eyes approaching. "This is the Prince," someone said.

"Someone get a healer!" another shouted.

Periander lay all the way back again. *How many times is this going to happen?* he wanted to know. *They've beat me this time. They've beat who I am.*

. . .

It was dark when he awoke. He couldn't move. He was lying in a bed, and, though the blankets were not constricted around him, he could not move.

"You're awake," a voice said. It was an old voice. "Drink this." Firm hands lifted his shoulders and held the nozzle of a wineskin to Periander's lips. The contents tasted like a giant's sweat. It was thick and bitter, salty and sour.

"I don't know how much you'll remember from this entire ordeal. You're weaker than any living man I have seen," the old man said. "It will be a while before you have all your senses back, and a while longer before you can move functionally. Hold on, though. Everyone wants you to hold on."

Periander waited in the darkness for a while longer, wondering if the man would say more. Why couldn't he recognize the man? Was it his injuries, his inhibited senses?

"I had given up on the Triumvirate," the man said. "I had decided it was time for new... leadership. A new age. I'm not supposed to have wanted this: even the secrets that guide me direct me to hold fast to this government. But men like Verin Theseus and Odyn X. Men like your father..."

Again, silence.

"I had given up on *us*, and saw fit to bring about a new order. Trion is a bull and Ivos a serpent. But they are catalysts for a new era. Or they were to be," the man said. Periander had some of his vision back: the man had whitening brown hair and a thin, white beard. "But I'm hesitant once more. Here, drink some more. It will help your strength come back. You need to put a lot of meat back onto those bones."

Periander drank more.

"You convinced me. *You,* the son of a usurper, taught *me* there can still be honest strength in this land. You've taught me there is still fight in the Triumvirate," the old healer said. "You've given me hope, Periander. I hope you kill our enemies as fiercely as you fought for your life tonight."

The old man left him.

. . .

Periander sat in a wooden armchair and ate a bowl of stew. It had been a month since the attack on his life in the streets of their capital, but he was still little more than skin and bones. Cat sat next to him, holding his free hand while he shovelled meat and broth into his mouth. It was not food for a Prince. It was food for an ill man.

Periander sat in a hall somewhere in the Tower of the Throne. It was not a large room, but was comfortable. The rounded walls and high ceiling reminded him of the Imperial Council Chamber where the Three Princes were to meet when they were not in the field. There were three dining tables in the room, but the only ones in the room were the Prince and his wife.

"You can't stay here forever," Periander said between mouthfuls. "Avernus cannot function without one of us there. And I don't like Artemys being on his own all the time."

"You don't like it?" Cat asked.

"They'll elect someone else, Cat. My father had enemies and I have accomplished nothing compared to him," Periander said.

"That's not true—" she protested.

"They'll elect a new Prince, not a Gothikar, not—"

"Great Glyph, Peri!" she blurted, releasing his hand. "All you care about is your politics and your war!"

Periander put down his spoon. The stew was making him ill. He had overeaten, as instructed by his healers, but he hated the feeling. "Cat, you know that's not true. I told you that Artemys was the only—" This time he cut himself off, but the damage had already been done.

"It's all about Artemys, again," Cat said, and stood up. She stepped away, wringing her hands together. "Periander, you have a *wife!* Maybe I don't like *you* 'being on your own all the time!' Maybe I want to be the reason your fight for your life! Or maybe, I don't want you to fight for your life anymore! Maker, Peri, this is driving me mad!"

"Cat," he said, leaning toward her. "Please, I did not mean—"

"I have had enough of this! Tell Theseus he can fight the wars. Tell them you're done. You have to be done!"

"I want to be," he said. *I thought I decided I was done,* he pondered, *when I was dying on the cobblestones of my own capital!*

"You want to be?" Cat repeated. "You want to be!"

"I am not trying to fight the Triumvirate! I am not burning Edessa! I am not poisoning the Strait with blood! I am not an assassin in the night!" Periander shouted. He lowered his voice. "I am trying to finish this, that is what I am."

She spun toward him, her dishevelled hair falling in front

of one eye and her lips curling. "It can't be finished, Peri. *It can't be finished!*"

Periander flinched. He leaned back into his chair and delicately pushed the bowl of stew away from the edge. "What do you want, Cat?" he asked. Though she started to answer, he kept talking, drowning out her words. "You want a man, a coward, boy, who's going to hold your hand while the giants burn your home down? You want someone who's going to only raise his hand to fight when they come to rape you? I have seen war; I know war! If you want someone who doesn't, *go ahead.* Go back to Avernus or wherever you want, and find someone who only cares about you. You have my blessing."

She was staring at him with an expression he recognized from war: horror.

He took a breath. "I'm serious! You deserve someone who gives you everything! That's not me. It can't be me. I married the Triumvirate before I married you. I'm sorry. If you want someone else, I want you to want someone else. So go. Please."

She took a step backward. "I can't," she said, tears running down her face. "I don't know how to reply to that." She started to walk away.

Periander stood up. His chair fell over. His legs shook, and he almost fell with his seat. He leaned on the table, no more than flesh hanging from bones. He stepped toward her. It was as physically painful as clawing his way along the cobblestones. "Stop," he said.

She did, but did not turn to face him. Her hands were raised to her face, hidden from him by her hair.

"I'm sorry," he said, this time softly. He trembled from weakness and leaned against the table. "Don't go. I need you. I can't fight this war without you."

She turned back toward him. "Why?" she asked, wiping tear stains onto the light green and white dress she wore.

He almost fell forward and put his hand on the table to hold himself up. "I am not fighting for the Triumvirate; something I frequently forget. Sometimes it takes four assassins to make me remember that fact. I'm not fighting for the land. I'm fighting for you."

"Can you?" she asked. "Can you fight a war for the land out of selfishness?"

"It's all I have," he said. "You're all I have. You and Artemys."

She stepped toward him. "You are a stubborn earth-spawn," she said. "Taking all this to make you say that you need me too."

"No," he said, "not stubborn. I'm lost." His own tears were there, around the corners of his sight.

She crossed the room again, embracing him and helping him to his chair again. She righted it. "Well, I'm here with you. Just never tell me to leave you. Not like that."

Periander was quiet. There was a hole in him, one that had not healed with Weveld's spells or herbal brews. He knew he was out of causes. He had gone from fighting for what was right, to fighting for land and country, to fighting to kill Trion or Ivos. He knew he was on his last breath. He was fighting for family. But he had realized something else as he fought for his life in the Everwood fall. Each step down—each cause he lost—weakened him. Cat's plagued him. "Can you fight a war for the land out of selfishness?"

When he had reached the gatehouse on that dark night, he had cried out and pleaded for help. The Maker had given him none.

20

Year of Olympus 573

Chaos reigned in the Hall of the School. Aella and Parsis were arguing about Weveld's betrayal. Kaen, his white hair revealed with his red hood thrown back, and several others were deep in a debate about Artemys's command. Vardin and a few others were just shouting at Artemys directly. Only two magicians still retained their seats; all the other high-backed, oaken chairs were empty. The tall, decorated ceiling of the Chamber echoed with their reaction to Artemys. He ignored it all as he collected his thoughts.

"Order!" he bellowed, at last. The Master Magicians quieted. "Order. That is *what* we are. Is this not correct? We *are* the Order of Magic. Not the mayhem, nor the conflict of it. I feel this strongly, as we all do. And we all feel the same fury, the same chaos at Weveld's betrayal. Magic should burn with chaos at such a crime!"

Two dozen faces received him in captivation.

"Please, all I desire is peace for us. I have more right to lead us than a traitor, but you all have more right than I. Allow me the trials, or disallow me them. But *please*," he said, "Let's discuss it with order."

Kaen was the first to get a word into the silence. "I would vouch for Artemys to take the Trials, and be our Crown Magician."

Artemys nodded to Kaen, and fully expected a burst of noise at Kaen, but the Masters maintained silence as Artemys had pleaded. They all understood that he had turned their own disciplines on them.

"I second it." Amidst surprise from all, Aella stepped forward.

"Thank you," Artemys said.

More silence. Finally, Theos of Galinor, who had been there at the Massacre in Eldius, at last voiced his support. "Artemys has remained a wild card, thus far," he said. "If he would cast his lot with us for good, I would see how he performed in our Trials."

"It must be unanimous," Aella said.

One by one, every Master agreed, some sincerely, some grudgingly. Some only agreed because Aella, or other Magicians they respected, had.

"Let it be noted," Aella said, "that we are all in agreement here. Artemys will take the Trials of the Crown. Should he succeed, he will become the eighth Crown Magician, and leader of our Order."

"Perhaps a short recess would be acceptable?" Vardin asked. The room sighed in agreement.

. . .

An hour later, the Council Chamber of the Order began to fill once again. The room somehow felt neater than it had before. It was brighter too. The cloud of Weveld had been lifted. Artemys waited by the windows on the north side of the School. A city had been growing there since his childhood, thriving around the wide cove in Vero Isle's west coast. There was an abundance of trade to be done with Order. Magicians had perfected the binding of books during his father's lifetime, using glyphs of air to cut paper thinner and bind codices tighter. Minerals and resources could be created with magic too. Looking down from the Hall, Artemys could see the buildings rising above the treetops and the port past it.

It reminded him of his Avernan port, which reminded him of her.

He had not thought of Kerres in ages, though a deep longing for her had filled him against his best intentions. Why did love feel like misery? He knew both, intimately. He had known Kerres intimately; he let his mind wander there for the first time in months. The taste in her mouth, the soft of her skin, the dimples in her back... *Maker, why her? She would toss me into the flames of oblivion if I was of no use to her.* Even before he had thrown her away, she had levied herself higher and higher in status by speaking of the Prince in her grasp. Breaking their relationship, now a full year past, had been the best and worst decision he had ever made.

"Are you ready?" Aella asked.

"As ever," Artemys replied. He banished *her* from his mind. "I will do my best, for this Order. For all of you," he raised his voice for the Masters seated further from the window.

"We will conduct the Trials here," Aella said, leading him to the center of the room. "The first Trial is glyph knowledge. You must name these glyphs as I show them."

From nowhere, a black area cut the air in front of Artemys and glyphs began to appear. Artemys was in this moment now, with no memories recalled or lusts revived.

"Water, guidance, vapor, ash, blood, silver," he listed, as the glyphs flickered before him. He voiced faster and faster, as the glyphs hurried up, challenging him. "Anger, ice, cloud, grass, fur, identity reference, magic reference..."

After many minutes passed, the void in the room filled with colour again and the Masters in attendance let out their breath. Kaen was smiling: Artemys had once assured him that glyphs could be learned like second nature, and that there were many more than their School even knew. On a spontaneous thought, Artemys wrote a spell he assumed was similar to their black sign and wrote his own glyphs into it.

"This one is sand, like from the great Southern Waste, not a beach," he said. "This one is seaweed. This one is scale, from a lizard or a fish. This is hate."

They all gasped in surprise. Artemys assumed no one showed more glyphs after the first Trial. "I could go on," he told them. "There is a world of glyphs out there, and the job of the Order is to learn them and categorize them. We have lost so much and we *must* regain it."

Parsis was laughing in disbelief. "I have studied the histories of our Order, and none have chosen the Trials of the Crown to do as you have just done. We must overlook your arrogance for the magnitude of this discovery."

Artemys bowed. "I cannot speak to that, but it seemed important to this Trial. Please, the second Trial."

Aella allowed herself a small smile. She had wrinkled skin, but a keen beauty to her that defied age. She was one of the strongest women Artemys had met. She said, "You must demonstrate your reasoning abilities in a variety of scenarios. You are travelling on a road..."

Abruptly, Artemys saw a road in the forest. The trees were a mix of pines and spruce: he was somewhere in the northern lands. He could still feel the space of the Chamber around him. He could smell the sweat of aged men and Aella's perfume, but could also see the clouds above Athyns. He could feel wooden floorboards beneath his feet, but when he looked down, there was only dirt around his sandals.

"You stumble upon a man being robbed by three bandits. You are not a magician or a warrior. Just a traveller," Aella said.

Artemys could see them, three armed men kicking a man who crawled in the grass. There was an overturned wagon and a dead horse, bleeding deep red into the dirt roadway.

"I must stop them," Artemys said.

"You do not have the physical capability to stop them. You are a passerby."

Artemys pulled himself from this vision as much as he could. He could hear the silent cough of aged Parsis, watching the Trial's proceedings. *I must think these Trials through. I must solve it how these Masters would have it solved,* he told himself.

"I will lie in wait, until they leave," he told Aella.

"The man is killed while you watch. The robbers set off into the woodland."

"I will follow them, to see where they hide." The vision showed him a lodge amidst dense foliage, a place that seemed cozy if it was not foreshadowed by bodies hanging from branches. "Now, I will turn back and set off to the nearest town. They must be warned of the robbers, and must bring them to justice. I can lead them there myself, if it is better."

"You are asleep in your room," Aella said. As suddenly as Artemys had been brought to that forested highway, he was looking at himself, a limp body asleep in a bed. "Your magistrate shows up at your locked door an hour after midnight."

Artemys' view shifted outside and he could see a mayor, complete with an escort of guards at the door to his house.

"He has an entire chest of gold for you, and a sealed letter." Artemys could see it all, though his other senses grounded him in the Chamber of the Order.

"What's the first thing you should open?"

Artemys could see the chest and the letter. What was he to demonstrate here? Pragmatism: the chest? Suspicion: the letter? Perspective: the door?

He paused, as he had so many times, and let his mind leave the room, leave the vision. He had been able to call upon these moments of clarity when he needed to outthink time itself.

"My eyes." Artemys said. *Clever riddle!* He smiled. "I must open my eyes before I can open the door."

Aella's voice jolted him again. "You are lost in a marsh," she said. Artemys saw a bog before him, gouts of vapor rising here and there, thick mud under his feet. He could not feel the squelch as he saw himself take a step ahead.

"Can I use magic?" Artemys asked immediately. She had specified it in the first test of reasoning, but had given him no parameters this time. Magic would be a quick solution to being trapped here.

The vision faded. "Good," Aella said.

"I barely had time to finish those scenarios," Artemys retorted.

"He's very bright," someone said.

"But you found the way to the solution for all three: discerning safety from danger, cracking a riddle, and realizing the riddle of a mundane situation," Aella explained. "Morality did not matter in any, but now it does." She broke a spell token and everything went black.

. . .

Artemys and his men followed the tree line, close enough to the edge to see the field where the main battle raged, but deep enough in the foliage to move camouflaged. From here, there was no rush of adrenaline to drown out the screams of the dying. Just a sickening march as they made the flanking manoeuvre they had been ordered to. Artemys examined his sword, Korbios.

It was clothed in a thick line of blood and dangling threads of hair. Where had it—the blood, not the blade—come from? Artemys could not remember a thing prior to this moment. Nor did he need to. He was the captain of this troop, and they had important work to do.

They came upon a crumbling brick cabin, grey and moss-eaten rock piled in the shadows of the forest's canopy. A man had died sitting against the wall, blood haloing his form, having clawed his way across the ground from the main battle.

"There's a troop, smaller than ours," Otho said, panting. "Half a mile ahead."

Artemys nodded to his scout. "We will take them out, quickly."

They marched on the double for that half-mile, and fell upon the enemies while they conversed. It was a swift skirmish. Korbios took two of the enemies with its insatiable thirst for red.

"Charge!" a voice shouted.

Artemys had only a moment to see the ambush rising from the foliage as he wiped his blade on a coat of the slain. "Ambush!" he shouted to his men, as another fifteen enemies surged toward them.

Three of Artemys's men died before they could stand. Artemys found himself stepping backward as he fended off blow after blow from two or three enemies. One of them took Korbios in exchange for a spray of blood against Artemys's cheek.

Artemys heard the snap of a branch behind him and felt something cold against the skin in his lower back. It was moving through him. He glanced down to find the point of a blade emerging from his side, dark with a thick ooze that spread around the wound. The frigid cold of the steel and shock turned to heat as the blade was pulled out, and Artemys found himself lying on the ground. The man who had stabbed Artemys from behind planted his feet on either side of Artemys and raised his sword to finish things off. He roared as he raised his sword again, and then Otho's short spear took him in the neck and he fell away.

Artemys laid and watched, removed from the situation, as Otho fought for both their lives. Where was Yotes? Where was Thieron? Those two were Artemys's best. Why were they not making this valiant stand?

He was paralyzed with pain. Why did it feel like the man had stabbed him with a brand, not a blade? Artemys held his hand over the wound, clutching his skin. He could still breathe... did that mean they had missed his lungs?

Otho lost his arm to an axe, and fell on top of Artemys.

How dare he die? Yotes should have died first. Any of the others. Otho was a scout, not a fighter. This was wrong. This was all wrong.

Artemys should have died first.

He lay there, conscious, waiting for one of the enemies to come for him. He did not know how much time passed. Finally, he told his ears to listen again and realized that now they were hearing silence.

Artemys pulled himself along the ground until Otho's heavy body was not on top of him anymore. The first man had also been above him, covering his legs, he realized. Maybe the enemies could not see him anymore, in the carnage. There were bodies everywhere. Artemys looked at himself and realized that he was bloodier than most of them. It seemed that most of Artemys troop had fled; there were more enemy corpses, marked with bright yellow tabards, than his own troop's bodies.

He rolled over. It seemed easier to shove himself up onto his knees this way. When he finally left the ground, his side made a loud squelch as it was sucked from the mud and blood. He stood up, and the pain got worse.

For a few minutes, Artemys just stood there, waiting for strength to collect when none would come.

He very slowly made his way back to that stone cottage. He limped over every rock and branch, and left a stain of blood on each tree he had to lean on. He found a few bodies on the way, bodies that had not been there before. They were marked with yellow.

The brick shack was in much worse shape now. There was a whole collection of bodies around the doorframe and a section of wall had fallen in where someone had collapsed against it.

"Captain!" someone called.

Artemys had sunk to his knees by the nearest tree without realizing it. He was seeing spots and coughing, but could still breathe. *I'm going to die...* he knew. Even if Rathar could heal him, he had a feeling in his chest that he would die. It was not just the pain of the wound.

His troop had him. They carried him into the stone cabin. Above Artemys, through the rotting ceiling wood, a weeping willow draped its vine-like branches on him. How could such a beautiful tree be here, in this hell? The darkness in the shadow of the tree was growing, blotting it out.

Then Rathar healed him, and light filled his vision again. The hole in his side was gone; the pain in his back and the heat of the wound left him. He released a curse as he woke from his stupor.

"Will I live?" he asked. It was an odd question after magical healing. Of course you will, was the usual reply. Something painful still bubbled inside of him.

But Rathar hesitated, and the feeling in Artemys's chest returned. *I am going to die here, lying under this willow.* "You've been poisoned," his magician told him. "It will kill you, but not as painfully as that side wound."

Artemys closed his eyes for a moment. This is it. All done. There were so many holes in his mind that he had not filled, that could not be repaired by Rathar's sorceries.

One thing bubbled through those holes in his head. Kerres. *"Maker!"* Artemys screamed, both inside and out. He would never get to see Kerres again. His love. His hope. Glyphs, it hurt. Not the poison that tingled at the back of his neck and drew coughs out of him. That felt like a scratch. Dying without Kerres...that was the sword through his gut.

He grabbed hold of Rathar's shirt and pulled him closer.

"Captain?" his soldier asked in fear.

"Give me magic," he told Rathar. "Now!"

Rathar stuttered that he could not.

Artemys shoved Rathar backward. *I need magic, and it needs me,* he knew. He had always known it—how had he forgotten it? "It was not a question. I am ordering you to give me magic!"

Rathar came up on his knees. "The statutes of the Order disallow it. I cannot give magic to anyone unless I deem them capable and worthy of becoming one of us. It is something—" He was cut off when Artemys grabbed him once more.

"Give me magic now, or perish," Artemys said, and placed a knife at his subordinate's throat. They all should die for letting

Otho stand and fight while they fled. All ten of the men in this hut were guilty of it. All hundred thousand in the battle were guilty too. Killing Rathar would be justice, not sin. "By all your glyphs, I swear it. I will kill you."

Rathar's face became very dark. Artemys had already grabbed his hands, so the poor man could use no spells. "Maker have mercy, I will," his magician told him. "Release me."

Artemys did so, but held the knife ready. "Any betrayal will warrant your death," he said. "Regardless of this blade, you would be acting against a superior." He *was* the captain.

Rathar traced a line in the dirt. Artemys watched in fear as he wrote complicated symbols all around it. Some were simple lines, but many were full of dots and curves. At last, Rathar whispered, *"Draz."*

Nothing happened. Rathar sank back, scratching away his spell with fingers spread wide. "It's done," he said.

Artemys smirked. "How do I know? You only said one word! Aren't spells like this a bit more complex?"

Rathar shook his head. "This spell uses many glyphs, glyphs we have long ago forgotten the name for. But it only needs one word: 'Draz.' It means, 'magic'. Here," he traced a glyph into the dirt again. "Hold up your hand and say, 'oken'. It's fire. I wrote other glyphs to make certain it won't be too much."

Artemys held up one hand. *"Oken."* His voice cracked. A small prick of fire appeared in his hand, hovering half an inch above the skin. He could feel its warmth, like a candle near his fingers.

How do I find Kerres now? How does magic change anything? He shook his head. He would be dead long before he could learn enough to find her. *Magic was not to find her. She's lost to me already. Magic is to do right. To fix this...hell.*

He wrote the glyph for fire again, this time without Rathar's safety spells. Then he wrote it again. And again.

"What are you doing?" Rathar asked. "Glyphs... please don't." Over his shoulder, Yotes raised an eyebrow and stepped closer.

"Stopping this," Artemys said.

Something, some force outside of this battle, made him pause. Was this really right?

Artemys had accepted it as right so long ago: kill the unjust. Ever since he had burned the slaver's face, he had been convincing himself how right it was. But here, leagues and years from that day on the Chase, was this the good course of action?

There is no good, Artemys said. *If I must choose between evil and ignorance, I must change the question.*

Another voice, somewhere deeper inside—or farther out— posed a different argument. *Killing is killing. If they are unjust for their murder, why are you just for yours? Is the answer to murder more murder, or...*

Mercy?

Mercy. Artemys trembled. Rathar and Yotes and reality were distant now. Only Artemys's mind remained, and the glyphs he had traced in front of him. Mercy could not end anything! It would let the murderers keep on murdering! Mercy was not the answer because it *could not* be the answer. *No. I will murder so no one else does. I will sin so that no one else can. I will be* damned *so that no one else will be!*

He was back in the cottage, bloodied and guilty men all around him. He was beside a battlefield where unspeakable horror was transpiring. He was a magician in front of glyphs.

He shouted, *"Oken!"* Fire consumed him, the men around him, the cottage, the willow, the forest, the battle. Fire wiped them all away.

Peace.

. . .

Artemys sat up. For one maze-like minute, he stared around himself in sheer confusion. There were old men and women staring at him. They were sitting in a high-ceilinged room. Artemys was already wearing a magician's robe.

Then he remembered. *That was a Trial.* The knowledge that Otho, Rathar, and the others were not real was sickening at first. For the duration of that Trial, only the battle had been real. Only Artemys the Captain.

Realizing the context made him even more ill. *That was a Trial for the position of Crown Magician,* he reminded himself. *A test of morality.*

"He failed it!" Vardin scoffed, half in surprise and half in disdain.

Aella spun on the Master. "Silence! There is neither failing nor passing the third Trial. We must analyze all that we have learned before making our decision," she raised a finger, *"in private."*

Duly scolded, Vardin held his tongue.

Theos helped Artemys to his feet. "You can wait in the hall if you are hungry, or in the public chambers if you're tired."

Artemys closed his eyes. He had failed? How could that be failure? The Crown Magician had to decide when war was acceptable, and Artemys's hatred of the battle in his scenario should be relevant. *Hopefully some of them understand...*

He stood up and walked toward the door. It would be a long wait.

. . .

"We are ready," Parsis told him. Artemys lifted his head from the tabletop. *Maker, what will they choose?* he wondered. He glanced around. The Hall of the School was busy, but no one paid Artemys any mind. Only a few of them could guess what was going on. He had to assume that none of those present now had been there when he carried Hevarus's body through. It had been less busy then, regardless.

His stomach rumbled. He had not even tried eating while he waited.

"They're waiting," Parsis said.

"Sorry." Artemys stood up and followed him. They climbed the spiral staircase in silence. Could Parsis not just relay Artemys's failure to him? Must he stand before them to hear it? Vardin must be eager to rub it in. If Weveld indicates their track record, Vardin would make an ideal Crown Magician!

At last, they reached the carved doors. Artemys held his breath as they entered the Chamber. Aella was the only one standing. Even Parsis plopped into his own chair.

"Artemys Gothikar, son of Prince Gothikar of Avernus," Aella intoned. "You are hereby elected to the status of Crown Magician." She paused.

What? Artemys's head snapped up and his jaw dropped. "I passed?"

"You passed the first two Trials in such excellence that the controversy of the third has been deemed irrelevant. While once an incredibly righteous leader might be required," Aella considered her words carefully, "anyone is better than your prior, and you have proven yourself one of us."

Vardin would not meet his eyes, but the room seemed abuzz with excitement. How would Artemys change things? What would he improve? Would he succeed where Weveld had failed?

"Let it be noted that you are also the youngest Crown Magician to be elected in the history of our Order," Parsis added.

Aella nodded. "I am certain some rest and reflection is in order for us all. Tomorrow, we will welcome you the Eighth Crown Magician. I will oversee your transition into his duties; thankfully the next meeting of the Triumvirate is more than four months distant. You should be able to embrace your position before then. May we take our leave, Master?" she asked.

Artemys blinked. Had he done it? Had he succeeded? Was this what he had always been working toward? Could he, as Crown Magician, fix the Dominion?

21

Year of Olympus 552

At least the giants were biding their time. Periander needed that time. He was sparring with Odyn in an open yard between the war tents. Odyn had the upper hand of course, with his superior strength and size. Periander was still weak and fought with dancing dodges and off-hand swipes or jabs at his opponent. Some of Odyn's soldiers had gathered, leaning on spears or standing with crossed arms as they watched their Princes fight.

Odyn slammed forward with his blade level, more of a steel punch than a slash of any kind. Periander stepped backward as Odyn came forward and spun to the left. He used Wolf's Eyes, a pair of high-stabbing moves that forced Odyn to break off his attack with parries. The brutish man frowned and his brown beard quivered as he took a few steps back.

Then he hammered forward again with the hilt of the sparring blade; the wood caught Periander in the brow and knocked him to his knees.

"Glyphs," Periander breathed in a puff of white moisture. He tossed down his sword.

"You're bleeding," Odyn said, his words clouding too. "But you're doing better. You'll be ready for battle within another month or two."

"I feel like I'm fighting a giant," Periander said and Odyn laughed. The mud felt damp around Periander's finger. He drew a line and then began etching glyphs along it. The healing spell was minor; it only needed to fix a bruise on his brow. He barely felt the tug on his strength. He was always weary now, but he did not feel ready to drop—even after the fight.

"Good," Odyn said. "There's still lots of them to fight."

Periander tossed his sparring sword to one of the others. "I'm out," he said. A few others stepped into the ring to get thrashed by the violent man.

The fighting yard was set amidst Odyn's war camp in the Cerden Mountains, under the grey skies of the winter's end. Only the white caps of the rocky peaks held white. Within the month, it would all melt. The Cerden range was a rocky shelf compared to the Maker's Forge or the World's Foundation. Those mountains held glaciers all year, but the snows here would be gone soon.

Periander left the yard and looked into some of the tents as he walked between the rows. Men sharpened their blades or slept. He saw a few reading, but not all of them knew how. Readers were more common in this era than in Akheron's day. Books were affordable by the common man now, but were still spreading in popularity. Many men just sat there, with a skin of ale or a mug in their hands, staring into crackling fires.

He saw lots of men he recognized. None he knew by name, but he found them all comparable to himself. They were tired. Some of them had known more years of war than years of peace before. They were beaten, hopeless and waiting for their turn to take a Trionus spear or a giant's hammer to some vital organ and, breathing peacefully at last, leave this harsh world behind.

Periander spat to his right. *It's not right.* He finally understood his father, the man who had rid them of the Kinship. *If there were a Maker,* Periander thought, *why would he let us endure this?*

Periander strode faster. Close to his own tent—he was visiting with the Olympian army while Illus and his men camped north of Galinor on the coast—Periander was intercepted by a short man with a thick moustache. "My Prince," he began, "I bring a letter from Captain Mordus."

Periander had finally given Mordus his own host of soldiers. He had promoted his friend to Captain after he travelled from Dagger's Edge to Galinor after the outset of the war at Oban Ford. But he had kept his friend in direct service; most Princes had a Court Magician—Erykus had just accepted Kronos

Accalia to be his—but Periander had magic himself. So, as his companion and aide, he had chosen a valiant fighter and survivor. Mordus had done well in the position, saving his Prince's life on many occasions. On the fateful night when assassins came for him, Periander had told Mordus to take a night of leave and enjoy the capital. It did not reflect poorly on Mordus's reputation, but it had changed Periander. He did not want a companion now, lest he drag them down with him.

Periander snatched the letter from Mordus's outstretched hand. Many messengers still related news by memory, but the inner circles of the Princes could easily afford written correspondence on spell-thinned parchment. He broke the beeswax seal and read his friend's words.

> *Periander,*
>
> *There's been no sign of giants here. Theseus is sending me farther north because my men can move faster than his army. The trip across the Strait was smooth; hopefully the rest of it will be too. We will travel up the West Trident and then across Sinai.*
>
> *Do not expect news from me any time soon, I will not be able to send word until I return to the Mydarius after my mission.*
>
> *Hope things go smoothly there and that you are recovering well from your ordeal.*
>
> > *Your friend,*
> > *Mordus of Eldius*

Periander sat down in his tent. He hoped Mordus did not feel slighted in being given such a task. He folded the letter again and set it on the table in front of him. His map was there, full of dots for various camps. There were large, red hashes where they had lost battles. Even one on the Strait of Galinor, where they had won and then fled.

There were very few dots or lines in the Maker's Forge. They really had no idea what was there.

Periander encountered a surprising thought as he sat there and looked at the map. He would later uncover it fully, but now he only knew the surface. How could a barren range of rocks host a million mountain men? Where did they come from? Most importantly, what would knowing more *mean?*

One of his guards outside said, "Another messenger, sir. From the Magician's Order."

"Enter," Periander called.

The man who strode in was not familiar to him. He had wide shoulders and a bald head. The magician wore the traditional orange of his Order. He bowed to Periander. "My name is Filus, milord," he said. "There has been an incident in Avernus and Lady Gothikar bids you come at once."

Periander stood up quickly, the map and its questions forgotten beside him. "An incident! What's happened?"

"Your son lives, but has been attacked. We have the culprit under custody."

"Glyphs!" Periander said, slamming his hand against the table for support. *This is not right,* he thought again. *Curse the Maker, enough of* this. "Write your spell, quickly! Guard!"

The guard stuck his head into the tent as Periander and Filus exited. "Sir?"

"Inform Odyn that there's been an attack on my family. They live, but I must return to Avernus immediately. Tell him to notify the other royals. If this is Trion, other families could be targeted," Periander explained.

"Ready," Filus said.

"Yes, sir," the guard said, and strode away.

"Let's go," Periander said. Filus whispered his words of magic and the camp was replaced with the city of Avernus.

There was a lick of frost on the few trees he could see, and trails of smoke rose from quaint brick chimneys into a fog that surrounded the Avernan Point. Periander didn't have time to see the rest. He strode past Filus, past the guards here and off of the stone platform. The Avernan Known Location was a rooftop rather far from the Palace grounds.

He followed the staircase around the outside of the building. A small garrison of guards had always been stationed here, those on duty stared at him as he strode past. "Horse!" he shouted.

A moment later, a man handed him the reigns of a horse. "I'll catch up," Filus called as Periander galloped away.

Someone attacked Artemys? he repeated, in a daze. *Why?* He kicked the horse, hard. It cried loudly and tried to go faster.

Men and women leapt out of the way as they saw him charging up the narrow streets. More than once, someone's arm or leg got hit by the steed; they pranced out of the way or tumbled to the ground.

Why would anyone hurt Artemys! Periander's grip on the reins was a white-knuckled fist. His other hand held his sword's hilt, unconsciously, where it sat in its sheath on his belt.

He did not know how long it took him, but he was uncertain if anyone had ever travelled across the city that fast.

He slid from the saddle even as the horse danced into the Palace courtyards, heaving and clouding the air in front of it with a fog. Periander wasn't breathing enough for the air to become obscured. Forgetting his appearances, he ran into the Palace and up into his quarters.

"Where is he?" he shouted. "Cat! Artemys!"

A guard or two appeared from nearby doorways and servants peaked out cautiously. "This way, sir," someone said.

He stepped into an infirmary. Artemys was lying on a white bed. Cat dashed across the room and, sobbing, wrapped her arms around him. She screamed into his shirt without making any noise, then raised her hands and started slamming them against him. Under her breath she mumbled things like "your fault" and "we aren't safe". He grabbed her flailing fists to stop her and held them together against his chest. "What happened?" he asked, lowering his head in a slouch to look her in the teary eyes. Her arms went limp against him, so he released them and took her chin between his hands. He looked into her eyes, but then over her head at his son's cot again. He appeared unharmed, simply asleep. "What happened?"

"A *guard* attacked him!" she said. "One of our own guards!"

"What!" Periander asked, staring at his wife again. "Why?"

"Glyphs!" she cried. "I don't know! Who can protect us if even our defenders turn upon us!"

"There must be a reason!"

"Maker, I pray it is a reason easily defeated," she said.

Periander stepped toward his son. "I don't pray. Not anymore." His words were unconscious.

"Peri, they attacked us in our home! You can't leave again! Glyphs, please!" Cat cried to his back.

"Shh," he said, kneeling by the cot. His son appeared at peace. "You'll wake him. We'll speak of this later."

Artemys stirred, his face contorted for a brief moment by some nightmarish phantom. He was seven; until today, his primary concerns had been reading and running.

"Artemys," Periander said calmly.

His son stirred again. "Father!" he blurted, when he opened his eyes enough. He rose off the bed and reached out to embrace him. "You came home!"

"Yes, I'm here," Periander said. "Are you doing all right?"

"I am tired," Artemys said. "Master Filus said that the healing would make me tired. But it's better now than before."

"You can rest as long as you want," Periander said. "But first, I want to give you a gift."

"What gift? Is it from the West?" Artemys asked, excited.

"No," Periander said. "Some people will say it's from the Maker. Some people say it's just from the world. It's a gift that will keep you safe, if you use it well."

"Really?" Artemys breathed. He propped himself up on his elbows, his eyes wide.

"You know what magic is, and you know how it works, right?"

Artemys nodded. "I read about it lots."

"I'm going to give you magic," Periander told him.

Cat gasped. "What? Periander, we should talk about—"

"Cat," he said, turning on one knee, "This won't change anything about his future unless he decides it should. This will only help him. He can study magic if he wants, or he can keep it as a back-up."

"Do you have magic?" Artemys asked.

"Yes," Periander said. "That's why I can give it to you. If you want it."

Artemys nodded. "I can protect Mother when you're gone."

Periander smiled. "Never mind that, Artemys. It will be sufficient to give anyone a second thought about you."

"...Like that man?" Artemys asked.

Periander felt his calm break. "Yes, like him. Glyphs, Artemys, I'm sorry he hurt you. I will deal with him soon, to make sure he doesn't hurt you again."

Artemys stared at him with an expression between

acceptance and uncertainty. "Mother told me it is not any of our faults, so you do not need to be sorry."

It is his *fault,* Periander thought, imagining a guard with Ivos's face standing over his son's small body. He trembled and looked away. "Here," he said, and placed one hand delicately on Artemys's chest. He wrote a line of glyphs. Catlin knelt and took one of the boy's hands in her own. She was crying, but it was a bit more than simple grief now. When the spell was done, Periander read, *"shoraz ath draz."*

Artemys closed his eyes briefly, then opened them again. "I do not feel any different," he said.

"Once you're feeling better," Periander said, "Filus can show you the basics. And you can learn lots from books. If it interests you more, you can talk to your mother or me about visiting a School for it."

"I can use magic now?" Artemys asked. He was looking at his hands as though they might be different now.

"You can do anything. Just ask for help if you need it."

"What did you do?" Filus asked from the doorway. "That is a sacred gift! Only a Master of magic should decide who should receive it."

Periander had Filus's neck in one fist before anyone moved. "None of the Nobles, let alone Princes, would object to what I have done. My son was attacked, and you will silence yourself."

"Father?" Artemys called. "Filus is a friend!"

"I know, son," Periander called, and released the magician. He was ashamed of his temper, but he was barely keeping himself from charging straight toward the guard that had hurt his son, wherever he might be. "I'm sorry you saw that."

"He healed me," Artemys repeated, smiling at Filus.

"I'm going away for a while," Periander said. His carefully chosen words grinded from his throat.

"Please do not leave again!" Artemys said.

"Oh, not to war. I need...to teach the guard not to hurt you again," Periander said.

Cat tensed, though she still knelt by the bed and cradled their son's hand. "Must you now?"

"Glyphs," Periander said, but shook himself. His son had heard! "I must," he replied.

"Father," Artemys said, but he paused.

"Yes?"

"Please don't fight the guard. All you do is fight, Father! The guard is sick, I think, and we should help him... right, Mother?" he said. He looked at Cat with pride. She had spoken to him about the difference between right and wrong.

"Some men are past help," Cat said, her voice distant.

Aren't we all? Periander thought, but shook his head and looked away. "Sometimes, when you're bad," he said aloud, "The only thing for you is punishment."

Artemys nodded. He had stolen food from the kitchens before, which had earned him a stern reprimand. He understood. It was a simple lesson, wasn't it? Periander couldn't meet his son's eyes, though, and he stepped out of the room without saying anything more. *I failed him as much as his attacker...I failed. I need to know how badly.*

"Filus," Periander said. The corridor was colder than the room and much emptier.

The magician brushed his arm as he stepped from the room. "Yes?"

"I need to know my son's injuries."

"No, you don't," Filus said.

"What do you not understand about this?" Periander grabbed the magician again. "I am your Prince. I am god to you! When I say or do something, you do not question me! Glyphs! What does Weveld teach you lot?"

"That the Order of Magic is oversight for the Triumvirate—"

"Against each other! Listen to me," Periander said with a deep breath. "I will break your neck the next time you talk back to me. I can find a hundred magicians to replace you, and *no one would stop me.* I may be weak right now, after assassins tried to kill me, but I am physically and *legally* capable of *breaking* you!"

Filus's face was turning red as the blood flow was obstructed by Periander's grip. He waited a few anxious breaths longer before releasing the magician.

"Now," Periander asked, glaring the man in the eye. "Tell me of my son's injuries, before you healed him."

Filus straitened and tugged his orange robe into shape

again. "He had a lot of bruises, all over his body," the man said quietly. "Four of his ribs were broken, one on one side and three on the other. His jaw was broken, and he was bleeding a lot. We made sure to clean him before he awoke. As for mental injury, I can only speculate."

"You won't," Periander ordered. He clenched his fists. These were injuries to make a grown man sick, let alone a child. *Maker, what have I done? I should never have left my family!* He ground his teeth together hard enough that it hurt. "Where is the man who did this?"

"What will you do?" Filus asked, visibly bracing himself.

"What it is within my right to do, as justice and law of this city and this country," Periander droned. "Don't worry yourself about that, you won't be there, and you needn't lose sleep over it. I don't sleep anymore, so it hardly matters. Where is he?"

"In the Keep's dungeon, not the Barracks's. We did not want to risk somewhere that other guards could get at him. Only our most loyal men watch him," Filus said. "I rinse my hands of what transpires there, and I reluctantly tender my resignation, Prince Gothikar."

"Fine," Periander said. "Get out of my Palace." They walked away from one another.

Periander descended the stairs almost as quickly as he ascended them. Someone had to pay for this. And Periander needed to know: *why?* The Keep's dungeon was in one corner of the building, not completely underground, but down a few steps from the main floor nonetheless.

"Sir," a soldier said, as he saw Periander coming. "Condolences on the day's unfortunate incident."

"Unlock the cell."

The man did not speak again. He turned the key until there was a heavy thud within the mechanism and then stepped away. Periander held out his hand until his loyal guard dropped it into his palm. "Wait in the Hall," Periander said.

The soldier strode away.

Periander stepped into the cell. It was a small room, but with ample elbow room for any dungeon needs. Rooms like this used to make Periander sick, but his life had become one. There were chains hanging from the ceiling and collected in the corners. There was little else in terms of decoration: no tables or furnishings.

The only occupant of the room stood in its center, above a small grated drain. He was a man like any other. Torn wool pants were his only possession now. His arms were raised above his head, held there by two chains.

"My lord Prince, royal Gothikar," the man said. There was a slur to his voice from alcohol, but it was distant. The man had already been beaten a bit: he had bruises on his right cheek and right side. Hopefully those marks had served to sober him up a bit more.

"You are?" Periander asked, only managing two words between his clenched teeth. His fists were lines of white marbles, his jaw a dull ache.

It was warm in here, wasn't it? He tore off the cloak he wore and threw it aside. His movements were jerky.

"Name's Rel ten Asirus."

"Not anymore," Periander snapped. He planted one fist in the man's gut and the other across the man's jaw. This was familiar to him. Fighting. Hurting. The pain and fear of Artemys's loss was not. It could never become familiar. *Glyphs, please let it never become even* remotely *familiar.*

Once the man—swinging in his chains—found his breath again, he pulled himself to a stop and glared at Periander. "You've taken that from me as well now? My own name?"

"What?"

"Your father, Akheron, he killed everyone I loved."

"I'll kill everyone you love," Periander said. "And I won't hurt your eyes so you'll see it all, clearly."

"Ha. You're a fierce one, aren't you?" Rel asked. "Your father was too. And mine."

"Who was your father? Some dung-eater from Tarroth?" Periander asked. "Was his blood as yellow as yours?"

"I serve no traitors—Trion or otherwise, and I am no more of a traitor than you and your usurper father!" Rel spat on him.

Periander drove his knee into the man's groin, as hard as he could. It took the fool a few more minutes to recover than the first two blows had. Before he had, Periander grabbed the man's hair and yanked his head back as hard as he could. "You attacked the son of your Prince!"

"I was the son of my Prince," the man said. "I was Prince

Aristorn's closest friend. He called me son. He called *me* son!
And your father killed him!"

"That is not what the histories say. There are no records
that imply my father killed a single member of House Aristorn!
We know the Buccaneers burned their estate on the Point. We
know about the Grey Night! No more."

"You're a fool if you think your father's hands were
clean."

"I don't," Periander said. "Neither are mine." He drove his
foot down on the back of the man's leg until there was a snap
and man screamed. This was how they broke Trionus's spies. No
head injuries: that would dull the pain. It was a science, like the
scholars who studied the world instead of magic. There were
roles to play and actions to elicit results.

Once the man finished his cries of pain, Periander gripped
his head in his hands again. "How many more of you do I have
to kill?" he asked.

"None," Rel gasped. His voice was quiet. "I'm the last. Not
even full Aristorn, but I still have more claim to this city and this
throne than you."

"I was willing to forgive trespasses like this when you
merely sent assassins after me in Galinor."

The man laughed a bit hysterically. "Did you like that? The
best of the best...they still couldn't manage to kill you.
Gothikars, it seems, are like pests. They just won't go away."

Periander shook his head. "We aren't pests," he said.
"We're a plague. Sometimes I wonder if we only bring death."

"Your son will," Rel said. "He's got generations of your
blood-red footprints to follow."

Periander slammed his fist into the man's gut as hard as he
could and roared, "You will not *speak* of my son!"

His voice echoed from the room. He pummelled the man
with as many blows as he had energy for. "You hurt him!" he
sobbed. "You could have broken him!"

At last he was out of energy, and he slouched away a few
steps. He panted for breath. His arms quivered, still clenched
with agony and fury.

"Will you break the trend?" Rel gasped, at last. His nose
was bleeding from both nostrils. "Will you...have mercy?"

Periander's arm slammed across his torso and gripped a

handle. Then it slammed back to his side, holding a knife. "No," he said. He closed his eyes and took a deep breath for strength. He found none.

He pressed the knife against the man's chest. It drew a drop of blood, resting between two ribs.

"At least I left a lasting impression on a few of you," Rel said. "You should've seen the look in your earth-spawn son's eyes."

With an incoherent scream, Periander stepped forward. He yanked the blade out again and then back in. His roar continued until he was out of breath. Then he shrieked more. On stiff feet, he stumbled back from his work. The man bled out quickly. Red pooled beneath him and dripped down the drain. Red dripped from Periander's hands. Red wiped onto his clothes when he tried to rub it off. With jerky movements, he threw down the blade. It clanked across the ground. Periander punched the wall, then sagged against it. The rock almost broke his hand. He cried into the stones. "Where do I go now?" he asked. "I can't fight there and here! How can I protect two places?"

If only Theseus could command the war! He couldn't. Odyn could, but Odyn wanted to, and that was no man to lead them in a battle against Ivos's ideologies.

It fell to Periander. He stepped away from the wall. Red smudges mirrored him there.

He stood straight again, but kept staring at the marks on the wall. Was this him now? A line of red, faint from dealing and receiving death? Cat was right. He should not have kept fighting after the first five years, let alone the first ten.

"You have to change," a voice said. It was the same voice that had spoken to him while he crawled through the golden streets of Galinor. A voice that could be his own for its familiarity. He turned toward the cell door.

A stranger stood there. He wore a plain green tunic and black pants. His boots were nothing of note, simple leather. His hair was sandy brown, and his face sharp and memorable. He had a scar running from under one eye to the edge of his cheek. He was staring at Periander, ignoring the body that hung, head bowed, in the middle of the chamber.

The stranger had seen Periander acting the way a madman would, not a Prince. "I—" Periander began, but cut himself off.

He did not know what to say.

"You have to change. They're all like this. You were supposed to be different. You *have* to be different," the man said.

"Who are you?"

The stranger blinked. "Terrus." The name did not seem true, but this was a man that spoke only words to be believed.

"Terrus," Periander said, raising one hand in front of him with fingers up and palm open. "You mustn't tell anyone how I was acting. They will lose respect for me. I must be strong."

"No. This is not strength," the man said, looking at the body. He looked back at Periander. "I have no one to tell. I am as alone as you are in this moment. But you should not concern yourself with how others perceive your behavior."

"You're right," Periander said. "I should behave as a Prince."

"Yes. You should concern yourself with only your own behavior."

Periander gasped, despite himself. The man's words cut as sharp as a knife. "You would judge a Prince?"

"I would judge a man. One who has already passed judgement upon himself," Terrus said. He looked at the blood on the wall.

Periander ran the back of his hands across his eyes to wipe away his tears. "You don't know anything about me. You haven't seen the war if you think I am *anybody* other than...this." He panned his arms around himself.

"You must change. You must win the war. You must go back across the Dominion."

"Not me. I haven't the strength. Don't send me," Periander said.

"Which is why you *have to change,*" the man said. *"Please."*

As suddenly as he had interrupted Periander's battle with himself, the man called Terrus disappeared. It was as though he had been there and then never been there. Just a shadow, instead of a man. An echo instead of a voice. Could it be magic? If Terrus had used it, the spell was far beyond anything Periander had ever heard of.

His words had been real though. Somehow, they seemed

more real than anything else in the room, even Periander. The man's last words had been more than wise words or advice; they had been a personal plea, rent from someone as hurt as Periander.

No one could be, a voice inside said. Periander silenced the voice with a new one. *I must change.* He shivered. How could the man's voice have gotten inside his head so easily.

"I can't, can I?" Periander asked the empty room and the dead man. "There's still a war to fight. Please, don't send me into the heart of things again." He remembered his list of reasons, causes to fight for. He had lost what was right and he had lost his instinct for survival. He had lost his desire to save this land and he was sick of his desire to kill Trion and Ivos.

If he couldn't protect his family, he had nothing left to fight for.

"You must change," the man had said.

"I don't want to," was Periander's reply.

But the man's words existed on that level too. They challenged him to change his wants too. A full *change* would mean wanting what he didn't presently want.

The convoluted train of thought left him with one impossible question. *How?*

22

Year of Olympus 573

For the second time in his life, Artemys found himself at odds with that stone block building in the heart of Attarax. The small, mossy village was more or less as he had left it. He could not pinpoint the memory of his last visit here. Instead of a singular event, after which he had not returned here, it was a slow tapering off. Under Weveld's guidance, he had begun to work with both the Order of Magic and the Disciples. Eventually, he was working with the former more than the latter. Then he had decided to vest a larger interest in his relationship with Kerres and his family members in Avernus. After that, he almost stopped visiting Andrakaz's cult altogether. The last time he had here had been before forging Korbios.

He stood in the valley of Attarax and found himself momentarily distracted by Korbios. He could sense the sword when he thought of it. He could sense his father.

Why are you in Delfie? he wondered. His father was there being shown to the public quarters.

Artemys let the thought go. He would deal with his father next. They had not spoken since before the Massacre of Eldius. He had not spoken to Kerres or Pyrsius since sending them away. *Maker, so much has changed since the first time I was at odds with these Disciples.*

He followed the pathway into the village, brushing the waist-high stone wall as he passed. He was Crown Magician now. It had been two days since his Trials, and he was still exhausted from that day. But he was strong in his purpose today.

He would deliver a warning and an ultimatum to Weveld. It would secure peace for now. If Artemys was still capable of predicting Weveld's behavior.

The Disciples watched him in confusion. Was he not the enemy now? Should they attack him or flee? He heard them whispering. Some of them ran ahead of him, to the main building. That was good; perhaps he would not need to enter it.

By the time he reached the double doors that led into the stronghold, Weveld was already there, breathing hard and holding tokens in both hands. Even he did not know what to expect from Artemys.

"Weveld. Prime Zealot," Artemys said.

"Crown Magician," Weveld returned, his voice cold. "You dare show your face *here?*"

Artemys smiled. "You cannot hurt me. Your whole Discipleship could not kill me. And attacking me would cost your *cult* greatly."

Weveld stepped closer. There were still several paces between them. The old man was livid.

"Do not test me on this," Artemys warned.

Weveld lowered his guard, though he did not put away his tokens.

Artemys raised his voice so that all gathered could hear him. "Once, the Disciples of Andrakaz and the Order of Magic may have been linked. That time is past. No more will you and your kin control both Orders, Weveld. Do not try to remove me. Do not try to corrupt my successor to your ways. From now on, you may not *touch* the Order of Magic."

Weveld raised an eyebrow. "Who will stop us? Just you?"

"My Order," Artemys said. It felt good to call it his. "I will teach them of the Disciples. I will teach them what I was taught here, so that we will recognize you and your ideals and suspect you for them. None of you are evil. None of you are the villains of folk tales. But, you attempt to control magic, to own it. My Order attempts to categorize and 'order' it. There is a difference, and no more will one affect the other."

"I am an old man, waiting to die," Weveld said. He tensed, clenching his fists around his tokens. "And you have taken my life's work from me."

"Your life's work was defending and upholding the

Triumvirate. By oath," Artemys noted. "And the Triumvirate is still here, defended and upheld after your life. Die in peace, for you have succeeded in your task. Die not in crime."

Weveld's face broke. For all his cravings of knowledge, he was also genuine in his love of country. He pocketed his tokens. He had lost all his fight now, and *was* just a man waiting for the end. He had accomplished far more than his failures and none of the rest really mattered. "Thank you," he managed. Artemys's words had recognized him.

"Furthermore," Artemys called to the Disciples. "You will reform your group. Now, you will be the Brotherhood of Andrakaz, for he has been gone long enough for you to serve him no longer. Now you are brothers of his cause, if you wish to think of it in such a way." He did not truly understand their obsession with the ancient sorcerer. He was a mystery, of course, but not a god. "What this will mean in a practical sense? No longer will Zealots hold knowledge and abilities that others cannot. You are all equals, for you are not a government. The Order of Magic may be, but you claim to serve magic directly. Why are some better than others? Henceforward, you are the Brotherhood of Andrakaz."

They stared at him. It would take them some time to embrace what he had said. But they would. Every Disciple, even Hevarus and Artemys, had envied the Zealots' power.

"Are you a member of this Brotherhood?" Weveld asked.

"No." Artemys turned away. "The Crown Magician must be *only* a man of the whole Dominion's wellbeing. But I *will* be watching..."

He returned to the School of Delfie with a word of magic. The air around him flickered in the shape of a square. The dry grass of Attarax Valley was replaced with lush green foliage and Caius's familiar face. "Welcome back, Crown," the Sentinel said.

Artemys smiled and offered his hand. "Caius. How is your wife?"

"She's well, sir." Caius gave him a firm clasp. "I will be a father within the fortnight."

"Incredible! Please, let Master Kaen know if you want some time off from your duties. He will assign someone else to your post."

Caius stiffened. "It will be quite all right, sir."

"Tell me, did my Father arrive?" Artemys phrased it nonchalantly, as though he had known of the visit earlier.

"Yes sir. He had a pack of supplies in case you were unable to see him today; that he put in the public quarters in the Hall, but I think he might have also gone to grab food. I'm certain he must have made quite the scene in Avernus when he, the very Prince of the Triumvirate knelt to write his own spell at the Known Location," Caius chuckled. "Not every day you see a man of his position cast a spell. They all fancy tokens."

Artemys grinned. "No doubt it will be the talk of Avernus for days," he said. "Do let me know if your wife has a girl or boy."

Caius bowed from his waist.

Before Artemys even reached the Hall, his father appeared in the doorway. "Father," Artemys called, as he approached. "What a surprise!"

Periander looked grim as ever. "Artemys," he nodded. "Perhaps some privacy would be acceptable? Or will you try to keep hiding from me?"

Artemys paused. His father was so direct. He was a general and a Prince and nothing less. But, Artemys would have it no other way. "We can talk in my study. Follow me."

He led the way through the Hall and out into the courtyard of the campus. He nodded to those he recognized. The Order of Magic consisted of thirty-one Masters, fifteen general Magicians, and more than fifty Apprentices; those were just the members of the Order, not the servants and staff that helped the School run as an institute. However, he was beginning to recognize many of them by name.

The first floor of the Tower of the Order was a small kitchen with a pantry and cellar below it. Artemys led the way up the stairs that followed the curved wall of the building up, past the second floor, to the third floor. Here were his own Crown Magician's quarters and quarters for his apprentice, should he accept one, and his servants' as well. Two-thirds along the hallway that ran the diameter of the Tower was the ornate doorway to his personal study.

He touched the doors, and they swung open on their own. "We will not be disturbed in here, nor will anyone overhear us," he said as the doors closed behind his father.

Periander took a moment to collect himself, pacing past Artemys and examining the study. His father has such broad shoulders; when Artemys was young and his father fought in the war, Artemys could not imagine any giant being larger than his father. The Prince turned back toward him; he had more scruff than he usually did, making him look a bit wilder, a bit more desperate. "What are you doing, Artemys?"

"Talking to my father," he returned. "You will have to be more specific."

"Maker. You disappear off the map for a year and now take over the *entire* Order of Magic!" Artemys could see the anger that his father was holding back. The Prince continued, "I searched for you exhaustively! After Eldius, I was...well, I was fearful for you. That kind of confusion and pain can do serious damage to us. Pyrsius was...distraught. And then, to not hear from you for days, weeks, and then months?"

"Did you think, father, that maybe I did not want to be found?"

Periander started nodding, but did not get a chance to say a thing.

"I failed you. I failed our goals. We had finally agreed to work together, to try to save people!" Artemys stepped backward. "And I cost so many their lives, but still stopped killers."

"Stopped killers?" Periander snapped. "No, you *killed* killers. My plan was not to hunt down evil-doers and give them their own treatment! Did you learn nothing from burning the face of that slaver, all those years ago? *This* is not the way, Artemys."

His father's words cut him. They did not give him guilt or self-doubt. They revealed a truth he had not wanted to accept. *My father is part of the problem,* he realized. There were the damned, murderers, and sinners; there were the corrupt, Odyn and the ilk of lords that sought more benefits in a world where they had all the benefits; and then there were the righteous, who falsely believed that solid hearts and intentions could solve something. "What would you know of *the* way, father? There is no way! There is only sin, and someone must sin to stop the sinners! In the, what, fifteen or sixteen years since the war, how much have you managed to change? *Anything?"*

"Enough!" Periander roared, with the voice of the warlord. The study fell silent again. Periander began pacing once more, following one of the bookshelves against the west wall. After a few moments, he raised his hand in front of him and turned toward Artemys again. "I may not have changed society for the better, but I haven't changed it for the worse."

Artemys stepped forward. "I have not—"

"People already lived in fear, before a lord murdered two commoners and ordered a crowd set afire. *Now,* that lord sits at the head of the most powerful force in the Dominion!" Periander exclaimed.

"Weveld *had* to be replaced! And no one else would be as aware of the true state of the Dominion as—"

Periander quivered, his hand turning into a fist. "Did you know that I fought side-by-side with Weveld in the war? He *is* a good man! He is one of the most loyal members of this government—"

"He *was*, perhaps. But has not been as loyal as you think!"

"You turned his closest friends against him!" Periander retorted.

"Apparently not all of them," Artemys said.

Periander stepped forward, reaching for Artemys and then froze. A dark look clouded his features, and he slowly lowered his arms. He mumbled something about mercy, then said, "You bring out the worst in men; I fear it is because you *are* the worst of men."

His father walked past him, touching the doors and leaving without a noise. Silence returned to Artemys's study. Artemys sank into the reading chair in the corner of the room. He was exhausted. And he was hurt, though he did not like to acknowledge it. How could he continue, when even his own father stood against him? *Maker, this world is* wrong, *so wrong.* He held his head in his hands. *My own father is one of them. One of those that must be replaced when the Triumvirate is.*

It was a day fast approaching, but not nearly fast enough.

23

Year of Olympus 553

"We should have all of our armies in the North!" Odyn snapped. "On the Blood Strait!"

Periander and Theseus sat at the triangular Council table. Odyn has his hands on the smooth Everwood, while he leaned across and argued with them. Outside, a flock of gulls circled the Imperial Tower, making enough noise to grind on Periander's senses like a nail file.

"My men and I are growing impatient. While your armies skirmish in the north, and even win some ground on occasion, my men win nothing! Because they fight nothing! I have not seen a giant in more than a year!" Odyn said. "Let my army join yours. Let me get some glory and power instead of watching my seniors treat me like a child."

"We are not treating you like a child," Periander said. Odyn was the youngest of them and often worried it made him inferior somehow.

"You are the one who won the Battle on the Strait," Theseus said, "Not I."

"No, you are the one that lost the Battle on the Strait," Odyn said, "When you demanded we all fall back—"

Periander threw his arms up as Erykus retorted the insult. "I saved the lives of all your men, and likely your life too."

"I'd rather die on the battlefield than—"

"Enough!" Periander shouted and slammed his palm against the table.

Everyone stared at him, including Weveld, who sat in the

Crown Magician's chair nearby.

"Stop bickering like children," Periander said. "Now I'm treating you like a child, Odyn. Not when I told you to keep our strongest and freshest army in the south Cerden."

Odyn sat down, remarkably. He listened to the reprimand.

"It's not a bad thing that you haven't seen the enemy," Theseus said. "That's the reason we sent you south, so that your army would be the strongest when it really counted."

"You haven't seen the enemy," Periander repeated, his eyes looking through the table and tower and into his memories. "Our two greatest defeats: the Battle at Dagger's Edge and the Burning of Edessa..."

"Yes?" Weveld murmured, while the others joined him.

"We did not see the giants until it was too late," Periander said. "We did not see the giants until they were *all* there."

"You think...?" Theseus began.

"They're in the south." Odyn said. "But that can't be. There's been attacks on the Blood Strait or in Sinai!"

"No giants in Sinai," Theseus mumbled. "Soldiers only."

"Weveld, a map please," Periander said.

The Crown Magician was smiling. He rose and opened the Everwood doors, called to a servant and closed the door seconds later, with a map in hand. Anyone the Council could possible need was already standing ready, such as the Royal Cartographer, Veren Nallar.

Weveld spread the map on the table for them.

"Theseus, mark your skirmishes, and I will mark mine," Periander said. They used a quill and flask of ink that Weveld produced from his cloak. Soon there were six or seven X's along the Blood Strait, North Cerden Mountains, and the regions northeast of Edessa. "And Odyn, you have truly not fought a single one?"

"None!" Odyn repeated, looking at the map.

"Have you lost any scouts?" Periander asked. That was another indicator of the enemy's horde.

Odyn pursed his lips and hummed. "One," he said. "His horse was spotted, dead, at the bottom of a crevasse. It was an accident."

"Did anyone see the man fall?" Theseus asked.

"No."

"Mark it on the map," Periander ordered.

Odyn drew a small circle a bit east of Tarasal, a remote mining village north of the Golden Plains.

"Glyphs," Theseus said. "I will send word for my men to sail south."

"Sail past the Galin before you set to shore," Periander said. "Here." He marked another spot on the map, a day's march south-east of the river.

"Why?" Theseus asked.

"The horde is trying to evade us and strike here, in Galinor. It's the only explanation. It's been a full three years since any significant sightings of them," Periander explained. "We are going to attack them on all sides."

"Where should I go?" Odyn asked.

"You're a Prince," Periander said. He knew how Odyn must feel, for he had felt the same potential inadequacy from Odyn's seasoned father. He would treat Odyn like a man. "Where should you go?"

"Well, if I pull out of the Cerden Mountains too quickly, they might notice, right?" Odyn said. "I will move gradually, every few days withdrawing. If we plan to catch them on the Galin, I will fall back as far as the final ridges and wait there until we know where they are. Periander, you will have to be the bait, if this is the plan."

"I know," Periander said. "I will march south along the Mydarius Coast and then the Galin until we encounter them. Weveld, is there any way we can communicate more quickly between our separate armies?"

"I have read about Scrying Stones," Weveld said. "I believe the Disciples of Andrakaz would have a firm enough grasp on this type of magic to help."

"How does it work?" Theseus asked.

"We use any object, such as a stone, but alter it in a very unique way. Usually, by putting a pocket of air or fire within. Then we can use a typical scrying spell," the Crown Magician explained.

"I'm not familiar with scrying," Odyn said.

"It's a vision-spell that focuses on a specific type of object. The more of that object there are, for example instances of water, the less likely you are to view your intended target,"

Weveld said.

"So by making an object that is neither popularly man-made, nor common in nature," Periander extrapolated, "you can write scrying spells that will allow our magicians to see each of us, and only us."

"Precisely," Weveld said. "I will get started on that immediately. Hopefully, I can get a Scrying Stone to each of you before you set out from the Tower. Just give them to your magicians. I would not want to invade the privacy of my Princes."

"Of course," Periander said.

"Maker willing," Theseus said, "We will meet again on the field of victory."

Periander frowned. *Even if the Maker doesn't will it, I still plan to stand on a field of victory,* he thought. Then, *You have to change,* bubbled to the surface of his thoughts again. He shook his head. Theseus and Odyn had already stepped to the door. Weveld waited for Periander to step through the Everwood doors before he followed.

The ritual of entering and exiting the Triumvirate Council Chamber was a silent ordeal. Periander waited for the others to vacate the hallway before he stepped forward for his turn. Each was a life-sized statue, carved of light-brown Everwood, of the Triumvirate's founders. First, the likeness of Valik Aristorn. He had a beard past his collarbone, and his hairline was reclining. Periander dropped to one knee. Was it true that Periander's father had orchestrated their downfall?

He rose to his feet and took two steps farther. The statue of Syril Ivos was a good foot shorter than that of Aristorn. He had a full head of hair past his ears and no beard. Periander knelt. How had his present day become so lost from those old ones?

The third statue was Tiberon Odyn, the first of his name. He was the tallest of the three, but was not as thick as his descendants. He had short hair and a small beard around his chin. Periander had looked at this statue so many times before. Who was this man? How could one man have made something that lasted so long and meant *so much?* It was only under Tiberon's guidance that Ivos and Aristorn joined forces. It was only under his leadership that they had defeated the warring Kingdoms of Midgard and united the whole Dominion under his

Triumvirate. Periander bowed. He stayed bowed longer for Tiberon. He knew the whole point of the Triumvirate was the equality of the Princes. But he stayed there and whispered a quick prayer, the first one he had in a long time. "Maker, make me more like this man," he breathed. He also prayed he had guessed the giants' strategy correctly.

. . .

The Mydarius Sea stretched toward the horizon. It had been a fortnight since their Council meeting, and their armies had moved south. Of course they had left troops to guard the north and keep up the appearances of their influence. Periander had again left Captain Illus in his stead. Captain Mordus had set sail with Theseus's men. From the coast, Periander had seen their ships sail by two days earlier.

Salantar rode beside him, humming a song from the saddle of a dun warhorse. Periander remembered the crude lyrics to it and mentally thanked the seasoned fighter for not singing the words aloud.

"Weveld," he called over his shoulder. They were only a day's march from the Galin River now.

"Yes?" the sorcerer said, riding up beside Periander. They were both mounted on black horses, Periander's bulkier and taller than the wizard's.

"Any news from the Scrying Stones?"

Weveld shook his head. His hair was now more grey than brown, and his beard was growing longer. "No sightings. Odyn's army is no more than a few hours march from here, but your scouts have already reported that. Theseus's men are ready. They are camping a day's march south of the river."

"Have any of the sorcerers spotted anything at all of the giants?"

"Nothing," Weveld said.

Periander shook his head. This was starting to feel wrong. He had a feeling of dread in his stomach. If the giants did not appear, it would mean they had lost major ground and wasted a lot of time travelling south. It could be a major defeat.

"They'll be here," Salantar said. "I can feel it."

Weveld scoffed. "You can feel battle?"

Salantar laughed. "You need some youth for it," he said. "You probably could've, in your younger days."

Weveld bristled. "I'm young still, and handsomer than you."

"If old badgers were appealing!" Salantar returned.

Periander burst out laughing.

"What?" they both asked him.

"I never thought you two would argue about appearances!" he said.

"It's not my fault I was imprisoned in hell for years," Salantar barked.

"Yes it is, actually," Periander retorted. "And Weveld?"

"My age should only reveal my loyalty to this country. I have served it all my life, unlike some of your companions," he said, ignoring Salantar.

"Are you doubting my loyalty, for my youth?" Periander asked.

Weveld gaped. "Of course not," he stammered. He struggled to keep his steed under control. He was hardly paying attention to where he rode. "I—well, you—"

"At ease," Periander said after a moment of humour. "You are both fools if you think you are attractive. I, on the other hand," he ran his fingers through his beard and they got caught in a tangle, "am the very example of beauty."

They all burst out laughing.

Ahead, the hill beside them curved northward and their view opened up to the flatland south of the Cerden. The clouds were magnificent towers in the sky or the tendrils of some glorious flying creature. In the distance, a cloud of smoke was rising along the rocky Cerden slopes from an indistinguishable village.

No sooner had Periander seen it than he heard a sound that chilled him to the bones and cut his laughter quiet. The dread that the enemy might not be here did not disappear, but it became a different kind of dread, a black, oily dread like spilt ink or the bottom of a bog.

War drums began to echo the hills.

24

Year of Olympus 574

"I do not want an Apprentice!" Artemys repeated for the hundredth time. It was a resigned exclamation this time. The other Masters had already made it clear that this would be a significant embarrassment to the School if he did not, something about tradition and honour.

He had explained to them that he had no interest in accepting a member of the Order to be his Apprentice. *They are already gifted,* he had explained. *If I am to train a new magician, I will gift them something they did not have.*

Aella stood near him in the courtyard of the School. "It's not exclusively for their good. I am a much stronger person having trained Gredyn."

It must be someone I can change for the better, he decided. Though it appalled him to imagine working with or helping the sort of person he hunted for justice, it was something that made sense to him. *In all things, I must make the world better.* Though bringing someone to justice was the right reply, trying to teach someone would have to suffice.

"Aella," he said, "I want to thank you for your support. The removal of my predecessor could have ended poorly, and my leadership could have been refused."

Aella bowed her head, but kept walking beside him. There was a group of Apprentices leaning against the fountain ahead, some of them older than Artemys himself. He steered his course onto an intersecting footpath, so Aella and he would not need to interrupt them. "You have saved this Order from his taint, and you have likely saved it from its own destruction. I had to be skeptical at first, but you have done nothing to warrant my mistrust. Until you do, you will have my trust."

Artemys smiled. "That is unsettlingly close to a threat," he said, but laughed so she would know it did not bother him any. "I am just glad that Weveld has not resurfaced or threatened us further."

"He's been staying in that distant village. That cult. Should we do anything about them? As the Order of Magic, they are our enemy, are they not?" she asked.

"They do nothing to harm us, nor harm magic. Should they, we will crush them." It had been several months since he had delivered his ultimatum, and the newfound Brotherhood had done nothing to concern him.

Someone cleared his throat behind them. It was Darian Barsos, his hair longer than when Artemys had had met him, and his skin redder. It was a hot summer in Olympus, where Darian served as Court Magician for Prince Odyn.

"Welcome back to the School," Aella immediately said. She and Artemys clasped his shoulder and asked how he fared.

"I am well," he said, "but my city is not. More riots and robberies bury the streets in broken glass and bodies. Our guards are stretched thin now. I have come to request a handful of mages to defend the Keep, should it come to that." His face was grim.

Artemys lowered his head. *Will this not end? I have done my best to help these rioters get justice, but they continue to create such chaos!* "I will go myself. It is time to end this. Do you have the name of a ringleader? Someone who is urging these anarchists on?"

Darian glanced nervously around the courtyard to make sure they were talking in silence. "Certainly you are needed here, Master?"

Aella was giving him a surprised look too.

"I am needed wherever the Triumvirate needs me," he said. "I am young and can handle myself better than my predecessor. Let us bring these men to justice. A name!"

Darian grimaced. "They say it is a rogue member of the Buccaneer Navy who has snuck into the city to escape his pirate enemies. I do not have a name, but we have three suspected places. These are places that we could not access with a horde of guardsmen, so they are the safest places for a coward like him."

Artemys nodded. "You must show me. Aella, you must oversee the School in my absence." *Another hunt!* He quivered in anticipation. *I must teach these fools some patience! They riot because the Triumvirate bullies them—what they need to do is wait for me to deal with the Triumvirate! Their solution solves nothing!*

Without waiting for a reply from Aella, Artemys performed the Known Location spell for Olympus and put his hand on Darian's shoulder to bring them both to the Olympian outskirts. This Known Location was set on a hilltop that overlooked some of the city from the west side; it was the furthest from the inner city of all the Locations.

The hilltop was mostly clear, but was fringed with the dense foliage of the jungle. No other place in the Dominion had trees like this spiky canopy full of colours. There were forests of deciduous trees along the southern coast of the Mydarius Sea, but here, north of the Forked River, the land was overflowing with life.

Olympus was so large it made any man feel small. It was twice the size of Athyns and three or four times the size of Avernus. The slums were more than two-thirds of the city, hundreds of thousands of people living in single-storey shacks of wood and rock. An occasional estate interrupted the squalor, towering stone walls and floors of their Keeps rising above. Most of them were surrounded by smoke and some of them were burning. In the distance, almost on the horizon, were the walls of the Upper City—full of three storey mansions—and the towering heights of Odyn's Palace within that. Somewhere beyond those Upper City walls was Bronzehill Keep, where Pyrsius hid Kerres from their father and visited her in secret.

"What are the suspected places this lout is hiding in?" Artemys asked, still surveying the city.

Darian coughed and pointed toward the horizon. "There is a warehouse on the river in the south end of the city that was well guarded by freelance mercenaries the last time our scouts could get there. On the waterfront to the north is a marina that none of our eyes-and-ears have heard from in months. Lastly, practically under our noses, the Red Stallion near the Upper City

Walls."Artemys turned to him. "You said the mob's leader was once a Buccaneer?"

Darian nodded.

"Well then, he will not be on the waterfront," Artemys decided. *The Red Stallion,* he recalled. *That is where I stayed when I hid in Olympus... I fought Hevarus near there, and I tracked a thief near there.* He remembered the barmaid he had considered asking to his room. He could not imagine the bumbling innkeeper cheering on a bloodthirsty gang.

"I will go to the warehouse. It is the two-storey one, with the trees around it?" Darian nodded again. "Go to the Outer Barracks and commission a troop of soldiers. Not guard, soldiers," Artemys instructed, "Head toward the inn in case I guessed wrong. I will meet you there."

"Good luck, Master," Darian said, and set off down the hill. The Outer Barracks was one of the defensive Keeps on the very fringes of the city. From it, Darian could make a direct march across the district to the Red Stallion.

Artemys waited until the Olympian magician was out of sight. Then he replaced his vision of the smoking city and jungle hilltop with glyphs. He moved his view forward, past the striding description of Darian and through the glyph-filled air. Wherever a column of smoke rose, the glyphs for air became descriptions of smoke and heat. Artemys focused in on the warehouse, but withdrew by a block. Here was a glyph-stone wall, fish-smelling glyph air, and glyphs for the rats which were tearing at a nearby body. He let the vision fade, and knelt to the much more tangible earth. He wrote all those glyphs, for the wall, fish, air, rats, flesh, rot...

Then he stood in that spot, smelling that stench and stepping away from the corpse. He could see the warehouse down a nearby alleyway and across the street. It was built out of rock bricks but had giant wooden support beams crisscrossing its front in horizontal and perpendicular directions. Oddly, there were no men in the street where Artemys had appeared—none living, that is—nor in the alleyway.

He cautiously approached the next street, at the end of the alley. There were two or three children running several blocks away, but there was no sign of anyone else. Artemys approached the warehouse. He traced the glyphs for air and force on the doorframe and sent the barred doors crashing back into the building.

A dazed guard stumbled to his feet in surprise. "What, who!" he stuttered, and jabbed forward with a spear.

Artemys sent him flying with another air spell. The man crashed into a stack of boxes, which were apparently full of something heavy for they did not collapse. He did, and, dropping his weapons, scurried toward a side door of the building. Artemys let him go.

This was not a bustling command post or propaganda nest, but instead an organized storage space. Artemys walked across the warehouse to make sure there was no one hiding within. Perhaps there was a secret basement? With growing dread, Artemys scoured the building to no avail.

Was I wrong? Is he on the waterfront? What if he is connected to the Buccaneer Navy? That cast the age of riots into a much darker light, an intentional undermining of the Triumvirate.

"No, no," Artemys said, and took a step back in his mind. He walked toward the blasted doorway. *There are no secrets from the Great Glyph, or...well, very few. There is no plot beneath the surface, save mine. I know this, because I have looked for this,* he told himself. There were no rioters, criminals or traitors here. *If the mob is not connected to the Buccaneers, then...they are at the Red Stallion.*

His stomach sunk as he did, to the dirty cobblestones. With a finger, he wrote the glyphs for the Red Stallion Inn in the mud and did not even regain his feet to read them.

When he did stand, the deserted river streets were gone. Now he stood in a debris strewn street. This looked startlingly close to the drawings he had seen of the People's Revolution of his grandfather's day. Akheron had incited a riot that led to a complete revolution against the Kinship of the Maker. He had gazed at an illustrious canvas depiction of a man in white, holding the ceremonial glass chalice of water and standing in a thoroughly bloodied street. There had been glass and wood scattered across crumbling cobblestones, and columns of smoke framing the scene. All of this looked similar to the Red Stallion as Artemys took in his new surroundings, but what truly captured the scene was the look on the Kinship man's face, the forlorn loss somehow painted directly upon animal hide.

Here, in Olympus, was the same distancing despair. There were Olympian soldiers strewn across the ground, amidst many more civilian corpses. The inn was burning, sail-like clouds of smoke rising above to grey out the sun. There was a group dragging some injured away down the street; they ignored Artemys.

Trembling, he climbed the steps. Darian had brought guards here, expecting nothing but a routine check in and found an angry crowd and, likely, their zealous leader.

There were no more soldiers amid the carnage now. And now Artemys saw burn wounds and maims, sizeable rocks and dissipating vapor. This was the aftermath of a magical battle. Darian lay against a nearby wall. A man lay across Darian's legs, one arm reached upwards. The man's hand was gripping a knife. It fit sleekly between the Court Mage's ribs.

Artemys closed his eyes and turned his head away before he opened them again. There, stuck in the wall between broken beams of wood and scorch marks was the barmaid that had helped Artemys that day. He had killed a handful of men since the Massacre of Eldius, but it had not been since killing those first two that he had felt like this. He almost emptied his stomach.

Then he heard voices. There were still some men on the floor above him, their muffled mouths conversing. Darian was dead, and by the trail of corpses he was the last of his troop to fall. Those were offenders up there, killers and rioters all of them.

Artemys wrote a few glyphs on the ground and stepped back. A cone of light angled upward from the ground and into the ceiling, cut away wood and brick so that a circular area of the layer between floors collapsed to Artemys level. Three men landed on their legs, hard, and crashed off of the circular section of floor they had stood on.

"Protect me," one of them shrieked as he tried to get to his feet. The others jumped forward, and Artemys set them both on fire.

He did not feel his rage as he stepped through the falling ashes. He only felt peace and the disruption of it. He only felt the guard who claimed lineage of House Aristorn, breaking a boy of seven's ribs. He only felt his father's justice.

The third man slipped on a brick from the storey above and fell on his behind. Artemys grabbed him by the collar and smashed him against the wall, only a few feet from Darian. Darian was part of the problem, killing men and women who deserved better, whose only crime was being bullied by the Triumvirate.

"Are you the *mastermind* behind this all? Behind running the streets of Olympus red with human blood?" Artemys asked. This man was part of the problem too, bullying the Triumvirate back, while its very nature defied being changed. The Triumvirate could not be taught; it must be killed.

"Who are you? A lord? *This* is what you do," the man replied, trying to collect some ounce of his passion. He indicated the debris of the tavern.

"I am trying to make a difference! You cannot fix a man by torturing him. You cannot fix a government by torturing it, any more than you could a man!" Artemys replied. "These riots, they are not solving anything, they are simply clouding the shark infested waters with blood!"

"I know that! A little blood will bring out the sharks, and they will bring a reckoning for the Triumvirate!" the man retorted. He had sharp eyes, a clever expression. His narrow jaw smiled as he spoke now; he thought he had Artemys. He thought they were on the same side.

"You are one of the sharks," Artemys realized. "The people are unruly, but you, you are one of the ones who likes the bloodshed and feasts on its results."

The man frowned. "You agreed with me, that the Triumvirate must be replaced."

"Yes, but not tormented. These riots have been going on for decades now, since the war. They are becoming worse and worse, but have not caused any change. Only more fear!"

"What do you think you cause?" the man snarled. "Killing people from the shadows? Killing the unjust, no matter their sins? You cause fear! I knew you would come for me, when I worked with the Buccaneers. We all knew that you would. Why do you think I turned to the people, instead of raiding them?"

Artemys shook his head. *The unjust* should *fear me. The Aristorn guard who beat me, he should fear me.*

The man shoved against Artemys hands. *"You* cause these riots. No one knows your name or your House, but your actions have the words of lords and Princes all over them. A nobleman seeking his own justice. How can we be ruled by such a man?"

"No," Artemys replied. *I cause this? Me?* He slammed the man back again. He was starting to feel sick again. "People like you cause it. Waiting for chaos to swim in."

The man laughed, his smile returning. "You are the great shark, we the lesser ones. You won't admit it, but the only way to finish the Triumvirate, to put it out of its torment," he said, throwing back his head to get dark sweat-drenched hair out of his eyes, "Is the chaos! That's why you kill, that's why you hunt the evil doers to make us all fear, to make us all more active. But you're the biggest one."

Artemys stepped back from the raving man. This radical, hypocritical fool spoke a truth that could break Artemys if he let it. A truth that had hunted him for years. He was part of the problem. He was a murderer, a plotter, a rebel, a sinner. He was one of the sharks. *But how can I fight the Triumvirate without fighting? That does not even make sense!*

The man was bleeding, he noticed, all down the wall behind him. He must have hurt himself when he fell. The tavern was groaning around them, shaking after the damage that Artemys's spell had struck to its very core.

Its very core. That was important. "Riots are on the skin of the Triumvirate," he told the man. "Wars, like my father's, danced in its organs. But to change it, to break it and rebuild it... we need only grip its heart."

The madman sank a bit lower against the wall. "Your father's? Who are you?" he asked again, knowing he had lost, knowing that he would die.

Artemys smiled. "Artemys Gothikar, the Crown Magician of the Order, the heart of the Triumvirate."

He threw beams of light to both sides, slashing out the sides of the tavern and turned his back on the man. As he walked into the street, the man shouted something incoherent, and the second floor of the inn collapsed on top of him.

Artemys swore he would not kill again, not until he could strike the entire Triumvirate down in one room.

Shards of glass pelted his back, but nothing hurt him. He

was hurt inside, knowing that he was part of the problem, knowing that, in truth, he had been failing his goals ever since killing those first two offenders in Eldius.

There was someone in the street now, turning to run as soon as she saw him coming out. Another member of the gang? The inn's roof was still breaking apart, but Artemys found himself running after her. She had her brown hair bound at the back of her head, but was wearing proper leather shoes, not heels nor sandals of any kind. She was not wearing a dress either; this was a girl familiar with getting around the streets, running, jumping and hiding.

It was the thief! Artemys kept running but looked into the Great Glyph, watching the glyphs for stone moving under his feet and the glyphs for fire as he dodged around a burning carpenter's shop. He had guessed it. As he looked ahead and saw the glyphs for the girl he was chasing, he recognized her as the same thief he had chased before killing Hevarus. He had let her go then, but this time he would not.

It was only instinct that governed this decision, his hatred of this mob and their backwards efforts to evoke change.

He ignored what he had learned from the mob's leader.

He let the Great Glyph fade, and stopped running. They were in an adjacent street, the thief running ahead. He wrote a spell on the ground, one that took some time. It referenced the thief's True Glyph, the glyphs that represented who and what she was. He gave it a good yank.

The thief tumbled out of thin air, in mid step, and barely avoided crashing into the wall right beside him. She managed to sidestep around the corner, tripped over her own feet, and deposited herself into a heap a few paces away.

Artemys strode forward and knelt beside her. "What you do is wrong," he said. "Stealing for yourself. Give me one good reason not to kill you."

She glanced up at him in terror and opened her mouth to ask who he was. She was bright though. That was not a reason. She looked at him with wide eyes and paling face.

He did not want to kill her. He had not studied her life as it had played out in the Great Glyph; he had done this with some of the criminals he hunted. But she was just a thief, from what he had seen. Did that deserve death? Artemys had to only believe in white and black and the two could not mix. If he opened himself up to grey... then the world would become all grey. He would lose good and evil for mediocrity. And she was not good, she was bad.

"My name is Tannes," she said, clenching her jaw.

"What?" he asked, confused.

She laughed, but it did not last long because of her fear. "You want a reason not to kill me. The best reason is me! My name is Tannes. My mother died of starvation three years ago. I almost starved to death last year." Her face darkened and she went on, "I have been raped twice. I have killed twice. I would like to be safe, and that is all I would like."

Artemys stepped back. There were two oceans roaring inside of him, fighting at one another. Mercy, his father had mumbled. Justice, his mind replied. She was a thief, she was a murderer. But she was a victim. And she wanted what anyone would want.

"I..." he trailed off. Tannes glanced around, likely judging if she could make her escape. She must have known she could not, for she waited for his rebuttal.

He did not have one. In the heart of the storm was Artemys's creed, which he kept returning to. *I will damn myself so that none need be damned again.* In this circumstance that offered two possibilities. *Kill her for her murders; though this makes me a murderer, it stops her from harming more.*

And then, the second option: *Don't.*

Letting her live would be as much of a sin as killing her, would it not? Artemys did not care about that. He only cared about the ends, not the means. Would she kill again, if he let her go?

Can something that is wrong become good? he wondered. *Maker, I hope so. For my own sake, I hope so.*

"I will not kill you, Tannes," he said. "But I will not let you go."

She stared at him. "Am I to be your prisoner? If you attempt to harm me, I will defend myself." She reached for her knife.

"No," he said. "I will not harm you either. But I cannot let you go, in good conscience, without ensuring you will not sin again. Besides, this will ensure you will not worry where your next meal will come from."

She shifted uncomfortably and reclaimed her feet. "If I am to be stuck with you, tell me who you are."

Artemys smiled. "Have you ever wanted to be a magician?"

She raised an eyebrow. "I have dreamed of it! Imagine, creating food with words and writing."

"You will become a magician then," he said. He smiled ironically. He would she if she could cross the divide and be redeemed. And he would satisfy Aella's council in doing it. "My apprentice."

"Who are you?" she repeated.

Artemys smirked.

25

Year of Olympus 553

The Galin lowlands had disappeared into the waves of battle. The nearby Mydarius understood how it was. Tides lapped the shore, back and forth. Some waves crashed in a loud din, while others were the gradual ebb and flow of sand covered and sand lost. On the lowlands, instead of the tide reflecting white and blue, it was the colour of blood.

Periander yanked his sword out of a fallen giant's shoulder and rolled out of the way of another's axe. The newcomer's attack crushed the bones in the fallen one's shoulders, and Periander's opponent yanked his weapon free, too. A spear caught the giant in the arm, and another in one foot. Flailing free of its attackers, the mountain man smashed away one of his new attackers and, a spear still in his foot, lashed out for the Prince again. Periander stepped backward, and the large axe clawed the ground in front of him. Two arrows appeared in the giant's chest with a thud, and he fell to his knees.

The giant cursed before he fell, foreign words that were just a rumble to Periander.

The Prince's squad formed around him, seven ragged men. Three had bows; the other four were armed with shields and spears. One was bleeding from the leg and limped, but the others were unharmed. That last giant had smashed away one of his men, but they did not even pause and struck forward at the next mountain man.

The giants did not fight in ranks. They swung their weapons too broadly to stand anywhere near one another. It was a slight disadvantage, for the Imperial soldiers could group up against individuals. They still had to be careful, for eager giants might strike forward without warning.

Weveld had his own squad of guards and burned away enemies whenever he could cast a spell without harming their own men. Periander could see the burst of orange in the smoky cloud that hung upon the battle. He was not the only magician who fought today. Members of the Order of Magic or the Disciples of Andrakaz threw their own spells at the giants or ran along behind the Imperial troops, healing soldiers who had fallen but still lived.

Periander did not see a lot of fighting: his squad was behind a few others. His men liked to protect him. They did not like him risking his life for them. It frustrated him, but it was one of the few things that his orders could likely not change. Ahead and to the left, Mordus and Salantar fought back to back, toppling mountain men every few moments.

In this smoke, there was no sign of Theseus or Odyn, or any of their soldiers. If all was working to plan, there would be three separate battles being waged, on three separate faces of the horde. And if all continued to work according to plan, the giants would start to panic when they realized they were trapped. Panicking would make them fight more desperately, more dangerously, but also recklessly. Fear. It would be a victory in itself to make this horde feel fear.

Scattered amongst the giants were troops of men wearing yellow. They did not seem to command the giants; rather, they fought alongside them.

An even larger brute appeared through the smoke, with a smaller mountain man beside him. They swept aside half of the squad in front of Periander's and easily defended themselves from the counterattack. The larger one was bald and wore tattered hides over a hide tunic. He stepped around the troop and, with a roar, lashed at one of Periander's archers.

The spearmen thrust forward and defended the bowman while he fell back. The other two archers released a few arrows, but they seemed to be little more than a distraction for their attacker. He brushed away the shafts, leaving two dark red holes in his side and upper leg and smashed aside a spearman with the giant wooden mace he wielded. The soldier's spear and arm disappeared, and he was crushed into the ground nearby.

Periander circled the giant cautiously, along with his remaining infantry. Their opponent was almost twice as big as them: huge, even by mountain tribe standards. He lashed out again, hammering the ground with a loud thud as his potential victim leapt aside. Periander slashed forward and got the giant's hand while his weapon was still outstretched.

The brute roared and released the weapon. The spearmen drove forward to seize the advantage, and the archers released another round of arrows.

As the giant fell, the smaller one broke away from the squad ahead of Periander's. He roared, *"Vashal!"* and charged toward Periander's men. Periander simply stared. It could have been a curse or it could have been the fallen giant's name, but Periander found the emotion in it recognizable. He had felt it from his son and he had felt it himself when his father was gone. It was the despair and pain at loss.

The young giant fought recklessly and fell moments later to Periander's soldiers. It made Periander feel sick: they had slain a father and his son. A thought occurred to him, one he wished had not. *What if they had a mother, a wife? A lover?* Periander fought to return to his, but what if they also did?

It's battle, he told himself. *Our men have families, too.*

Nearby, a bolt of light smashed the ragged squad ahead of Periander's to pieces. Its aftermath left a dark spot in his vision, running through the air to the hands of a man wearing a dark robe. One of *their* magicians.

"We need him alive," he told his men. "I will catch his attention and absorb his attacks with my own magic. Flank him if you can, or attack him when he's off guard—we need him alive!"

They nodded to him. Periander grabbed three tokens from his pouch. Two were defences of rock: effective against most attacks. The third he snapped first. It sent a spike of metal through the air.

The enemy sorcerer saw it coming and knocked aside with a blast of air. Periander could not see his face, but the man wrote his next spell with jerky hostile movements. He knew who he was fighting. He sent an orb of fire toward Periander, as large as a man.

Periander snapped his second token. A wall of rock appeared in front of him. The fire was hot enough that the front of it became molten when it struck. A few holes appeared, spitting liquid rock back at Periander. He bit back the pain of the heat and stepped out of the way of a glob of hot rock that could probably have killed him. As the rock began to teeter, he hurried to write a spell of air. This spell could kill the man if it worked, but Periander was counting on his opponent countering it.

His air attacked the rock right in front of him and sent a blanket of half-molten rock hurtling through the air. Periander could not even see his enemy—the wall was still between the two. All around, giants and squads of Imperial soldiers were making room for this duel. Magicians cut swaths through battles and caused a sphere of death when they ran into one another: the common soldiers knew to keep their distance.

The magician cast a spell of water to cool the rocks, but before he could use air, the crumbling stone wall collided with him.

Periander ran forward, but dropped to the ground as another of the man's lighting blasts crackled toward him. The enemy magician was pulling himself up through the rubble. One of Periander's soldiers charged toward him from behind, and reached for him.

The loose storms on the ground exploded outward as the man defended himself with an air spell. Periander's soldier flew a few feet and hit the ground hard. He did not move. Periander was bruised by a few falling stones, but he charged forward again. The sorcerer thrust out another surge of light.

Periander broke his third token, and another section of rock appeared in front of him. The lighting did not even blast through, let alone harm Periander. Hiding from his opponent's sight, he drew his sword and shouted, "Now!"

It could not have worked better. A few of the squad started to run forward, uncertain, for Periander had not warned them of this specifically. More importantly, the magician spun to check for others rushing him from behind like that first soldier had. Periander charged away from his stone protection and reached the sorcerer before the man saw him coming.

He slashed at the man's hands first—even a subdued magician could still cast spells. The man screamed as his fingers were broken, bloodied or cut. Periander had not attacked hard enough to dismember the man, simply to remove the threat of magic.

He grabbed his enemy and, kicking at the man's legs, knocked him to the ground. The magician grunted, spittle appearing in his beard that Periander could now see beneath the hood. He did not recognize the man. He grabbed the knife from his belt and knelt over the spell-caster.

"Who are you?" Periander asked.

The magician simply spat upward and got his spittle back in his face.

"Tell me who you are!" Periander said. "Glyphs, who do you work with? Why would you betray your own species?"

The man kept his mouth closed.

A few of Periander's soldiers stepped closer. "We could torture him," one said.

"We haven't the time," Periander said, looking around. His other squads were doing their best to defend this position, but they could not remain here indefinitely. He adjusted his grip on the man's robe and hauled the enemy closer to his face, then paused. The man wore a tunic beneath his robe. It was a distinct grey colour, one that Periander had seen before. In a fluid motion, he slashed the man's throat and stood up.

His men were staring at him. They had heard his words and then watched him kill the man; they had not seen what he had. Which was all the better.

The Disciples of Andrakaz work for our enemy, he realized. *They are operating on both sides of this war.*

"Sir?"

"You will come with me. When we reach Mordus's squad, reinforce his men, as I will be taking him with me."

"Sir."

It was not a long way to Mordus and Salantar. They had to avoid a few heavy corpses in their path, a few living giants, too. The din was unbelievable. The giants were shouting as they fought—they were getting desperate. Odyn and Theseus must be fighting successfully as well. The enemy had not expected them here.

Mordus saw them coming and, after defeating a small group of Trionus's soldiers, pulled his squad out of the fray toward Periander. "What brings you to this side of the battle-lines, old friend?" he asked, clasping hands with Periander. He was a handful of years older than the Prince, and had, in recent years, taken to calling him "old friend".

"Dire news," Periander replied. Salantar was wiping blood from his sword onto the thin, brown grass beneath them. He looked up at Periander's words. "I need both of you to come with me, and, Mordus, bring your most trusted men only."

Mordus shrugged and bellowed a handful of names. A few squads broke off from the fight and were replaced by others. "These will do," he said. There were about twenty men now, not counting Periander's, who were joining the fight as ordered.

"What is it?" Salantar asked. He was one of the few who did not trim his beard shorter during the warmer months.

"The Disciples of Andrakaz work for the enemy. They have all along, I suspect," Periander said.

"Glyphs!"

"We're done!" Mordus added. "Will those who fight with us turn on us?"

Periander frowned. "I do not know. But we must turn on them."

"Now?" Mordus asked.

"We are winning a victory here. We might not be able to if we must fight a force of magicians as well," Salantar said.

"I know. Which is why none of the Disciples must know what we do until we strike."

"As soon as we do, they will wreak destruction on our men. If even one of them sees our attacks before we get to him..." Mordus was visibly shaken by this. He looked how Periander felt.

"We need some way to disguise our actions then," Salantar said.

Periander nodded. "We will. Perhaps we can deal with two issues at the same time then."

Mordus pursed his lips. "What second issue?"

"Weveld's loyalty."

There was a moment of silence. "I will go to him," Periander said. "Salantar, you will come with me. We will give ourselves a tactical advantage against the giants, a spell that will cloud this field in mist. I will give Illus the order to target the giants' legs, for only they will be visible beneath the cloud."

"That's brilliant," Mordus said. "The giants won't be able to see us, but we can see them!"

"I've wanted to try it for some time, but this the first battle where Weveld fought at my side, and he's the only one with an understanding of magic capable of it," Periander said.

"And it will give us a guise to position our men at each of the Disciples," Salantar said.

"I hope so," Periander said. "Do not move on them until the cloud forms. And if it does not, Mordus, come look for me. I fear the thought of Weveld's allegiance to our betrayers."

"The Maker's speed, Periander," Mordus said, and reached out his hand.

Periander took it and patted Mordus on the back. "You as well, 'old friend.'"

Mordus strode away, his men in tow. They would likely spread across the battlelines in search of the Disciples. Periander turned to Salantar, who was still holding his blood-smeared sword.

"Let's go," Periander said, and led the way.

Weveld and his squad had pulled back from the fight for a brief respite. He was seated on a large rock when Periander found him, legs dangling toward the ground.

"Sheath your sword," Periander ordered Salantar. He reluctantly obeyed.

"Weveld," Periander called, and the Crown Magician reclaimed his feet.

"Prince Periander," Weveld returned. He walked away from his squad and met Periander with an outstretched hand. "What brings you out of the conflict? For me, it was my age."

"We need a larger advantage," Periander said.

"Really?" Weveld asked. "Our armies are attacking from all three sides! The giants are panicking and falling like flies."

"But our men fall quickly, too," Periander said. "I fear the giants can regroup a second force much easier than we can. These are our only armies—we mustn't lose them."

"Very well," the Crown Magician said. "What do you suggest?"

"The giants' height and our lack of it are two advantages that cancel each other out, or put us at a disadvantage. I would like you to write a spell that will obscure the vision of the giants, at their height. Then, we can still fight while they will have a massive disadvantage."

"Large scale spells are incredibly dangerous," Weveld said. "There are many unexpected side effects, as you should know from when you learned magic. I could kill everyone here if I were not careful, and that is the least of my concerns. A spell the scale of a battle could leave a permanent effect on this region. We could change the world by accident, create something like the Southern Waste!"

The Southern Waste was referred to in a select few surviving texts as a lush forest like the lands surrounding Olympus. It was widely cited as the danger of large scale spells.

"Which is why we must not fail," Periander said. "This is why I came to you with it."

Weveld pursed his lips. He didn't look at the battle or the land, only at Periander. "I can try," he said at last.

For the next fifteen minutes, Weveld wrote glyphs on the ground. He restarted a few times, clearing his slate with the edge of his palm. He picked out a few strands of grass once he finished, before he stood. The grass could not affect the spell, only Weveld.

His words began with *"Arnabo-dara..."* but then blurred together so fast that Periander could discern none of them.

Even before he finished speaking, trails of mist were rising from him into the air in front of them, billowing together and across the field. Weveld finished reading the earth, and glanced back up at Periander. Before long, the sky was shrouded from view and even the air around Periander became obscured. He could see the ground fine, and the legs of nearby soldiers. Weveld and Salantar stood close enough to be visible.

"The Disciples serve the enemy," Periander said. He drew his sword. "Did you know?"

Salantar bared his steel too.

Weveld stared at him. "They have been fighting on our side all day!"

"And fighting for the horde," Periander said. "Did you know?"

Weveld looked at the glyphs written on the ground and Periander tensed. He could have written other spells there as backup. Magicians were dangerous, so dangerous.

Weveld looked back up again. "You're killing them, aren't you?"

Periander nodded. "They have betrayed their state, their oaths, and their race. We will defeat two foes today."

"Yes," Weveld said, his features sinking to a red fury. "We will. I can help fight them. My Order has been betrayed perhaps more than yours, Prince."

Periander did not move, still. His sword was at his side, ready. "You will fight *with* us?" he asked.

"Of course," Weveld said, brushing between them. "You don't think I knew, did you? You told me to find more magicians, and I did." Periander and Salantar matched his pace. Ahead, the crescendo of battle grew. Blasts of fire flickered through the thick mist—the only lights that could pierce it. The giants' war cries had turned to screams of pain and anger.

Weveld cut a hole in the horde. Periander worried it might be a charade at first. He doubted it after Weveld set the first Disciple they came across on fire. He forgot about it after Weveld crushed the second with a pillar of rock.

The enemy no longer fought. Many of the giants pulled themselves along the ground on bloodied legs to be later finished off by groups of parading Imperials. Those that still walked pressed their fellows backward until they could not any longer.

Many giants escaped, punching through the western most ranks of their opponents and fleeing into the foothills of the Cerden Mountains. In the aftermath, Periander bellowed to his soldiers of their victory. They had finally won a true battle. A great battle. The giants would spend years recovering. The Disciples would think twice about whom to side with again. Weveld clasped hands with Periander. Salantar and Mordus embraced. Captain Illus bowed until Periander grabbed his shoulders.

When Periander went to sleep that night, after a feast with Odyn and Theseus, he forgot about their politics, about their victory and about the Disciples. "You have to change," a strange man had told him. "Please."

He wasn't sure why he thought of it after the battle. He tucked the blankets tighter around himself.

26

Year of Olympus 577

Galinor was a lavish city. The seat of the Triumvirate afforded the capital certain luxuries, luxuries from every corner of the Dominion. There were carriages winding the wide streets below and men and women lounging on the rooftops. Artemys could see a woman bathing on a rooftop pool. He smiled; it had been a long time since he had last seen a woman bathe.

Artemys stood at a window in the Tower of the Throne. It was not a large window, and not a decorated one. Just an opening in the rock walls that afforded him a view of the city and the isle of Galinor. He could see the Mydarius stretching to the horizon. To Avernan men and women, the Mydarius was small. Artemys had grown up with both seas: the Mydarius and the Valharyn Ocean. The latter was larger than all the land of Dominion, from what maps showed. Since the Age of Myths, a fortune had been spent on exploring, searching for treasures in the lands beyond the Dominion, but no one had crossed the Valharyn, the desert to the south, or the tundra to the north. Or, in the least, no one had returned to tell of it.

He turned away from the window. He stood in the Council Chamber of the Tower, the true chamber of the Triumvirate. He wondered how many other Crown Magicians had stood at this window and contemplated the world while the Princes spoke.

It did not matter. Artemys was powerless to change anything. He was powerless to be the last Crown Magician, to fix their civilization, to cure the Triumvirate.

And, as he stood in this Council Chamber for the fifth time, he realized that he also could not kill the Triumvirate. Odyn sat in the seat of Olympus, Theseus in the seat of Athyns, and Periander in the seat of Avernus... he could kill these three.

"We need to act," said Theseus for the fourth time. "We need to stop these riots and whoever is causing them. It feels like we have not had peace since I was a child."

"There is no war," Odyn chided.

"And we must pray it does not come to that," the Prince of Athyns replied.

"There is no simple way to stop them," Periander said. Artemys and he had not spoken as father and son since that fight, three years prior. They were only Crown Magician and Imperial Prince now. "We *must* address their concerns. Provide food at cheaper costs, provide shelter for those with none. Our treasury cannot be that low, can it?"

Odyn's dynasty provided a large percentage of the Triumvirate's wealth, largely because their city was the largest. "The war exhausted my father's treasury and left my generation wanting. Only now are we regaining some of what we spent."

Periander shook his head and lowered his gaze from his peers.

Artemys paced toward his own chair, set aside from the Three Princes. The Crown Magician's job was to keep them in line, but not to be one of them.

Artemys knew he could kill them. He had the skill to. Only one of them was a magician, and he was not an experienced one. He could handle the physical act of killing them, and he could handle the mental act as well.

"But we know now that there are individuals behind this, do we not? We know the people live in fear of the vigilante of Olympus," Theseus said. "And we know there is propaganda in circulation, radicals seeding another revolution."

Artemys was that vigilante, though they knew it not. But he had never sought or published for revolution. If he had his way, he would kill those radicals too.

"The vigilante has not struck in years," Odyn pointed out. "He might be dead."

"Stopping these issues will not stop the unrest," Periander repeated. "I'm beginning to fear that the peasantry are correct: their lords neglect to help them."

Odyn raised an eyebrow. "I might suspect those words if I did not trust who spoke them."

Artemys could also handle the emotional impact. Killing Odyn would feel good: the man was much wealthier than Artemys and much more selfish. Killing Theseus would be harder. He was a good man, and more willing to act than the others. Odyn would only act if it served himself; Theseus would act if it served good. And Artemys's father...would not act. Killing him would be difficult for Artemys, but not impossible. His father now stood between him and the Dominion.

"The *only* way to calm the people is to show them that we do care. And you say we cannot afford it," Periander said.

Theseus threw up his hands. "The revolts are the water in a river, the vigilante and the zealots are wind blowing it faster. Stopping them may not stop the river, but they may slow it. Buy us time to buy their favour!"

Periander raised his head from its bow. "The Triumvirate is dead," he said.

Shocked silence followed.

Everyone in the Chamber stared at him. This was the High Prince, the hero of the Triumvirate, the greatest man any and all of them had known.

"I do not know if it was the war or not. Maybe we poisoned it earlier. Or maybe the government's very constitution is flawed," he said, meeting their eyes. "But we are the puppet-masters of a corpse, now."

"How can you say that?" Theseus snapped, a look of horror and betrayal on his face. "You were ready to sacrifice all of our lives for it, and now you say it's nothing but rot?"

Periander sighed. "I would sacrifice us all again," he told them. "The Triumvirate has done more for humanity than any civilization before it. We must revive it if we can. But we must also recognize that this is not a government to serve us. It is to serve the people."

Artemys stepped up to the table. "This Triumvirate has not served the people since my grandfather let it! It resulted in the death of a religion and all who followed it. That is the price of serving the people. Are any of you willing to pay that price?"

They glanced at him. The Crown Magician usually played a small role in the discussions of the Imperial Princes, but he was allowed to play *a* role.

Theseus raised an eyebrow. "It could be said that the Nobles of Avernus tried to stop the People's Revolution. That may not have been the Triumvirate serving the people, simply Akheron serving them. Do not forget that the Nobles need not elect Princes by blood, but by any reasoning they see fit. They sought to stop your grandfather, not aid him."

The Nobles of each city elected the Princes. They usually just elected that Prince's heir, but could override the system if need be. The Princes had a large impact on how the Nobles fared, so it was usually a symbiotic system. However, they had tried to cut Akheron out of power during the Revolution.

"If people had something to believe in now," Odyn said, "we would have peace."

Periander sunk a bit in his chair. "We cannot claim to address that conundrum," he said. "Akheron did not serve the people, but convinced them they were serving themselves instead of him. Even now, we believe the lie he fed us."

Artemys almost laughed. He had not noticed the angst his father felt for his grandfather. It somehow seemed ironic. "So without him, there would have been no Revolution?" he asked, incredulously.

Their reaction surprised him. "No," they said in unison.

"There wouldn't have," Theseus said.

Artemys stepped back from the table again. The Nobles had the power, and it was tactically impossible to kill them one at a time. The remaining ones would be able to quickly defend themselves when they realized what was going on. Even Artemys was not powerful enough to destroy all the armies of the Dominion. The Nobles held the power, and, by definition, they could not serve the people directly.

"I still cannot believe you have given up on the Triumvirate," Theseus said to Periander, shaking his head. Periander said nothing.

Artemys could do it; he was physically and mentally capable of clearing the Chamber. He *could* kill them, but it would not change a single thing. The Triumvirate would go right on dancing on the misery of its citizens. Artemys bowed his head. To truly execute the Triumvirate and force a new government to form, he would need to arrange the deaths of all three Princes and all nine Nobles, *at once.*

They continued their debate, but it meant nothing to Artemys anymore. The Princes were pawns and fools.

"How did it go?" Tannes asked after.

Artemys and she stood in the courtyard below the Tower. He had a momentary vision of wood crashing against the bloodied cobblestones before he shook his head and saw the clean-swept yard once more. There something gloriously final about the vision, and it left him with warmth in his despair.

"Artemys?" she asked.

He glanced up. Tannes had brown eyes, a deep hazel, and a sharp chin. He broke the gaze and led the way to a secluded corner of the courtyard.

"That well, then?" she asked.

Artemys shook his head. "We are ruled by...blind men," he said, kneeling to write a spell. "My father; he's the smartest of them. He knows this government is flawed, failing..."

She nodded.

He stopped his spell writing. "You should do this," he said. She knelt and started tracing her own line of symbols. There were no marks, of his or hers, but it was the intent that marked a spell.

Artemys continued, "But if I put Periander Gothikar and the Vero Murderer in a cell together, they would discuss philosophy until the end of time!" The Murderer had taken seven lives from the streets of that Port before Artemys took his.

She flinched. "And the others?" She stood up.

"Theseus is a man of action, but he is blind to how these riots are any fault of the government's functioning. He idolizes the Triumvirate," Artemys said.

She whispered, *"Bor'elep lorazar,"* and they stepped through into the courtyard of the School of Delfie.

"Odyn is the worst of them. He is selfish and he is hungry," he said quietly enough that Caius would not hear. The magician was leaning against a nearby tree reading a book, and gave Artemys a brief bow of his head.

"Well, *this* has to stop," she said. Tannes understood him in a way even Kerres had not. She understood that things had to change. If they stayed the same, humanity would be swallowed in their own sins. Artemys was still uncertain how strongly she would support further sins to evoke that change, but he was content with that. It meant she was a better person than he, despite how he had found her.

"I know," he said. "But I do not know how. I learned in the past that plotting achieves almost nothing. And, more recently, murder is sowing more problems than solutions. I need to strike in the very heart of it all," he said, careful not to name names here in the hub of magic.

"But how?"

Artemys raised his hands to his head and pressed the base of his palms against his forehead. "I do not know!" *Should I just hunt them down? It will not work!* "I thought that I had achieved something in hunting injustice. I did not. Then, I thought I had achieved something by becoming Crown Magician..."

"But?"

"I cannot change a thing," he said. "I might be able to stop the Princes from making things worse, because I can control the election of a High Prince, if it comes to that. But I cannot fix *anything!*" he breathed. He felt so weakened by it, he could barely walk.

"It takes time," she said. "You can influence the Princes gradually."

Artemys shook his head. They paused on the threshold of his own little tower. His tiny quarters, here in the middle of the ocean, in the middle of a realm of sinners, in the middle of nothing. "The years tick by," he said. "And my hands are as red as they can be. I have been defeated by myself and by this world. I am powerless."

He stepped into the shadows.

27

Year of Olympus 553

Five days after the Battle of the Galin, Periander and the Imperial Princes returned to the capital. Galinor was exactly how they had left it. The Everwood trees were in full bloom; their white leaves had not started turning to gold yet. Periander smiled as he rode through the city on the back of a black horse. He saw smiles now, heard cheers. A few men went to their families in tearful embraces.

"We need to get to the Tower," Mordus said. "The other Princes have been waiting..."

"Let them wait," Periander said. "We need this victory to mean something now. The war wages on."

"Does it?"

"The giants have more armies. Our scouts still vanish. We are still fighting for the west," Periander explained. Despite his own point, he clucked to his mount, and they picked up the pace a bit.

A woman ran between the tall trees and grabbed one of the dismounting soldiers nearby, planting kisses across his face.

I need to get back to Cat, he thought. But then he frowned. She had likely heard of the slain guard in the dungeon last year. She had sent a letter, but he had not read it. *No, I mustn't get back to Cat until all of this is over and I can truly* change.

His mood was fouled. He kicked his horse and trotted up the hill with Mordus in tow. They reached the Tower of the Throne, passing into the courtyard around it and dismounting. A stable boy bowed to him and took the reins of the horse. Mordus tossed him a coin, which apparently warranted a second, even deeper bow.

Periander stepped inside of the Tower. The first level was a guard house, to defend the structure at all costs. The second level had a small kitchen and quarters for the servants. Mordus remained in one of the Halls below the actual Council Chamber, separating from Periander without a word. Periander bowed to Tiberon, to Syril, and to Valik. Had they fought wars like these? Had they known the cost of it? Which one of them had stabbed a helpless man—a criminal, a fiend, a devil—and sunken into the bloody drain beneath?

"Periander!" Erykus Theseus cried in delight. He clasped hands with Periander, and the latter forced a smile.

Odyn was next, clapping both of Periander's shoulders and booming, "We finally won one!"

Weveld nodded to him.

"Let's be seated," Periander said. They stepped toward the triangular table, though none of them sat.

There was a map spread across it, by default now, and a pitcher of wine. Theseus leaned over the tabletop and grabbed it, pouring four cups full. "A toast," he said, "to our triumph."

Periander smiled. Erykus's cheer rubbed off on him. He accepted a cup and touched it to his comrades'. They all had a small sip. For this council, drinking too much could have dangerous ramifications for reputation. The decisions within this room dictated law within every corner of the Dominion, and anyone drunk within it would be cast out.

"Another toast," Odyn said, "to Prince Gothikar. It was his strategy that brought us glory."

"Do not toast on my behalf," Periander said.

"Come now, any man who increases my power will gain my respect."

"Do not," Periander repeated. "I will not be rewarded by whim, especially one such as that."

Odyn frowned. "You draw close to insult there, Gothikar."

Theseus spread his arms. "Come now," he said. "Let's not do this now. Odyn and I have talked, and we have decided something. We have an announcement to make."

Periander had been leaning against the table, but he stood straighter.

"We have the giants on the run," his friend said, "as far as we know. We accomplished this in cooperation, and, frankly, under the command of one man. Odyn and I believe the same man can keep them on the defensive and, perhaps, end this war. We have chosen to elect a High Prince."

"Wha—" Periander blurted.

"Weveld, would you approve such an action?"

Weveld grinned. "Of course. This is wartime. If ever there should be a High Prince, it is now."

"I vote Periander Gothikar for High Prince," Odyn said.

"And I," Theseus said, "second the vote."

Periander stood there stunned. He could barely breathe. Of course he had known he was giving orders to them before the battle, or even during the past few years. But he had not seen this coming. "Why?" he managed.

Theseus laughed. "Don't look so surprised," he said. "You have already been fulfilling the role of High Prince. This changes little but title."

"Exactly!" Periander said. "This changes nothing but accolades for me."

"Accolades you deserve," Weveld contributed.

Periander shook his head. "I am half the man you think I am. I am not the High Prince."

Odyn rolled his eyes. "I told you, Theseus. He hasn't the ambition."

"He has the necessity," Erykus said, setting his jaw. Periander saw a gleam in his eyes he had not before. Theseus believed in this, *fully.* "And that is why he should be," he said, looking over his shoulder at Odyn.

Odyn shrugged.

Theseus turned back to Periander. "Periander, you have talked in our bouts of politics, when we were young, that if any man should be High Prince, he must not want to be. He must need to be."

"I don't need to be," Periander said. "I don't need any of this." *Yes, you do,* a voice told him. Was this the change he was mean to accept? How would this help anything? Periander strode toward the door. He was done playing their political games. He could command armies without being a High Prince. They would all listen to him.

Valik Aristorn stared at him with wooden eyes. Unblinking, unwavering. The statue seemed to be speaking to Periander, not through movement, but through thought. Gothikar replaced Aristorn, for this? For storming away from Councils and refusing titles? Akheron had replaced the Aristorns for their seat as Prince. No one but Akheron knew why: it could have been out of desire, greed, or even necessity.

Periander turned back to the room and his friends within. "I accept," he said, his voice catching in his throat. "I will be your High Prince. I will command all your armies. I will win this war. And then, the moment it is over, I will step down again."

They stared at him and nodded. Weveld glanced at the plain wooden chair. The Throne. *Not yet,* Periander said. *I haven't the strength to sit there yet.* He turned back to the corridor and bowed low to Aristorn.

28

Year of Olympus 581

It was Artemys's name day. Thirty-six years ago, he had been brought into this world and given this name, the only one he had. Twenty-nine years ago, he had been beaten, bloodied, and broken by an Imperial guardsman, slighted by the success of Prince Periander. Eleven years ago, he had sought out the Brotherhood of Andrakaz to learn hidden truths and seek change. Eight years ago, he had become the Crown Magician after killing one of his only friends. Four years ago, he had realized that he had been wrong for the past thirty years. He had been trying to change something he could not, something perhaps unchangeable. He had been trying to make good and had been making evil. He had killed, he had killed so much.

He stood on a balcony in Galinor. This was the Keep of the Order, an ancient building in capital city. He could see the Tower of the Throne from this balcony, rising above him. Unattainable? He closed his eyes and prayed it was not. Everywhere he looked was chaos. Everywhere was the guardsman, the Aristorn, the boot in his ribs.

The Keep of the Order had once been the main holdfast of their Order. Eventually, the administration had shifted so fully to the School of Delfie that this tower had become nothing more than a property owned by a large civic institution, a nothing. Artemys could not help but wonder if the Disciples of Andrakaz had a hand in the shift. Every Crown Magician before Artemys had served the Brotherhood.

Artemys looked down into the streets. Was he done? Had

he played out all of his cards and lost? He needed to talk to someone other than Tannes; she was a good girl, a magician, and a friend. But she was so much less than he. She was simply a recruit to him. An experiment to see grey turn to white. So far, a promising experiment, but not what he needed now. He gripped the railing between him and the void, inhaled deeply, and forced himself to turn away.

The air tasted like baking, like grapes and pastry. It did not stir Artemys. He spent a lot more time in thought and a lot less time eating.

I have turned everyone away. He stood in the corridor beyond the balcony, but did not walk. He had nowhere to go. *My father only wishes to persuade me, to convert me. My brother only wishes to be rid of me and my magic. Kerres...* he touched his stomach. That thought made him hungry, oddly. Or sick. *I love you, I love you still. Maker curse me. I must not go to you, for you will destroy me.*

He started moving again, even if it was aimlessly.

. . .

Pyrsius was still living in Bronzehill Keep more than Avernus. He had duties in the Gothikar fief, but he spent his private life in Olympus, in Kerres's arms. She had found what she was looking for in him, Artemys knew. A royal, a powerful man, a good man who was not even aware of how she used him.

Today, he was shopping for her in one of the many markets of the city.

Artemys wandered several dozen paces behind him. *How did I come here? Why?* he wondered. *Just to see? Or to talk to him?*

He could scarcely believe that Pyrsius might hold some answer for him. *But did I come here for answers?* he wondered again. He came here because he was alone in the world, and Pyrsius was too, even if he did not know it.

"Alms, please," someone said. Artemys blindly handed out a coin, and started to walk away. He froze. Had he become so jaded? He would drown himself before he let himself become his father. He turned back to the beggar. "I am sorry for your circumstance," he told the beggar. "I wish you fortune, for you deserve it as much as any."

The beggar stared at him in confusion. He had a crooked tooth in the front of his gaping mouth, and grey stubble all over his face. "Bless you," he said.

Artemys smiled and turned back to the road.

Pyrsius stood right there, the passersby splitting around him. He held his hands on his hips, the hilt of the sword at his waist intentionally clear. He met Artemys's surprised gaze with a masculine aggression. This was not the boy who hunted stags on his father's Chase. This was the to-be Prince of Avernus, the son of the High Prince, the lover of an astounding woman. Pyrsius was Artemys's equal in this moment. "Brother," he said.

Artemys smiled. He already felt better. "Brother."

"Did you teleport here?" his brother asked. He had grown a narrow beard around his chin. It made him look even more distinguished..

He truly does fear magic? Artemys realized. "Yes," he said.

"You shouldn't have," Pyrsius said, and turned to go.

Artemys stood up and matched his brother's pace. "We have not talked in years," he said, still a few steps behind.

"That's true," Pyrsius said and slowed enough for Artemys to come abreast of him.

"I do not know why."

Pyrsius smirked, but did not reply. "Not since the Massacre," his brother said.

"I am sorry for that," Artemys said. Pyrsius stopped walking and glanced at him. Artemys glanced away from the woman pulling a cart up ahead and met his brother's eyes. "I truly am."

Pyrsius rolled his eyes, and they kept walking. They passed the woman with the cart; it was full of small, green fruit with rough-looking shells. Artemys had not seen such a plant before, but there was a whole variety of plants north of the Forked Rivers that did not grow anywhere else in the Dominion.

"What do you want, Artemys?" Pyrsius asked.

"How have you been, brother?"

Pyrsius stopped walking again. He was trembling. "I've been well. I'm busy. You? That's good. Are we just going to stand here and exchange predictions on the weather?"

Artemys stepped back. "I am *trying* to branch out again. I drove the people most important to myself away, and I want to go back to the way things were. So, if you have something to say to me, than say it."

Pyrsius grabbed Artemys by the arm and steered him into a nearby alleyway. There were rats picking at the rotting carcass of a predator bird; it looked like a hawk of some kind. It was shadowed. There were boards placed across the rooftops above, blocking most of the light.

"You want to connect? You want to build new bridges?" Pyrsius said. "I'll burn any connections you try to make to me, *brother*. Ever since I was a child, you have tried to ruin the world around me. I'm just trying to get by here! As a Prince, it's complicated. Which must be *why* you see fit to make my life more difficult!"

"What?" Artemys asked. "What are you talking about?"

Pyrsius sneered. "When I was a child, you abandoned me for magic. I remember days of us playing on the Palace grounds, then you left. Aside from visits, the next major *moment* we shared involved you burning the face of one of our citizens!"

"I had to study magic, because Father took away the Princehood and gave it to you! Magic is all I was left!" Artemys defended.

"Well, I am *sorry,"* Pyrsius said. "And then Kerres comes to me, crying. You used her and broke her when you got bored of her!"

"I—"

"Despite how I felt about you then, I was still terrified in Eldius. I thought I had lost you for good in Eldius. I was terrified when I saw you, saw the bloody men around you. I thought they had killed you already!"

"I'm sorry..."

"I did not realized until the fires had burned out, and you were long gone...that they *should* have killed you. *That* would have been justice."

"Yes, it would have," Artemys said, lowering his head.

"Oh, what new Artemys is this?" Pyrsius snorted. "A version I have not seen until now, a version I have yet to believe."

"Listen." Artemys wanted to plead, he wanted to ask for

some pity or forgiveness...but he had never given pity or forgiveness, and his brother would not now.

"Leave me alone," Pyrsius said. "And leave Father alone. He has been damaged by your building of bridges. He should have burned them too. He should have burned you."

Artemys staggered back. "Enough," he said. "Leave me."

"No," Pyrsius said. "This is my home now. You invaded it with magic, now you will leave it, too."

Pyrsius grabbed Artemys's shoulder with one hand to hold him steady and then lashed out with a fist. Artemys found himself on the cobblestones, bleeding like the predator bird.

"That was for how you treated Kerres," he told Artemys. "Now scram."

Artemys wrote a spell and appeared in the forest near the School of Delfie. *Let Pyrsius fear my magic,* he prayed. *Let him fear me.*

29

Year of Olympus 556

The giants fought skirmishes now, not battles. They picked away at the Cerden Mountains still. They were biding their time. Rebuilding a new horde. If the Imperials could manage to replenish their armies after their initial defeat at Dagger's Edge, the giants could too.

High Prince Periander Gothikar had called for his Council to meet on the war front this time, not the capital. It was a bit more difficult for Odyn and Theseus, whom he had summoned away from their own cities. With a High Prince, the other Princes could divide their attention and give their fiefs some aid, even if it was in the simple form of morale. They had to travel to Galinor via magic, then via horse to the High Prince's camp near Mount Cerde.

Periander awoke the morning they would arrive like he did any other morning. He stepped into a pair of trousers. His thick leather boots were getting worn, but he laced them up all the same. He chose a dark tunic and pulled it over his head, then a thicker one over it. Lastly, he donned his dark green cloak. He stood up.

He was going to tell them he was done. He was returning to Cat. This war did not need him anymore. It had been three years since the Battle on the Galin, and the war front had become a game of biding time, choosing land, skirmishing back the tribes' advances. Each time he had tried to advance, to finish the war as he had planned with his comrades, he encountered enough armies to force him to withdraw. He could only win battles he chose, such the Galin.

So now he camped at Mount Cerde and longed to go home. And he would. He was High Prince, and they could not stop him.

Periander stepped out of his camp. The mountain towered above him. It reminded him of the Maker's Forge peaks he had seen all those years ago. It felt like a different life. They were calling this the Unending War now, instead of the Trionus War. This was the seventeenth year of the war. Periander closed his eyes. If he still fought in this war next year, he would have spent as much of his life in the war as he had before it. There was snow at the peaks of the mountain, descending the slopes. The snow at his camp's elevation had melted away and been pulled downhill into creeks and streams.

Periander spent a few hours sparring with his men. He was fierce now, far stronger than he had been in years. He had been a shrivelled man for years, from the Loss of Edessa past the assassins that had come for him in Galinor. Following the attack on his son, he had worked himself into a frenzy.

He fought three of his soldiers at once, thrashing them one by one with the solid wooden sparring sword. There were metal rods in the middle of them to give them a bit more weight, but not enough to injure anyone seriously.

Captain Illus tried his hand against the Prince. The aged general was still a blade master and gave Periander a bit more trouble than his soldiers had. Periander's attacks had such strength that Captain Illus had to keep moving back or to the side from his attacks. An occasional slash caught Periander off-guard, but none he deemed "fatal". Illus was deft, that was certain. They were both perspiring, dancing across a solid span of dirt with the clack of blades.

Periander found himself thinking about his life more than the fight, and fell into the defensive to give Illus some breathing room. *When did my life become this war?* Periander wondered. He parried and tapped Illus's arm with his blade. The Captain smirked and stumbled to one side. *I use to care about things like... learning.*

Illus caught his shin and Periander winced. He thrust back in retaliation and put some distance between them.

What is right? Periander wondered. This fight had cleared his head a bit. He clacked blades with his opponent again. *What is right, here? To keep fighting unto the end of time? Surely not. I used to be a* good *man. When did I lose sight of that?*

When Ivos betrayed us all, instead of just me. When I burned Trionus City. Periander paused and was rewarded with a ringing blow to his shoulder. He pranced back, quickly, waving his blade to discourage a follow up attack. *Maker,* he thought, *I burned a family alive.*

He had no more thoughts for a while. He started to feel the rising snows again, the darkness he had awoken within that morning. The resignation. It felt more *right* than what he had done.

That's truth, isn't it? He strode forward and struck downward with his blade. Illus lost his footing, and touched the ground with his opposite hand to stop his fall. *Enough!* Periander snapped, and cracked his blade over his Captain's.

Illus lost his own sword to the earth and folded his ringing hands. "You've broken your weapon, sir."

Periander's wooden sword was splintered halfway up the blade, though still held together by the iron rod within, now bent. He tossed it aside. "Good fight, Captain!"

"Very good," another voice called as Periander heaved Illus to his feet.

Periander turned to find Odyn clapping his hands.

"I dare say you'd be a match for me," the other Prince said.

"I did not notice you had arrived," Periander said. He removed his gloves and gripped his comrade's hand. He gave it a bit of force; he wanted Odyn to feel his strength today. His assertion.

Odyn smiled. "Theseus said he would wait in the pavilion you have raised for this meeting. Your gladiator was kind enough to show him the way."

How long was I fighting? "Well, let's get to it," Periander said. He led the way down the slope until they reached a large pavilion marked with red flags. Within, Erykus and Weveld waited for them, seated at a rectangular table large enough for half a dozen men. There was a keg of ale in one corner that the other Prince had already poured from. Odyn stepped up to it as soon as they entered.

"You're likely wondering why I summoned you this far," Periander said.

"It must be important," Weveld noted.

"I'll cut straight to it. I am done fighting this war," Periander said.

"Periander," Erykus began, leaning against the table's edge.

"This has been my life for the past fifteen years, and the past three as High Prince have accomplished nothing, save giving you three respite. I need respite now. I am done."

Odyn turned from the keg. "Hold on, Periander. We have rebuilt our homes during these three years, but there is still much to do. The Dominion is stretched thin and exhausted by the war as much as we are."

"Then I can only imagine the state that my home is in," Periander said. "The state my wife must live in."

Odyn sat down, and put his muddy boots on the table. Erykus planted his hands on the table. "Our lands are starving. Yours is the farthest from this war," Odyn said. "Your fishermen have staved off misfortunate. They're a hardy folk. All of the food in the west is going toward supporting you here."

"I am not saying we give up on the war," Periander said. "Simply that I am."

"Trion hasn't. His hordes still press with his fervour," Odyn said. He raised his hand before Periander could speak from his open mouth. "Or Ivos, or whoever it is that desires our heads so much!"

"Everyone does," Weveld said.

"I do not doubt their fervour," Periander said. "I doubt mine. They can continue this war until the end of time, it seems." He paused. "This has perplexed me for a few years now. We often forget they are 'men,' mountain men. They must eat something... but...how can they feed this many soldiers?"

Theseus shrugged. "We have no way of knowing."

"But we do have a way of finding out, don't we?" Odyn asked.

"What do you mean?" Periander asked.

"Forget fighting them for a minute," the Prince of Olympus said. "They defend any route that our armies could travel. But what if we were only trying to explore, not invade."

"A map," Periander called. A servant appeared from the opening of the tent and handed Periander a rolled parchment map. Periander spread the map on the table. "Where do you think?" he asked. "There's only rock! Where could we possibly explore?"

"Without fighting the giants," Odyn added.

"I don't imagine they patrol the Trion River very much. Taking any substantial force along there would leave our entire warfront undefended," Theseus said. "We could follow it the whole way into the Maker's Forge."

"The Fields of Heaven," Periander said. "I read about that in a chronicle of Oban Hokar. He found a paradise in one of the valleys, full of tall and beautiful people...most scholars think it's another one of his fictional additions..." Hokar the Explorer was infamous for writing about things that no one was certain could be real. The Age of Myths thwarted understanding though.

Periander fell silent, lowering his chin. He knew where this was going.

"Giants? Beautiful?" Odyn asked.

"Have you ever seen a female?" Weveld asked.

"No. Have you?"

Theseus looked up from the map. "We could be onto something here. We need to send someone there."

"A troop?" Weveld asked.

"More, but not too much more," Odyn said.

"Someone that can represent us," Theseus said. "Perhaps one of us?"

"It must be one of us. The decisions made, should we find a *city* of giants...they could end the war," Odyn dropped his feet to the ground, and straightened his posture.

"We could cut out the enemy's economy from beneath them," Theseus said. He took a drink of ale and slammed his mug down to the table.

"Who will go?" Weveld asked.

Not I, Periander thought. *I am done with this. Don't send me.*

"I am marrying some woman within the month," Odyn said, "to ally the second wealthiest house in Olympus to mine. I will cancel it if I must."

Don't send me. Then, *Please, you have to change!*

"Someone will need to take command of this war front too," Theseus said. "But I have a reelection meeting with the

Nobles of my city this year...They are still frustrated with my lack of an heir, and I must persuade them I am still the necessary Prince."

"I will go," Periander said, despite all his will not to. "Send me."

All three stared at him, Weveld with a smile, Odyn and Theseus with surprise. "Periander, you said you were done!" Erykus blurted.

Odyn only grunted in surprise.

Periander closed his eyes and heard his voice say, "I was there at the start of this, I might as well be there at the end."

"I will take your place," Theseus said. "You have already given all you need to give."

"I am the High Prince," Periander said. "I will order you not to, if you insist."

Weveld stepped forward. "I will join the High Prince. This will be a dangerous ordeal, I suspect. I will make certain he survives it, even if he does not want to."

"Very well," Periander said. "I'm sure we can use some magic."

"You'll take two troops?"

"Three," Periander said. "I will ask for volunteers. We need men who want to go."

"Why?" Odyn asked. "You don't."

"Exactly. I must surround myself with those who do."

"I do," Weveld said. "I've seen this war suck my homeland dry for long enough."

Periander turned to go. "Who will stay in this theater of war?" he asked, turning back.

Theseus stood straight again. "I will, until Odyn has married. Then, perhaps we can trade places, and I will see to my affairs in Athyns." He glanced at Odyn, and the Olympian nodded.

. . .

Later, Periander opened Cat's letter. She told him how much she missed him, how much Artemys missed him. She wrote that he had left home to attend the School of Delfie. That made Periander proud; he remembered a few months he spent for basic glyph training there. But Artemys, he hoped, would aspire to be greater than he. Cat told him to do his best and stay safe and return home soon. Periander closed his eyes. How could he do all of those things?

He picked his quill from its well and wrote his own letter.

Catlin,

I miss you so much. I told Theseus and Odyn today that I was done fighting in the war. I told them I was coming home to you, and that they could finish things themselves.

I lied. By the end of the discussion we had strategized a way to end the war. I cannot write details here, lest this letter fall into untrustworthy hands. But I can write this: my final task in this war will take me further from you than I've ever been, and I'm not sure how long it will take. It could take years, though I pray it does not.

I will do everything in my power to return to you, but my primary duty, as always, is to this land. I cannot rest safe with you until the Triumvirate can rest safe.

I pray it can soon.

> *Yours always,*
> *Periander*

30

Year of Olympus 582

"It's just that you haven't been well," Tannes said. "I'm worried for you."

"You," Artemys said, "Are worried for me?"

"It has been two years now, since you returned from that Triumvirate Meet. You go about your day, you teach the general magic class, you train me for a few hours, and then you retire to your quarters. You spend days on your own, without a word to anyone!"

Artemys stood up and paced toward his window. They stood in his Tower of the School quarters. It was more than half a year since he had sought out his brother in Olympus. It was spring, and the forest outside was budding. The sun was starting to sink, casting an orange light against one side of the oak tree nearest the building. It looked complete.

"I appreciate your concern," Artemys said. "But there is nothing you can do."

He heard her soft footsteps and felt her hand on his shoulder. "Maybe you just need a distraction," she said. "You have become so obsessed with the state of affairs that you have forgotten your own state. When was the last time you talked to Kerres?"

Artemys brushed her hand away by spinning away from the window. They were standing close enough to embrace. "Do not bring her into this," he said.

"Do you still love her?" Tannes asked. "I know you have thought about me and I know how lonely y—"

Artemys closed his eyes. Anytime he imagined himself with Tannes, he only saw Kerres again. He would not and he could not betray her. He opened his eyes and made them ice. "You will not speak like this again," he told Tannes. "If and when there is a way for you to help me, I will not hesitate to speak to you...but not this."

She stepped back. She seemed genuinely saddened. It did not seem that she loved him or was trying to tempt him. She only wanted the best for him.

"Tannes," he said, and she glanced up. "I am glad to have one friend to rely upon."

She smiled. "I am as well."

A few minutes later, he was alone again. This time he felt it. He contemplated summoning her again, but that only sickened him. In truth, the School and his status of Crown Mage demanded enough of his time to allow him a day-to-day life. He did not spend hours thinking about the state of affairs as he once had. He could not anymore; it would break him like a twig.

Because he was weak.

How weak? he wondered. *Weak enough to be tempted?* Kerres was still there in his head. Tannes had made him think of her, and now he could not stop.

He turned away from his window again. His quarters felt like a den. There was a table to one side, drawers near it, shelves above it, and a scattering of chair around the room. *Just one peek,* he told himself.

The Great Glyph appeared before him, almost unwilled. He saw Kerres, dining with her father in Olympus. His businesses had flourished, and he now operated in both Avernus and Olympus. The name Rysarius had become a popular one and a wealthy one.

Artemys sank into one of the cushioned chair in his quarters and watched them. She was so unaware of him, he knew. He wondered if she ever thought of him; the Great Glyph did not show thoughts to him.

Time passed slowly. Artemys blurred the lines between Delfie and Olympus and waited outside until Kerres left her father's estate for Pyrsius's. The sun had almost set, and the world was turning blue when Kerres came through the estate's gate wearing a white cloak. She glanced both ways and froze when she saw him.

He stood up from his lean and waited as the moment drew onward. It had been nine years since he had last laid his actual eyes on her and she was no less stunning. She had wide eyes, but crisp enough eyebrows to look dangerous and not dallying. Her chin and cheeks were angular and symmetrical, her skin pure. He remembered how soft that skin was.

"What do you want?" she asked finally, with a toss of her braided hair. "Or are you here just to reminisce as you did last year with Pyrsius?"

Artemys could not break his gaze, but he felt shame. He should not be here. But he needed someone to show him the way...Pyrsius could not, but maybe Kerres could?

"I just need to talk to you," he said. "Does it have to be *for* anything, Kerres?"

She smirked. "It always was like that. There was always a reason for everything. Until there was a reason to send me away," she said. He opened his mouth to protest, but she continued, "I still do not understand what that reason was."

"It was my own foolery," he said.

"Oh, I knew *that* all along. Is that the reason you came all the way here, to tell me that?"

Artemys trembled. She had nerve. A fire that could not be extinguished. Artemys did not want her any other way. "Silence," he said. She obeyed. He still had some authority, and he was glad for it. "Despite everything, especially how it ended...we had something special. That has to be worth something."

She pondered in silence, still standing cautiously in front of the gateway. They were still within view of her father's guards. He was surprised she travelled on her own; Olympus was a tremendously dangerous city.

"Fine," she said. "Walk with me—can I trust you?"

He nodded. "I would never harm you—"

"Without reason," she said.

He fumed as she turned and started walking away. He had no choice but to stride alongside her.

"You have as long as it takes to get to Bronzehill," she said. "I will not have Pyrsius knowing of this."

Artemys smiled. "It is good to know some things can

remain between us."

"Careful," she said. "I only protect one of your secrets. I will not protect others."

"What?" Artemys asked. "What secret?"

She glanced at him out of the corner of her eyes. "You are going to become King...or so you say," she said.

"I..."

"How has your progress been, toward that goal?" she asked.

He glanced around. The streets were abandoned except for the occasional carriage or the scrounging beggar. "Well, I am Crown Magician," he answered.

Kerres laughed. "So I have heard."

They were quiet for a few minutes.

"Kerres," Artemys began. "I have made a great many mistakes. More than I could count on these hands."

"Are you going to apologize for treating me the way you did?"

"Yes. I have already accepted that it was my fault."

"It was," Kerres said. "And you cannot get me back again."

"That's not what I meant," he blurted.

"But it is what you want," she said. He could not meet her eyes any more, but she seemed willing to offer them for his interest. "I know how I make you; I can see the way you look at me, the lust you have for me, and the pain you feel."

"I..." Again he could only trail off. "It is not just that," he said, not bothering to argue his feelings with her. It was an argument he could not win. "I am lost, Kerres."

"And I cannot help you," she replied. They stopped walking in front of an empty bakery. Only a trace of the doughy aroma remained.. "You hurt me, Artemys. You hurt me worse than anyone has. I hope you find the help you seek. I hope you become King. I honestly wish the best for you...but I cannot love you again."

"I do not understand," Artemys replied. *She wants power...*

"I know you cannot. Because when you knew me, I wanted to be a Lady, a Princess, a Queen," she said. "But now I'm content to love Pyrsius. I'm content to just live. I have changed, Artemys."

"No..."

"Yes," she said. "People change."

No, they do not...Can they? Can I change? "How?" he asked.

"I told you already," Kerres said. "I cannot help you. Farewell. I hope you find what you are looking for." She started to walk away.

"Wait." She turned back toward him. "You were right, I am lonely. Give me one last kiss, Kerres. Please."

Her eyes widened. He could see the thoughts now. Should she? Would it be a betrayal of Pyrsius, or just a memory of Artemys and she?

She took a step back toward him, placed her hand on his shoulder and leaned forward. She smelled a bit like garlic from her dinner, but still like perfume. Still like Kerres. Her lips were dry; they stuck to his. They were warm, too. Her mouth was hot and wet. For that moment, with her touching his shoulder and touching his mouth, Artemys was not alone anymore.

Then she pulled away, her eyes and nose red-rimmed. She licked her lips. "Goodbye, Artemys," she said, and then she was gone.

And he was alone still.

31

Year of Olympus 556

Periander's expedition left the town of Grey River a full month later. They had sailed from Helius up the Strait, leaving in the night so as not to be spotted from Edessa. It was a large distance, but they could not risk anything on this mission. They had steered clear of Nori until they had noticed a distinct lack of movement or smoke. The town was abandoned. A trickle of refugees had arrived in Covin, Athyns, and Galinor over the past few years. Some from Edessa and some from its outlying villages. It seemed that Trion and Ivos had begun losing their grip on their Imperial holdings. They passed Trionus City—the mountain still looked broken where its Keep had once stood. The abandoned ruins chilled the entire expedition, and they only pulled to the coast to camp once it was out of site. Then, after three weeks of sailing along the Blood Strait, they reached the mouth of the Trion River.

Grey River had been no more than a scattering of gutted shacks, abandoned shops, and burnt corpses.

Among Periander's group were three Imperial Captains: Mordus, Illus and an Olympian Captain named Corlin, along with their respective groups of soldiers; just over half a thousand men altogether. Salantar and Weveld rode at Periander's side. The latter had a handful of magicians as backup, all in the orange robes of the Order. They had hunted the Disciples down as thoroughly as they could following the Battle on the Galin.

East from Grey River they sailed. Their troops were divided between five galleys. They made good progress for the first week, covering about twenty miles a day and camping on the Trion River's banks. His comrades dined with him each night, and occasionally guest soldiers that the Captains thought deserved special recognition by the High Prince.

Many of them spoke in excited tones; they admired him, loved him, and envied him. He tried to have patience with it. Morale was good for efficiency, so he praised their services. He lamented their sacrifice.

A month after leaving Helius, they started sailing northwest. The land was open still. Plains reached toward a mountainous horizon and occasional groves of evergreens dotted the landscape. Some of the men were starting to catch mild scurvy, or at the least ailment. Though it could be cured by Weveld's magicians, Periander decided to slow their progress.

"We need our men healthy," he said. "We will hunt and forage what we can as we travel."

Every few days they would stop, send out scouts and then parties of hunters to follow. On those days, while Periander waited, he would find himself left breathless at the sights. He had never been anywhere like this before, where grass stretched to the horizon, smooth like silky skin, shining with the rays of sun that danced between enormous, white clouds. Had it been here all along? For the Maker's delight and none other's?

He knew the history of these lands, he knew the facts. He knew that the mountain tribes came down into them every few years before the war, and Imperial troops had politely asked them to withdraw. They were Triumvirate lands, they would say. Pioneers surveyed it. Periander's campaign had already passed occasional settlements—all abandoned now—and empty mines along the occasional shallow ridges or crevasses. This was one of the main frontiers. Trion had been a settler. He had uprooted his Household from Galinor and sought out into their new lands.

Tiberon Odyn had secured them. He had offered the tribes a place in the Dominion and they had refused. So these lands belonged to the Triumvirate now. Theseus had once told Periander some details from his analysts. Within fifty years, these lands would have cities like Trionus or Edessa all across them. They needed the frontier. Then the war had interrupted it.

Night fell.

The next day they sailed northwest again. After another

month, Captain Illus estimated they were halfway to the next turn of the river, when it wound to the northeast for fifty miles or so. Periander decided they would stop. He ordered the construction of fortifications.

"We will camp here," he said. "For the next month, scouting parties will explore both the Sinai foothills to the east and the Maker's to the west." He made it clear these were not to be individual scouts but groups capable of self-defence. They could not lose scouts this time: anyone they encountered had to be stopped before they could report the arrival of Imperials.

There was more than one close call. Once, when Periander was abroad on the plains directly north of their Trion River fortification, they spotted a group of tall-walkers to the east, moving further north at a rapid pace.

Salantar, who stayed close to Periander's side, spotted them first.

It was a strenuous afternoon. The giants could travel at a less exhaustive speed while still outmatching human legs. Periander, the gladiator, and the twenty men with them had to jog for most of the day to catch up.

The giant turned on them when they realized they would not reach their destination in time. It was a rough fight. They outnumbered the enemy only slightly, but it took more than a single soldier to bring down a giant. They killed the creatures, but not without casualties. Salantar made sure that Periander escaped unharmed, despite taking a few bruising close-calls himself.

They did not return to the fort until after dark and found search-parties setting out to look for them. Mordus breathed a sigh of relief when he saw Periander stride into the camp.

After another month, they sailed northward again. When they reached the river's bend on their maps, Periander again ordered a fortification built and the region scoured. It was a shorter distance to the Maker's Forge Mountains this time, rising ridges of rock that towered over the flatlands and the foothills notwithstanding. It was still a long trip to the mountain pass where the Trion River escaped the Maker's Forge.

Within the first week, winter struck like a clap of lightning. It was brighter and sharper than any winter they had ever endured. The days spent huddled round fires in the Cerden

Mountains became memories of Avernus's warm winters and frosts. This was a special kind of hell, crawling through golden leaves and tainting them with blood, watching that hole in the dungeon drain. This was enough to make a man lose his mind. They rarely left their tents. They lit bonfires. Men started dying of the cold after only a few weeks. By the time the allotted month had ended, they were so buried in snow that they decided to keep camping.

The heart of winter passed. The snows began to melt, but the cold remained, a fierce creature that stalked the pathways of their camp. One day, Periander had looked out from his tent and realized why the camp looked so familiar.

When he was young, and Captain Joran had been killed, he had killed their attackers and later married Joran's daughter. One of the men he had killed had been a simple farmer from a lake-valley in the Southern Spine. He had given the assassins information of Periander's passing there, and served as guide to them. Periander had had no regrets after killing the man, only at Joran's death.

Years later, only a year before the war began, Periander had toured his lands like his father had many times, to give his people a face for the name "Prince Gothikar." They had stumbled upon the ruins, in the Southern Spine, of an abandoned farm. The man he had killed had not returned to it, and the others had starved to death or abandoned it before they did, too.

This miserable camp, between the Maker's Forge and the rest of the world, looked as desolate as the farmstead's ruins. Periander had stood amongst them, as he stood at the opening of his tent now, and wondered how his actions had caused such a thing to come to pass.

"They're up there," Mordus breathed one day, storming into Periander's tent in a burst of cold. "Giants."

"Glyphs, how many?"

"There's structures. Shacks, inhabited caves!"

Periander strode from his tent. The snow, though recently cleared from the camp with magic, was boot deep again. Flakes drifted from the sky, though he would not describe it as snowing. Would he mar the floating specks of light with a splash of blood today?

Mordus led the way. His men were waiting, having just

returned. Illus was there too, but his clothes, like Periander's, were not layered with frost and snow.

They hiked for most of the afternoon. Eventually, after climbing quite a ways uphill, Mordus ordered a halt. "You lot rest here. I'm going to show the Prince," he said.

Illus, Mordus, and he pressed on for another few minutes. The slope they were on bent northward and then west; they were close enough to the hill's peak for Periander to notice the turning of land in such a way. Of course, there were only snow-caked trees visible.

At last they stopped again. This time, Mordus knelt and pointed down the slope a few paces ahead. Periander and Illus followed suit.

In the valley in front of them was a tribe of giants. As Mordus had described, a number of inhabited caves seemed the primary focus. There were outlying structures of wood and fur. Some were thatched, but many had sloped, wooden roofs like the buildings in Agwar Watch. Once again, Periander was reminded of that disastrous expedition. The first men he had killed.

There were no guards. The only giants outdoors were hard at work: one was cutting wood, and another had tied an enormous wolf up to a frame and was draining it. There was smoke, but it blended with the white. No wonder they had not spotted this place from the river.

"Should we move on them?" Illus wondered.

"No," Periander said. "If we find nothing in the heart of the mountains we can explore here more. This is a village only. We must find their capital."

"We could question them," Mordus said.

"All such attempts have been unsuccessful," Periander replied. "The giants are not intimidated by us. We can cause them pain or kill them, but none we have yet encountered have betrayed their kind."

"We've only encountered warriors." Illus led the way back to the troop. "Perhaps their commoners would be more prone to interrogation."

The thought made Periander sick. "We will scout first," he said. "I will not sink to that depth unless I must."

There was little he would not do, if he must. That was a

chilling thought. He had once governed himself by something greater than necessity. *You have to change...*

They returned to their fort, and kept guards in those slopes. They could not risk the village spotting them.

Eventually, the snow began to melt. It was still the season of winter by their calendars, but it became a weaker winter. The Trion River expanded with melted snow, and they set sail again, this time northeast. It took them only a few days of rowing to reach the next bend in the river—back to the northwest.

At that bend, they found a town. The giants had constructed a wall of stone, dragged for miles from the nearest quarry in any of Periander's calculations. Their scout returned before their galleys reached it, and they spent a few days contemplating further action.

"We should attack," Mordus argued. "We need to stay on the river as long as we can move our boats!"

Illus nodded.

The Olympian, Corlin, debated against it. Surprisingly, Salantar took his side. They were seated around a table in the cabin of one of the galleys. "I want to strike at Trion's throat when he thinks I'm still leagues away," the grizzled veteran said, as he picked at his teeth. He had filled in his missing teeth with wooden replacements back in the streets of Helius. Periander had told him that he could afford emerald teeth if the gladiator had desired it. Salantar had only scoffed and said, 'Might almost make me look rich. Wouldn't want that.' He had brought a dozen of his fellow ring fighters on this campaign. They were a force to be reckoned with; there was little doubt when one noticed the giant knuckle bones each kept around his neck. They kept count of their kills like it was a Maker-forsaken game!

Weveld remained indifferent about the town they discussed. For most of this campaign, he had been acting passively. He wanted Periander to make the decisions, but was content with whatever they might be.

"We will attack," Periander decided. "Any refugees that flee will lead us to their home, and any warnings they give will be received far too late to summon armies from the south."

"If there are no armies this far north," Corlin said.

"If there are no armies here," Periander allowed. He stood up and grabbed his trusty lamellar armour from a nearby chest, while his council bowed and scurried to their own quarters to arm themselves. He had gone through a dozen sets of it during the war. Thankfully, it was not the most expensive armour.

Swords, on the other hand, *were* expensive, and he had used dozens of them too.

"Everyone ready?" Periander asked. Their troops were arrayed in sets of ranks, various units. The latter ones were armed with torches and would set about burning buildings once they reached the battle, while the former troops would focus on hostilities.

He got nods from his Captains.

"Listen up," he called, walking along the front of the arrangement. "This is going to be different than our other battles. This is going to be an assault, not a battle. This is going to be an invasion. The giants came into our homes, into Grey River, Nori, and Edessa, to name those we have seen...and they burned them! Glyphs, let's burn them too!"

His men bellowed in reply. There was a hill between them and the village, so they could only see the smoke. Their cries might be heard, but it would not matter soon.

"Follow your Captains. Torchbearers, don't be reckless, let the fighters deal with enemies!" he ordered. "Let's go kill some giants!"

The ground thundered by beneath them. Periander and Salantar ran in the front, with his squad of guards close behind. By the time they crested the hill, a few giants had armed themselves and come out to face them. There were only a handful of them, though they put up a good fight. Periander claimed a kill, though Salantar's gladiators took down three or four between them and fought over the knuckles. Their five hundred men were more than enough to punch through the giant's line within minutes.

The wall gave them no hindrance. There was a large opening for the river, several hundred feet across. It had a band of snow and ice they could walk across on the edges—the river swelled to almost twice its current size in the spring.

They charged into the village, and the butchering began. Many of the inhabitants locked themselves within their wooden shelters. The buildings all had single storeys, but they were taller than human single-storey constructions to accommodate their height. Periander saw some of his men start axing a door, but most of them left those garrisoned for the torches at the back of their incursion.

They reached a larger building on the farthest side of town. It had large, wood carvings across its walls in the giants' language: Periander recognized none of it. But he did recognize the function of this house—it was the leader's.

And here he came. A huge man stormed out of the house, twice Periander's size. Most giants loomed several feet taller than him, but this chieftain was the biggest he had ever seen. He was covered in scars from wolf, bear and blade. It was no stretch for Periander to imagine this mountain man fighting a grizzly with his bare hands.

Salantar and his gladiators spun wide into a circle, trying to flank the giant. The chief reacted by thrashing around in large circles with his club. He caught one of the fighters and sent him crashing into the wall of the longhouse.

Periander blasted at the giant with a burst of air to distract him. While the chief charged toward Periander, Weveld let fly a blast of his own. The giant was knocked perpendicular to his charge at the Prince and collided with his own house. The wall depressed under his weight and cracked as he fell through it. They advanced cautiously through the growing cloud of smoke. Illus took the lead, as Salantar was checking on his fallen comrade.

Something shot past him and Illus disappeared. Like a pendulum, the giant's mace came back from the blow, swing past Periander against, the giant stormed out of the longhouse.

"Illus!" Periander shouted. "Weveld, see to him!" He drove his sword straight into the giant's leg. It slid past the bone and out the other side. The giant roared, and the world spun away for a minute.

When everything stopped moving, Periander was lying against one of the other buildings. He looked up and saw Illus laying there with blood all over him, his eyes looking in different direction and his mouth hanging slanted.

Weveld had a hand on him, but was simply staring at the dead man in shock. Periander dragged himself to his feet. His ears were ringing, but after a quick pat of himself he found no injuries. He looked up.

The beast was dragging itself on one knee while the leg that Periander had stabbed trailed red through the snow behind him. The sword still protruded. Its clothes, simple wool, were tattered from arrows and slashes, and its face was full of rage and pain.

Salantar ran forward, shouting, with a double-handed sword and brought it down on the creature's head.

The battle was over. They had lost a hero and burnt a tiny village.

32

Year of Olympus 583

The Gothikar Study still astounded Artemys. It put the Crown Magician's Study to shame. How could that be? Four centuries of Artemys's Order fed his study. Akheron Gothikar had purchased this one with a fortune he had produced from nowhere. It was a reminder to Artemys that he had accomplished nothing.

His father worked at the nearby desk. A single lantern flickered from one corner of the desk. It looked like a letter he was writing.

Should I interrupt him? Artemys wondered. *Will he have time for me?* When Artemys had gone to his brother, he had not known why. When he had tracked down Kerres, he had known why, but had been unwilling to ask for it directly until Kerres had brought it up and dismissed it for him. But Artemys was no longer sliding into the pit. Now he was falling, tumbling down a slope of shale stone.

"Help me." He needed someone to catch him, to pull him back up.

"Artemys?" Periander asked, rising to his feet in surprise. "When did you get here?"

"I have failed, Father. I am lost," he said. He could not stop himself. He could not stop the tears that came sobbing up. "Help me..."

And his father did. He took Artemys in an embrace. He told him that people can change and that there is hope. He told

Artemys that time could help. They spent the night in discussion. In fighting. In settling. In truth. Artemys found quiet, and his father found his son.

Over the following weeks, Artemys moved his belongings back to Avernus. He needed his father now, like he had as a child. His father had not been there then, but was walking beside him now. He left Aella in charge of the Order, but continued working with them on a provisional basis. It was a leave of health—not unheard of.

A few months later, he shared a dinner with Pyrsius and his father that did not end in fighting. His father shared the meal in silence mostly.

It was the Year of Olympus 584. Pyrsius laughed with him as they sparred in the courtyard of the Palace. His brother had returned to the city as well. Kerres was still troubled by Artemys. Artemys felt healthy again. He felt strong. He had no desire to kill anyone. He still had a desire to help, but there must be other ways to help. His father had given him hope.

It was the Year of Olympus 587. The riots had stopped. Artemys and Periander had replenished the treasuries by selling spell tokens to the general public. No dangerous ones, just tools. Magic for anyone. Any man, woman, or child could break a token and cast the spell. As the Imperial treasury recuperated, the Dominion could afford to give jobs out to the citizens again. They set up infrastructure projects, road that needed to be built, or resources that needed to be harvested. And the riots stopped. For the first time in almost a hundred years, the Triumvirate had peace again.

It was the Year of Olympus 589. Kerres laughed at his joke. The four of them were sitting in the courtyard of the Avernan Palace: Kerres, Pyrsius, Artemys and *her*. The woman who would love Artemys for who he was, not who he could become. She would see the newly formed parts of him, the strength and tranquility he had found in defeating the darkness. This man did not need to fight in order to create peace. This man did not need to stop injustice with death. He could stop injustice with his will. And she, whoever she was, loved him for it.

It was the Year of Olympus 593. Artemys had a son. He was forty-eight and he brought a new man into the world. What should his name be? Hev. Hevarus Gothikar. His achievements would blind out any of his family's. They would change more than Akheron's revolutions. They would win more than Periander's war. They would supersede Artemys's Order. And it made Artemys more proud than the sun. The love he felt for Hevarus was unlike anything he had ever felt. He had only experienced that kind of love once, when his father had forgiven him.

It was the Year of Olympus 595. Somewhere, a guard kicked a boy to the ground and then kicked him again.

"Help me please," the boy was saying to his father.

Artemys let the Glyphs in his head fade. They had shown him the future *he* could have. A right life. He could get better. He could change. He knew it now. But it was not a future he could accept.

He was standing here, at the last ledge into that dark pit.

His father stepped around the desk, his arms open for an embrace. Offering a hand to pull him up from that pit. "Thank the Maker," he said. "Son..."

If Artemys accepted his father's embrace, it would mean his salvation. But it would also mean a flawed future. It would mean his failure. His ultimate redemption and failure.

He would not. He *could* not. He had to drive a wedge between himself and this last hope.

"What does that mean?" he asked, withdrawing from their embrace. "I ask for help and you thank the Maker?"

Periander paused. He lowered his hands a bit in confusion. "I just mean that I am glad you have realized...you were seeing the world wrong..."

"I was seeing the world wrong?"

His father frowned. "Artemys, I'm not trying to say you were wrong...I've been praying for you, and I'm thankful my prayers have been answered."

Artemys paused. This conversation would hurt his father as much as it hurt him. *Dare I turn away his hand? That will leave me alone, truly alone.* "I am alone," he told his father. "But my goals are right. I will fix this land. I *must.*"

"I told you at Delfie, you are only going to harm yourself and others with the way you see the world. You don't believe in good anymore and you hate the smallest sins enough to sink to any depth to stop them," his father explained.

"The best way to stop them," Artemys retorted. "You will not dirty your hands to interact with any sin, so you can solve nothing."

"You think I will not dirty my hands?" Periander asked incredulously. "I fought a war—"

"A war that cost this nation its morality and hundreds of thousands of lives!" Artemys returned. "A war that solved *nothing.*"

Periander grabbed him by the shirt and shoved him backwards. They collided with a bookshelf hard enough that two books fell. "It saved *all* the lives that were *not* lost, you ungrateful..."

"Release me," Artemys said, fiercely knocking his father's hands away. "You cannot help me. You are blind! All I want is a father, and all you can be is a general!"

His father stepped back, stricken. "I pray it is not so."

"It is! I just want a family!"

"I pray that you see the truth. You do not want a father, you want an accomplice, and I will not become him. I will not become everything I have fought against. Not for you, not for anyone. Perhaps it is best that you are on your own," Prince Gothikar said. "The only thing worse than having a corrupted son would be watching him corrupt others."

"Father!" Artemys replied. "Please." It was both a lie and the truth. *Please help me. Please stop me. But please do not.*

"Artemys," his father said. "Are you truly determined to fight the Triumvirate?"

"Yes," he said. *It must be undone. Like the Kinship before it, the people need it to be stopped.* "Will you turn me over as a traitor?"

"If it comes to it. Glyphs, if it comes to it."

"Then you should fight me now," Artemys said, drawing his knife and a spell token. He had not willed them to his hands, but his words were his own. "For I will fight you tooth and nail any day you stand between me and the light."

His father disarmed him in a fluid moment. He was a soldier, to the core. Artemys found himself pinned against the wall again, his father's arm across his chest and hand cupping his neck; this time Artemys could not shake his father's strength. "I will not harm you, not if I can avoid it. Leave me. Please leave me," he told his son. "Please...*change.*"

Artemys found himself released. He had so little strength in this state, in this trembling dread, in his chosen damnation. He sank to one knee as all of his father's strength left him.

"The Maker have mercy on you, for I cannot," Periander said as he walked away.

Artemys was a husk, a shell now that everything had been stripped away. There was no more friends, no more family. His Apprentice held him up, his tasks gave him time, his life wasted away. He would find a way to stop the guard from beating the child, the man from raping the woman, the Triumvirate from scourging the Dominion, the world from cursing *him*. He recalled Tannes's words. *"I would like to be safe, and that is all I would like."*

Artemys could not be safe in this world, and he could not find a way to change it. He stood on the edge of that pit, where the slope he had been sliding down turned into a chasm. He looked into it, and leapt. He did not want someone to catch him. He knew now it was not a pit of his own design, but a pit of the world's. He did not want to live here anymore, so he would let this pit claim him. He would find the bottom.

33

Year of Olympus 556

Periander's breath frosted in front of him as he watched Weveld write the spell. A hole appeared in the earth when the magician spoke his worlds. Together, Mordus and he lowered Captain Illus's body into it. Weveld conjured a small, stone post to mark the grave.

"Who was his second?" Periander asked, trying not to inhale the smoke from the village they had sacked.

A man stepped forward from the soldiers working in the husk of the village. They were clearing a way for the ships to come through, though the river was now thin enough the boats travelled single file only. Illus's second had short, dark hair, a thin beard, and sharp eyes. "Rychard of Tarroth, sir. I'm a great admirer."

"Captain Rychard now," Periander said. "Will you kill giants for me?" he asked.

"Of course, sir," Rychard bowed. "I only hope I can achieve the same repute as my predecessor. He was a great man."

"He was," Periander said. "How is the river?"

"We are almost ready to sail again," Rychard said. Mordus shook his hand and introduced himself.

And sail they did. It was slow going as the approaching spring filled the river with fast water, running south. Sometimes the banks were too steep to camp on them, and they would simply drop anchor and sleep aboard the ships. A week passed. Then another. It was the new year, 557. Periander had been fighting this war for eighteen years. When it had started, he had been eighteen. A boy. He had not felt young then, and he certainly did not now.

Then they reached a huge ridge, a cliff that loomed at least forty feet above them. There was a waterfall ahead; they could hear it roaring, though, of course, their ships could not reach it. The river was set in a canyon, and there was no room to disembark, so they were forced to drift back down the river for a full day. They camped on the first banks they came to and moored the galleys upon the low beach.

They marched up the slope until they reached the cliff. From here it was not as impractical to climb. Periander watched the water falling as he went up. It was like an ocean's worth surged past him. The snow was almost entirely melted now, and the cliff was covered in clumps of mud and ledges that could not be trusted.

No one fell, thankfully, and they camped that night on the edge of the Maker's Forge.

Periander was awoken at dawn by a scream. He leapt out of bed, threw his lamellar over his breeches, grabbed his newest sword, and ran out of his tent. There, he froze.

He could not see a foot in front of him. There was only white. A fog—no, a cloud! It was thick enough to block the sunlight. Everything was sunken white, almost grey. He could hear others scurrying from their tents and arming themselves. Were they under attack?

Periander wasn't sure. "Someone talk to me!"

"Orly fell," someone called. "It was his scream!"

"Fell, from the cliff?"

The reply came affirmative.

"Mordus, Rychard, Corlin!" Periander shouted. "Weveld! Get to my tent, but be careful! As for the rest of you, I want a line of guards to form on the edge! Stand close enough to see each other, and stop anyone from walking off. Anyone not standing guard, pack up the camp! I won't have more of you lot falling to your deaths the easy way!"

A chorus of shouts replied and the camp scurried awake.

"Periander," Mordus said with relief, as he came out of the haze. "What's this then?"

"The Cloud Lands," Periander said. He stepped back into

N A V R E U G D E N H I L

his tent and marked it on the map. Oban Hokar had talked of it: a mountain pass several miles long that was shrouded most days by clouds. He shrugged into proper woolen trousers and donned his gloves and cloak.

Once those he had called had arrived, with the addition of Salantar, he gave his orders. "We need to press onward. These clouds will not pass today, or tomorrow. And this is the worst tactical position if the giants come this way. We will march through the pass as far as we can today."

"We'll lose men in the fog," Rychard said.

"How much rope did we bring from the boat?" Periander asked.

Corlin shrugged. "Several coils, each a few hundred feet. We weren't certain if this cliff was the only climbing we'd be doing."

"Every soldier will tie the rope to himself," Periander decided, rolling up his map. He tucked it into the nearby pack. "It will be slow progress..."

"Very slow," Salantar said. "Why don't our soldiers just get a sense of direction?"

Periander reprimanded him with a glare. "But every life is valuable now on this campaign."

As they strode out of the small tent and Periander set about collapsing it, Mordus said, "Have you heard what they're calling your campaign?"

"No, and I don't—"

"I've heard two: 'Gothikar's Vengeance' and the 'Royal Victory.'" Mordus helped him fold the tent up.

Periander tucked it into his pack and shouldered the heavy load. "It's neither of those things. It's 'Periander's Last Try' if anything."

"You used to smile," Mordus said.

Periander shrugged, looked away from him, and started walking toward the north side of camp. "And I used to read, love, feast. I was a fool."

"If that's foolery, I hope you lose your senses again, someday," Mordus said. "You've become a foul one. A strong, unwavering statue. Sometimes you need to think like a man again."

"That's enough," Periander said, turning on him. Mordus

wasn't standing behind him. Instead, Terrus stood there, the mysterious man with the scar and forlorn look. "You have to change," Terrus had once said.

"You!" Periander breathed. His gasp drew a hole in the cloud between them.

Terrus looked just as... *incarnate* as he had before. It was an odd way to describe a man. But Terrus somehow *was* the struggle within Periander He *was* the invasive cloud around them, opaque, but all encompassing. "You need to be a human again."

"What are you doing in my camp?" Periander blurted, reaching for the man. His mind wrinkled when he realized that Terrus was standing further away from him than he had first judged, and his hands were gripping thin air.

"You need to care again, about your friends, about this kingdom. Not just about finishing your task. You need to *feel* again. Feel loss, not just disadvantage," Terrus said, his voice quiet.

"I have no friends," Periander retorted. "I have subordinates."

"You are the one deciding so," Terrus said. "They still think you're their friend. They still think you're... *human.*"

"Stop telling me what I need to be," Periander said. "If you know how this world is, and how good men are, you can lead this army."

"That's not my life. That's yours," Terrus replied. His voice became desperate again, like it had when he had first talked to, first *begged* Periander. "You have to change, Periander. Where you are rock, you must become water. Where you are justice, you must become mercy. Forget all of this, if you decide, but please...decide."

"'You have to be a god or a devil?'" Periander quoted. "My father told me that, but I will not tell my son. It's a lie—there is no water, there is no mercy, there is no god. Only devils."

Tears slid down Terrus's cheeks. "I'm alone again," he said, fading back into the cloud. "I always have been... Please, Periander, *please* change!" And then he was gone. There was only cloud.

Periander stepped forward, and there was only this infernal white covering the world. That man could not continue doing this! Dropping in and out of Periander's life and plaguing him like Periander's own conscience!

Then Mordus appeared again. "Glyphs, this fog! Regardless, I was just saying, 'you used to smile.' I think you ought to again. Find some day-to-day thing to be happy about," his subordinate was saying. "I can tell you a joke if you want."

"No, Mordus," he replied. "That will not be necessary."

"See, that's what I'm talking about..."

Periander raised his hand. "Listen up, men!" he shouted. "We're setting off. Tie yourself to the rope that your Captain provides!"

Within the hour they had left the camp behind. Mordus tied in directly behind Periander, while a few guards insisted on marching ahead of the Prince. Salantar and his mercenaries made their own line nearby, though they refused the rope. Meanwhile, a set of linked lines appeared for the various troops, and the army crawled forward across the Cloud Lands.

It was incredibly slow progress. They had to keep stopping to wait for groups that had veered too far north or south. They followed the river, still, it wound upward. Sometimes it was a gradual incline, sometimes a steep cliff. It was impossible to tell how far uphill it actually went because no one could see more than an arm's length or two ahead. There was a lot of stumbling, falling, and bruising, but thankfully nothing serious. The valley they were in seemed very wide, sometimes, and they risked losing the river's edge once or twice. Thankfully, the various rapids along the way made enough noise to draw them back. Sometimes, however, the mountains on both sides of them drew so close together they had to lengthen the army into thinner ranks and march through narrows in the river itself.

They heard wolves a few times and a variety of birds. There was a scattering of evergreen trees along the valley floor, fed by the moisture in the air that must rise everyday if such a cloud were to continue.

"Look," Mordus whispered.

Periander glanced up from the ground at his feet. There was something walking nearby, man-shaped but only a little over half Periander's size. In the thick haze, it was only a shadow moving parallel to his. As he watched, he could see its head turning, looking at them then ahead and then at them again.

"If I cut the rope to grab it," Periander whispered back, "it will run, won't it?"

"Probably," Mordus said. "Is it a child?"

Periander did not dare call out to it in case it fled. He needed to catch it. He very gradually turned left; not toward it, but to eventually intersect with the path it walked. As he suspected, the specter walked further from him to keep its distance. The group of guards tied further ahead on the rope turned to see why the rope was pulling them. Without a word, they gave him the slack to continue turning the line on the rope to the left.

The shadow kept its distance. Then it saw soldiers on its right, for Periander was now walking against the incoming line of soldiers farther back. Before it could run out of the tightening knot, Periander dashed to the left. He closed off the circle.

"Who goes there?" he asked, drawing his sword. The short figure shrunk as he advanced, crouching to its knees. It made no reply.

Periander stepped closer still, and the layer of cloud between them thinned.

In front of him cowered a man—no, a creature of some kind. It was wiry, thin arms and legs and an oddly shaped head. The soldiers that drew closer gaped at it as well; Mordus shouted, "All hold!" to stop the other troop-lines. The small creature flinched at the loud noise.

Periander sheathed his sword again. "What are you?" he asked, kneeling closer.

The skin on the creature bore no resemblance to his own. It was sandy in colour and texture. There were clumps—not unlike warts or bruises—of dirt and rock all over it. One large one above its left eye, another bulging near its collar bone. The creature's eyes were tiny, black, and beadlike, though when he glanced to the side at an advancing soldier, Periander saw whites behind. The creature glanced back at Periander and made a rasping sound from his mouth. He had teeth, some sharpened like a predators, with molars in the back.

"Glyphs!" Salantar exclaimed as he arrived. "What by the Maker is this!"

The creature dragged its legs with it as it clawed across the ground away from the newcomer. It was unclothed save for a band of fur around its waist to protect from the elements.

Corlin and Rychard appeared. Rychard blurted, "What kind of foul earth-spawn is—" and then froze.

Periander's jaw dropped as he glanced from Rychard back to the stubby being. He looked at the texture of its skin and the sand that fell from it when it moved. "You're an earth-spawn..." he breathed.

"Earth-spawn are actual creatures?" Mordus questioned. "I thought it was just a...name."

"I did too," Periander said.

Weveld approached through the cloud, saying "Earth-spawn is a derogatory term becoming widely used to mean..." then he fell quiet when he saw it. "Or that's what our scholars thought." He knelt near Periander and looked at the earth-spawn.

The creature made its rasping sound again, then a series of odd syllables that did not make any sense. They did not even sound like a uniform language.

"The term appears in almost every book that is say, two hundred years old," Weveld explained. "It is often used in association with some lower class. We assumed it meant commoners, or basics, which is why it became the insult it is..."

"But it's real. Look at it!" He glanced back at the creature. The earth-spawn scratched its shoulder and the lump of rocky dirt came free, plopping to the ground. It did not seem adversely affected in any way.

"If this is an earth-spawn," Weveld said, "then they were once scattered across the entire Dominion and had some form of society. This appears to be nothing more than an animal."

"It's all right," he told the spawn. "We won't harm you." He reached toward it.

Its tiny eyes widened, then slammed shut and it collapsed across the earth, splaying its limbs. Periander laughed. "It's pretending to be dead," he said. He smiled, the little fellow was so comical.

The ground nearby exploded and men went flying. The rope went taught and yanked him down beside the earth-spawn, who, with a blood-curdling screech darted away between the legs of soldiers. Others were screaming, some in pain. As Periander's hearing returned to him, he heard, "Giants!" shrieked at the top of someone's lungs.

Periander rolled to the right and left his pack where he had lain. A dead soldier was lying near it, having knocked the Prince down. He yanked his sword from its scabbard with a rasp like the earth-spawn's.

Another bundle of soldiers were sent flying. Periander was yanked toward them, and went down on one knee again. He stood up and spun, pulling the rope into hand and tensing it between his torso and grip. He slashed down on it and was free.

There were shadows, four or five of them, swiping at the lines of soldiers with hammers and maces.

Mordus ran past Periander. "We have to stop them," he blurted, and Periander ran beside him. Mordus bellowed, "Cut yourselves free, men! But don't lose sight of one another! Let's cut these giants down to our size—"

His words cut short as a hand grabbed him by the head and yanked him away. Periander sprinted after, driving forward with his sword. The giant that had Mordus only grunted as Periander slashed lengthwise across his knee. He raised his arm and, like he held a rock or a ball, hurled Mordus away.

Periander went cold, like ice or death. He followed through with his slash by taking two steps past the giant and then spinning in mid motion and leaping. His sword pierced the creature's lower back. Periander yanked out his knife and drove it in an arm's reach above himself. He pulled his sword free and climbed another thrust higher. By the time he reached the giant's shoulders, they were both lying on the ground and the creature was unmoving.

One of the others screamed *"Vashal!"* and charged at Periander.

The High Prince ignored him and turned his back toward him. His men would protect him, and the second giant would fall.

Periander dashed to Mordus's side. His legs were buckled and broken, one armed snapped, and his head hung at an impossible angle. His eyes were open.

"No!" Periander screamed. "Maker, no!" he hung his head and pressed both hands against his captain. He trembled. Not his subordinate. *His friend.* When had he become so jaded to life? When had he become so foolish? *I have lost my senses,* he realized. *I have lost who I am.*

Sobbing, he reached out with a shaking hand and closed Mordus's eyes. Then he just stared at the corpse for a minute, in silence. In horror. In grief.

He threw back his head and shrieked incoherently. It was not rage or vengeance. It was sorrow, pure, human sorrow. He sunk from his folded knees to his backside and supported himself at an angle with one hand. He had lost a friend today, a brother.

Periander glanced at where his men stood in audience, but he looked at the fallen giants. He did not feel fury, for the first time in a long time. It was a distracting emotion from what he really felt. He looked down at Mordus's broken body. *"Vashal!"* he cried.

34

Year of Olympus 584

Halfway down his fall into the void, Artemys inhaled a thought. A question and answer that might be true, but might not be.

He needed to know.

Artemys was seated in the hall, a cup of mead and a plate in front of him. There was a half-eaten leg of chicken there, and a stew-soaked, half-eaten loaf of bread. A bit of gravy was running down his grizzled chin. He knew he was the talk of the commoners. Their brilliant Crown Magician run amok. The youngest magician to pass the trials and perhaps the youngest one to lose his mind, they said. *But not the first*, he reminded himself, as comfort, before returning to the thought that had interrupted his meal.

He needed to know the extent of the truth. Weveld had taught him there were no limits on magic save those that the Disciples had imposed. Limitless power. They spoke of a buffer that prevented too much from being drawn at a time, but the power, they claimed, was infinite. Artemys had never believed in such a thing. Spells were words, certainly speech was limited.

But maybe he had been wrong to turn to his family or the one he loved. Maybe it was more simple, and all he need do was turn to magic. Artemys smiled to himself and wiped his chin with a rag before sending it sailing over the tabletop in front of him.

He willed the Great Glyph in front of his eyes and chose a spot that appeared on no maps, a flatland far to the west. Then he snatched the knife from the table in front of him and dragged it in a straight line along the table. He immediately felt the eyes of his servants, cooks and guards on him.

Tannes raised an eyebrow. "A spell?" She was clever enough to know he was not just cutting a table. That was foolishness. This was the central line of a spell.

Artemys began drawing lines and stabbing dots into the wood along the line. When he had finished, he glanced at his apprentice. She had already finished her meal, her plate sat cleanly in front of her, her utensils placed nicely on top of it. "Stay here," he told her, and then read his spell, *"Elep hayen elkobo loraz." Move me to this place in the Great Glyph.*

And he moved. One moment he was seated at a table, slumped on a wooden bench, and the next he was seated in thin air. He landed on his behind; tall grass and ferns moved aside for him. He glanced at the small knife in his right hand. He tossed it away and stood up.

Here, so far from the Dominion, no one would see him. No one could possibly be watching and he needed to know the truth about magic. Had some *Maker* truly given them the gift of creation?

He blew the grasses away with a simple wind spell. He would need a large canvas for this spell, and the open dirt beneath the field would serve him well.

It involved multiple center lines. He used the glyphs more liberally, tracing in a description rather than a combination of elements or orders. He treated it like an art instead of a tool. There would be rock here, but air here. There would be trees and earth and ice and cloud. There would be water, running in a brook. There would be beauty.

Time crawled slowly by until he stood up and dusted his muddied hands off on the silk robe he wore. He stared down at the long lines of glyphs and whispered, *"Be,"* before beginning to read the spell.

He finished with, *"Aroke-bakan."* He held his breath and looked up at the fields to the west.

The light seemed to blur in a particular spot, what he would compare to only be the size of a hut's side. This spread until half the horizon in that direction was fuzzed like he was looking at the world from underwater. Dark grey and brown began to appear like drops of blood tainting his view. Soon the whole blur was the shade of stone and green began to thaw certain regions of it.

Artemys had to suck in a breath before he fell over.

Flat sheets of white trimmed the top of the shimmering spectacle. Tendrils of cloud escaped the bubble and drifted into the heavier clouds in the sky. The blur began to withdraw like a slowly melting snowflake. Each colour and each line became clearer, the angles of rocks piercing up into the sky, the green clusters of trees on the slopes, the icy embrace that clothed the peak.

Artemys stared at the mountain he had created and smiled.

There was hope. There was true strength somewhere in this reality, true power now unconcealed. And he could draw upon it. What did it matter that none shared his vision? What did it matter that everyone would rather exist in the shadows than the light that Artemys could cast?

This magic, this godliness that he had discovered...he could create anything with it. But, as he examined the base of the mountain, he realized he would need to break what was already there to do so. There was an ugly line of dirt between the green fields and the stony slabs and thick forests of his mountain.

He had hoped all his life that he would be able to take power without bloodshed, without expense. He knew that to be false now. He would need to break their Dominion. He would need to throw down the Triumvirate, and seize control.

He had been a fool. The answers did not lie with friend or family, but in magic itself. How had he forgotten the truest metaphor of them all? He was a sword. He did not fear the bottom of the chasm he imagined himself falling within; he was a blade, and he would *kill* whatever lurked there.

As he wrote a spell to return to the School of Delfie, he contemplated the costs of his new plan. *Enough of letting things play out to their own accord, letting plotters have their plots.*

This time there was a grinding when he cast the spell, a shivering in his gut, and then in the air around him. The surrounding view began to look like the School of Delfie, but got stuck for a moment. He could see the mountain and the School Hall at the same time. The image pulsated like a parchment bent back and forth so a wave rippled its surface.

Then, with a jolt so jarring it should have made a sound, he flickered back to the windy courtyard in front of the Hall.

"Milord," Caius gasped. "You've returned."

Within moments, a handful of amazed apprentices and craftsmen appeared. Aella was the first to step out of the Hall's main doorway, her weathered features pursed with perplexity. "Master, we tried to use the same spell you wrote, but *none* of our spells worked. Still none of them do."

Artemys frowned. He had not considered that. "A spell token please. Any will do." One of the apprentices handed him a water token. He broke it and directed the spell at the earth, but no pool of water appeared there. He waited a moment. Perhaps it would delay like his teleport had. But the spell did nothing.

Weveld was right about that also. There was the entity or energy that the Disciples referred to as *The Hunter.* Andrakaz, in an age past, had created a limit on the magic that could be created at any given time, so humanity would not destroy itself. "Do not worry," Artemys told the crowd, running some quick logic through his head. They were taken aback by his words. He had just broken a simple spell token and it had done nothing. "Do not worry. Within the hour, I suspect, our spells will work once more."

Night was starting to settle, though he had not noticed it when had been building the mountain.

Tannes emerged from the crowd. "How did you teleport like that? Your spell was not one for the Known Locations!"

There were only five known places that magicians knew spells for. Supposedly there were many more lost in time to them. "I have discovered more."

Aella stepped down another step toward him. She wore the traditional red robe of a Councillor. "Spells to where?"

He thought quickly of places that could serve the Dominion well. "Tarroth, Eldius, Gev, Ivos...these cities. I know of a few others, but they are inconsequential. I only travelled across the island with that spell from the table. I needed some time to think."

The crowd gasped in awe. In their eyes, he was no longer the youngest Crown Magician, but perhaps one of the greatest. His predecessors had lost magic, lost the Known Locations until there were a handful, lost spells like the Great Glyph... Artemys had not retained that trait. With an afternoon, he had proven the greatest truth to himself, and ascended to legend.

They'll need to die. The thought hit him in the gut, as disruptive as the travelling spell had been. He must have shown it too, for Aella and Tannes both stepped towards him. The latter even offered her shoulder. He gripped it with a hand, started to lean, but then released it. He had not touched a woman since Kerres.

Tannes stared at him, slowly lowering her hand.

"I must leave you once more," he told the crowd. He did not break his gaze on his apprentice. "I will retire to my quarters. My day has exhausted me."

Then, as the crowd began to dissipate, he lowered his eyes and walked past Tannes. He needed to be separate from her. He needed to be separate from any of them. *They will all need to die.* He stood at the opened threshold of the Tower of the Order and sighed before stepping through.

There was a limit on magic. To break and rebuild this land would require it all. The fewer men and women that used magic, the more of it Artemys could use. Enough magic to silence every murderer, whether they be Prince or pauper.

He began the ascent of stairs to the third floor, where the Crown Magician's chambers sat.

The first rule of magic was only the elect may use it. There was a spell that any wizard knew which connected another man or woman to the language of the Maker. It was not an ability granted by birth, or something that could be obtained by knowledge. It was a spell that passed from one generation to the next, a gift from gods to men, the talent to activate glyphs with one's voice.

If enough magicians were removed from the equation, the use of magic would dwindle or die. But so long as a single magician lived, it would not be lost altogether.

He reached his chambers and shut the door. "No. I cannot." That voice repeated it though, *They will all need to die, so that the next age can live.*

What were the other ramifications? Those he could not consider? *If I create a void of magic, a lull where no magicians use spells, and all of that energy, the energy to make mountains was unspent... would the universe counter it?* Would nature do some creating of its own? Would other, ignorant, wizards learn new glyphs, a cyclical system to spend that extra energy?

He did not bother sinking to the floor against his door or rummaging through the shelves near his bed for some clue hidden in a book. He just stood there. "How can I make this choice? How can I choose the future like this?"

Someone knocked on his door. He opened it.

Tannes's arms were stretched to either side of the doorframe, but she dropped them as it opened. She had tied her black hair back on her way up from the courtyard. "Who were you talking to?"

"No one," Artemys replied. Almost everyone referred to him as "my lord," even a few members of the Council. He was glad Tannes did not. "Myself," he confessed.

She smiled. "You seem distressed. I haven't seen you act like that before."

"I have realized something difficult. There are...certain costs to doing what I must," Artemys said, closing the door after her.

"What must you do?"

Kill them all. Kill you. He looked away from her. *How can I?*

"There," she said. "You had that same look when I offered you support in the courtyard, and again when you opened the door."

"Tannes," he trailed off. "You would think me mad." He crossed his small antechamber and leaned against the wall.

She started shaking her head. "I'm your apprentice; I don't get to think that. You can tell me whatever you need, if it would help."

Artemys smiled. "Who are you, that you would accept a burden so carelessly?"

"I'm not accepting it carelessly—"

"I meant: without any strings attached?" he asked. *Kerres, Pyrsius, Weveld...even Father. They all have strings attached.*

Tannes smirked. "I'm on the good side, that's why." She laughed. "What kind of question was that? Is there no one doing things just because?"

Artemys bit his lip. He squeezed his eyes for a moment so they would not tear, then opened them. "I fear I would only corrupt you. By the Maker, my world is full of strings, questions, collateral damage...there is no 'good side.'"

"Collateral damage? Is that what this whole...upset is about? You aren't willing to pay the price for what *must be done*?"

"You are too straightforward with your Crown Magician." It was half jest.

Tannes stepped back a pace. "I will leave if you say the word."

Artemys felt his humour with this situation dry up like water on a grill. "Very well then. Leave."

She blinked in surprise, her slanted smile gone. "I'll be in my own quarters, if I'm needed."

She closed the door on her way out, and Artemys felt as alone as he had before she arrived. And just as confused.

There was a war coming.

He grabbed a sheaf of paper from the end table by his poster bed, and began to write names upon it with the nearby inkwell.

"The School of Delfie, Athynian Academy, Olympus Guild." *The three largest.* "The Tower of Glyphs." Avernus was far behind the others in its arcane studies, but it too had a school. "Spell-master in the Edessa Arena, the Circle in Ivos."

I'm missing some, he knew. There were clusters in every little town. His study had more books. It was just down the hall.

He strode out of the quarters, with his list of targets in hand. There were two doors before his study: a servant's quarters and a storeroom. The door to his study was carved with the symbols of magic, like the Kinship of old. An open circle for air, a triangle for fire, a square for rock, a dark circle for water. This study had been used by every Crown Magician since the School had been built. The doors had spells traced onto them too, they could be moved by words or the slightest touch, and sealed as easily, too.

Artemys strode into his study, the two doors parting at the touch of his palms. There were no lamps lit; the only light flickered from the corridor.

A man stood in the middle of the clutter, clothed as dark as shadows so that only his face was visible—sharp, ageless features, piercing eyes, a scar beneath the left.

Artemys had seen this man before, a bumbling traveller who accepted his offer of teleport from a distant inn to the city of Avernus. A man who had watched him—not in fear, or confusion...but in analysis.

"You," Artemys breathed, closing the doors with a breath of magic.

"You think you know me?"

Artemys clenched both his fists at his sides and leaned toward the man. "My father and his before him decided their places in the world. This implies...obstacles." *Magic will counter.* Artemys had wondered what would happen should he break all of the rules. Would nature counter, would magic become easier somehow so that the extra energy were consumed?

The man still did not move a muscle, eyes piercing.

This is how the equation will balance. An enemy. "Every other soul is but a pawn," Artemys continued, stepping closer. He had to kick a book out of the way. "But you—you are my adversary."

Now the man nodded. "I did not expect you to speak truth."

"You know of what I speak, so you must know that I will burn every magician, man or woman, in the flames of the Great Glyph to seize. What. Is. Mine!" Artemys hissed. "To take my place, to take my world." He was the storm of Delfie the day his mother died, he was the fire burning the slaver, he was the hammer on Korbios, he was Kerres's betrayal.

"And you," the man whispered, creeping closer with each word. "You must know that I will die a hundred deaths," now, in the very eye of Artemys's storm, "to stop you."

And he was gone. No flash of magic or blur of glyphs.

Artemys stood in his study, unmoving. A dozen minutes passed as he stood alone in the darkness. He had an adversary, which meant he had a plan. He had to have done something in order to cause this nemesis. He knew that they had to die now. He knew it. He looked at the paper still held in his right hand and cast it aside. *The first step when someone knows your plan is to change it.*

The magicians will all die, but I will not do it. Who already hated magicians? Kerres. Kerres and Pyrsius. If a magician were to kill Pyrsius...Kerres would never stop hunting Artemys.

Artemys knew that she would ruthlessly do anything for vengeance.

Then, after that moment of silence, he threw open the study's doors again, stormed down the corridor and bellowed, "Awake!"

Servants stumbled into the corridor in shock, guards stormed to their posts, his Great Glyph-enhanced senses felt a dozen scrying spells activate as his subordinates tried to determine if they were under attack. Magic was working again, that was a good sign. Artemys shoved his way into Tannes's quarters. She was wearing a robe, having just risen from bed. She held a lantern toward him as he rushed in.

Artemys held a finger to his lips to quiet her, and placed his hand against the wall. He drew an imaginary central line and scrawled glyphs across it. *"Truis,"* he whispered. Silence. No one's scrying spells—spying spells—could hear the words they would speak now.

"What is happening?" Tannes asked once she understood his spell to be complete.

Artemys took a breath, still leaning on the wall. "You spoke of costs. You spoke of collateral, and that some things *must* be done." Artemys believed these things, but he needed to know Tannes could handle his orders before he gave them.

"Yes, why?"

He turned toward her. "Do you truly believe that death can buy life? That crimes can cause justice?"

Tannes nodded. "Yes. Look at what your grandfather did. He fought a war and a revolution that nearly tore apart this land. But the Revolution was needed—look at how many responded to his call when he threw down the first Stead!"

Artemys's grandfather had seized the Princehood of Avernus for the Gothikar family; he had done it with spies, deceit, and murder. Artemys thought that Akheron had tried to do something about the issues Artemys saw, to fix the way they had structured society or change human nature itself, but his efforts had been in vain. *Mine will not. Mine* must *not.*

He turned back to the wall, breaking from her eyes. "You must go to Bronzehill at once. I will write a spell for you. You can teleport directly there."

"How do you know all of these spells?" she asked, but

nearly interrupted herself with a more prominent question: "Why am I going there?"

You must kill Pyrsius. Artemys took a breath and opened his mouth. "You must kill Kerres," he said.

He thought *What?* at the same time she spoke. He thought she said the same thing, but he could not hear it. *Why Kerres? Why would I say that?* His mind raced out of the room for a moment, churning through everything he had planned, all the seeds he had planted. All the words Kerres and he had spoken.

Killing Pyrsius would make Kerres wild. Killing Kerres would...

Pyrsius had seen a crowd of rioters massacred by magic. Pyrsius had seen Artemys burn a man's face with his hands. Pyrsius had lost his brother to the school of magic, even before he had found his brother. Pyrsius had lain awake, wondering why sorcery caused the problems in this world.

And most importantly, Pyrsius was the next Prince of Avernus, with the resources of an Imperial Prince at his whim.

"You must kill Kerres," he said more sternly. *She must die. If I want someone to destroy magic, Pyrsius is the one who can do it.*

"*Why?*" Tannes asked. "You *love* her!"

Artemys remained silent. He had known since the first time they had split that she was his weakness. *What good is a sword with a chipped edge? Korbios's edge cannot chip. Magic gives it the strength to never chip.*

She grabbed his shoulder and turned him toward her. "What good could her death possibly accomplish?" Tannes asked.

Artemys brushed her hand away and leaned close. "The wars have never ended. But now they are just under the surface. I was nearly slain by a mob. I killed a cultist to prove our Crown Magician was a traitor. All because I will not play by their rules. Something has to change. This is how."

Tannes shook her head. "I don't understand it though."

He laid both his palms on her shoulders, knowing she would not return from this task. She would be the first casualty. *No, Kerres will be the first.* It made sense in a dark way. "You do not have to understand."

Tannes sat down on the edge of her bed. "I have killed

before," she said.

"I know. And I know it was difficult for—"

"I will do it," she said, "if you swear it is for the right reasons."

"Glyphs, I swear it." He did not even breathe as he traced the glyphs on the wall. This was a longer spell, but he spoke it quickly, nearly under his breath.

A square section of air flickered to darkness, not lit by the lamp Tannes had set nearby. It was waiting for a traveller to enter it, before it flickered to Bronzehill in Olympus.

"You must use a spell to do the deed," Artemys said. *Be certain that Pyrsius knows that magic took his lover*. His brother already hated and feared magic, this would motivate him to do something with his wrath. And he had the resources of the realm at his disposal.

Tannes stared at him, but nodded and stood up. As she walked toward the teleport, Artemys's heart got the best of him. He gasped, "Please, make it quick for her..."

Tannes glanced at him, and then stepped to Olympus.

35

Year of Olympus 557

They reached Heaven's Fields a month after they escaped the Cloud Lands. Periander spent his days in silence. Not alone though. He had some of his friends with him: Salantar and Weveld. He tried to smile at their jokes or stories, for Mordus's sake. He felt anger once or twice but, as that odd Terrus had said, he simply had to make a *choice.*

Heaven's Fields sat below him. They had killed its sentries in the outlying valleys. Even those guards had seemed on edge: whatever lurked in this region knew that the Imperials had arrived. When they were finally granted a view of the valley, Periander almost sat down on the spot.

This was surely the capital of the giants. The valley stretched to his right, and the opposing peaks sported snow despite the quickly approaching summer. The first thing Periander noticed was the bright blue lake in the middle of the lowland. He could almost describe it as green. When Oban Hokar and his ilk had explored this land he had called it a paradise, a field-covered valley that captured the hearts of man.

None of Heaven remained here.

The lands were covered in wooden scaffolding, constructions, and buildings. Layered upon each other, it reminded Periander of an Olympian slum. Nowhere else had he seen such dense population. The outlying valleys had shown signs of farming. Perhaps they provided food for the giants that lived here.

There were columns of smoke from furnaces and ovens.

There was the stench of rotten food and waste. Even from this vantage, Periander saw dead bodies in some of the ditches on the south side of the valley. This was no utopia. This was squalor.

"Corlin, Rychard, Salantar, Weveld. Five guards a piece. The rest of you wait here." Periander set his pack down and started down the slope. Those he had called scurried to join him.

There were trees, mostly pine and spruce. The clouds overhead were grey, but the sun made the top of them white. By the time they neared the tribal city, a party of giants had gathered to greet them. A few were armed, but many of them looked fearful.

Behind them, Periander could see sewage running from one of the structures down a street. A smaller giant was watching it, and occasionally picking things out of it.

Those that had gathered were scrawny. Two of them were female, though Periander would not describe them as beautiful as his comrades had once jested. "What happened to this place?" he asked. "Why are you all cramped here?"

"All valley," one of them said. "All valley."

Periander shrugged with his arms out. He did not understand.

"He means," Weveld said. "That all the valleys are like this one."

"What?" Corlin asked. "How can that be?"

"For there to be an army of that size, their needs to be a civilization *this* size," Weveld explained. "The horde that went to war with us was the fighting force of these people. Look around. Can't you see why?"

"I see the enemy," Salantar said, heatedly. He drew his sword.

"No," Periander said. "Sheath it."

"No," Salantar returned. "These *things* burned by home."

"Salantar. Sheath it." The convict's sword slid back into its sheath, but he glared at them and muttered curses under his breath.

"Enemy," one of the females said, her voice as low as Periander's, though not the rumble of the male that had spoken. She pointed to the northeast.

There was a group moving up a ridge there, on the double. "Those are Trion's soldiers, sir," Rychard said. "Those are

Imperials."

"No, they're not," Periander growled. "They're the enemy."

"That's not what I meant," Rychard said. "I'm so—"

"Corlin," Periander said, "Run ahead and get our troops ready."

"Will we attack this place?" Salantar asked.

"No," Periander said. "We will attack our true opponents, Trion and Ivos."

"Do you think they're here?" Weveld asked with a raised eyebrow. "Wouldn't they still be in the south fighting the war?"

"Ivos will be here. He'll always be where he thinks it's safest."

Salantar was ahead of Corlin, heading uphill at a jog. Periander turned back to the giants. A crowd had gathered as they talked. Periander bowed his head to the woman who had spoken. "Thank you," he said, though she could not understand his words.

He turned and followed his friends back up the hill.

. . .

It was a hard march to catch up to the yellow-cloaks. Periander was exhausted, mentally and physically, by the time his army reached them. They finally burst out of a thick, pine forest and found the yellow-coated army holding a defensive position. They had lines of shields and spears. A volley of arrows fell toward Periander's men. Weveld raised an air shield, but some of the men fell before it caught the artillery.

"Form ranks," Periander shouted, and his captains obeyed. Mordus's men now answered directly to Periander.

They marched forward at Weveld's direction as he kept wards to defend them from ranged attacks. They crawled, like an injured cockroach, bristling with shields. Periander marched on the right flank, like an antenna.

This was a traditional battle, not the guerilla warfare they were forced to adapt to against the giants. This was a gritty tug of war for land and the upperhand. Once his ranks reached the enemy's, they shoved forward. The men in the front ranks were crushed between shield or spear. Some made room for fighting, but it was more of a shoving contest.

"Rychard, order your men to the far flank," Periander called. Rychard barked his order and his men obeyed on cue. They split off from the fighting and drove to west.

To protect their side, the enemy force had to turn on an angle. "Now," he told Weveld.

They both wrote spells, along with one of the surviving magicians in Weveld's company. A storm of air and fire surged against the yellow-cloak's closer flank. Those who had footing-space to flee ran onto the spears of Rychard's men.

To his credit, the enemy commander maintained control of his men to the very end. Periander watched him—a man in dark-painted armour—as he barked orders to his men. A veteran group thrust directly into Corlin and Periander's main force, the meat of the army that had stopped to cheer at the fiery destruction wrought by the magicians.

"Hold strong, men!" Periander shouted. "Rychard, now!"

His bellow echoed, but thankfully it was enough; Rychard and his men charged north as quickly as they could, disengaging the enemy's far flank. The enemy commander reacted exactly as Periander expected. He was paranoid; his tactics and battle formation had confirmed it. And it fit with what Periander had predicted of the entire battle. *Ivos will try to protect himself.*

He ordered his men to fall back and defend him. Rychard's movement was a launching point for a full attack from behind, so the commander yanked as many of his men back into defence.

Then Periander heard "Now!" echo from the enemy army, between the screams of dying men.

He did not expect what happened next. A second fist of veterans shot out from the chaotic remnant of the enemy's formation. It struck straight for Periander. Weveld lashed out with fire again, but his sidekick took a sword to the gut and disappeared beneath the charging mens' feet. Periander hacked at spears that neared him and used his own wooden shield to fend off attacks, but he was falling back step by step. Corlin ordered men to his rescue, slashing perpendicularly into the charging ranks of the enemy's surprise attack.

An axe caught Weveld on the head, and he fell to the ground. Periander ran toward him as he sunk. "Protect me!" he bellowed, and the Imperial soldiers complied. The Trionus soldiers were forced away by Corlin's men.

Periander yanked a healing token from his belt as he tenderly pulled the axe free of Weveld's head. It was brittle stone, so brittle but so powerful. He snapped it between two fingers and the grey dust fell onto Weveld's bloody cloak. The man's head sealed shut and, though a section of grey hair was missing and a scar formed, he inhaled sharply and opened his eyes.

He wiped a hand across his face to wipe away all the blood and then accepted Periander's hand. The Prince helped him to his feet.

Rychard and his men had driven at the back of the enemy's force when they saw what was happening on Periander's side of the battle. The enemy formation was broken and men were fleeing in every direction. Many were hunted down by cheering and shouting Imperials. Periander closed his eyes. They were all the same—hunting down giants and humans alike. They had been doing this for practically twenty years. No change. He watched Salantar dash after a cluster of men and cut them down one by one.

Periander, looking away from those that fled, walked through the chaos with his sword held ready. No one came near him, enemy or friend. He saw maimed men trying to put themselves back together. He saw dead bodies and dying ones, men from both sides. He saw the things he had not let himself see for the entire war, the things that threatened to bring out his rage. He saw Captain Joran dying. He saw himself crawling through the streets of Galinor.

He saw the empty ruins of a farming village, the first desolation he had caused.

The enemy commander was slumped on his knees, cradling an injured arm. His guard still surrounded him, but fled as soon as they spotted Periander. He must have been a fearsome sight, walking nonchalantly without a shield—when had he lost it?—and drenched in blood.

Ivos removed his dark helm and tossed it aside. His grey hair was slick with all his sweat. It dripped from the scruff on his chin. He was weeping. He threw his sword down in front of Periander.

Periander stood there for a long minute. Could he really

change now? Could he really *choose?* He looked down at his own sword, and then back at his enemy.

"Where's Trion?" he asked.

"He died," Ivos said. His voice was a whine. "Years ago! He was an old man before this war and passed away with a fever one winter. At least five years ago, I swear."

"Would you lie to me, even now?" Periander asked.

Ivos closed his eyes and shook his head. He opened them again. "He's long dead, I swear it. I would not lie!"

Another long moment of silence passed. Periander was oblivious to the dying battle or the men who were watching. He *had* to change. Mercy. He did not even think of that odd stranger saying it. This was a choice that had been waiting for his heart since he was young. Mercy.

"Is this enough?" Periander asked the old man. "Are you done yet?"

Ivos only shook his head. "Get it over with," he said.

Periander ground his teeth together and, sword lowered but brandished nonetheless, stepped closer. *"Are you done yet? Have you stolen enough lives from this world? Have you broken enough people?"*

"I never meant for this," Ivos stammered. "I thought we would win... but now my stomach turns at even that thought."

"You should die for what you have done," Periander said, "and I long to kill you. But...enough death." He spat to one side.

Ivos's eyes widened. He looked confused.

"Are we done?" Periander asked.

"Yes. I swear it," Ivos said.

"Get out of here," Periander said. He sheathed his sword. "The Maker can judge you for all of this. You've brought enough evil into this world; you might want to spend your final days bringing some good into it."

"W- what?" Ivos stuttered. He was still perplexed by Periander's words.

"I'm sure someone will try to kill you before long, and, if you don't get out of here, it'll be sooner rather than later," Periander said. He turned to walk away. "Get out of here, snake."

As he walked, he heard armour clank and feet run. He doubted his men would harm the traitor after Periander's words.

Periander smiled. He had changed, somehow.

"You bastard!" A fist slammed into his face.

Periander wiped away blood from his nose. His men were holding Salantar's arms, though the livid man was still advancing on Periander. "He killed my family! He killed my people! I had to watch it from a forsaken cell! Glyphs!"

More Imperials contributed their strength. It took five or six men to hold the gladiator back.

"You let him live, you traitor!" Salantar roared. He spat on Periander.

Periander held his nose and felt the warmth of his blood. "I'm sorry, my friend. You'll come to forgive me, I hope. You'll come to understand." He felt tears. He whispered a prayer for the first time in years. "Please help him understand," he asked the Maker.

"You're no friend of mine!" Salantar screamed as the soldiers dragged him away. They left the bloody battlefield behind.

36

Year of Olympus 584

This is me.

Kerres woke up. Had she heard something? She lay awake for a moment, breathing into the cold air. It was soft and warm under the blankets. She had been dreaming, she realized. What had she been dreaming of?

She dug in her elbows and pulled back against her pillows until she was nearly sitting. It had been a nightmare, not a dream. She fumbled at her night table, nearly knocking the chalice aside. She did not though, and took a sip of the cold liquid.

"Are you well?" Pyrsius asked in a muffled voice.

She glanced at him. His face was half-pressed into a feather pillow.

"Yes," she said. "I am going to check on Lanteera."

His voice was more awake now. "You're certain everything is well?"

Kerres ran fingers though his dark hair. "Yes. I'll return quickly." She swung her legs out of bed.

"Return to me quickly," he mumbled, breathing slowly. He spent more and more time in Avernus and only visited for nights. Prince Periander knew nothing of his granddaughter's existence and they conspired to keep it that way, even if it meant young Lanteera would know nothing of her heritage or even her father.

Kerres wrapped a white fur robe around herself and grabbed a nearby unlit lantern. Lanteera's room was through their antechamber, across the hall, where servants could attend her without disturbing Lady Rysarius. Kerres waited until she was in the antechamber before setting the lamp on the shelf and lighting the oil with a spark. The Keep got cold at night, and dark.

Artemys had been too close when he had visited last year... *Thank the Maker we hid her in time.* He could not know of Lanteera. Kerres smirked as she stepped into the icy, stone corridor. *Perhaps that was my nightmare.*

She reached for the door to Lanteera's chamber, but her hand stopped. She gasped, but couldn't. And then she couldn't breathe. In the corner of her eye, Kerres could see a woman standing, or leaning rather, against the wall. The woman had tears in her eyes, but something harsher too.

Kerres felt a pain growing in her face and chest. She still could not breathe. She struggled to move, but the air around her was as hard as rock. Who was this? Finally, Kerres recognized her. It was Artemys's apprentice, and that harshness in her eyes, that was him.

She tried to speak, and it took all of her strength to utter, "Not—" *my child, please.*

Artemys watched as Tannes wrote the spell. A spell had conjured this vision for him, so he could be with Kerres at the end. He could see her eyes, trying to comprehend. He watched as her face began to flush and the same tears that wrapped her eyes sprung to his. "It has to be done..." he whispered.

A tear fell from her eyes and Artemys cursed, "Glyphs."

With the strength to raise mountains, he tore a hole in the air and stepped into that distant hallway, behind Kerres, in Bronzehill.

Tannes could see him, but Kerres could not. Artemys opened his mouth to call off his assault as Tannes' eyes saw him.

But his mouth hung open. *Can people truly change? Has she changed? Have I?* He spun away, almost doubled over with his hand over his gut. He thought the pain would kill him. *If I could change, I would have before this moment.*

It has *to be done...* Was that in his mind, or spoken? He fell through the air to his Crown quarters again, hands on the floor. "Gah! I'm sorry Kerres, I'm sorry, I'm sorry..." He forced himself to keep watching.

Pyrsius awoke, sliding out of bed without a second thought, like he *knew* something was wrong without hearing a sound.

There were dark tendrils at the edge of Kerres's eyes. This was her nightmare. This was her dream. *Not Lanteera, please.*

Was it a baby's cry that had awoken her? Or a murderer's call?

"It *has* to be done," her attacker said, but it was directed at them both.

Pyrsius charged through the door to the antechamber, his breath held in terror.

Kerres felt her arms jerk, but they did not move in the hallway. They were held tight by the air. Her attacker seemed to jump, and stumble back. Hands brushed Kerres from behind, and it seemed to release the air's hold on her, but it did nothing for the silence of her lungs.

She sank back against the wall as Pyrsius's hands released her. She saw a knife in his hands.

Their attacker released a burst of fire at him; Pyrsius walked right through it, his clothes flickering with embers for a moment. He grabbed hold of their attacker—Kerres tried to cry out but could not—and jammed the knife under the magician's chin, cutting her breath away without a beat to realize she had died.

Lanteera is safe.

Pyrsius spun back toward Kerres, but the darkness had nearly obscured all of her sight. The spell was still there, holding her lungs closed. Her vision seemed to bulge and warp. Her arms and legs were jerking freely now. His hands, wet with blood, grabbed her arms and pulled her tight against him. He was speaking, but Kerres could hear nothing except for the last words she would in this world: another voice, the one that had awoken her from her sleep, the harsh one:

"This is me," Artemys told her, and let the Great Glyph fade from his eyes. He had very nearly stopped Tannes. He had

very nearly broken the sword he was trying to be. He had almost become a weed of grass blowing in the wind.

But he was steel. *I have to be.*

He stood now, in his Crown Magician's quarters. He had packed a chest with clothes, food and books. Pyrsius would be driven mad by this; it would grow to consume and define him. He would come for Artemys first, but it would not be enough for him. Nothing would be, until no wizards were left to draw breath.

Artemys would need to leave. The Keep of the Order would be his new home—it was an ancient building, founded with their Order itself in Galinor, the seat of the Imperial Council. It had been practically abandoned since its use during the Trionus Wars.

Artemys had played his last plan: Pyrsius. Now all he had to do was wait.

Steel was good at that.

37

Year of Olympus 557

By the time they returned to Heaven's Fields, a different group was waiting for them. There were two giants wearing burgundy and a small group of warriors. There were not nearly enough to threaten Periander's force, as rag-tag as the remnants were. They had won the war today.

It was twilight, and the sun was setting on the Maker's Forge, sinking toward the western horizon, beyond the icy peaks.

Bathed in orange, Periander, accompanied by his two Captains and Weveld, strode to their meeting place. The giants had chosen a flat ledge halfway up the slope, far enough from the impoverished city to be considered neutral ground.

The two chieftains waited for Periander to make an action. They did not speak, only watched. One had a thick brow across his forehead. The other had a much longer beard and loomed a foot taller than his comrade.

"I am Periander Gothikar," he told them, "leader of the Triumvirate."

One of their group, a warrior wearing white furs, translated his words into the rumbling language of the giants. The larger chieftain nodded and replied in kind, with a stream of syllables Periander could only guess at. They were afraid of him and his men. They could raid the giant's city if they chose.

"This is Tokl Niffis, head of our Tribes. What intend you...respected leader?" the translator spoke. He was no master of the common language. "We given you the betrayer."

Periander drew his sword. It was still bloody. The giants all tensed. The larger chieftain lifted the axe he held. Periander drove his blade into the thick dirt with a scraping sound. "Enough humans have died," he told them. Rychard, Corlin, and Weveld gasped.

The giants dropped their weapons to the earth as well and the chieftain added a quick word or two. The translator said, "And enough of our people."

"That's what I said," Periander nodded. Again, his comrades gasped. The translator pressed his hands together, drawing looks from his fellows. It was an expression of some kind that Periander could only guess at.

When their leader heard the translation, he folded his hands together and looked skyward, then back at Periander. He let out a long string of words and the translator explained, once he had finished, "You will be known among our tribes as Gothikar-Giant-Friend, for you have...seen us. Is the war done, respected leader? Or..." he searched for words, "can we speak of it?"

Periander raised his hand to indicate a pause and turned to his companions. "Remember," he said, "that I am the High Prince." They stared at him.

The High Prince turned back to the leader of the giant men. "Your tribes can settle the lands surrounding the Trion River, not Sinai. You may also have the Cerden Mountains. You must never set foot near Galinor, nor Gev, nor may you cross the Golden Plains. Are these conditions acceptable? They are as close to Trion's original ones as I can accept."

Rychard stepped forward. "We need these lands!" he blurted. "Where will our people settle!"

"Are we really going to surrender to them?" Corlin questioned. "Those are all Trion's conditions, save the capital!"

"Silence!" Periander hissed. If his lands reflected even half of what had become of Heaven's Fields...it would be justice. They had room. They could sacrifice for a change. They had to.

They had to change.

The lead giant listened to the translation of Periander's terms, then fell to one knees. He spoke his next words with excitement and gratitude. *"Vashal* of the giants," the translator said, then paused to search for a word Periander could understand. At last he said, "Hero."

Periander fell to his knees and his men, by tradition did so too.

The translator continued. "We accept these terms. May we never spill one another's blood again."

Periander nodded. "Thank the Maker," he said.

The chieftain forced a smile the way Periander's kind smiled. "Thank. The. Maker," he managed, and looked skyward again. He looked back to Periander and offered his hand.

Periander pressed his hand against it, though he could not reach round enough to grip it. "If you ever need, ask for me amongst my kind, Tokl Niffis, and I will come."

The translator relayed the words to the chieftain. Together they reclaimed their feet and Tokl rumbled a reply. "And you, Gothikar Giant's Friend, may ask for Niffis, and he will reply. Go in peace."

"Go in peace," Periander said.

Corlin and Rychard ranted protests the whole way back to their camp. Weveld remained oddly silent, wrapped in thought. If Periander picked up on any emotion from the old man, it was thankfulness. He understood, somehow.

Periander ignored his friends' objections; later he would have to persuade Theseus and Odyn it was the right decision. For now though, he simply watched the sunset in silence. *Cat,* he thought, *I'm coming home. I'm finally coming home.* He smiled.

One day, the following year, he was walking through a crowded feast room and he saw Terrus's face in the crowd for a moment. When he turned to confront the strange specter, it was gone. Terrus left words behind though, echoing through Periander's head. "Thank you," the mysterious man said. *"Thank you."*

38

Year of Olympus 588

Artemys had lived for three years in the Keep of the Order, watching and waiting. Pyrsius had slain a handful of wizards, but had yet to move on any of the powerful ones. He would. Artemys knew he would. Pyrsius was plotting now, building his own web as Artemys once had, hunting those he saw as unjust, as Artemys had also done. Artemys had not realized then that webs were meaningless. Only knowledge and action mattered.

He rose in the morning and stood on top of the Keep for sunrise. To the west were a dozen ridges of rock—the Cerden Mountains—to the east was the Mydarius Sea. Across the city of Galinor, Artemys could see the Tower of the Throne, taller than his own Keep. That Tower held the Council of Princes whenever they should meet to vote on matters relevant to the entirety of the Dominion.

One day, he would creep higher than this tower, to that one.

He watched the sun creep higher above the horizon. No one could see him up here, and if he shouted the wind would steal his voice away before it could be heard. He was perfectly alone.

The top of the Keep was a square composed of stone battlements, with wooden beams bridging the empty center. Artemys had conjured three large rocks in an array. He remembered the wooden floor beams groaning under the weight, but they were silent and still now.

On each, he wrote a spell. The first displayed Prince Odyn, the second Pyrsius. These two were key. The third was set to siphon through any uses of magic; sometimes such a spell showed Artemys something of interest, but he did not give it a large amount of attention.

Odyn had been particularly interesting to Artemys recently. He was a troubled man, the eleventh of his name in the dynasty that had started the Triumvirate. Tiberon Odyn, the conqueror. The histories said that he had slain three Kings himself. This Odyn was a child grown large. He possessed the strength and ferocity of a barbarian, but he knew he could never emerge from the shadow of those that came before him. There was a lust for power there that could prove useful.

Artemys had contacted Odyn already. He had sent him a letter signed with an anonymous "A," asking him if he desires Kingship. In the letter, he had advised Odyn to contact Pyrsius, as a means to an end. It was the sort of thinking Odyn responded well to, an easy solution to a complex problem. He had, in turn, sent a letter to Pyrsius. They would strike some sort of deal, Artemys was certain. It was of no matter to him. He could defeat them with ease once they had done the job of ruining the Triumvirate.

A surprising turn of events had occurred a few weeks following that. The Brotherhood had also contacted Odyn and offered him their support in the coming days. Artemys was uncertain why they would help kill magic; perhaps it was a ploy to access more energy, as Artemys was doing. It was irrelevant. For now, they were a benefit, not a threat. Should they ever become a threat, Artemys had already proven his own power to them.

He spent a few hours on the roof, watching. *Any detail could be useful.* He was reminded of this lesson by the crucial piece of the Pyrsius puzzle, the flaming hand on their hunt.

Just before he turned away for a noon meal, he noticed something odd on the leftmost rock. It was the Southern Waste, a desert stretching south from the World's Foundation. Nothing had ever been found in that waste, or beyond it.

The spell was watching for the use of magic, but now it only looked down on the shadows of sand dunes. As he watched, a shape appeared out of nowhere. It was a person on their knees, with a line through their torso—a weapon of some kind. They collapsed to the sand and lay still.

Artemys smirked. "Who is this?" he whispered. He

tweaked the spell for a better view, with a whisper of a few glyphs, and froze.

There, on top of a random dune of dirt, was the man from his study and the teleport to Avernus before that. The man with the scar. Artemys's adversary. He was just lying there, transfixed with a sword, blood pooling beneath him.

The spell flickered to the next use of magic, a woman using a wind spell to move a rock from her field.

"No, no," Artemys mumbled. "That is not right." He retried the spell, but his adversary still lay there in the desert, staring blankly ahead.

Do I go to him? Do I heal him?

Of course not, he decided.

The next day, as the sun rose, he checked that spell first. If Tannes were still alive, he might explain himself by saying, "I am only curious." He would not admit he was part terrified and part obsessed.

The man still lay there. *Do I at least investigate his body further? By visiting him, I would not need to heal him...*

He shook himself, and spent the rest of the morning watching his father and Pyrsius. Pyrsius had been spending more time in an archive, compiling a list. Artemys knew it was similar to the list he had once dared to write. He had burned that list— none could know the Crown Magician had dared compose it.

He spent the afternoon avoiding that spell. The Southern Waste was of no significance. No corpse could ever be found there. He trained with a sword on some scarecrow-like targets he had found in one of the lower levels of the Keep. He had been chiselled with muscles during his days living in Attarax. It was a harder life there. In the years since, he had grown weak. But he was improving.

He went into the Galinor Market district during the afternoon, careful to disguise his face with a hood and a spell. He had to keep his living quarters stocked himself, something he had not done in a long time.

The third morning, he could resist even less. He sat up in bed, and conjured the Great Glyph. The man's body was still laying there. *Does this mean I won?* Artemys wondered.

He packed a few things into a bag and teleported directly to the dune.

The sun was hotter here than anywhere he had ever felt. Slaving in the lumber yard in Attarax had been bad. This, somehow, was worse. He tossed his pack of supplies aside and sank into the sand beside the body. How could this man be here? The scar running down one cheek to his chinbone, the eyes, staring blankly now, not piercing, the weathered face?

"Who were you?" Artemys asked. There was, of course, no reply.

The weapon that had done the deed had a remarkable hilt. *Korbios! How?* The same sword Artemys had given to his father was now firmly embedded in the man's chest. No, in his heart.

Is this some gift from the Maker, telling me I've succeeded? There was no logical way to explain how Artemys's adversary, who had threatened Artemys in the core of his safety, could have come to this moment, transfixed with Artemys's own blade, in the desert.

Artemys stood up, then crouched beside him. There was no breath, but there was also no stench and no glaze in his eyes. *He's still alive!* Artemys realized.

He grabbed Korbios's hilt and pulled. The sword would not move. There was dry blood caked around the blade and its entrance to the man's body.

Artemys leaned back, putting his legs into it, and the blade finally released with a sickening squelch. He stumbled with its release, nearly falling to the earth. No blood left the wound; it was a dry injury now, weathered by days spent under the desert sun.

A red paste sleeved the end of the sword, marring its beauty. *I need to clean it*, he decided. He traced some lines in the sand a few feet from the body and whispered, *"Al'oken."*

Water bubbled up from the marks he had made in the sand and began to trickle past Artemys's feet. Before long, there was a brook weaving its way between the dunes.

Artemys put his knees into the hot dirt, hiking his red robe up enough that it would not hinder his posture. He first took a cupped handful of water to quench his thirst. Then he placed the sword in the water and scrubbed his adversary's blood away. He had to be very careful not to touch the blade's edge. It was as razor sharp as the day Orestys had forged it.

Once it was finally clean, Artemys sat back in the sand and

stared at the quiet man. The man's skin was burned from the sun, but his face was peaceful: he had lain here awake long enough to come to terms with his situation. He wrote a line of glyphs in the sand and whispered their words. A bulk of rock appeared nearby, with a bulge to create some shade. There was a small niche under the bulge, enough to give someone shade.

Artemys dragged the body into the shade. There was quite a pool of red where the man had lain. Artemys kicked some sand over it. He wrote a healing spell, touched the man's chest, and whispered the words.

The flesh resewed itself, leaving an ugly scar. There were spells for healing scars with new flesh, but Artemys did not bother.

He nearly turned away, but noticed a line emerging from either side of the scar—above and below. It was too thin to have been caused by any sword; it was like the skin itself had traced something there. Artemys quickly healed the scar, further exhausting the man's body. It would be some time before he awoke.

As the scar faded, Artemys was shocked to see a line of glyphs written across the man's chest. There were glyphs there that Artemys had never seen before!

Among those he recognized were a spell that would allow this man to see the Great Glyph as well. Another made the man immune to any mortal death—only magic spells could kill him. Artemys lifted Korbios again; the spell did not make this man invincible. He could feel pain and suffer injury, but he could not die.

Artemys stood up and climbed the dune a bit higher. He opened the pack and dug out some meat, wood, and kindling, and got to work on a fire.

An hour later, he heard movement down the slope. He slowly stood up and turned to face his adversary, expecting the worst. He had a few spell tokens in hand, just in case. His adversary climbed the dune, staring at him blankly. There was no recognition in that face.

"By the Maker, how'd you find me?" the man said. He seemed younger than the force of reckoning in Artemys's study.

"A lot of scrying," Artemys replied. *I cannot warn him of my web, but let him fly where he will. I should appear the friendly rescuer.* "Have a seat. I'm heating up some venison."

As they sat, the young man said, "My name is Dryn..."

Artemys settled into place. Finally, a name for this enemy's face. "I know who you are. And we have a strong connection..." Artemys said. He paused, wondering what affect his words might have. "My name is Artemys Gothikar."

In a splash of sand, Dryn fought to get up and ended up sliding back from the fire before he could climb to his feet. "Great Glyph! Artemys Gothikar is dead!" the young man exclaimed. He reclaimed some of his composure and, with a growl in his voice, asked, "Who are you really?"

I'm dead? This man...he thinks me dead? Artemys shrugged. "I'm Artemys."

"He was an old man in the forest, who gave me..." The man trailed off, his eyes narrowing. His arms settled at his side, resolutely. "He died. I saw him die."

"An old man?" Artemys could not help but smile. *If I were an old man, this Dryn would be much older.* But he needed to know more. What would make this stranger say more... "Perhaps that was me."

Dryn's eyes widened. "Travelling time...it never occurred to me, but it makes sense now... I should have considered that I'm not the only one who can travel through time."

What? Glyphs, what? Artemys held his tongue. *Travelling time? What does that even mean? This man can move between times...?* Was it like a teleport, or a dream? Was it exhausting, energizing, painful? *This man thinks I can travel time too...?* He invited the man to sit again. "I have seen many things in my days, but never one like you. Tell me who left you like that, here in the desert."

"It was... your brother, Pyrsius..."

Artemys laughed. *So the war on magic succeeds?* "Pyrsius defeated you? Dryn, Dryn...Pyrsius does not even have magic."

"He has tokens," Dryn blurted. "Powerful ones. And your sword!"

"The sword has a mere ward of protection from it breaking. The Order would not even call it a magic sword," Artemys said. *How could this man, who somehow set me on edge in the heart of the Delfie School...how could he be defeated by my* brother?

"You found me...you saw what he can do...what I've been

through!" the young man's face was pained now.

"So after all this, you think you can be beaten by tokens? You can best him, Dryn," Artemys said. *Someone has to get rid of my brother after all of this is done. He will be a chipped blade by then. Might as well get this adversary to do it.*

"Have you seen that? In the future?"

I make the future, fool. I am the future. He could not let this man, let alone anyone, see that side of himself. Artemys took a breath. "I know how much you have suffered, but there is more at stake than your life or even that of your friends. Pyrsius does not stand a chance. You need to plan though. Pyrsius's brilliance is his plotting. Take that away and you only need to wait out his tokens."

Artemys had once wondered if the Hunter that kept only the limit of magic would somehow counter a lull caused by the death of all magicians. Would it create something to use up that energy? As he stared at Dryn, Artemys realized he knew the answer. *By stealing energy for myself, I create my own adversary.* Dryn, and his travelling through time, consumed enough of the energy left by the death of magicians. *But the magicians are not even dead yet!*

"And Odyn? His armies have rallied near the Glyph Gate to the Sinai Mountains. My friends found them." Dryn paused, then corrected himself, "Or rather will. Right now... in this time period, we just reached Ithyka. But in my present war is about to break out."

"Really...?" *Odyn. Armies? In any ordeal, Odyn and Pyrsius would both seek the easiest solution. The easiest for Odyn would be to force a vote of the Triumvirate to go in his favor.* Artemys could help force that vote, to push out the diplomacy of the Triumvirate. "He did not become High Prince as he plotted?"

Dryn smiled. "No, I stopped him. In my time, I'm the Crown Magician, as you were in yours."

What? Great Glyph... Dryn was a fool enough to tell all. And it made Artemys incredibly surprised. *It does not matter... The title Crown Magician is a robe, and it is not the most colourful one.* "I see." So Odyn will move his armies, likely with Pyrsius's support. Artemys had to frame this in Dryn's idealistic terms though. "So is it possible that Theseus will defend the

Northlands?"

"I doubt it. The allied forces of the south would outnumber any defences of the north, especially if the enemy emerges in Sinai instead of facing Edessa. If I am able to defeat Pyrsius as you say, then I'd still have to face Odyn...and then perhaps I could save Athyns."

To Artemys, any rush for time seemed in vain for a man of Dryn's apparent abilities. He picked the venison from the fire, splitting it between them. "Defeat Pyrsius and Odyn, and I suspect the remaining enemy will yield to Theseus. The Three Nobles of each city will no doubt grant him the High Prince-hood in order to reestablish order in the realm."

Dryn raised an eyebrow and swallowed his bite from the hot meat. "Are you certain? The Nobles of Avernus and Olympus would side with Theseus? Even after all this time?"

Artemys explained that they would be bound by law, but he was practically interrupted by Dryn's next remark.

"I can't travel forward. That is why I haven't investigated the timeline more. Any date I go back to...I'm stuck there until the time elapses." Dryn was apparently thinking beyond Artemys's words to the task of dealing with Pyrsius in his own time period. Apparently he would have to live until he reached whatever time he was from.

He quickly summoned the Great Glyph into his vision and searched for Dryn. There was a villager named Dryn ten Rayth, wandering south from a northland district, right now as they spoke. The road to Athyns, which Dryn had already referred to, was at least a month long. "You are what...two or three months in your past?"

Dryn nodded. "Two and a half."

"Then you have a portion of time to try to overcome your hindrances." Artemys was getting bored of trying to point out to Dryn things that any time-travelling prodigy should already know.

"And when I get back to the present?"

Artemys smirked. "Save the realm." *I will be there, waiting. And once you kill my enemies, I will kill you.* He glanced down at Korbios, still sitting in the sand beside him. Conquest. It was only fitting to use this as his sword from now on. In this time, while Artemys sat here, or on top of his Keep in

Galinor... Periander also had a version of Korbios. Artemys's was the blade that had come back in time with Dryn.

"I think I know where to go..." Dryn murmured.

"Good. I have fixed your wound, and..." *To keep him unaware of this web...* "put you back to right." Artemys stood up with his sword. *I need to leave first, a mysterious wizard travelling time.* He kicked dirt onto the fire. He shouldered his pack and picked a spell token from his belt. It was a teleport spell, back to the Keep of the Order. He glanced back at his adversary and tried not to laugh. "May the Maker protect you, Dryn Rayth. Defeat our enemies."

Artemys stepped through to the Keep and remained silent as he wandered down the dimly-lit corridor. He had meant that last line. Everything Dryn was doing only worked in Artemys's favor. Dryn did not know his actions were in vain, that he could not possibly save the Triumvirate from Artemys. "Defeat our enemies," he repeated. The Hunter had set up an adversary for Artemys. But the adversary now worked for him.

"Save the realm, Dryn," he lied. "Save the realm."

N A VREUGDENHIL

ACKNOWLEDGMENTS

First thanks go to the first reader. Joseph, you're a great friend and I've enjoyed our "stand-up" worthy humour. Thanks for all the help you've poured into reading this book and the last and your excellent feedback.

My biggest thanks must go to my readers, of course! Shadow Glyph was incredibly well received and the entire process was a thrilling dream come true. From opening the first box of books to reading the first bad review—my love of writing has manifested in one blessed year thanks to all my supporters!

Dylan Tracey, kudos again on the map. Even the new, detailed sections I've made were simple stencil cuts from your great work! Also, you're a useful one to bounce ideas off of! Keep up your own writing; I'm still waiting to read it! And never pick a fight with the ladder. It'll win.

Bro! You know more of the plot than anyone, I think. I'm glad you enjoyed reading the first book anyway, and I hope you enjoy this one too. Mom and Dad, thanks for your support, as always! I look forward to talking this one over with you once you've read it. To my entire family, I have too many thanks to write in a book this size, but I will say I love you all and am so grateful!

To all of my friends, both when I was writing and editing this, thanks for your help! Friends: Hanna, John, Dan, Aaron, Gerreke, Jeff, Dylan, Kayla, and the Tangents; coworkers: Paul, Dan, Michael, Justin, James, Nicholas, Bree and all the rest! Thanks to you all, and best wishes!

Lastly: unhealthy amounts of Hans Zimmer, Muse, Billy Talent, Emery and the Used were used in the creation of this book (different bands for different characters or feels). Thanks for your ingenuity, your inspiration, and your noise.

Once again, thanks to any readers of this book. If you've read up to this page, you'll have a better idea of who I am than vice versa, so I hope you've enjoyed what you experienced and tune in next time!

358

N. A. VREUGDENHIL grew up in Trenton, Ontario, and is currently finishing a Creative Writing BA at the University of British Columbia in Kelowna. He started writing novels at age 10, and, ten years later, published the first of a series of five, *Shadow Glyph* (2012). *Gothikar* (2014), the second book in the *Shadow Glyph Series* is his second publication.

facebook.com/shadowglyph

www.ithyka.com

Made in the USA
Charleston, SC
09 January 2014